Praise for
THE TRIDENT DECEPTION

"A terrific thriller debut. Campbell does an amazing job balancing character interaction with high-octane action, all the while keeping the technical jargon to a level understandable by nonmilitary readers. This is the best novel about a submarine since Tom Clancy's classic *The Hunt for Red October*."

—*Booklist* (starred review)

"Fans of submarine thrillers who are saddened by the demise of Tom Clancy will welcome Campbell's debut." —*Publishers Weekly*

"No one puts the reader inside a submarine like Rick Campbell does in *The Trident Deception*. I couldn't put it down. Compelling and thrilling, this novel is a must-read." —Jack Coughlin, *New York Times* bestselling author of *Shooter* and *Time to Kill*

"*The Trident Deception* is a fistfight of a thriller. A masterpiece." —Dalton Fury, *New York Times* bestselling author of *Kill Bin Laden* and *Tier One Wild*

THE
TRIDENT
DECEPTION

RICK
CAMPBELL

St. Martin's Paperbacks

This is a work of fiction. All of the characters, organizations, and events portrayed in this novel are either products of the author's imagination or are used fictitiously.

THE TRIDENT DECEPTION

Copyright © 2014 by Rick Campbell.
Excerpt from *Empire Rising* copyright © 2014 by Rick Campbell.

For information address St. Martin's Press, 175 Fifth Avenue, New York, NY 10010.

Library of Congress Catalog Card Number: 2013031934

ISBN: 978-1-250-06127-0

Printed in the United States of America

St. Martin's Press hardcover edition / March 2014
St. Martin's Paperbacks edition / February 2015

St. Martin's Paperbacks are published by St. Martin's Press, 175 Fifth Avenue, New York, NY 10010.

10 9 8 7 6 5 4 3 2 1

To my wife, Lynne, who has supported me all these years and sacrificed so much, allowing me to chase my dreams.

To Brett, Caitlin, and Courtney, I pass along the advice that led me to write this novel:

—*What would you do, if you weren't afraid?*

ACKNOWLEDGMENTS

Many thanks are due to those who helped me write and publish this novel:

First and foremost, to Ned Steele for the inspiration to pick up the pen; to my wife, Lynne, and my children for their support through the long hours; to Nancy Coffey, without whose assistance I would not be a writer; and to my agent, John Talbot, for his belief in this book and for taking a chance.

To the many wonderful people at St. Martin's Press. First, to my editor, Keith Kahla, for making this novel twice as good as it was. To the many departments at St. Martin's Press; editorial is only the beginning: to Young Lim and the art department for the incredible cover, to Rafal Gibek and William Rees and the rest of production, to Steven Seighman and design for the interior layout, to my marketing and publicity team—Paul Hochman, Loren Jaggers, Justin Velella, Cassandra Galante, and Courtney Sanks—for the many hours they've dedicated on behalf of *The Trident Deception,* to Hannah Braaten, for her cheerful assistance as I attempted to navigate my way through a new literary world, and to the countless sales reps I'll never meet. And finally, to the publisher of St. Martin's Press, Sally Richardson, and the editor in chief, George Witte, for making this book possible. Thank you all so much.

To those who helped me get the details in *The Trident Deception* right: to Commander Pete Arrobio, who walked me through the P-3C submarine prosecution procedures, to Royal Australian Navy Lieutenant Commander Josh Wilkinson, who guided me through the Australian submarine scenarios, and to U.S. Navy Captains Murray Gero and Steve Harrison for refreshing my memory and helping me get the new technical details right. (Some of it isn't right, on purpose—see Author's Note in back.) And to Douglas C. Waller— the nuclear weapon release procedures in *The Trident Deception* are those authorized for public dissemination in his novel, *Big Red*.

To my writer friends in Purgatory and The Pit, thank you for your support on this long journey; for sharing the good times and pulling me though the bad times. I wouldn't have made it without you.

And finally, to the men and women in our armed services, and especially the Submarine Force. My heart and thoughts will always be with you.

PRINCIPAL CHARACTERS

(A complete cast of characters is provided in the addendum.)

UNITED STATES ADMINISTRATION

KEVIN HARDISON, chief of staff

CHRISTINE O'CONNOR, national security adviser

STEVE BRACKMAN, senior military aide

DAVE HENDRICKS, deputy director, National Military Command Center, Pentagon

MIKE PATTON, Section Two watchstander, National Military Command Center

ISRAELI ADMINISTRATION

LEVI ROSENFELD, prime minister

EHUD RABIN, defense minister

BARAK KOGEN, intelligence minister

ARIEL BRONNER, director, Metsada

COMSUBPAC

JOHN STANBURY, Commander, Submarine Force Pacific

Murray Wilson, senior Prospective Commanding Officer Instructor

USS *KENTUCKY*

Brad Malone, Commanding Officer

Bruce Fay, Executive Officer

Pete Manning, Weapons Officer

Tom Wilson, Assistant Weapons Officer

Herb Carvahlo, Electrical Division Officer

Steve Prashaw, Chief of the Boat

Alan Davidson, Radio Division Chief Petty Officer

Tony DelGreco, Sonar Division Leading Petty Officer

Bob Cibelli, Sonar Division Petty Officer

Roger Tryon, Missile Division Leading Petty Officer

FAST-ATTACK SUBMARINES

Ken Tyler, Commanding Officer, USS *San Francisco*

Dennis Gallagher, Commanding Officer, USS *North Carolina*

Brett Humphreys, Commanding Officer, HMAS *Collins*

EAGLE-FIVE-ZERO (P-3C AIR CREW)

Scott Graef, Tactical Coordinator

Pete Burwell, Communicator

WASHINGTON, D.C.

As a full moon cast faint shadows across the narrow paths winding through Rock Creek Park, Russell Evans checked over his shoulder again as he ran at nearly a full sprint. The young man almost lost his footing on the rocky path above the creek bed, his dress shoes slipping on the damp stones. Stopping behind a thick copse of trees, Evans rested his hands on his knees as he waited for his exhaustion to fade, his heart racing as he gulped the cool night air. Dropping to one knee, he thought about the poor choice he'd made tonight and the danger he now faced.

It had seemed like a wise decision at the time. The man he had chosen to confide in was the one person who had the authority to investigate further. But Evans had misinterpreted the flicker in the man's eyes when the information had been laid before him, assuming the seasoned government official shared his concern over what he had discovered. Now Evans believed the man's concern was not for the danger the

security breaches represented but for the discovery of
the breaches themselves. Evans now realized that had
he been older and wiser, had he confided in someone
more trustworthy than powerful, he would not be in a
desolate park in the middle of the night, fleeing for his
life.

Evans pulled out his cell phone and scrolled through
his address book, the faint light of the BlackBerry display illuminating his face in the darkness. This time, he
selected a person he knew he could trust without question. A draft e-mail appeared. The first line of the message he typed was short and cryptic, only seven
characters long. He was about to expound when the snap
of a twig brought his head up.

Pressing the BlackBerry display against his chest, he
scanned his surroundings. But his eyes saw nothing in
the dark shadows. He slowed his breathing, keeping it
shallow in an effort to listen more closely, but all he heard
was the babbling of Rock Creek as it wound south toward the Potomac. As he debated whether to finish the
e-mail or resume his flight, a voice reached out from
the darkness.

"Stand up."

Searching in the direction of the voice, Evans spotted its source. In the trees twenty feet away stood a man,
his arm raised, pointing a pistol. Evans stood, then took
a step back.

"Stay where you are!"

The man's voice was familiar, but Evans couldn't
place it. His eyes strained to identify the man, but the
moon's faint illumination was insufficient.

"Who are you? What do you want?" Evans asked.

"Who have you told?"

"About what?"

The man stepped closer, his face becoming clearer. "Tell me who you have told, and I'll spare your life."

Evans almost laughed. He knew he would be dead in a few minutes regardless of what he revealed. As he held the cell phone against his chest, he slid his thumb along the keyboard and pressed Send. The message was incomplete, but it would have to do. He had run out of time. He dropped his phone on the ground as he replied to his assailant, hoping the sound of the BlackBerry hitting the path wouldn't be noticed. "I told no one. You caught up to me too soon."

Evans crushed the phone between the heel of his shoe and the rocky trail with the full weight of his body, until a sharp, impossibly loud crack echoed through the quiet park.

"What are you doing?" the man asked.

"I stepped on a stick," Evans replied, with no expectation he'd be believed.

"I can see I've wasted enough time with you already."

It appeared Evans had assessed the situation correctly; he would not leave Rock Creek Park alive. But the e-mail had been sent, offering hope the information he had collected would be successfully analyzed. Not that it mattered, Evans stepped toward his executioner, hoping to determine his identity. As the man's features slowly materialized into a recognizable face, Evans began trembling. He now understood what was at stake, what they were planning to do.

"It's a shame I have to kill you," the man said. "But when we're about to kill millions, what's one more." The man squeezed the trigger gradually, until he felt the firm recoil of the pistol in his hand.

Standing over Evans's body, the man verified the single shot had done its work. He then scanned the ground with a small flashlight, spotting the fractured BlackBerry. Stooping down, he retrieved the phone, attempting to turn it on. But the phone refused to energize. Realizing what Evans must have done, the man slipped the broken phone into his pocket, confident it could be repaired enough to reveal whom the young man had contacted and what information had been shared.

10 DAYS REMAINING

1

JERUSALEM, ISRAEL

Under normal circumstances, the thirteen men and women seated in the conference room would have been dressed in formal attire, the men wearing crisp business suits, the women turned out in silk blouses and coordinating skirts. They would have struck up lively conversations, attempting to persuade their colleagues to accept one proposal or another, their animated faces reflecting off the room's varnished chestnut paneling. But tonight, pulled away from their evening activities, they wore sports slacks and shirts, their hair wet and windblown, their faces grim as they sat quietly in their seats, eyes fixed on the man at the head of the U-shaped conference table.

Beads of rain clung to Levi Rosenfeld's Windbreaker, left there by a spring storm that had settled over the Middle East, expending itself in unbridled fury, sheets of rain descending in cascading torrents. Prime Minister Rosenfeld, flanked by all twelve members of Israel's National Security Council, fumed silently in his seat as he awaited details of an unprecedented threat to his country's existence. He wondered how such critical information could have been discovered so late. At the far left of the conference table sat Barak Kogen, Israel's intelligence minister. Although Kogen was not a member of the Security Council, Rosenfeld had directed him to attend tonight's meeting to explain the Mossad's failure.

At the front of the room, a man stood before a large flat-screen monitor. Thin and short, wearing round wire-rimmed glasses, Ehud Rabin's physical presence failed to reflect the power he wielded as the leader of Israel's second-strongest political party and as Israel's defense minister. Ehud waited for Rosenfeld's permission to begin.

Rosenfeld nodded in his direction.

Pushing his glasses onto the bridge of his nose, Ehud stated what everyone in the room already knew. "The Mossad reports Iran will complete assembly of its first nuclear weapon in ten days." The lights in the conference room flickered, thunder rumbling in the distance as if on cue.

Rosenfeld looked at his intelligence minister. "Why did we discover this just now, only days before they complete assembly?"

Kogen shifted uncomfortably in his seat, his eyes scanning each member of the Security Council before coming to rest on Rosenfeld. "I apologize, Prime Minister. Nothing is more important than preventing Iran from acquiring nuclear weapons. But Iran has deceived us and the rest of the world. We were fortunate to discover the true extent of their progress in time. We will be more vigilant in the future."

There was something about Kogen's quick apology rather than stout defense of his Mossad that gave Rosenfeld the impression he was hiding something. But perhaps the evening's tension was clouding his intuition. He turned back to Ehud. "What are our options?"

Ehud pressed a remote control in his hand, stepping aside as the monitor flickered to life, displaying a map of Iran. "Weapon assembly is occurring at the Natanz nuclear complex." A flashing red circle appeared two hundred kilometers south of Tehran. "Uranium for additional weapons is being enriched at Isfahan, and plutonium is being produced at their heavy-water plant near Arak." Two more red circles appeared in central Iran. "Eliminating the facilities at Arak and Isfahan will be easy, but destruction of their weapon assembly complex at Natanz will be impossible with a conventional strike." The map zoomed in on the Natanz facility, a sprawling collection of innocuous-looking buildings. "Iran has built a hardened complex beneath the Karkas mountains, connected to the main facility by tunnels. While a conventional strike will collapse the tunnels, it cannot destroy the weapon assembly complex."

"So how do we destroy this facility?"

"Since the complex cannot be destroyed with conventional weapons, that leaves one option."

Rosenfeld leaned forward in his chair. "What are you proposing?"

Ehud glared at the prime minister. "You know exactly what needs to be done here, Levi. We have a responsibility to protect the citizens of our country. There is no question this weapon will be used against us, either directly or indirectly. We *must* destroy this facility before

Iran completes assembly of this bomb, even if that means we have to employ one of *our* nuclear weapons."

The conference room erupted. Some council members passionately agreed with Ehud while others chastised him for proposing such an egregious break in policy. Rosenfeld slammed his fist on the table, silencing the room. "Out of the question! We will not use nuclear weapons unless they are used against us first."

Ehud's eyes narrowed. "Then millions of our people will die, because Iran *will* use this weapon against us. We can either strike now, before our men, women, and children are murdered, or afterward. If we do not strike first, their deaths will be on your conscience."

The defense minister's assertion hung in the air as Rosenfeld surveyed his council members, some of them staring back, others with their eyes to the table. Whether they agreed with Ehud or not, they could not avoid the underlying truth.

If Iran assembled this weapon, it would eventually be used against Israel. That was something Israel could not allow. But a nuclear first strike! Although the prime minister and his Security Council had the authority to authorize the use of nuclear weapons, morally . . .

Rosenfeld looked down one side of the conference table and then the other, examining the faces of the men and women seated around him, eventually returning his attention to Ehud. "Are there no conventional weapons capable of destroying this complex? Not even in the American arsenal?"

Ehud's lips drew thin. "The Americans have the necessary weapons. But they will not provide them to us while they engage in *discussions* with Iran." Ehud's voice dripped with disdain as he mentioned America's attempt to convince Iran to abandon its nuclear ambitions with mere words.

"Do not discount our ally so easily," Rosenfeld replied. "I will meet with the American ambassador tomorrow and explain the situation."

"You are blind, Levi." Ehud's face tightened. "The Americans have abandoned us, and you fail to recognize it."

"That's enough, Ehud! Provide me with the information on the weapons we need, and I will broach this with the United States."

Ehud nodded tersely.

Rosenfeld stood. "Unless there is more to discuss, I'll see you tomorrow morning."

The council members filed out of the conference room, until only Rosenfeld and Kogen remained.

Turning to Rosenfeld, Kogen said, "Prime Minister, may I have a word with you, privately?"

"Of course. What would you like to discuss?"

"It's best we not talk here."

Footsteps echoed off the gray terrazzo floor as the two men, each lost in his own thoughts, walked down the Hall of Advisers toward Rosenfeld's office. On their right, paintings of Israel's prime ministers hung in shallow alcoves, beginning with the image of their country's first premier, David Ben-Gurion, who guided Israel through its War of Independence. At the far end of the hallway, a conspicuous bare spot on the wall marked the location where Rosenfeld's portrait would someday hang.

Glancing at the shorter and heavier man walking

beside him, Kogen thought Rosenfeld had aged more than could be attributed to the normal passage of time. But that was easily explained. Shortly after his election six years ago, the prime minister had weathered a three-year intifada. Then there was the personal loss he had endured, compounded by his dual responsibilities as father and prime minister. Yet despite the toll of his years in office, the older man walked with a determined pace and slightly forward lean, as if barreling through unseen obstacles in his path. The brisk pace was his only exercise; workouts were always something to be scheduled in the not too distant future. As a result, he had steadily added padding to his midsection. But Kogen knew Rosenfeld considered his weight acceptable as long as his waist remained narrower than his shoulders. Fortunately, Rosenfeld had broad shoulders.

Kogen, on the other hand, had retained his youthful physique, lean and muscular. The taller man, always impeccably dressed, he projected an air of competence and confidence. To the uninformed, Kogen was the more ideal image of a prime minister. But his service had been limited to the military and Israel's intelligence service; he'd been appointed intelligence minister shortly after Rosenfeld's election as prime minister.

Reaching the end of the hallway, Rosenfeld and Kogen passed through a metal detector and into the Aquarium, the security guard's eyes displaying no hint of curiosity about their arrival so late on a Monday evening. The Aquarium section of the PMO, the Prime Minister's Office building, where foreign leaders visited their Israeli counterparts, contained a plush, well-appointed lobby, offices for Rosenfeld and his closest aides, and a communications center that allowed for minute-by-minute contact with the Israel Defense Forces. Kogen reflected on the many decisions Rosenfeld and previous prime ministers had made in that small room, guiding Israel through its turbulent history; decisions that paled in importance to the one that would be made tonight.

Following the prime minister into his office, Kogen sat stiffly in the chair across from Rosenfeld's desk, scanning the content of the modestly furnished room as he collected his thoughts. The furniture was spartan and utilitarian, the desk and chairs made from natural un-stained maple, unadorned with intricate carvings. The shelf behind Rosenfeld was filled with books arranged in no particular order. The office, with its indecipher-able filing system and simple furnishings, reflected the prime minister perfectly—it was difficult to gauge his reaction to complex issues, yet straightforward once a decision was made. Although Kogen had known Rosen-feld his entire adult life, he could not predict his friend's response. Rosenfeld's decision would determine whether four years of painstaking preparation had been in vain.

Heavy drops of rain pelted the prime minister's windows as Rosenfeld waited for Kogen to speak. As impatience gathered in Rosenfeld's eyes, Kogen steeled himself. He cleared his throat, then began. "We must destroy Natanz, Levi. You know better than anyone the sacrifice we will endure as a nation if Iran is allowed to develop nuclear weapons."

Rosenfeld glanced at the framed portrait of his family, still sitting on his desk. "You're not telling me anything I don't already know, Barak."

Lowering his voice, Kogen continued, "Iran is a cesspool of contempt for Israel, intent on exterminating our people. Natanz *must* be destroyed before this weapon is assembled. We do not have the necessary conventional weapons. Therefore it must be destroyed with a nuclear strike."

There was a long silence as Rosenfeld contemplated Kogen's assertion. Finally, Rosenfeld spoke. "I will not authorize the preemptive use of nuclear weapons. From a political and moral standpoint, that is something we cannot do."

Kogen leaned back in his chair, a sly smile emerging on his lips. "I never said *Israel* would launch the nuclear strike."

Rosenfeld blinked, not comprehending Kogen's statement. "Then who?"

The younger man's smile widened. "America."

A puzzled expression worked its way across Rosenfeld's face. "America? The president would never authorize this."

Kogen hesitated a moment before continuing. It was finally time to reveal the Mossad's most closely held secret. "The president's authorization isn't required, Prime Minister. Only yours. The Mossad stands ready to initiate an operation that will result in America destroying Natanz. Your authorization is the only step remaining."

Rosenfeld stared at Kogen for a long moment, then his eyes went to the portrait of his family again. No one understood better what was at stake than Rosenfeld, and

Kogen knew he was struggling. Iran didn't have an army massed on Israel's border. They didn't have a nuclear arsenal in the process of being launched. Yet the threat Iran posed was severe. It had to be dealt with, and deceiving America into employing one of its nuclear weapons was the perfect solution.

It didn't take long for Rosenfeld to come to a decision.

"Absolutely not!"

Frustration boiled inside Kogen. Still, he harbored hope Rosenfeld would eventually come to the proper decision. The Mossad plan was a radical proposal, and the prime minister would need time to accept it. After a few days of reflection, Rosenfeld would see the wisdom in Kogen's solution.

Showing no outward sign of his frustration, Kogen stood. Before turning to leave, he said, "In ten days, Prime Minister, Iran will complete assembly of this weapon. You have until then to decide."

2

BALLISTIC MISSILE SUBMARINE–USS *KENTUCKY*

Just off the south shore of Oahu, as the sun began its climb into a clear blue sky, the USS *Kentucky* surged through dark green water, the seas spilling over the bow before rolling down the sides of the long black ship. Standing on the Bridge in the submarine's tall conning tower, Lieutenant Tom Wilson, on watch as Officer of the Deck, assessed a large gray warship crossing the submarine's path ahead. The ship's Captain, Commander Brad Malone, stood next to Tom, binoculars to his eyes, likewise studying the U.S. Navy cruiser four thousand yards ahead, inbound to Pearl Harbor. Standing behind them atop the conning tower, or sail, as it was commonly called, the Lookout scanned the horizon for additional contacts. But the cruiser just off the port bow was the most pressing concern, and Tom decided to alter the *Kentucky*'s course to maintain a safe distance.

Pressing the microphone in his hand, the lieutenant passed his order to the Control Room below. "Helm, left full rudder, steady course two-six-zero." Tom turned aft to verify the order was properly executed, watching the top of the rudder, poking above the ocean's surface, rotate left. Behind the ship, the submarine's powerful propeller churned a frothy white wake as the *Kentucky* began its slow arc to port.

Tom knew the *Kentucky* would not turn quickly due to its tremendous size, which could not be appreciated while the submarine was underway or alongside a pier. Like an iceberg, most of the ship was underwater. Only in dry dock was the immensity of the submarine apparent—almost two football fields long, wide as a three-lane highway, and seven stories tall from the keel to the top of the sail. A tenth of a mile long, the submarine did not maneuver easily. But that hadn't been a factor in the tense weeklong exercise the crew had just completed.

Two weeks earlier, the *Kentucky* had slipped from the quiet waters of Hood Canal in Washington State, passed Port Ludlow and the Twin Spits into the Strait of Juan de Fuca, and entered the Pacific Ocean en route to her patrol area. Less than a day after getting under way, however, they were diverted to the Hawaiian operating areas for an unexpected week of training. The *Kentucky* had performed well during the exercise and had just offloaded a group of students onto a tug outside the entrance to Pearl Harbor. Finally, after months of training in port and the unscheduled diversion at sea, the *Kentucky* was heading out to relieve another Trident ballistic missile submarine on patrol.

The submarine's rudder returned to amidships, and the young Officer of the Deck turned his attention to the submarine's new course: westerly toward its patrol area.

Commander Malone dropped the binoculars from his eyes. "It's good to be back at sea, isn't it, Tom?"

Tom turned to the ship's Commanding Officer.

Not really.

Several weeks ago, as the crew prepared for another two-and-a-half-month long patrol, the tension between Tom and his wife had escalated. Nancy's disillusion with Navy life had grown sharper with each deployment, and now that she'd given birth to twin girls, the stress of his pending departure had sparked an explosive confrontation. Tom had finally agreed to submit his resignation when he returned from sea. This would be his last patrol.

Malone stared at him, and Tom realized he hadn't answered the Captain's question. "Yes, sir. It's good to be under way again."

The older man smiled, placing his hand on the young officer's shoulder. "You don't have to lie to me, Tom. I know it's not easy."

A report from below echoed from the Bridge communications box. "Bridge, Nav. Passing the one-hundred-fathom curve outbound." Tom acknowledged the report, then glanced at the Bridge Display Unit, checking the *Kentucky*'s progress toward the Dive Point.

"Shift the watch belowdecks," Malone ordered. "Prepare to dive."

Tom acknowledged the Captain's order as Malone ducked down into the ship's sail, descending the ladder into Control. Tom squinted up at the sun; it'd be two long months before he saw it again. Two months of fluorescent lighting and artificially controlled days and nights. Two months before the *Kentucky* returned home, the crew greeting their wives and children waiting on the pier. As much as he enjoyed his job, it paled in comparison to the joyful reunion with his wife, and now his two young daughters, at the end of each long patrol.

With his thoughts lingering on his family, Tom dropped his gaze to the horizon, then flipped the switch on the Bridge box, shifting the microphone in his hand over to the shipwide 1-MC announcing circuit.

"Shift the watch belowdecks," Tom ordered. "Prepare to dive."

Twenty minutes later, Tom descended the ladder into Control, stopping five rungs from the bottom. He pulled the heavy Lower Bridge hatch shut, spinning the handle until the hatch lugs engaged.

"Last man down, hatch secure," he announced to the new Officer of the Deck stationed on the Conn, a one-foot-high platform in the center of Control, surrounding the two periscopes. Tom signed the Rig for Dive book, then reviewed the status of the rest of the submarine's compartments. He turned to Commander Malone, standing next to the Officer of the Deck. "Captain, the ship is rigged for Dive."

Malone nodded thoughtfully. "Since this is your last patrol, why don't you take her down?"

How did he know?

Neither Tom nor Nancy had told anyone, but Tom wasn't surprised. Malone seemed to know everything about his ship and the crew that manned it.

He grinned. "I'd love to, sir." After receiving a quick update on the ship's status, he relieved as OOD, this time in Control instead of on the Bridge above, informing

Malone once the turnover was complete. "Sir, I have relieved as Officer of the Deck."

"Very well. Submerge the ship."

"Submerge the ship, aye, sir."

Before submerging, Tom surveyed his watch section in Control. Fire control technicians manned two of the four combat control consoles on the starboard side of the ship, calculating the course, speed, and range of contacts held on the ship's sensors. The Quartermaster, responsible for determining the ship's position and monitoring water depth, was bent over the chart table near the Conn. In front of Tom sat the ship's Diving Officer, supervising the two planesmen—the Outboard watchstander, who operated the submarine's diving control surfaces on the stern, and the Inboard watchstander, or Helm, who operated both the rudder and the depth-control surfaces on the submarine's sail. On the left side of the Diving Officer sat the Chief of the Watch, who was responsible for adjusting the ship's buoyancy, both overall and fore-to-aft, and operated the submarine's masts and antennas.

After carefully reviewing the status of his watch section, Tom announced loudly, "All stations, Conn. Prepare to submerge."

The Quartermaster examined the ship's Fathometer, announcing, "Two hundred fathoms beneath the keel," and the Chief of the Watch reported, "Straight board, sir. All hull penetrations sealed."

Satisfied his watch section was ready, Tom approached the port periscope, which was already raised, turned the scope until it looked forward, then pressed his face against the eyepiece, peering through the scope with his right eye. "Dive, submerge the ship to one-six-zero feet."

The Diving Officer nodded to the Chief of the Watch, who announced, "Dive, dive," on the 1-MC, then activated the ship's diving alarm. The characteristic *ooooggh-aaahh* resounded throughout the submarine, followed by "Dive, dive," again on the 1-MC. The Chief of the Watch opened the vents on top of the main ballast tanks, letting water flood up through grates in the ship's keel, and the *Kentucky* gradually sank into the ocean as it lost buoyancy. As the waves passed over the submarine's bow, the escaping air rushing out of the main ballast tank vents shot geysers of water mist high above the *Kentucky*'s sail.

"Forward tanks venting." Tom swung the scope around, looking back over the ship's stern. "Aft tanks venting."

The *Kentucky* gradually sank into the ocean, and soon only the submarine's sail was visible above the surface, the waves now passing over the top of the Missile Compartment deck.

"Deck's awash."

The *Kentucky* continued its descent, the top of the submarine's sail disappearing into the ocean as the Diving Officer announced, "Passing eight-zero feet." Waves began breaking over the top of the periscope, increasing in frequency as the *Kentucky* slipped into the depths of the Pacific Ocean.

"Scope's under."

Returning the periscope to a forward view, Tom folded the handles and reached up, rotating the periscope locking ring counterclockwise, lowering the scope into its well. The Control Room was quiet, except for occasional reports and orders between watchstanders. Tom listened closely to the Diving Officer and the Chief of the Watch as they monitored the submarine's buoyancy, determining whether they needed to flood water into or pump water out of the variable ballast tanks.

"Shutting main ballast tank vents," the Chief of the Watch reported, sealing the tanks in case the ship was grossly overweight and an Emergency Blow was required to restore buoyancy.

The submarine gradually slowed its descent until it leveled off at 160 feet. "On ordered depth," the Diving Officer announced. The *Kentucky* had submerged without a hitch, the evolution executed flawlessly.

"Well done, Tom," Malone said. "Get relieved and meet me in Nav Center with the XO and department heads."

In the Navigation Center behind Control, Tom joined Malone beside the chart table, along with the ship's Executive Officer and the submarine's four department heads. On the right of the ship's Commanding Officer stood the Executive Officer, or XO. Responsible for all administrative issues and the daily execution of the ship's activities, Lieutenant Commander Bruce Fay was the submarine's second in command. Beneath the CO and XO in the military hierarchy stood the submarine's four department heads, all on their second submarine tour with the exception of the ship's Supply Officer, the only non-nuclear-trained officer aboard.

The most senior department head, Lieutenant Commander John Hinves, standing to Malone's left, was the ship's Engineering Officer, or Eng, responsible for the nuclear reactor and propulsion plant, as well as all basic mechanical and electrical systems throughout the ship. The other three department heads were all senior lieutenants. Pete Manning was the Weapons Officer, or Weps; Alan Tyler was the Navigation Officer, or Nav; and Jeff Quimby was the submarine's Supply Officer, or Suppo, although many had not yet broken the habit of referring to the man responsible for serving the pork and beans as the Chop. Tom, one of nine junior officers aboard the submarine for their first three-year sea tour, was the only JO in Nav Center because of his assignment as Assistant Weapons Officer, responsible for the more detailed aspects of the submarine's tactical and strategic weapon systems.

As the six other men waited quietly around the chart table, Malone opened a sealed manila envelope stamped TOP SECRET in orange letters, retrieving a single-page document containing the ship's patrol orders. Until this moment, no one aboard the *Kentucky* knew their assigned operating area, where they would lurk for the duration of their patrol. Malone skimmed the document, pausing to read aloud the pertinent information.

" 'Transit through operating area Sapphire, then commence Alert Patrol in Emerald.' " Malone turned to the ship's Navigator. "How long to Emerald?"

Tyler measured off the distance on the chart between the *Kentucky*'s current position and the entrance to Emerald.

"Ten days, sir."

3

FAST-ATTACK SUBMARINE—USS *HOUSTON*

"So what have you learned?"

Captain Murray Wilson stood between the *Houston*'s two periscopes, his arms folded across his chest, glaring at the ten Prospective Commanding and Executive Officers gathered in the submarine's Control Room. The atmosphere in Control was subdued, with most of the ten PCOs and PXOs staring down at the submarine's deck. As Captain Wilson dressed down his students, the *Houston*'s crew sat quietly at their watch stations, painfully aware their performance during the Submarine Command Course had been dismal as well.

"In twenty engagements over the last week, the *Kentucky* consistently defeated you, sinking this ship every time. A ballistic missile submarine, not even one of our front-line fast attacks, handed your ass to you." Wilson shook his head, then asked his question again. "So what have you learned?"

One of the PCOs, headed to relieve as commanding officer of the USS *Greeneville,* spoke. "We need to better position the ship, taking advantage of the ocean's thermal layer. The *Kentucky* gained her advantage through better employment of her sensors."

"True," Wilson replied, "but that's not the answer I'm looking for."

An uneasy silence settled over the Control Room again until a second PCO spoke, this one headed to relieve as commanding officer of the *West Virginia*. "Countermeasures aren't very effective against our AD-CAP torpedo. You have to be more aggressive in your evasion tactics when you're being shot at with advanced digital torpedoes."

"Another good observation," Wilson said, "but still not what I'm looking for."

Silence returned to the Control Room as Murray Wilson, the most senior captain in the Submarine Force, waited for the obvious answer from one of the students in the twelfth Submarine Command Course under his instruction. Each year, the Submarine Force held four command courses, ensuring each officer tapped to relieve as a submarine commanding or executive officer fully grasped the knowledge and tactical guidance necessary to successfully lead his crew in combat. The three months of intense training culminated in a weeklong exercise at sea, the students split between two submarines, pitted against each other day and night, their Torpedo Rooms filled to the gills with exercise torpedoes.

The *Houston* was supposed to go head-to-head against another fast attack, the *Scranton,* but an electrical turbine casualty sent the *Scranton* to the yards for repair, and the *Kentucky* was hastily drafted into service. When the students assigned to the *Houston* learned the *Kentucky,* which specialized in launching missiles instead of hunting enemy submarines, had replaced the *Scranton,* their reaction was glib; they were confident they would defeat the *Kentucky* without breaking a sweat.

They couldn't have been more wrong.

Wilson's gaze swept across his now humble students, stopping on Commander Joe Casey, headed to the USS *Texas,* one of the *Virginia*-class fast attacks. He'd been the most boisterous of his students, loudly proclaiming they'd crush the *Kentucky* in every scenario.

"Commander Casey. What's the most important lesson you learned this week?" Casey looked up, and Wilson knew from the look in the young commander's eyes that he had learned his lesson.

Casey said, "Don't be too cocky."

Wilson smiled. "That's exactly right, gentlemen. Never underestimate your opponent, which is exactly what you did this week. When you found out the *Kentucky* replaced the *Scranton,* you expected a cakewalk. Going up against a ballistic missile submarine instead of one of our fast attacks was going to be like what, Commander Bates?"

Doug Bates, standing next to Casey, looked up and answered quietly, "Like shooting fish in a barrel."

"Things didn't turn out quite the way you expected, did they? Just because the *Kentucky* is a ballistic missile submarine doesn't make her any less capable than a fast attack. All of her department heads have served on fast attacks—and don't forget, I trained her commanding officer and executive officer. True, her sonar and combat control systems are a generation behind what we have on our fast attacks, but they are capable enough in the hands of a crew that understands the ship's strengths and weaknesses, and most important, doesn't underestimate their opponent. When you lead your submarine into the Western Pacific or through the Red Sea into the Gulf, you'll be pitted against what could easily be considered an inferior adversary, lacking the sophisticated equipment and training you enjoy. But all it takes is one mistake, one incorrect assumption, one *torpedo* to send you and your crew to the bottom."

Wilson's ire began to build as he contemplated the fate of his students. He ought to fail them all, permanently ending their careers, a fitting reward for their inability to lead their crew in combat. But as he scanned the faces of the sullen and embarrassed officers, he wondered if instead of this being his worst class, it was his best. No other group of Prospective Commanding and Executive Officers had learned this critical lesson more thoroughly than the men standing in front of him.

"Excuse me, sir." The *Houston*'s Junior Officer of the Deck interrupted Wilson. "The Captain requests your presence on the Bridge. The *Kentucky* has returned to periscope depth and is requesting release."

Wilson acknowledged the officer's report, then finished addressing his students. "When we get back to port, I want a complete reconstruction of each encounter, with detailed analysis of what you did wrong and what you could have done better in each scenario. You have seventy-two hours to complete reconstruction of all twenty events."

A moment later, Murray Wilson emerged onto the *Houston*'s small Bridge cockpit, squinting as his eyes adjusted to the bright daylight, joining Commander Kevin Lawson, the *Houston*'s commanding officer.

"Looks like I've got some work to do," Lawson said, a look of embarrassment on his face. "I know I've got a new Sonar Chief, but I didn't realize how far the sonar shack's proficiency had fallen. We'll spend a few weeks in the sonar trainer before our next deployment."

Wilson didn't reply. He knew Lawson would take a turn on his crew as soon as they returned to port. Instead, his eyes searched the horizon for the *Kentucky*.

"Bearing two-seven-zero relative," the Lookout behind Wilson said.

Turning to his left, Wilson spotted the *Kentucky*'s periscope and antenna just off the *Houston*'s port beam, only a few hundred yards away as the ballistic missile submarine headed out to sea for her long strategic deterrent patrol.

Lawson passed the handheld radio to Wilson. "The *Kentucky*'s on channel sixteen."

Wilson took the radio, holding it close to his mouth. "Outbound Navy unit, this is inbound Navy unit, over."

A familiar voice crackled from the radio; Murray's son, Tom, responded to the *Houston*'s hail. "Inbound Navy unit, request release, over."

Wilson replied, "Outbound Navy unit, you are released for other duties. Godspeed and good hunting, over."

There was a burst of static, followed by Tom's response. "That's not an appropriate wish for this class of submarine, but thanks anyway. See you in a few months, sir. This is outbound Navy unit, out."

Wilson handed the radio back to Lawson, then

watched the *Kentucky*'s periscope grow smaller as the submarine headed out to sea, finally disappearing altogether as she descended into the murky ocean depths. A brisk wind whipped through the fast attack's Bridge, sending a chill down Wilson's spine. He rubbed both arms as he looked up, noting a towering bank of dark gray cumulus clouds approaching from the west, the direction the *Kentucky* was headed. But Wilson's son and the rest of the submarine's crew wouldn't even notice the storm churning the water's surface several hundred feet above them.

"The cold front's rolling in fast," Wilson said, turning to Lawson. "Let's get in before we get caught in the storm."

4

WASHINGTON, D.C.

National Security Adviser Christine O'Connor sat in her West Wing office with her elbows propped on her polished rosewood desk, rubbing her temples with her fingertips in a slow circular motion. As she gazed out her window overlooking the White House south lawn, hoping for relief from her pounding headache, she took no notice of the gray skies and steady rain that had moved in overnight. Instead, her thoughts dwelt on the upcoming meeting with the president's chief of staff; the reason, she was sure, for her painful migraine.

Searching through her desk, Christine located and then downed four ibuprofen with a gulp of lukewarm coffee. Although she felt far older today, she was only forty-two, not that most people would have guessed; only the thin lines around her slate-blue eyes gave her age away. Still, it felt like her time in the administration had aged her more than it was worth. As Christine brushed a strand of auburn hair away from her face, she wondered, not for the first time, if she had made the right decision.

Two years earlier, in the incoming administration's temporary spaces off Pennsylvania Avenue, Christine had sat nervously across from the president-elect, answering pointed questions from the man she'd met only moments earlier. She hadn't expected the interview to go particularly well; she disagreed with the president-elect's positions on national security on almost every point and made no effort to imply otherwise. However, there must have been something about her straightforward responses and poised demeanor that sealed the deal for the president. Christine had accepted the appointment, even though she knew it would be difficult working in an administration whose political views she didn't share. Unfortunately, she hadn't counted on the animosity between her and the president's chief of staff.

Kevin Hardison was the kind of type A personality who cared only about results. As the president's right-hand man, he was unencumbered with the obligation—or the talent—to maintain personal relationships. He didn't seem to care whose feelings he hurt or careers he ruined in his quest to achieve the administration's goals. Although Hardison treated the rest of the White House staff fairly, with equal disdain, he seemed to have reserved a special spot in that black void where his heart should have been for Christine.

This wasn't the first time she had worked with Hardison, and the previous experience had been altogether different. The two had met on Congressman Tim Johnson's staff, working in his office in Rayburn Hall. Christine, fresh out of Penn State with a political science degree, had been paired up with Hardison, ten years her senior, to learn the ropes. The two had gotten along well, developing what she thought was a strong friendship.

So it was no surprise to Christine that Hardison had recommended her to the president. However, Hardison had assumed she was still the malleable staffer she once was, and that he would be able to force her to acquiesce to his policy initiatives. Hardison hadn't responded well to his rude awakening once she assumed the role of national security adviser.

As Christine navigated the hazards of disagreeing with the powerful chief of staff, it didn't take long to determine why the president had selected her for his national security adviser. As a congressional staffer, Christine had specialized in weapon procurement programs, analyzing and recommending adjustments to the budget. Her weapon system expertise had proved valuable to the current administration, as few, if any, on staff knew the difference between a Tomahawk and a Standard missile, between a Sidewinder and an AIM-9X, or even the basic difference between a mortar, a howitzer, and an artillery gun, the latter distinction being crucial to those fighting in the mountainous regions of Afghanistan.

Perhaps even more important was the experience she had gained as the assistant secretary of defense for special operations and low-intensity conflict, along with a two-year stint as the director of nuclear defense policy. Her track record working for both Republicans and Democrats was noteworthy, and her ties to the Defense

Department's congressional supporters were extensive. Her ability to liaise effectively with key representatives and senators on both sides of the aisle had proved useful to the president, who, as a former governor of a Midwestern state, was considered a Washington outsider.

One of the staff secretaries entered Christine's office with a stack of files in her arms. Seeing the bottle of ibuprofen, the secretary came to a quick and correct conclusion. "You're meeting with Hardison, aren't you, Miss O'Connor?"

Christine nodded, smiling weakly. The chief of staff had crafted yet another plan to restructure the nation's intelligence agencies, no different from the last in any meaningful way, and was awaiting her endorsement. That endorsement would not be forthcoming. She believed the endless reorganizations, despite the impressive names and ambitious proclamations, did nothing more than change the tablecloth. The only way to make significant changes was to break some china. But the venerable intelligence agencies had far too many congressional allies for any meaningful reorganization to occur.

As Christine prepared to review the four reorganizations since September 11, 2001, the secretary clutched the files against her chest, evidently not noticing Christine wasn't in a particularly talkative mood. Christine was about to politely request the files when she spotted Hardison, headed down the hallway toward her office, a frown on his face.

"Speak of the devil," the secretary whispered. "And he doesn't look too pleased."

*   *   *

Hardison entered Christine's office, wasting no time on pleasantries. He grabbed the remote on Christine's desk, pointing it at the TV on the wall across the room. A reporter appeared on-screen, umbrella in hand protecting her hair and makeup from the steady drizzle, the spandrels of the Calvert Bridge arching gracefully behind her. "To recap today's gruesome discovery, the murder victim discovered in Rock Creek Park has been identified as twenty-two-year-old Russell Evans, a White House intern. Police officials have provided few additional details, but we'll keep you up-to-date as new information is obtained. This is Doreen Cornellier, Channel Nine news."

Christine stared at the TV in disbelief. Russell . . . murdered?

The TV went black, and Hardison tossed the remote control back onto Christine's desk. "Leave," he said to the secretary, who was still clutching the files.

Christine stood to accept the files. She numbly thanked the older woman, who avoided the chief of staff's stare as she hurried out of the office.

"When was the last time you talked with Evans?" Hardison asked.

She placed the files on her desk, then focused on Hardison's question. "Friday night. I stopped by his desk on my way out and he said he'd be working late."

"What was he working on?"

"I had him reviewing nuclear weapon policy initiatives we have under development. Why do you ask?"

Hardison's eyebrows furrowed. "Call me paranoid, but someone just murdered your intern, and I'd like to convince myself his death was unrelated to his work.

That he didn't piss off a powerful constituent or lobbyist group."

"You think his murder was politically motivated?"

"No, it was probably just a mugging gone wrong. But we're meeting stiff resistance to some of the legislation we're pushing forward, and I'd like to know if he was working on anything sensitive."

"I don't think so, Kevin." Christine glanced at the dark TV. "Do you want me to look into it?"

"No, I'll take care of it. Get back to work. Did you approve the intelligence agency restructuring?"

"No," Christine replied coolly.

Hardison approached Christine behind her desk, stopping a foot away, a scowl on his face. The strong scent of his aftershave assailed her. "Why are you here? Why did you take this job?"

Standing her ground, Christine refused to be intimidated by Hardison's physical presence. "Because the president asked me to. Because he, unlike *you*, values dissent, wants to hear the other side of the story and not just the stilted one-sided crap you feed him."

The muscles in Hardison's jaw twitched. "The president has the vision, and I do the heavy lifting. I've melded this White House staff into a formidable team, and you refuse to join that team, bucking my policies at every turn."

Christine glared up at him. "You mean the *president's* policies. Or do you?"

"Don't mince words with me, Christine. Either get on board, or get out of the way."

Christine pressed her lips together as several inflammatory responses flashed through her mind. Instead, she took a more personal approach. "What happened to you, Kevin? We used to be friends, working together to achieve the same goals."

"That was twenty years ago, Christine. I've become a realist, while you cling to your idealistic dreams. I achieve results, while you do nothing more than make my job difficult."

It was pointless to continue the discussion. She settled into her chair. "Is there anything else you'd like to discuss?"

"I want your concurrence on the restructuring proposal."

Christine smiled. "Don't hold your breath."

Hardison gritted his teeth, then turned and left.

Leaning back in her chair, Christine rubbed her temples again with both hands. Maybe Hardison was right. She felt like a salmon swimming upstream, making no headway against the current of well-intentioned, but ultimately damaging, policies being pushed forward. Then again, she had taken the job not because she thought she'd be able to implement policies she believed in, but because she believed in damage control. If she could derail just a few of the administration's disastrous initiatives, her suffering would be worth it.

As Christine dwelt on her misery, her thoughts turned to Russell Evans. The young man's mysterious death weighed heavily on her, and her heart went out to his parents. She couldn't imagine their grief upon opening their front door to a police officer delivering the unwelcome news.

Pushing her thoughts about Evans aside, Christine

checked her e-mail, picking up where she'd left off Friday evening. After she'd replied to a few e-mails, her hand froze as the mouse cursor passed over a message with no subject.

It was from Evans. Sent last night, just after midnight.

Christine clicked to open the e-mail and was greeted with a white screen containing a single phrase: E DRIVE.

e drive?

Checking the TO: and CC: fields, Christine noted the e-mail had been sent only to her. Turning her attention back to the solitary phrase, she contemplated why Evans would send her this cryptic e-mail. Perhaps the message was incomplete.

Or maybe it was everything she needed to know.

Opening the My Computer icon on her desktop, she searched through the drive directory. The C and D drives were folders on the computer's hard drive. The E drive was her CD drive. Christine pressed Eject, waiting as the drive tray slid out.

There was nothing in it.

She tapped her index finger on her desk, wondering if Evans meant *his* E drive. Stepping outside her office, Christine scanned the desks in the adjacent West Wing alcove where several interns and office staff worked, her eyes coming to rest on the computer beside Evans's desk. Her intuition gnawed at her, warning her to consider carefully to whom she revealed Evans's e-mail, as well as the results of her search. After verifying no one else was within view, she stopped by Evans's desk, pressing Eject on his computer.

A disk slid out.

Christine placed the CD into a plastic case resting on

Evans's desk, and a moment later she was back in her office. When she slid the disk into her computer, a windowpane opened on her monitor, displaying the contents of the CD. There were several dozen files, their names consisting of random letters and numbers. Christine double-clicked on the first file, but nothing happened. She tried to open it with various applications, each failing to respond or returning a pane of gibberish.

As she searched, a Recall notice from Evans appeared in her Outlook in-box, and a second later, the notice and Evans's original e-mail were gone. Christine blinked at the screen in stunned silence, until two things became clear.

The first was that whoever had killed Evans had his BlackBerry.

The second was that there was something very important about his CD.

Christine picked up the phone and dialed the familiar number to the office in Langley. A few rings later, the call was answered.

"Director Ronan, this is Christine. I have a favor to ask of you."

5

TEL AVIV, ISRAEL

Greg Vandiver's eyes cracked open against their will, fluttering shut again in response to the bright shaft of sunlight streaming through the second-story bedroom window overlooking Rabin Square. Rolling to his side, Vandiver forced his eyelids back open again, the color of his bloodshot eyes matching the numbers on the digital clock next to his bed. A painful pounding reverberated through his head, and it took a moment for him to realize someone was banging on the bedroom door—Joyce, no doubt. Vandiver sat up quickly, immediately regretting it as his head began throbbing in sync with the vigorous knocks.

Suddenly remembering he was not in bed alone, Vandiver turned and studied the young woman sleeping peacefully next to him, a thin sheet covering her naked body. Her straight, glossy black hair was spread across the white pillow as if it had been neatly arranged for a photo shoot. Almond-shaped eyes and caramel-colored skin rounded out her sensual beauty, a sharp contrast to the man admiring her. At five foot six and 180 pounds, U.S. Ambassador Greg Vandiver was not a particularly attractive man. Constantly on a diet that included too much wine and dessert, he had steadily added weight to his frame. Yet, at fifty-five, his smile retained its youthful exuberance and his thick black hair had yet to be invaded by the first strand of gray. His wealth and political influence compensated for his bland physical features—it never failed to amaze him how young women found money and power almost impossible to resist.

The pounding on the door resumed, this time accompanied by a rattling of its hinges. Vandiver stooped down, pulling on a white cotton robe he had deposited on the floor the previous evening. "Enter!" he shouted, immediately regretting his loud response as his head pulsed. The woman next to him stirred in her sleep, licking her full, luscious lips.

The door swung open, and Vandiver's executive assistant entered the bedroom. It took only a second for Joyce Eddings's eyes to take in the all-too-familiar scene. "You need to get moving, Ambassador. You have an unscheduled meeting with the prime minister in an hour and a half at his office in Jerusalem."

Vandiver studied Joyce's face; as usual, she expressed neither approval nor disapproval. Glancing at the clock again, he verified he had thirty minutes before departing for his meeting. But first, he had to make arrangements for a token of appreciation for his female guest. "Can you send—"

"Roses or carnations?" Joyce asked, pad and pen already in her hands.

Vandiver pondered for a moment, recalling his late-night escapade. "Roses. And get her phone number."

"Her name?" Joyce asked, the corners of her mouth turning slightly upward as she prepared to wait patiently while the ambassador struggled to answer the simple, yet always difficult, question.

Vandiver's eyes fell to the young woman still asleep in bed, trying to pull her name from last evening's fog. While he never forgot a face or a body, names were another matter altogether. Finally, he located the first memory of last night's encounter—her warm, firm handshake, the movement of her eyes as she quickly surveyed his body, her glistening lips parting as she introduced herself. Aah, yes.

"Alyssah." A beautiful name for an even more beautiful girl.

Ambassador Vandiver lifted up the bedsheet, admiring Alyssah's exquisite body one last time before beginning his day. Letting out a heavy sigh, he let the sheet fall.

An hour later, the harsh morning sun reflected off the flat desert landscape as a black Mercedes-Benz sped southeast along Highway 1, following the path of the ancient Roman highway connecting the coastal plains of the Mediterranean and the sandstone buildings of Jerusalem. Vandiver relaxed in the backseat of the armored S600 as Joyce, seated beside him, shuffled through several folders on her lap, searching for the answer to his last question. Vandiver knew it was unlikely the issue of foreign military financing would come up at this morning's meeting. However, he preferred to be prepared.

While showering and shaving, he had narrowed the list of potential topics, with this being the seventh and least probable on his list.

Joyce succeeded in locating the desired brief, pulling it from the folder with an exaggerated gesture. As she traced her finger down the sheet looking for the amount of economic and military aid provided by the United States to Israel and its neighbors each year, Vandiver reflected on how the U.S. government, not unlike himself, routinely used its wealth and influence to seduce or, to more accurately describe the process, procure reluctant friends.

The 1979 Israel-Egypt peace treaty was hailed by many as a historic turning point, bringing the long-awaited peace desired by both Arabs and Israelis. But most people didn't know this international agreement had been, in part, procured by the United States. Each year the treaty remains in effect, Egypt receives two billion dollars in aid and Israel four billion, the bulk of which is foreign military financing—a grant that must be spent on U.S. military equipment. A clever way, Vandiver had to admit, to buy friends and influence their behavior while simultaneously feeding the American defense industry.

As Vandiver reflected on the tactics employed by the powerful United States against its weaker enemies and friends alike, he found it ironic they were passing the Route 38 interchange, taking travelers south to the Valley of Elah, the site of David's epic biblical battle against Goliath. Only fourteen miles from Jerusalem and flanked by rolling Judean hills, the verdant valley slopes gently downward to a carpet of red anemones and multicolored lupines, through which wanders the seasonal brook where David gathered the stone used to slay Goliath.

Israel, despite its size, was no David, easily fielding the most capable military in the Middle East and the only country in the region with nuclear weapons. The outcome of a conflict with any of its neighbors, or even a multinational coalition, was not in doubt. However, Vandiver had learned from his lead Diplomatic Security Service agent that Israel's National Security Council had met unexpectedly late last night. The prime minister's request they meet so quickly after the Security Council meeting worried him. It was likely America's assistance would be requested. What could possibly be beyond Israel's capability?

Twenty minutes later, Vandiver's car rolled to a halt outside a building that looked more like a run-down factory on the side of a highway than the headquarters of Israel's executive government. Vandiver knew that aside from the luxurious Aquarium, the accommodations in the prime minister's headquarters matched the building's outward appearance. Climbing out of the sedan, Vandiver was greeted by Hirshel Mekel, the prime minister's executive assistant, and another man, Mekel's aide. After the requisite introductions, the young aide guided Joyce toward the Media Situation Room as Mekel escorted Vandiver into the Aquarium.

Entering Levi Rosenfeld's office, Vandiver crossed the room, extending his hand. "Good morning, Prime Minister."

Rosenfeld rose, stepping out from behind his desk to greet his American friend. "I'm glad you could meet this morning on such short notice."

Vandiver shook Rosenfeld's hand vigorously. "No problem at all." Glancing to his left, Vandiver noticed a man sitting in a chair against the wall.

"Barak Kogen," Rosenfeld said, "my intelligence minister."

Vandiver eyed the head of Israel's Mossad warily for a second before returning his attention to Rosenfeld. "What can I do for you today, Prime Minister?"

"We have a serious situation," Rosenfeld said, "and we need the United States' assistance."

"How can we help?"

"Please, sit." Rosenfeld returned to his seat and Vandiver sat in a chair across from Rosenfeld's desk. A steward knocked, then entered with a tray of coffee and pastries, which he deposited on the end table next to Vandiver's chair. After pouring the ambassador a cup of coffee, the steward retreated, and Rosenfeld waited patiently while Vandiver's hand hovered over the pastries, finally selecting the most appealing one. Now that Ambassador Vandiver had a cup of coffee in one hand and a pastry in the other, he devoted his full attention to Israel's prime minister as he spoke.

"We have been concerned, Ambassador, that Iran will develop nuclear weapons, fearful they will be used against Israel. We have discovered that Iran is less than ten days away from completing the assembly of its first nuclear bomb."

Vandiver interrupted the prime minister, waving the pastry in his hand in the process. "Iran wouldn't dare use nuclear weapons against you. They know the United States wouldn't stand by—that we'd retaliate." Vandiver paused, realizing how his last statement, meant to reassure their ally, might have sounded to the Israelis. *After Iran wipes out part, if not your entire country, we'll teach them a lesson.*

Thinly veiled disgust spread across Rosenfeld's face. "We cannot let Iran obtain nuclear weapons. Unfortunately, the Iranian weapon complex is deep underground, protected by hardened bunkers. The conventional weapons in Israel's arsenal aren't powerful enough to destroy this facility, so we need your assistance. We need four of your newest bunker-busting bombs . . ." Rosenfeld glanced down at a sheet of paper on his desk, "the Massive Ordnance Penetrator, by the end of this week."

Vandiver placed the half-eaten pastry back onto the tray, his friendly demeanor transitioning to a cool façade. "I'm afraid I already know the answer to your request, Prime Minister. I've discussed this topic extensively with Washington, and the answer is no. Our administration is committed to peaceful negotiations with Iran, and will not authorize the transfer of any weapons to Israel that could disrupt that process."

"I see," Rosenfeld said tersely.

Kogen joined the conversation. "Ambassador Vandiver, I noticed your choice of words. You said the United States would not *authorize* the transfer of the weapons we seek. What is the United States willing to transfer to Israel *without* official authorization?"

Vandiver straightened his back. "It appears I've chosen my words poorly. Let me rephrase, to be perfectly clear. The United States will *not* provide Israel with additional offensive weapons, either officially or un-officially. Am I speaking clearly enough now?"

Kogen leaned back in his chair, the friendly expression on his face fading to an impassive mask. "Clear as crystal, I believe the saying goes in your country."

Vandiver turned back to Rosenfeld, whose face was slowly reddening as he absorbed the ambassador's response. More than thirty years earlier, President Reagan's use of the term "evil empire" in characterizing the Soviet Union, and later, George W. Bush's coinage of "axis of evil" had been ridiculed by many, their overly simplistic view of the world failing to reflect the complexity of modern politics. But Vandiver knew Rosenfeld shared that view, that he believed the two American presidents had assessed the situation with remarkable clarity—right versus wrong, good versus evil. And Israel's war against Islamic fanaticism was a quintessential example of the struggle between good and evil. A struggle the United States was now refusing to support.

"You claim to be Israel's closest ally," Rosenfeld fumed, his frustration bleeding through as he spoke, "yet you abandon us in our hour of need. Let me make something perfectly clear to *you*, Ambassador. Israel has the means to defend herself, and the fallout"—Rosenfeld hesitated for a moment as if reconsidering his choice of words—"the blood we shed will be on *your* hands if you do not provide us with the conventional weapons we need."

There was an uneasy silence as Vandiver assimilated the prime minister's last statement. Rosenfeld's choice of words did not go unnoticed, but they couldn't possibly mean what Vandiver thought they did. "Are you saying Israel will use nuclear weapons to destroy the Iranian facility?"

Rosenfeld greeted the ambassador's question with an icy stare.

The hair stood up on the back of Vandiver's neck. This was not just another diplomatic drill, putting a face on the administration's policies. Israel was *actually* contemplating the use of nuclear weapons in a proactive attack to defend itself. The Arab and world response would be unpredictable; a half dozen scenarios played out quickly in Vandiver's mind, all of them bad. Very bad. But one thing was clear—no matter what followed Israel's use of nuclear weapons, the outcome would be catastrophic for Middle East peace and stability. Israel could not be allowed to conduct a nuclear first strike.

Vandiver's eyes narrowed. "The support you have within the United States, both from its people and government, not to mention the four billion dollars in defense aid you receive each year, will evaporate if you attack Iran with nuclear weapons."

Rosenfeld stood suddenly. "Thank you for coming, Ambassador. I presume you know the way out?" His hands remained at his sides. No warm handshake and friendly smile would follow this morning's meeting.

U.S. Ambassador Greg Vandiver stood, glaring at Rosenfeld, then turned abruptly and left.

Barak Kogen rose and closed the door to Rosenfeld's office, locking it. Turning back toward the older man, he waited as the prime minister collapsed into his chair. The meeting had gone exactly as he had expected. The Americans could no longer be counted on to defend Israel, and now his foresight would prove valuable. The Mossad's operation had been tabletopped a hundred times, and after the addition of a few contingency plans, the outcome was always the same. All that stood in the way was the prime minister's approval.

Assessing the older man's crestfallen appearance, Kogen decided to press Rosenfeld again for approval. "It appears the only way to defend Israel is through the use of nuclear weapons," he began. "And who do you want the world to blame for this attack? We have the opportunity to defend ourselves and pin the blame on our so-called ally, who abandons us when we need their assistance the most."

After a moment, Rosenfeld replied, "We cannot defend our people by unleashing a nuclear holocaust, Barak. You seem unable to recognize that moral restriction."

"No, Levi, I disagree. You seem unable to recognize the choice you face. You must choose either Israel's *survival* or *destruction*."

After a moment's thought, Rosenfeld shook his head slowly. "I disagree, Barak. I'm prepared to authorize conventional strikes to protect our people, but not a nuclear attack. We will monitor Natanz closely, and if they move their weapon from the facility, we will strike quickly."

Kogen's eyes glowered, his frustration increasing as the hope Rosenfeld would authorize the Mossad operation faded. "We may not be able to detect the weapon's movement and strike before it is used against us. We have the opportunity to destroy this bomb and eliminate the risk to our people, but you must authorize the operation soon. Think this through carefully, Levi, before you let this opportunity pass."

6

JERUSALEM, ISRAEL

It was just before noon as a black BMW 7 Series sedan navigated the busy Jerusalem streets, fighting its way toward the original walled city in the heart of the Israeli capital. The previous week's storm had left behind a plain blue sky from which hung a solitary yellow disk, spreading welcome warmth across the city. Tables from roadside cafés spilled out onto the sidewalks, nearly every chair occupied as the city's population celebrated the sun's reemergence after a weeklong hiatus. The crowded sidewalks had dried for the most part, and pedestrians skirted the few shallow puddles that remained as Rosenfeld's sedan passed by unnoticed.

In the backseat of the armored car, Rosenfeld tried unsuccessfully to relax. He had slept fitfully, his dreams filled with images of Hannah, and had awoken tired and irritable. If that weren't enough, his meeting with Ehud Rabin this morning had been contentious, their conversation focused on military options available to destroy the Iranian nuclear facilities. His defense minister and old friend continued to insist the only way to destroy the facility at Natanz was with a nuclear strike.

As the BMW turned left onto Agron Street, Rosenfeld checked his watch. He was looking forward to a temporary distraction from his duties as prime minister, having decided to join his children for lunch at Sandrino's, just inside the ramparts of the Old City. As his face brightened with the thought of seeing his twin daughters, he couldn't help but think how much they resembled Hannah and how much she would have enjoyed watching them grow up.

It had been three years since Hannah died, killed indiscriminately by a rocket launched from Gaza. He should have spent more time with Sarah and Rachel after Hannah's death, but his duties as prime minister consumed him. He poured his efforts into retaliation against the Palestinians who murdered his children's mother, hoping the justice he wrought would lessen the sorrow of their loss. But he realized too late that what his daughters needed most wasn't revenge, but simply him. Now he scheduled time in his busy week for his children, attending their school activities and dropping in on them when he could. He looked forward to enjoying the simple and satisfying role of father this afternoon, temporarily setting aside the complicated and frustrating role of prime minister.

Just inside the Jaffa Gate of the original walled city of Jerusalem, sixteen-year-old Khalid Abdulla stepped off a Number 20 bus onto the busy sidewalk, his six-year journey almost complete. As he walked east along David Street, pedestrians passing by failed to register the rage smoldering inside the young man, noticing instead his polite smile. Nor did they note his lean build as they hurried by, because today he carried thirty extra pounds of weight under his loose-fitting jacket.

After a short walk down David Street, Abdulla stopped just inside one of the street-side cafés, his attention drawn toward two girls sitting at a table near the front of the restaurant, each girl wearing her long black hair draped over the front of her left shoulder. One of the girls looked at him and smiled, the radiant stare of her large brown eyes soon joined by her twin sister's. For just a moment, Abdulla forgot why he'd come, mesmerized by the girls' beauty. But then his hatred broke the spell, pulling his thoughts six years into the past.

Abdulla was only ten when he heard the gut-wrenching scream from the adjoining room, a mother's unmistakable wail of grief and unspeakable loss. Moments later, his mother swept him into her arms, her damp face pressed against his, whispering the words that ignited his hatred. His only brother was dead, killed by Israeli soldiers forcing their way into Gaza, their tanks crushing everything in their path. As she pulled away, she appeared older; frail and broken. Abdulla wiped his mother's tears from his cheek, and with them, his childhood. His purpose in life, and death, for that matter, had crystallized that instant.

Sitting at a table near the front of the café, Sarah followed her sister's eyes across the crowded restaurant. She knew before she turned her head what had caught her sibling's attention. Rachel's widening eyes, the faint blushing of her cheeks, her lips parting into an inviting smile—she'd spotted an attractive boy. It had never seemed unusual to Sarah that they could read the subtle changes in each other's facial expressions and mannerisms, communicating without uttering a word.

One glance at her sister at the end of the school day could tell Sarah many things; that Rachel had done well on her math test, that she'd spoken with Amir after English class, and that he had finally asked her out. Yet they talked incessantly, rattling on about how their day had gone, filling in the missing details. From the moment Sarah woke until her thoughts faded to dreams, she was never far from Rachel. God had designed them that way, she had concluded, connected to each other by an invisible, inseparable bond.

Off from school for the Lag Ba'Omer holiday, Sarah and Rachel had ventured into the Old City, shopping in the upscale stores along David Street, eventually arriving at Sandrino's. Unlike most adolescents, who shied away from being seen with their parents in public, Sarah and Rachel looked forward to the occasional lunchtime rendezvous with their father. To others, he was the prime minister, but to them, he was simply abi, the Hebrew word for father. When translated to English, Sarah knew it meant "the one who gives strength to the family." Now that the dark days following their mother's death had passed, he was there for them, giving them strength when they missed their mother the most.

Tonight would be one of those times, as they gathered with their aunts, uncles, and cousins to celebrate the end of the plague that had killed Rabbi Akiva and twenty-four thousand of his students. Aaron would be there, an attractive boy not unlike the teenager standing just inside the café entrance. There was something about the strange boy who stared at them, a dark brooding in his eyes that captured Sarah's attention. He had suffered a terrible loss, she could tell, the type of loss shared by many in Israel, for who had not lost a friend or a loved one in the bitter and pointless conflict between Jews and Arabs?

The boy's eyes left the two girls, scanning the restaurant, evidently searching for a table. Sarah considered asking him to join them. After all, there were two empty chairs at their table and he was rather attractive. But she thought better of it. Rachel didn't need any encouragement; she went through boyfriends like fashion accessories, and it seemed the boy across the café had suffered enough heartache. She noticed Rachel was about to rise and ask him over. A hand on her forearm and a quick look convinced her otherwise.

Abdulla turned away from the two girls; they were Jews, after all, and therefore their beauty should hold no appeal. Besides, his attraction to the twins would be irrelevant in a few minutes. Abdulla made his way to the back of the café, where, standing against the wall, the effect would be magnified. He stopped, turned around, then reached into his jacket pocket, his fingers sliding through the slit in the pocket lining.

Sitting at a table near the back of the café, Katherine Jankowski fed her six-month-old son as she waited for her antipasto to arrive. Matthew, strapped into a high chair, was waving his hands in the jerky and uncoordinated way infants do when they're excited, his eyes locked onto the spoonful of pureed carrots his mother was pushing toward his open mouth. Katherine would normally have been accompanied by her friend Alanah, but as Shabbat gave way to Lag Ba'Omer, Alanah had joined the half million Jews who make the pilgrimage each year to Mount Meron in northern Israel. Katherine's husband, Jonathan, had graciously volunteered to fill in during Alanah's absence, but he was running late, which was not an unusual occurrence.

As the waitress dropped off the antipasto, a teenager passed by Katherine's table. She watched him stop at the back wall and turn around and reach into his jacket pocket, searching for something. He surveyed the café in an odd way, and his thin face was somehow incommensurate with his girth. Her subconscious hammered at her, warning her that she was missing something important. As she studied the young man, searching for a clue to the uneasy feeling, he looked up toward the restaurant ceiling, his face radiating utter joy and contentment. His hand stopped fidgeting, evidently finding what he searched for. Katherine's eyes widened as the pieces fell into place.

She reached for her son.

But it was already too late.

A bright orange flash illuminated the windows of Rosenfeld's BMW. A second later, he lurched forward against his seat belt as the sedan screeched to a halt. Rosenfeld peered through the side window in an attempt to obtain a clear view of what had happened. Pedestrians were running toward and past his car, away from a mass of black smoke that spiraled upward less than a block away.

Climbing out of the sedan, Rosenfeld strained his eyes to identify the location of the blast. He spotted the sign marking the restaurant Bellaroma. And there was the Essex. But he was looking for Sandrino's, which was between the two.

Rosenfeld pushed past his security detail, jogging toward the source of the chaos, dodging the men and women fleeing in the opposite direction. An explosion had destroyed one of the cafés. Rosenfeld's pace increased as his desperation mounted, and he soon found himself in a full sprint toward the carnage a hundred feet ahead, his security detail matching his pace. A moment later, he spotted the shattered red-and-green Sandrino's sign on the ground.

The sidewalk and street were littered with broken glass, splintered wood, and the twisted metal remnants of tables and chairs; fires burned inside the destroyed café. The shrieks of terrified onlookers gave way to the cries of the wounded—screams of agony mingled with low, muffled moans. Somewhere among the carnage—*God, please spare their lives*—were his two daughters. Rosenfeld reached the first woman lying unconscious on the pavement. His pulse pounded as he turned over the teenage girl, relief coursing through his body as he stared at a stranger's face. He hurried to the next body a few feet away, then the next.

Then up ahead, there was someone who could be his daughter; long, straight black hair, the lavender sweater he'd bought each of them for their last birthday. As Rosenfeld turned over the fourth body, his blood chilled in his veins. A young girl looked up at him, recognition in her eyes as she stared at her father. She was still alive, but . . .

Rosenfeld fell to his knees, drawing his daughter onto his lap, resting her shoulders on his thighs and her head in the crook of his arm. He knew she was his daughter by the sweater she wore, the topaz ring on her finger. But her face was too mangled for him to determine which of his daughters he held. She lifted her hand, her blood-smeared fingers caressing the side of his face as if to comfort *him,* to help assuage the grief that would soon overwhelm him. Her mouth moved, but no words came out. Only the horrid gurgling of air pushing past fluid, until she finally closed her mouth, forcing the blood out and down the side of her face. She kept her eyes focused on his, and Rosenfeld watched as the illumination within her beautiful brown eyes faded, until the light was extinguished altogether and her hand fell to the ground.

A strange hush fell on the scene of devastation. It took a moment for Rosenfeld to realize his mind was selectively filtering the sounds, letting through only those that seemed to matter. A man sobbed as he knelt in the middle of the street, stroking the cheek of a woman who lay beside him, her eyes open and unblinking, staring at the cloudless sky. Nearby, a woman on her hands and knees retched noisily, her vomit splattering against the curb. Slowly, the low moans of the injured could be heard all around him, and then, faintly in the background, the high-pitched sirens of approaching ambulances grew gradually louder until the full terror registered in his ears.

Rocking his daughter in his arms, Rosenfeld searched

for her sister, finally locating her ten feet away. Rachel lay on her stomach with her head turned to the side, her eyes frozen open in death's stare, her face surrounded by a crimson pool spreading slowly across the gray pavement. Dragging Sarah over to her sister, Rosenfeld clutched both daughters tightly against his chest, attempting to squeeze the pain from his body. His breathing came in short, ragged gasps; there was no air. The curb and stores along the road began to tilt, slowly at first, then at an increasing rate as the world, it seemed, spun out of control.

Worst of all was the guilt. It swirled around him, threatening to consume him in a maelstrom. The small, seemingly inconsequential failings first—if only he hadn't arranged to meet his children for lunch today—then the larger, more complex issues: if only he had dealt with the Arabs more effectively, more *harshly*. But in the end, all that mattered was that it was *his* fault. He had failed, both as a father and as prime minister. He had failed Hannah three years ago, and now his children. Looking around at the dead and dying, he realized he had failed them all.

Kneeling in the middle of the street, his face turned up toward the godless sky, tears streaming down his face, he could not escape it. Like a black plague devouring everything in its path, his guilt consumed him.

7

JERUSALEM, ISRAEL

A morbid quiet had descended upon the PMO building. The staff spoke softly among themselves, their voices falling silent in the vicinity of the prime minister's office. Standing alone in front of Rosenfeld's door, Kogen knocked softly, waiting for a response that never came. Opening the door slightly, he peered into the dimly lit office, illuminated by a small lamp on the credenza behind the prime minister. Rosenfeld was sitting at his desk, his shirt collar unfastened, his tie on the floor beside him. Although his features were shrouded in shadow, Kogen could see the hatred burning in the older man's eyes.

Two hours earlier, the scene at the PMO building had been frantic once staffers realized the bombing had occurred at the prime minister's lunchtime destination. A few minutes later, Rosenfeld's security detail had called in, relaying his safety. The relief was short-lived, however, when they remembered Rosenfeld's daughters were meeting their father for lunch. Soon, their worst fears were confirmed.

Rosenfeld returned to the PMO building an hour later, trudging through the Aquarium toward his office. The front of his white shirt was stained dark red, the side of his face coated with a thin sheen of dried blood. Kogen had stood at the forefront of Rosenfeld's staff. But like the rest, he could find no words to express his sorrow. Rosenfeld hadn't given them the chance, his eyes avoiding theirs as he made his way past them. But now, as Kogen looked into the prime minister's eyes, it was easy to see—as well as understand—that something had changed.

Kogen stepped inside Rosenfeld's office, closing the door quietly behind him. The Mossad had done its work quickly and had determined who was responsible. Who would be held accountable, however, was the more important question.

"Prime Minister."

Rosenfeld stared across the room, giving no indication he noticed his presence.

"Levi."

The older man's eyes drifted toward him.

"I offer my deepest sympathy for your loss. Both of your daughters . . ."

Rosenfeld's eyes fell away.

"We know who is responsible." Kogen paused, waiting for a response before continuing.

Rosenfeld's gaze shot toward him, his eyes displaying a clarity they lacked just seconds before. "Who?"

"We were able to trace the path of the suicide bomber using the security cameras along David Street, tracking him back to a Number 20 bus, then farther back to the Central Bus Station, where a car dropped him off."

"Who is responsible?" Rosenfeld repeated, his rising impatience evident in the tone of his voice.

"The driver of the vehicle is Issa Nidal, a high-ranking member of the Izz ad-Din al-Qassam Brigades."

"Hamas?"

"Yes, Prime Minister."

Rosenfeld jerked forward in his seat, startling Kogen. The prime minister spoke in a low voice, hatred dripping from his words. "I want this man and every Hamas leader eliminated by week's end. Every one of them dead. Is that clear?"

Kogen nodded slowly. "Yes, Prime Minister. We're already coordinating with Defense."

Rosenfeld slumped into his chair, the fire extinguished from his eyes as quickly as it ignited. "Anything else?"

Kogen hesitated. He had no doubt Israel would track down and eliminate Nidal and his leaders, perhaps not by the end of the week, but eventually. But attacking Hamas was like scraping away the pus from a gangrenous limb. Iran was the sickness, and Hamas and its attacks on Israel only the putrid symptoms. Kogen knew, just as Rosenfeld did, that Hamas's campaign of terror was financed by Iran, and the Izz ad-Din al-Qassam Brigades received their training and weapons directly from Iran's Revolutionary Guards. Iran was intent on destroying Israel, and there was no doubt their nuclear weapon, if assembled, would somehow be used against Israel. The Iranian weapon assembly complex must be destroyed—that much was clear—and the Mossad had carefully crafted an opportunity.

However, the operation they had nurtured for years was on the verge of discovery. Kogen's contacts in the United States had determined a White House intern had sent a cryptic e-mail to the president's national security adviser. If she were to obtain and decrypt the information the intern had collected, the operation would be exposed and their opportunity lost. The plan could still succeed, but only if they acted quickly. And now, with the blood of his children staining the prime minister's clothes, there would be no better opportunity to obtain his permission.

With only a twinge of guilt, Kogen pressed forward. "We must discuss what I proposed last night. There's a possibility the operation has been compromised."

"It's no longer an option?"

"It is still viable, but we must initiate the plan now, before it is exposed. There's increased risk with executing early, but we've incorporated safeguards that will counter that risk. The operation will succeed. But you must decide."

"How long do I have?"

"You must decide today, Prime Minister. You must decide now."

"What are the details of this operation?"

"With all due respect, I think it's best you not know the specifics. But I can assure you it will be impossible to trace the genesis of America's attack back to Israel." Kogen approached Rosenfeld, stopping at the edge of his desk. "But I must make one thing clear, Levi. Once we execute, there is nothing we, or the Americans, can do to stop it."

After a moment, Rosenfeld leaned forward, hatred

smoldering in his eyes again. "They have taken everything from me, Barak. I will not let another suffer as I do at the hands of this evil. I will no longer do nothing as our people bury their husbands, wives, and children." Rosenfeld continued, his voice flat, surprising Kogen with its sudden lack of emotion. "I will approve the operation."

Kogen pulled the authorization letter from the inside breast pocket of his suit, unfolded the sheet of paper, and slid it toward Rosenfeld. Reaching across the prime minister's desk, Kogen retrieved a pen from its engraved stand. Fittingly, it was a goodwill gift from the American ambassador to Israel. He laid it on the paper, next to the signature block, and watched as Rosenfeld quickly signed the memorandum.

8

USS *KENTUCKY*

As the *Kentucky* cruised westward five hundred feet beneath the ocean's surface, Lieutenant Tom Wilson sat in one of the two chairs on the ship's Conn in Control, one chair designated for the Officer of the Deck, the other reserved for the Captain. Sitting on the port side of the Conn, Tom supervised his watch section, eventually turning his attention to the Helm, stationed in front of the Diving Officer of the Watch. The Helm—usually one of the most junior enlisted men aboard—was responsible for maintaining the ship's course and relaying propulsion orders to the Throttleman in the Engine Room, who would open the main engine throttles accordingly.

Tom had to admit the ship's propulsion orders had been confusing at first, with the intuitive interpretation usually incorrect. The *Kentucky* was transiting west at ahead two-thirds, which wasn't two-thirds of the ship's maximum speed but two-thirds of standard speed. Ahead standard was fifteen knots, and ahead full, well, that wasn't the ship's full speed at all but the speed that could be attained with the reactor coolant pumps in slow speed. The ship's maximum speed, ahead flank, could be achieved only after the reactor had been brought up to 100 percent power, generating heat as fast as its coolant pumps, operating in fast speed, could safely remove.

The time of day was also something that took awhile getting used to. Now that the *Kentucky* was no longer operating in the local waters around Hawaii and was headed out to her patrol area, the clocks had been shifted to Greenwich mean time, to which all other time zones are referenced. The Navy's radio broadcast and operational orders were tied to GMT, so that every navy ship around the world knew when to execute its orders, regardless of the local time. Although the clock said it was an hour after lunch, Tom's body told him it was already 3 A.M. It would take a few days for his biological clock to adapt.

As the young officer returned his attention to the rest of his watch section, a report blared over the 4-MC emergency circuit.

"Fire in the Engine Room! Fire in Propulsion Lube Oil Bay!"

The *Kentucky*'s general alarm sounded, alerting the crew and initiating emergency responses from the personnel on watch. Tom reacted instantly, shouting out his orders, bringing the submarine shallow so they could ventilate the ship, if required.

"Helm, ahead standard! Dive, make your depth two hundred feet!"

The Helm rang up ahead standard on the Engine Order Telegraph as the Diving Officer directed his planesmen, "Ten up. Full rise, fairwater planes." The Helm pulled the yoke back to the full rise position while the Outboard watchstander adjusted the stern planes, and the submarine tilted upward, rapidly increasing its angle until the deck was pitched at ten degrees up.

As Tom leaned forward ten degrees to counteract the ship's up angle, he spoke into the microphone lodged in the overhead. "Sonar, Conn. Make preparations to come to periscope depth."

Sonar acknowledged and a moment later reported two contacts. But the ship's spherical array sonar, mounted in the bow, was completely blind in the aft sector, or baffles, blocked by the submarine's metal structure. With the *Kentucky*'s towed array stowed for the transit to her patrol area, Tom had no idea if there were any close contacts aft of the submarine that might run over them on their way up to periscope depth, and he had to find out.

"Helm, left full rudder, steady course one-seven-zero. Sonar, Conn. Commencing baffle clear to port."

Malone arrived in Control and joined Tom on the Conn, activating a small speaker to monitor the communications between Damage Control Central and the Engine Room. Turning the volume down low so Tom wouldn't be distracted from his approach to periscope depth, he listened intently to the reports from Damage Control Central:

"The ship is rigged for Fire and General Emergency. All compartments sealed."

The Diving Officer reported passing through three hundred feet, then announced, "Two hundred feet, sir."

"Steady course one-seven-zero," the Helm reported.

"The fire main is pressurized. Hose teams One through Four entering the Engine Room."

As Tom waited while Sonar searched for contacts in the previously baffled area, his thoughts drifted to the Engine Room. Of the different types of fire, an oil fire was the absolute worst. The flames would spread quickly, following the oil as it coated the Engine Room surfaces. Heavy black smoke would roil upward, collecting in the top of the Engine Room, gradually descending until the entire compartment was choked in dense black smog. The four hose teams would be approaching the fire by now, the narrow white beams of their battle lanterns cutting through the thick black smoke. Two hose teams would attack the fire from Engine Room Lower Level, one from the port side and the other from starboard, while the other two hose teams did the same in Engine Room Middle Level, hoping to contain the fire before it spread into Engine Room Upper Level.

Their approach would be slow, hampered by low visibility from the dense smoke. It would be especially treacherous in middle and upper level if the fire spread, as the men advanced along narrow walkways suspended in the air between the hull and the Engine Room machinery. Their advance would be further complicated by the bulky air cylinders on their backs and the stiff, heavy hoses they dragged slowly aft as they negotiated the myriad turns and changes in elevation.

"Heavy black smoke in the Engine Room. Visibility limited to five feet."

If the crew failed to contain the fire and it spread out of control, the temperature in the Engine Room would reach 1,000 degrees, four times what it took to melt a person's skin. They would be forced to abandon the compartment, letting the fire ravage the Engine Room until it consumed the oxygen it needed to survive, eventually extinguishing itself. The evacuation would be frantic, the crew desperately attempting to account for the original personnel on watch and every man who entered the compartment to combat the fire. The Engine Room's watertight door would glow red-hot as the fire destroyed the submarine's essential equipment—the main engines, electrical generators, and water desalinizers. The *Kentucky* would be forced to blow to the surface, the once powerful warship a drifting hulk, waiting to be towed back to port, its missiles offloaded, and the submarine most likely scrapped.

"The fire has spread to Engine Room Middle Level."

Scanning the sonar display on the Conn, Tom noted two traces on the monitor, then called out, "Sonar, Conn. Report all contacts."

"Conn, Sonar. Hold two sonar contacts: Sierra four-one, bearing one-one-zero, classified merchant, and Sierra four-two, bearing two-five-zero, also classified merchant. Both contacts are classified as far range contacts."

Tom acknowledged Sonar's report, then reached up and twisted the port periscope locking ring clockwise, waiting while the scope slid silently up through the ship's sail, folding the periscope handles down as the scope emerged from its well.

"Hose Three has ruptured. Securing Hose Three."

"Helm, ahead one-third. Dive, make your depth eight-zero feet. All stations, Conn. Proceeding to periscope depth."

Silence descended on Control as the deck tilted upward. The submarine was vulnerable during its slow ascent to periscope depth, unable to rapidly move out of the way if a surface ship was nearby on a collision course. There would be no conversation in Control, except for the occasional depth report, from the time the Officer of the Deck ordered the submarine's ascent to periscope depth until, peering through the scope as it broke the surface of the water, he announced there were no close contacts. Even though Sonar had reported no close contacts, the algorithms were sometimes wrong and the submarine's sonar was not foolproof; occasionally very quiet targets, particularly warships, went undetected.

"The fire has spread to Engine Room Upper Level. Opening the Engine Room watertight door. Sending in Missile Compartment Hose teams Five and Six."

Years ago, Tom would have rotated on the periscope during the ascent. But protocols had changed. Peering into the eyepiece, Tom looked straight ahead, adjusting the scope optics to maximum elevation. He looked up into the dark water, scanning for evidence of ships as the *Kentucky* rose toward the surface.

"Smoke has spread to Missile Compartment. All personnel in Missile Compartment don emergency air breathing protection."

"Passing one-five-zero feet," the Diving Officer announced.

A small disk of light became visible, the moon's blue-white reflection wavering on the surface of the water, slowly growing larger as the *Kentucky* rose from the ocean depths.

"One hundred feet."

Tom twisted the left periscope handle, adjusting the optics downward so he'd be looking at the horizon when the submarine reached periscope depth.

"Eight-zero feet."

"The fire is contained."

As the periscope broke the surface of the water, Tom began rotating the periscope, completing a revolution every eight seconds, scanning the dark horizon and sky above for ships or aircraft.

"No close contacts!"

Conversation resumed in Control, now that the submarine was safely at periscope depth, and Tom slowed his rotation, periodically shifting the scope to high power for long-range scans.

"The fire is out. Hose Team One is stationed as the reflash watch."

That was the report Tom had been waiting for, as they needed to ventilate the submarine to clear the heavy black smoke, but they couldn't afford to bring in fresh air and oxygen that would feed the fire while it burned.

"Dive, prepare to emergency ventilate the Engine Room with the diesel. Prepare to Snorkel."

The Diving Officer acknowledged, passing the order to the Chief of the Watch beside him, and the order reverberated throughout the ship over the 1-MC a second later. Reports flowed into Control as the crew prepared to purge the heavy smoke from the submarine and bring in fresh air. A few minutes later, the Diving Officer announced, "Sir, the ship is ready to ventilate with the exception of raising the Snorkel Mast."

Malone clicked the stopwatch in his hand.

As he examined how long it had taken to put out the

simulated fire and prepare to ventilate the submarine, his displeasure was evident on his face.

"Not fast enough," he said. "Take her back down to five hundred feet and run the drill again."

Tom acknowledged the Captain's order, then swung the periscope around until it was facing forward. He folded up the handles, reached up, and rotated the locking ring counterclockwise. As the periscope descended into its well, he called out to the microphone in the overhead, "All stations, Conn. Going deep."

Before issuing orders to the Diving Officer and the Helm, he glanced at Malone, seated in the Captain's chair on the Conn. He still wore the frown on his face.

It was going to be one of those days.

Four hours later, Tom sat next to the Weps at the table in the Officers' Wardroom. The day's drills were over, and all but three of the submarine's fifteen officers gathered for dinner. Two officers were on watch, one forward as the ship's Officer of the Deck, the second aft as the Engineering Officer of the Watch, supervising the reactor plant and the propulsion spaces. The two officers on watch would arrive for dinner only after being relieved by the two oncoming officers currently seated at the table. There were only twelve chairs, and with two officers on watch, that left the fifteenth officer, Ensign Lopez, as the odd man out. As the most junior officer aboard, he would have to wait and eat dinner at the second sitting with the two offgoing watchstanders.

At the head of the table, the Captain was joined by the senior officers on his end with the junior officers at the other. Seated by seniority, the XO sat on the Captain's right and the Engineer on his left, with the Weps and the Nav next in line. The junior officers at the far end of the table engaged in their own conversation, occasionally breaking into laughter, while the Captain discussed the performance of Tom's watch section with the ship's senior officers.

They'd run the fire drill three more times until the crew was exhausted, the hose teams drenched in sweat after hauling the heavy pressurized hoses while wearing their thick flame- and heat-resistant fire suits. They had managed to shave two minutes off their original pace, still not enough to please the ship's Captain. He required nothing less than 100 percent effort on every occasion, and his expectations were almost impossible to meet. But as demanding as the SOB was, Tom found it hard not to like Commander Brad Malone. He judged and criticized everyone evenly and consistently, and when an officer or an enlisted struggled in the performance of his duties, he took the time to point out what improvements were required and how to make them. On the rare occasion the watchstander or watch section lived up to his unreasonable standards, he was quick to praise them for their superb performance.

As grueling as it was to run and rerun the endless drills, Tom knew and appreciated the reason why. The single most important rule for submariners was to make the number of Surfaces equal to the number of Dives. Everything they did throughout the days, weeks, and months underway was focused on ensuring they could accomplish their mission and still be alive to surface the submarine and return home.

Another day of drills was over. Tom had thought life

would be dull on patrol, lurking in the ocean depths, hiding from everyone, waiting vigilantly for orders he prayed never came. But the opposite was true. Sleep was a precious commodity as the crew constantly trained: fire, flooding, reactor scram, steam-piping rupture drills. And when they weren't running engineering or ship drills, the crew manned Battle Stations Missile and Battle Stations Torpedo, attempting to accomplish their mission and defend themselves in endless scenarios, combating a never-ending affliction of things that went wrong. Then there was the classroom training—tactics, reactor plant, and in-rate professional topics. Hours upon hours each week.

No, life on patrol wasn't dull. But even though the hours were long, the sleep scarce, and the training constant, Tom enjoyed it. There was something exciting about being the Officer of the Deck in the middle of the night, a twenty-seven-year-old lieutenant in charge of a two-billion-dollar submarine, taking it to periscope depth, with his eye pressed to the periscope as it broke the surface of the water, the safety of the ship and crew in his hands. Or manning the Bridge on the surface at night, the stars shining brightly above, the phosphorescent trail in the water marking the submarine's passage as it headed toward port after a long patrol, the distant lights on the shoreline growing steadily brighter as the crew returned home. It made the endless drills and the training worth every minute.

An hour after dinner, Tom wiped the sweat from his face with his shirtsleeve as he rounded the aft end of Missile Compartment Upper Level, starting his twentieth lap. There was enough space in the compartment, and the length was long enough, for a decent run. One mile was seventeen laps around, and Tom had decided to take advantage of the submarine's non-Alert status to get in five miles.

Although the ship had two treadmills, Tom enjoyed running the old-fashioned way. Once the submarine commenced her strategic deterrent patrol, the treadmills would have to suffice, since running in the Missile Compartment would be forbidden. The sound of Tom's feet pounding onto the steel deck would be transmitted through the ship's hull, and as faint as that sound was, it could give away the submarine's presence. As he passed down the starboard side of the ship, he paid no attention to the missile tubes or their contents. His thoughts were two thousand miles away, with his family, and how he would break the news to his father.

Tom was third-generation Navy. His grandfather had graduated from Annapolis and retired as an admiral. Tom's father had also attended the Naval Academy, and while Captain Murray Wilson wanted his son to follow in his footsteps, he hadn't cared which community—air, surface, or submarine—as long as Tom carried on the family tradition. Unwilling to disappoint his father, Tom had also attended the Naval Academy, graduating at the top of his class, eventually reporting to the USS *Kentucky,* BLUE Crew.

Trident submarines had two crews, BLUE and GOLD, to maximize the time the submarine, with its nuclear-tipped missiles, spent at sea. While one crew was out on patrol, the other received replacements for the personnel who transferred or left the Navy, then began the training cycle that melded the new crew into a team. The Off-Crew spent its time in various trainers, including weeklong navigation, tactics, and strategic launch sessions, and were formally recertified just before the other crew returned to port.

Tom would return to port soon, but not soon enough. The patrols were long, the time away from his family difficult to reconcile with his obligations as a husband and especially a father. Tom and Nancy had married a week after he graduated from Annapolis, in one of the June weddings that followed the graduation ceremony each year. Nancy took an immediate dislike to Navy life, from the long hours Tom spent studying at Nuclear Power School to the shift work at the Moored Training Ship that followed. But her distaste for Navy life intensified once the long patrols began, and her attitude had soured even more during the last patrol. Nancy had given birth to twin girls while Tom was underway, and she hadn't yet forgiven him for not being there during her difficult pregnancy. Nancy had made her position clear: It was either her and their two children or the Navy. Both were not an option.

The revelation Tom was getting out of the Navy would stun and devastate his father, and the last thing Tom wanted was to disappoint him. But given the alternatives, there was only one choice. He didn't relish the conversation he would have with his father upon his return to port, but there would be time enough to find the right words.

Tom wiped the sweat from his face as he rounded the aft end of Missile Compartment Upper Level again, passing the twelve missile tubes on the starboard side of the submarine before returning past the other twelve tubes on the port side.

Fifty laps to go.

While Tom paced the decks in Missile Compartment Upper Level, the ship's Captain sat with the XO in the Wardroom discussing Malone's retirement plans over a friendly game of cribbage. This was Malone's sixth and last patrol aboard the *Kentucky*. He had his twenty years in and would retire after his change of command upon return to port, going home to Iowa to take over his father's farm. His parents were getting on in years, and Malone's two sisters had no interest in continuing the family farming heritage. Working the earth and growing crops were a far cry from Malone's last twenty years, yet he and his wife, Karen, also from the Midwest, looked forward to leaving the metropolitan area with its fast-paced life and returning to the countryside, where people had time to chat. He would miss the Navy, and especially the dedicated men he worked with. At the same time, he looked forward to the next phase of his life.

Malone picked up his next set of cribbage cards, pausing for a moment to savor the unmistakable omen of good luck. He had just been dealt a twenty-nine-point hand, his first ever in twenty years of play. The odds of being dealt a twenty-eight-point hand were fifteen thousand to one, and the even rarer twenty-nine-point hand, considered a good luck omen among submariners, one in a quarter million. As Malone looked down on his twenty-nine points, he could not but reflect on the hot summer day in Mare Island Naval Shipyard years earlier, his submarine one of the last to complete overhaul before the historic shipyard closed down, the victim of a shrinking submarine fleet and associated industrial infrastructure.

He had watched his Captain escort an elderly woman off the boat following lunch, returning moments later to the Wardroom, where Malone waited. As the Captain eagerly unwrapped a thin package left on the Wardroom table, the brown wrapping paper pulled back to reveal an eighteen-by-twenty-four-inch nautical chart covered in glass and surrounded by a plain, worn wooden frame. Annotated on the chart were two merchant ship sinkings in the Yellow Sea between China and Korea, and the yellowed edges of the chart combined with the lack of a separate North and South Korea told Malone the nautical chart was a very old one. Dates were inscribed on the map beneath each sinking: 19 and 21 March 1943, and the dates and locations tugged at his memory until he finally recalled their significance.

In 1943, while the U.S. Surface Fleet slugged its way westward across the Pacific, Executive Officer Dick O'Kane and his Captain, Mush Morton, led the submarine *Wahoo* on her fourth war patrol deep into Japanese-controlled waters in search of enemy ships. In particular, they were looking for the prized merchant ships, the lifeblood of the island nation of Japan. By mid-March, transiting into the Yellow Sea, the crew had nothing to show for the long weeks at sea, morale deteriorating as each day passed. Their spirits lifted on March 18, when Dick O'Kane, playing cribbage with his Captain, was dealt a rare twenty-nine-point hand. Lady Luck made good on her promise—the *Wahoo* sank her first merchant ship of the patrol the following day. A scant two days later, O'Kane was dealt a twenty-eight-point hand, the *Wahoo* sinking a second merchant ship within the hour.

The two cribbage hands had indeed been omens of good luck for Dick O'Kane and the crew of the *Wahoo*, and as Malone studied the framed document in the Captain's hands, he noticed two sets of playing cards affixed to the chart, five cards in the top right corner and a complementing set in the bottom left. Only then did he realize what the Captain held in his hands. The elderly woman was Dick O'Kane's widow, and she had left the Captain with her husband's twenty-eight- and twenty-nine-point cribbage hands, dealt to him aboard the *Wahoo* on March 18 and 21, 1943.

Malone played out his twenty-nine-point hand, pegging from behind and winning the game. As he leaned back in his chair, the cloud of uncertainty that accompanied the beginning of each patrol, as the ship and its new crew members settled into their routine, finally lifted. He slowly pushed the cards across the table toward the XO. As for Dick O'Kane and the *Wahoo*, this would indeed be a lucky patrol for the USS *Kentucky*, BLUE Crew.

9

ARLINGTON, VIRGINIA

Mike Patton stood in the rain on the curb along South Quincy Street, hands in his coat pockets, wet hair plastered to his forehead as water trickled down his face. He made no attempt to shelter himself from the weather, because he was in an altogether different place. Or to more accurately describe it—the same place, but a different and better time. As he stared across the busy street at the empty restaurant patio, he could still see her sitting across from him that night, see the sparkle in her eyes as she smiled, hear her laughter spilling into the street. Two weeks after their dinner at Carlyle's, Mike had returned to Washington alone, wearily ascended the steps to his dark and morbidly quiet brownstone off Dupont Circle, and entered the nightmare that never ended. Now, three years later, he had received the phone call he'd been waiting for. He would soon complete his task and finally sleep in peace.

It should have been perfect. For their twenty-fifth

wedding anniversary, Mike booked a nine-day Mediterranean cruise, sailing from Athens and visiting the
Italian cities of Messina, Naples, and Rome before continuing westward for port calls in Monaco and Barce-
lona. But first, they had flown to Israel to visit Theresa's
aging parents. That detour had ruined everything.

Thirty years earlier, Theresa had left her homeland
to attend Cornell University, and it was Mike's good for-
tune, he always said, to have sat next to her that first day
in freshman English. It was easy to strike up a conversation with the vivacious young woman who seemed at
ease in the foreign country she had arrived in only four
days earlier. By the end of the week, the two had established a friendship that blossomed into romance. They
married following graduation, after Theresa made the
difficult choice between the man she loved and the country she loved. Theresa's thoughts were never far from
her family and homeland, and as they booked their anniversary cruise, she had requested they add a leg to their
trip and visit her parents in Jerusalem.

Less than three hours after arriving in Theresa's
homeland, their lives were forever changed. After getting settled in the guest bedroom of her parents' apartment and spending a few hours catching up on family
news, Theresa had insisted on rushing out to find the perfect gift for her niece's bat mitzvah. It was this search that
led them to the less frequented stores on the outskirts of
Jerusalem's shopping district. Theresa's memory of the
city was no longer accurate, and they found themselves
on an unfamiliar street. But she was certain the desired
store was only one block over, and they would arrive
there after a quick shortcut through the narrow alley con-

necting the two streets. As they turned into the cool, dark alley, it was the last time Mike held his wife's hand in his.

Mike heard it, but never saw it coming. His only warning was his wife's startled scream, and as Mike turned in her direction, his head jolted forward from a blow that could have easily fractured his skull. He awakened an unknown number of hours later, lying on his side on a dirt floor in a small room, his hands tied behind his back, duct tape covering his mouth. The back of his head throbbed with every heartbeat, and as he tried to make sense of the sideways world that swam in his eyes, the image of his wife eventually steadied.

She was kneeling on her hands and knees only a few feet away, sitting back on her ankles as she looked up at two men circling her, their faces concealed behind black keffiyehs. They probed her with questions, eventually making the only inquiry that seemed to matter. It was easy to see that Mike, with his ruddy Irish complexion, was no Jew. But Theresa's dark hair and eyes combined with her slender build begged the question. As Mike struggled to scream through the tape covering his mouth, warning her to not answer, Theresa, proud of her heritage, confirmed their suspicion. That had been enough to seal her fate.

Black hoods were shoved over Theresa's head and then Mike's. He struggled in vain while his wife's screams became fainter and fainter as they dragged her to another part of the building. Now, three years later, all that remained were the memories, memories that haunted him each night, memories that always began as Mike was woken from a restless slumber and dragged down a long hallway.

Bright, sterile lights blinded Mike as he was pulled to his feet and the dark hood was removed from his head. His eyes slowly adjusted, and the first images of what would become forever seared into his mind materialized out of the white haze. He stood at the back of a small, dilapidated room, its walls coated with a thin layer of cracked brown cement, a rack of spotlights supported by a metal stand glaring down on its occupants. In the middle of the room, Theresa sat on the only piece of furniture, her waist tightly bound to a chair, her hands tied behind her back. A streak of dried blood ran down her chin from cracked and swollen lips, evidence of her less than cordial treatment. But it was the fear in her eyes that worried Mike the most as they flitted between her husband and the other men in the room.

In addition to the two men holding Mike's arms, still bound behind his back, there were three other men in the room. Two stood motionless on either side of Theresa's chair, their hands clasped behind their backs, and a third stood in front, a video camera held down by his thigh. All three men were dressed in the traditional garb of Muslim extremists that had become so familiar on television: black long-sleeved salwar kameez shirts tucked into baggy white sirwal pants. Black keffiyehs covered their faces, exposing only their eyes. A sword, still in its sheath, leaned against the wall in the far corner of the room. As Theresa looked up at her captors through puffy, cried-out eyes, she examined first one, then another man, searching for a clue to her abductors' plans.

A door in the back of the room opened and another man, dressed like the others except entirely in black, emerged from the dark recess. Stopping by the corner of the room, he retrieved the sword. The man in front raised the camera to his right eye, and the red recording indicator illuminated. Twisting to the side in her chair, Theresa attempted to determine who had entered the room and what his purpose might be. Locating the man as he walked toward her, Theresa's eyes followed him until he stopped on her left side. Her eyes widened when she spotted the object in his hands, her panic cresting as the sword slid from its sheath with a tinny metallic scrape.

A low moan escaped her lips, cut short as she began struggling violently, almost convulsively, to escape from her bonds. The man tilted the sword in his hands, adjusting it until the harsh spotlights reflected off the metal into his victim's eyes. Theresa intensified her efforts to escape, her chair rocking on its legs as she struggled in vain, calling for her husband to come to her aid, to somehow make everything turn out all right. Mike tried to leap to his wife's defense, but his hands were still tied behind his back and the two men restrained him, strong hands gripping his arms.

The man with the sword nodded, and the two men began to untie Theresa's hands. Her resistance eased, unsure of her captors' intentions.

Hope shined in her eyes.

Mike brightened with the thought that their captors had only meant to frighten Theresa and record her reaction. Perhaps they would take her back to the dark room where she'd been beaten, where she would wait until a ransom was obtained or a political prisoner freed.

Or perhaps not.

After the men untied her hands, they pulled her arms out until they were extended. Placing their hands on the back of her shoulders, they forced her to bend at the waist until her upper body and neck were parallel to the floor. Turning her head to the side, Theresa looked up at her executioner, desperation on her face. As tears streamed down her cheeks, she begged for her life. The man responded by gripping the sword firmly in both hands, lifting it upward. Theresa's eyes filled with the kind of terror that comes with the certainty of death, and she lost whatever self-control she had left. Screams mingled with cries for mercy, and her feet slid frantically in the sand that coated the hard dirt floor as she attempted to push herself back and away from her fate. But the two men held her firmly in place.

The sword's upward movement halted, high above the executioner's head, and he waited. Theresa's fear suddenly turned to rage, and her head turned toward the man, cursing him, spittle flying from her mouth as she condemned her captors to the fiery pits of hell. The executioner stood there, sword held high, waiting for Theresa's rage to run its course, to transition into despair. Mike could tell he had done this many times, and relished every moment. Theresa eventually spent her curses, sobs occasionally escaping as she turned her face down toward the ground, her head sagging as she prepared to die.

A blow to Mike's stomach forced him to his knees, where, as he kneeled across from his wife, the worst part of it all began. Rough hands worked behind him, and then his arms were suddenly free and the tape ripped from his mouth.

They had untied his hands because they knew—

As if the horror of what was about to happen wasn't enough, they knew that once his hands were free, Mike would instinctively reach for his wife, caress her flushed cheeks as she kissed his palms, that he would hold his wife's tear-streaked face in his hands.

Theresa looked up at him, her eyes suddenly radiating a serene calm. "Don't be afraid," she said, as if Mike's blood, rather than hers, would soon be soaking into the parched earth. "This is supposed to happen. It is God's will."

Mike groaned, unable to find the words to express his despair, or his feelings for the only woman he had ever loved. Or ever would.

But Theresa's luminous green eyes simply stared at him. "You will know what to do," she said. "It will soon become clear."

Mike struggled with the meaning of her words. *What would soon become clear?* He prepared to ask her to explain, but never got the chance.

A whistling sound filled Mike's ears. It took him a moment to recognize its significance, to realize it was the swift movement of the executioner's sword through the air. He never saw the blade moving, never saw the bright glint of the sword as it sped downward. Instead, he saw his wife's wedding ring sparkle from the corner of his eye as her hand twitched.

They knew—

Theresa's face suddenly became heavy in his hands, and Mike noticed the sword was no longer held high, its tip now buried in the dirt floor, a six-inch-wide swath of crimson coating the blade. His wife's lips parted, as if to speak, but no words came, and he could no longer feel her warm breath on his skin. The color drained from her face, the animation fading from her eyes until she stared at him with dull, lifeless orbs.

As he held his wife's head in his hands, horrified yet incapable of releasing it, her face began to blur as tears collected in his eyes, then streamed down his cheeks. His body shook, his breath coming in short, shallow spurts. Rocking back and forth on his knees, he was unwilling to believe Theresa had been taken from him; that he would never hear her laughter, never hold her in his arms again. The pain of his loss was unbearable, and he couldn't imagine living without her. As his mind swam with ideas on how to end his anguish, Theresa's words came back to him.

You will know what to do.

It seemed there remained a single purpose in his life; some act he must accomplish before he could join his wife. *But what?* It was too hard to think. Perhaps Theresa was right, and it would soon become clear. Slowly, Mike's resolve solidified and his breathing steadied, determination replacing despair. Whatever he was supposed to do, he would figure it out.

Later that night, Mike was pushed from a van on the outskirts of Sderot. Dazed, he stumbled to the nearest police station, incoherently recounting the ordeal. But enough of what had happened eventually became clear. As Mike sat alone in a hotel on Yoseftal Street, authorities found Theresa's severed head rotting on a deserted street corner in Gaza, and it wasn't long before an Iranian-sponsored terrorist group proudly claimed responsibility. There wasn't much to go on, as Mike and Theresa's abductors had kept their faces covered, and Mike had no idea where they had been held. There were far too many crimes committed and loved ones lost to expend effort chasing a murder with no leads, and the case was soon abandoned.

Six months after his wife's murder, after the bruises had healed and he had passed a battery of psychological tests, Mike returned to work at the National Military Command Center in the Pentagon. But he had lied to everyone; the dream had never stopped. Each night, he relived that day in excruciating clarity, the nightmare torturing him with the terrifying last moments of Theresa's life.

Each night when Mike awoke from his nightmare, the ceiling fan greeted him, spinning slowly in circles that never ended. Then one night, a turbulent nor'easter tore through the city. As the rain drove against the windowpanes and the ghostly shadows of trees bent in submission to the howling winds, his town house lost power, and the fan drifted to a stop. It was at that instant that everything suddenly became clear, just as Theresa had promised. A stranger stepped from the shadows the next day, as if he'd been waiting patiently for Mike's epiphany.

The man was no longer a stranger, and his call earlier today requesting they meet had given Mike hope that the next time his mind drifted into darkness, there would be no dreams. For this afternoon's meeting, Mike had picked the restaurant where he had proposed to Theresa and where they had eaten dinner the night before their fateful trip. As he started across the street, still lost in thought, the blaring horn of an approaching car startled him out of his reverie. He stood there for a split second, part of him wanting it all to end now, splattered over the front of the vehicle. But he stepped back just as a dark green Volvo sped by. There was one task he had yet to complete; not until then could he join his wife.

Mike requested a table in the far corner of the restaurant that offered a clear view of the entrance, something he knew his companion would insist upon. The few patrons were scattered widely throughout, none within earshot. Mike ordered a glass of red wine and had taken his first sip when he saw his friend, if one could call him that, pausing near the hostess to scan his surroundings.

William Hoover—Mike doubted that was his real name—was the type of man you could pass on the street and never remember having seen. Caucasian, of medium height and build, with brown hair and eyes, he could blend in almost anywhere. He interacted with Mike cordially, but in the loving way one deals with a family pet, caring for its every need, yet willing to put the animal to sleep when the time came. Mike didn't care. He figured he was using Hoover even more than the younger man was using him.

Hoover sat without greeting, placing a brown satchel on the floor next to his chair. He appeared uncharacteristically tense.

"Is the *Kentucky* in range?" the man asked.

Mike shook his head. "Not yet. It'll be another nine days."

Hoover sat in his chair reflectively, as if making a mental calculation. "You will send orders to the *Ken-*

tucky as planned," he said finally. "However," he added, "you must execute today."

Mike shook his head. "We must wait until the *Kentucky* is in range before we send the order."

Hoover replied firmly, "You must execute now."

Mike paused, preparing to describe the situation like an elementary school teacher explaining a basic mathematical concept to her students for the first time. "The *Kentucky* just began her transit to her patrol areas, and the United States will have nine days to respond if we send the order now."

"You must execute now," the man repeated.

Exhaling slowly, Mike tried to control his frustration. Sending the launch order now would jeopardize everything. "You guys don't know what you're doing."

"We know *exactly* what we're doing." The man almost hissed the word. But then his voice calmed. "There are elements to this plan you are not privy to. I assure you the *Kentucky* will reach launch range. There is nothing the United States can do once you transmit the launch order."

The conviction in his voice convinced Mike to acquiesce. After all, it was their plan.

Mike's lack of response conveyed his agreement, and Hoover opened the brown satchel, retrieving a small black nylon case and a white envelope. "Here is what you need. Do you have any questions?"

Mike shook his head, his mouth dry.

The man returned the contents to the bag, then stood and left, leaving the brown leather case next to his chair. Mike sat at the table a few minutes longer before asking for the check.

A moment later, Mike stepped outside Carlyle's, the satchel gripped tightly in his hand. He paused on the sidewalk along the busy street, looking up into the overcast sky, blinking as the cold rain hit his face and eyes, until a gust of wind knocked him off balance. He pulled his coat tight around his neck, tucked his head down, and set off toward the Colonial parking garage—and his last remaining task.

9 DAYS REMAINING

10

ARLINGTON, VIRGINIA
WASHINGTON, D.C.

The afternoon rain had moved on, leaving behind broken clouds through which the sun gave notification of its slow descent. As Mike Patton stood outside the South Entrance to the Pentagon, he considered delaying his arrival for an hour; the 9/11 Memorial park was just around the corner, offering a clear view of what he hoped was a spectacular end to the last day of his life. But while there was something fitting about watching the sun slip below the horizon just before he completed his final task, he realized a late relief would catch his supervisor's attention, and that was the last thing he wanted tonight.

Following the meeting at Carlyle's this afternoon, Mike had returned home, shed his wet clothes, and dressed for work, leaving the darkened brownstone and his dreams behind. He left the door unlocked, because he no longer needed the worldly possessions within. All that mattered were the contents of the briefcase he carried in his right hand. Gripping the satchel even tighter, he let his thoughts of the sunset pass and turned toward the Pentagon's entrance.

At that precise moment, Christine O'Connor was busy at her desk in the White House, anxiously awaiting the end of another contentious day. As expected, her meeting with Hardison this morning had not gone well, especially after the chief of staff had insisted on discussing the intelligence reorganization, even though she had made her position perfectly clear. The meeting had not ended until Christine, frustrated beyond belief, had asked Hardison which part of her answer he didn't understand, the N or the O.

Notwithstanding her meeting with Hardison, Christine's thoughts never strayed far from Evans's murder and the disk she had found in his computer. An hour after her phone call to Director Ken Ronan yesterday, a CIA courier had stopped by to pick up the disk, which Christine had discreetly handed over; Ronan had agreed to place priority on the analysis. As she was winding things up for the day, Christine was interrupted by the beep of her intercom, followed by her secretary's voice.

"Miss O'Connor, an Agent Kenney is here to see you."

"Send him in."

A man in a dark gray suit entered her office. "Good afternoon, Miss O'Connor. I'm Agent John Kenney. Director Ronan sent me over." He opened his wallet, flashing his CIA badge.

Christine reached over her desk to shake his hand. "Please, have a seat."

Kenney unbuttoned his jacket as he took the chair in front of her desk. "We've examined the CD you gave us, but it's left us with more questions than answers."

"What was on the CD?"

"There was one encrypted file, with the rest of the files being merely time stamps. However, the time stamps correspond to the dates and times the Defense Department databases were probed for information by an external source. We've correlated the object of these probes, and it's become clear that someone was searching for specific information."

"What information?"

"Do you know what the code word *digashi* stands for?"

Christine stopped breathing, just for a second. She reached for her coffee cup, hoping Kenney hadn't noticed her reaction. "I'm sorry, Agent Kenney, but I can't help you."

Kenney smiled. "Your word choice is subtle, Miss O'Connor. Most people would have said they had no idea what this word meant. You said you can't help me, which implies something completely different."

Christine smiled back. "I'm afraid the security clearance required for this topic is well beyond the issues you normally deal with."

Kenney reached into his wallet again and retrieved his ID badge, tossing it onto Christine's desk. "I have a top secret clearance, authorized access to Sensitive Compartmented Information. I'm pretty sure I'm briefed into whatever program you need. Go ahead, check."

Christine swiveled her chair toward the computer

monitor on the corner of her desk, flipped through a couple of windows on the display, and typed the CIA agent's social security number on her keyboard. A few seconds later, she turned back to John Henry Kenney.

"Okay, you're cleared."

"And . . . ?"

Christine leaned back in her chair. "*Digashi* is the code word for a nuclear first strike."

"A nuclear first strike?" Kenney echoed her words. "By who?"

Christine folded her arms across her chest. "By us."

In the Pentagon basement at the end of Corridor 9, Mike Patton swiped his badge and punched in his pass code. He opened the door to the Operations Center of the National Military Command Center, then paused for a second before stepping into the room he would not exit alive. He could not predict how many of the other men and women in the room, some of them close friends, would share the same fate.

Mike stopped at the top of the new Operations Center. The Pentagon had completed its seemingly never-ending renovation, and the Ops Center had moved to its new, multitiered space in the basement level, patterned after the stepped NASA control rooms. The center dropped down in three increments, with each of the first two tiers holding ten workstations, five on either side of a center aisle, with the Watch Captain's workstation located on the bottom tier. An eight-by-ten-foot electronic display of the world hung on the front wall, annotated with the status of the nation's nuclear assets. Four Trident submarines were at sea in the Pacific Ocean: two on Alert patrol, a third on the way home, and a fourth, the one Mike was interested in, outbound from the Hawaiian operating areas.

Most of the watchstanders were still turning over, including the Watch Captain, a Navy rear admiral in the process of being relieved by an Air Force brigadier general. After surveying the men and women at their workstations, Mike made his way left along the top of the center to the third workstation in the first tier. Placing his briefcase gently on the floor, he pulled up a chair. "Evening, Isaiah. What have you got?"

Isaiah Jones looked up from his monitor. "No change in DEFCON, the *Tennessee* has relieved the *West Virginia* in LANT, and we've got one down silo in North Dakota. Pretty quiet all around." After a few more minutes discussing the more mundane details of the last six hours, Isaiah signed out of the watch log on his computer, then packed up his bag, along with an empty package of Doritos and a crumpled-up Coke can. "See you tomorrow, Mike."

"Take care, Isaiah."

Mike kept himself busy, waiting until the last member of the previous watch section departed, leaving him alone with the other nineteen watchstanders and the Watch Captain. Retrieving the black nylon case from his satchel, he opened it, exposing what looked like a small plastic insurance card and three nasal inhalers. He pulled out the card and slid it into his pocket. Leaning back in his chair, he clasped his hands behind his back, pretending to stretch out his shoulders, then stood and sauntered toward the entrance at the back of the room.

Stopping with his back next to the security door, Mike removed the thin card from his pocket and held it next to the electronic lock mechanism. Ten seconds was all it would take to destroy the electronic circuitry, he'd been told, but he held it there an extra five seconds for good measure. Sliding the card back into his pocket, he returned to his seat, then removed the smallest nasal inhaler from the case. After looking around to ensure no one was watching, he pressed the tip of the inhaler against his neck. The warmth spread quickly throughout his body. Retrieving the largest inhaler, Mike stood again, slowly walking behind the two rows of watchstanders as he pressed the inhaler plunger, releasing the odorless gas into the room.

Agent Kenney's face displayed no hint of emotion at Christine's explanation of *digashi*. "I wasn't aware we had nuclear first-strike options."

"Technically, there's no difference," Christine replied. "It's a matter of timing. The launch orders are the same. Whether it's a first strike or a retaliatory depends on who launches first."

Kenney nodded, absorbing the perspective. He reached into the breast pocket of his jacket and pulled out an envelope, retrieving a single piece of paper and handing it to Christine.

"This is the content of the encrypted file. We're running background checks on these individuals, but are any of these names familiar?"

Christine studied the list of ten men and women. "I'm afraid not."

"What about the letters 'I S'?"

Looking at the list again, Christine noticed each name was preceded by the letters I S. The letters could represent any number of things, and without additional clues she drew a blank.

"Let me see what I can find out." She placed the paper near her keyboard, selected the appropriate window on her monitor, then typed in the first name on the list. The defense personnel database responded immediately.

Ronald Cobb—NMCC

She typed in the second name.

Andrew Bloom—NMCC

After she'd typed in the third name, her stomach tightened.

Bradley Green—NMCC

She stopped after the fourth entry.

Kathy Leenstra—NMCC

Kenney watched as Christine sat there, no longer typing. "What is it, Miss O'Connor?"

Christine turned in her chair, facing Kenney again. "These individuals are employees at the National Military Command Center in the Pentagon, responsible for generating nuclear strike messages to our intercontinental ballistic missile silos, B-2 bombers, and Trident submarines." She stared at the list again, trying to figure out the meaning of "I S" in front of each name. Her eyes widened as it dawned on her.

Inner safe.

Nuclear launch orders would not be considered valid unless the code at the bottom of the message matched the codes contained in double-walled safes in the missile silos, bombers, and submarines, with no one person having both combinations. The only way to write a valid order was to open both safe doors in NMCC, allowing access to the sealed codes inside. These ten men and women apparently had the combination to the safe's inner door.

Swiveling back to her computer, Christine pulled a number from her contact list. Picking up the phone, she dialed the Watch Captain at the National Military Command Center. The phone rang, but there was no answer. Christine hung up and dialed again. After ten rings, still no answer. She slammed the phone down. "We need to get to the Command Center."

While the other members of his watch section sat slumped in their chairs or over their consoles, Mike worked at his desk, ignoring the phone that rang at the Watch Captain's desk. He finished the message except for the last part and closed the codebook. Approaching the safe at the front of the room, he entered the combination and unlocked the safe. Inside was another door, with another combination dial. Reaching into his shirt pocket, he pulled out the envelope Hoover had given him and retrieved the single sheet of paper. He ran his finger down the list of ten names before returning to the first. His finger lingered at the top of the page for a moment before he pulled the first inhaler from the kit, the one he'd injected into his neck, plus the third vial, this one with a sharp tip at the end.

Searching the room, he spotted his best friend, Ron Cobb, the first name on the list. He walked over to Ron, who was slumped over his workstation, and injected the inhaler into his neck. Thirty seconds later, Ron's eyes fluttered open. Grabbing Ron roughly, Mike pulled him upright in his chair; Ron's head was bent back, his eyes looking at the ceiling. Mike held the vial with the sharp tip against Ron's neck. "Ron, can you hear me?"

Ron's eyes gradually moved down toward Mike's face. He brought his head forward, stopping as he met the pressure of Mike's hand against his neck. Ron looked slowly around the Operations Center at the unconscious men and women at their workstations, his drowsy appearance transforming into a bewildered expression.

"What the hell—"

"I need the combination to the inner safe, Ron. What is it?"

Ron stiffened as his gaze shifted back to Mike. "I can't tell you," he sputtered. "You have the combination to the outer safe. No one person can have both combinations." Ron's eyes roamed around the Operations Center, spotting the safe and its open outer door. "What are you doing?"

Mike pressed the applicator against Ron's neck. "This injector contains a poison that will kill you in seconds. Give me the combination."

"I can't, Mike! Then you'd have access to the nuclear authorization codes!"

"Yes you can. And you've got ten seconds to give me the combination."

"We've worked together for fifteen years," Ron replied, the panic rising in his voice. "Our wives were best friends. I've got four kids at home!"

"You're right, Ron. And it would be a shame for Arlene to have to bury you, with your children standing beside her as they lower your coffin into your grave."

"I can't, Mike! Please!"

11

ARLINGTON, VIRGINIA

A black Suburban, its blue lights flashing, crossed the 14th Street Bridge at the end of rush hour. Forcing its way across three lanes of heavy traffic, an identical Suburban followed closely behind. Christine, sitting in the passenger seat of the lead vehicle next to Agent Kenney, ended her phone call without a word, her eyes fixed on the rapidly nearing Pentagon.

En route, Christine had contacted the deputy director of the National Military Command Center, who, while perplexed by the Watch Captain's failure to answer Christine's phone calls, was convinced it was nothing more than a simple connectivity problem. The deputy director was in a meeting a few blocks away in Crystal City but had agreed to meet Christine at the Operations Center. He had called back just before Kenney's SUV peeled off I-395 toward the Pentagon. Personnel inside the Command Center were also failing to answer the classified lines, and the deputy director's concern had skyrocketed. Kenney had picked up Christine's rising tension and was pushing his vehicle as fast as traffic moved out of his way.

A few moments later, the Suburban squealed to a halt at the Pentagon's River Entrance just as the second SUV, containing two men, ground to a halt behind them. One of the men joined Christine and Kenney as they ascended the River Terrace three steps at a time, while the second remained with the vehicles. Christine and the two agents sped through the Pentagon entrance as they flashed their badges to security personnel, then, after dropping down three levels via the A Ring escalators, headed out along Corridor 9 toward the outermost ring. They eventually reached the end of a long hallway, where two Marines stood in front of a large security door.

"Open the door," Christine ordered.

"We can't," the Marine on the left answered. "The door won't unlock, and there's no response from inside."

"Are you sure you have the correct code?"

"Yes, ma'am."

"What's standard protocol if you can't gain access?"

The Marine looked at Christine uncomfortably. "The deputy director will be here any minute. It'll be his call on what to do next."

As the Marine finished speaking, a man approached, running down the corridor, stopping next to Christine. He was out of breath as he spoke. "I got here as soon as I could, Chris."

Dave Hendricks, the deputy director of the National Military Command Center, was a relatively handsome man in his forties, about six feet tall, of medium build, wearing a blue sport coat and a coordinating tie. After a curt introduction to Agent Kenney and learning the door refused to respond to the Marines' security code, he attempted to open the door using his code, with the same result.

"Any ideas?" Christine asked.

"Blow the door," Hendricks replied, looking in Agent Kenney's direction.

Kenney motioned to the agent beside him, who spoke into his suit jacket sleeve.

Inside the Operations Center, Mike placed the list of names next to the safe, flattening the creases in the paper. He glanced at the safe, the inner door still shut, then at Ron and Andy Bloom, their stiff bodies on the floor. Psychological profiles had been run on all ten men and women who knew the combination to the inner safe, and the names on the list were arranged in order of who was most likely to crack and trade the combination for his or her life. The profiles of Ron and Andy were obviously incorrect. But Hoover had assured him the odds of all ten men and women sacrificing their lives to protect the combination were minuscule, with a 99.7 percent probability one of them would acquiesce. Mike would obtain the combination; it was only a matter of time.

Mike ran his finger down the list of names to the next one.

Third time's the charm.

Outside NMCC, a third CIA agent had arrived with the requested materials, and after placing the small block of C-4 explosive onto the door lock mechanism and inserting the detonator, Agent Kenney headed down the corridor and around the corner into F Ring, where

Hendricks and Christine waited with the Marines and the two other agents. The Marines and agents drew their firearms, then Kenney pressed the trigger, its thin wire trailing to the C-4, detonating it in a rumbling explosion. A cloud of smoke engulfed the corridor, debris ricocheting off the walls. The smoke slowly cleared, and a partially open door materialized out of the haze.

The two Marines surged forward, one stopping on each side of the door. The one on the left peered into the Operations Center, then shoved the door open and moved inside, his weapon pointed across the room.

"Freeze!"

The second Marine joined the first, pointing his pistol at a man at the far end of the room. There were about twenty other men and women in the Operations Center, all of them slumped in their chairs or sprawled on the floor. The lone man suddenly pressed something against his neck, then fell to his knees, collapsing against the wall.

As Michael Patton's vision began to cloud, a warm satisfaction spread through his body. He would have revenge against the country that encouraged the murderers who had extinguished Theresa's life, the country that supplied the Palestinian groups with the weapons and money that made their terror possible. His rage was intense at first, but he had learned to look at the issue dispassionately, convinced that the laws governing people's behavior were no different from the laws of physics.

For every action, there is a reaction.

Israel had reacted thousands of times to the senseless

slaughter of its people, their response diffuse and ineffective by the time it reached the savages who manipulated the strings of hatred. But the savages had crossed the line when their vitriolic hatred took Theresa's life, and they would soon pay dearly. Hoover had requested a launch order be sent to the *Kentucky,* and Mike had complied. But he had made one small, yet significant, change to the message.

As the darkness closed in, Patton was convinced this reaction would make a difference.

Those responsible would finally suffer the repercussions of their actions.

It didn't matter that millions would die in the process.

Mike had done the right thing.

He was certain.

One Marine rushed to the front of the room, carefully checking the man for weapons and signs of life, while the other Marine and the three CIA agents checked the other personnel. Christine scanned the facility, assessing the situation, trying to determine the man's intent and the extent of the damage inflicted. Aside from him, three other men appeared dead, a strange blue tint to their skin. The other men and women were unconscious but appeared alive as far as she could tell.

Near the man at the front of the Operations Center was a small circular trash can with a charred black residue inside, and a sheet of paper with random letters and numbers lay next to the radio communication panel at the front of the room. Christine's eyes shot toward the adjacent safe, spotting the two open doors, the inside barren. She immediately looked back at the communication panel, where a small green light blinked, indicating a successful transmission.

It took barely a second for her to realize what the man had done.

"Shut down all transmitters! Do not relay that message!"

Hendricks reached for the phone, but Christine knew it was already too late.

12

USS *KENTUCKY*
PENTAGON

It was midnight aboard the *Kentucky*. Tom slept in his stateroom under two blankets; it was always cold in the Operations Compartment, the space kept cool to keep the electronic consoles from overheating. The stateroom was small—calling officer's berthing aboard a submarine a stateroom was misleading. The eight-by-eight-foot room was cramped, housing three beds stacked on top of each other against one wall, two desks with ledges that folded up out of the way when not in use, and a pulldown sink. The three men couldn't stand at the same time without bumping into each other. Still, it was far better than enlisted berthing, where each man claimed a six-foot bunk, a five-inch-deep compartment under the mattress for storing clothes and personal articles, and a three-foot-tall locker for hanging dress uniforms.

As the senior officer in the stateroom, Tom claimed the middle bunk and Lieutenant (JG) Herb Carvahlo took the bottom, leaving newly reported Ensign Lopez to climb into and out of the top rack. Each bunk was a seventy-eight-by-thirty-inch aluminum coffin with one open side, adorned with a sliding curtain drawn shut when it was time to sleep. A bunk light, for reading in bed, was mounted on the bottom of Ensign Lopez's rack, a scant twelve inches above Tom's face.

Tom slept lightly, turning onto his side. He and the rest of the crew were still adjusting to Greenwich mean time, but they would never fully acclimate. Aside from the senior officers and chiefs, the crew lived an eighteen-hour day, divided into three sections: six hours on watch and twelve off. But even if Tom had been sleeping soundly, the announcement blaring across the 1-MC would have jolted him awake.

Alert One! Alert One! reverberated throughout the ship.

Tom bolted out of bed as Ensign Lopez landed on the deck beside him. Carvahlo rolled out from his rack at their feet, the three of them throwing on their blue coveralls hanging behind their stateroom door. The three men hurried to Control, arriving just as Malone and the XO entered, followed quickly by the rest of the officers not on watch.

Based on the 1-MC announcement, Tom knew they had just received an Emergency Action Message, but the *Kentucky* would remain in its normal watch section rather than manning Battle Stations Missile while the message was decoded. Most EAMs were informational in nature, keeping the crew abreast of political and military strife anywhere in the world with the potential to escalate to nuclear war. They would man Battle Stations Missile only upon receipt of a strike order. The watchstanders in Control waited for the submarine's officers, operating in pairs, to decode the EAM, most likely just another routine informational message.

Tom paired up with Carvahlo, forming the first decryption team, stopping at the forward section of Control outside the Op Center, a small room adjacent to Radio. Chief Davidson, the Radio Division Chief, eyed Tom through the peephole and opened the door, allowing Tom and Carvahlo entrance to the cramped space, capable of holding only the three of them. Tom went to the safe containing the codebooks, entered the combination, and yanked open the door. Pulling three codebooks from the safe, he handed two to the decryption teams outside the Op Center and the third to Carvahlo. He and Carvahlo would break the message, while the other two teams stood by in case additional transmissions were received.

Chief Davidson exited the Op Center from the back door that opened into Radio, returning a moment later with the EAM, ripped off one of the Radio Room printers. Tom and Carvahlo sat at a table in the Op Center and began decrypting the random letters and numbers, character by character, translating them into English. Carvahlo wrote the decrypted message in the codebook, occasionally glancing up as Tom confirmed the proper translation of each section. Carvahlo's pen slowed and his hand began trembling as he translated the last portion of the message. He looked up at Tom, doubt and fear in his eyes. Tom put his hand around Carvahlo's, steadying his roommate's hand.

Although Tom remained outwardly calm, he struggled to keep his breathing steady. This wasn't supposed to happen. They all knew what the submarine carried;

what they were trained to do. They would launch if ordered. But did anyone really believe they would receive that order? It wasn't supposed to happen this way, either. There was supposed to be ample warning: political unrest or conventional armed conflict that spiraled out of control. Informational messages would stream across the broadcast, keeping the ballistic missile submarines at sea informed. DEFCON would be gradually increased, the Mod-Alert submarines shifting to Alert status and the remaining ballistic missile submarines sortied to sea. They would have time to prepare mentally, ready when the order finally arrived. Not like this . . .

The message had decoded properly. But it still had to be authenticated, the codes in the EAM compared to sealed codes stored in the doubled-walled safe aboard the *Kentucky*. Tom stood and spun the tumbler on the double safe, ensuring Carvahlo couldn't observe the combination, and opened the outer door. He looked away as Carvahlo spun the tumbler to the inner door and opened the safe. Reaching in, Tom retrieved a thin two-inch-square packet, looking remarkably like a wet-nap, with the appropriate markings identified in the EAM. Taking the EAM and the codebook, both Tom and Carvahlo held on to the small authenticator and exited the Op Center, turning over custody of the open safe to the next pair of officers.

As they approached Malone and the XO on the Conn, the watchstanders in Control eyed them carefully, aware from Carvahlo's pale face that something was wrong. Tom stopped at the edge of the Conn and handed the message and the codebook to the Captain.

Tom's mouth was dry, his tongue thick. He spoke

slowly, trying not to let his voice quaver. "We've received a combined Informational and Strike message. The message is a properly formatted, valid EAM."

Malone's face betrayed no hint of emotion. He stood rigidly, staring at the decryption team in front of him. The XO stood next to Malone, his eyes wide, staring first at Tom, then at Malone. The Captain lowered his eyes to the codebook, which he placed between himself and the XO, waiting for the XO's acknowledgment.

After a long moment, the XO spoke. "Ready," he said, his voice cracking. He cleared his throat. "Ready, sir."

The submarine's Commanding and Executive Officers reviewed the decoded message together in silence, verifying each section had been properly decrypted.

"The message is a properly formatted, valid EAM," the XO announced.

"I concur," Malone said.

Tom's eyes had drifted to the deck as the Captain and the XO verified the message was valid. But now he looked up at Malone and the XO again. It all came down to the next step. A valid EAM was only half of the requirement. For the crew to launch, it also had to be authentic—the codes at the bottom of the message had to match the codes inside the sealed authenticator. Tom prayed they didn't.

"Request permission to authenticate."

"Authenticate," Malone replied.

Tom peeled open the wafer he had retrieved from the safe, revealing the authentication codes. He called them out, one by one, comparing them to the codes contained in the EAM.

The codes matched.

"The message is authentic." Tom forced the words out of his mouth.

"I concur," the XO said, followed by Malone.

Malone stared at the decrypted EAM, digesting the message's contents. Every pair of eyes in Control, even those of the two planesmen, rested on the ship's Captain, awaiting his response. The submarine's ventilation and cooling fans whirred softly in the background, and the sonar screens flickered silently behind him. Malone finally looked up and asked the decryption team to formally inform him and the XO of their orders.

"What are the launch instructions?"

Inside the National Military Command Center, less than a minute had passed since Hendricks began breaking the coded message, yet it already seemed like hours. Christine paced nervously behind him, pausing to glance over his shoulder with each pass. The deputy director's pen moved quickly as he broke the encryption, character by character, writing the message in English into the codebook. But even the English on the paper told Christine nothing; the strategic and nuclear terms were foreign to her. "What does it say?"

Irritation momentarily flashed across Hendricks's face. "I'm working as fast as I can, Chris. Just give me a minute."

Christine resumed her pacing. The two of them were alone in NMCC, aside from the seventeen unconscious and four dead men and women. Medical help had been summoned, which would arrive momentarily, greeted by the pair of Marines and the three CIA agents waiting outside. Christine didn't want anyone listening to her conversation with Hendricks; until the message was decoded and they knew what they were dealing with, she wanted to be sure no one else became aware of the contents of the transmission.

Hendricks's pen stopped moving. "Dear God," he said quietly.

Christine peered over his shoulder. "What does the message say?"

The phone beside Hendricks rang. "Yes?" Hendricks was silent for a few seconds. "I see." He hung up and looked up at Christine. "We were too late. The message went out."

"What does it say?"

"The *Kentucky* has been directed to launch."

Christine couldn't believe what she was hearing. One of their submarines had been ordered to launch its missiles? Her knees turned weak and panic stabbed at her. Visions of a hasty, but well-deserved, retaliation, followed by an all-out nuclear war, flashed though her mind. Steadying herself, she gripped Hendricks's shoulder, then sank into the chair next to him, her thoughts blank for a few seconds. But then her mind snapped into action.

"How many missiles were released?"

"All twenty-four."

"Against who?"

Hendricks checked the message again. "She's been assigned an Iranian target package. Her missiles will destroy the entire country."

Christine blinked several times, trying to comprehend what one of their Trident submarines had been directed to do. Annihilate an entire country. But relief washed over her at the same time. Iran could not retaliate, and the United States was safe. That selfish thought was accompanied by guilt; while America would emerge unscathed, Iran would be reduced to an uninhabitable wasteland. They had to stop the launch, somehow countermand the order before the *Kentucky* acted. "How long before they launch?"

"If the *Kentucky* is within range, she'll begin launching within minutes."

"We have to stop it. Can you send a cancellation message?"

Hendricks's eyes went to the empty safe, then to the charred residue in the trash can. "That man knew what he was doing. He destroyed all the authentication codes. If we send a message without the correct codes, the *Kentucky* will ignore it."

Christine began pacing again. "Is there a backup set of codes somewhere?"

"There is, but it'll take two hours to get them here. I'll have the message ready to go with the exception of entering the authentication codes. But if the *Kentucky* is within range, there's nothing we can do to stop her from launching."

Christine realized their only hope was that the *Kentucky* was not within launch range and would not get there within the next two hours. She looked up at the electronic display at the front of the Operations Center. Four Trident submarines were at sea in the Pacific and another four in the Atlantic. In each ocean, two submarines were in their patrol areas while two were either en route or returning. But instead of their name or hull number, each submarine symbol was labeled with a set of random characters and numbers. Which one was the *Kentucky*?

"What fleet is the *Kentucky* assigned to?" Christine asked.

"Pacific."

"Get me the SUBPAC Strategic Watch Officer."

A moment later, Hendricks handed the secure handset to Christine, and a man's voice warbled over the long-distance encrypted line. "Lieutenant Commander Coleman, SUBPAC Strategic Watch Officer."

"This is Christine O'Connor, National Security Adviser. I need to know if the *Kentucky* is in her patrol area."

"I'm sorry, ma'am. But I can't provide that information over the phone."

Christine lost control, yelling into the receiver, "This is a secure phone, and if you don't want to end up at admiral's mast by the end of the day, you damn well better answer my question! Is the *Kentucky* inside her patrol area!" Her face had turned red and her fingers white as she gripped the phone.

There was silence on the line for a few seconds before the Watch Officer answered. "No."

"Will she reach her patrol area in the next two hours?"

Silence on the line again.

"Answer my question! I don't want to know where the submarine is, just if she'll reach her patrol area in the next two hours! Yes or no!"

"No, ma'am."

Christine exhaled, then hung up the phone.

"The replacement codes will be here soon," Hendricks said, "and then we'll send the cancellation message."

Christine glanced at the man who had killed himself, who was still slumped against the wall. "Why would he send a launch message to a submarine that wasn't in launch range, knowing that we'd send a cancellation message within the next few hours?"

Hendricks shrugged. "That's for your CIA friends to figure out, once they track down who's behind this. In the meantime, you had better inform the president."

Christine nodded slowly, then picked up the secure phone, dialing the familiar number.

The conversation was brief and terse, with Hardison interjecting at the end; the president had placed her on speakerphone in the Oval Office so his chief of staff could overhear. Christine's instinct had been correct, sending the Marines and CIA agents outside NMCC. They would send a cancellation message, and no one would be the wiser. An extensive *cleanup,* as Hardison had put it, would be required to sweep this incident under the rug. Christine had almost corrected the chief of staff, replacing his choice of words with the proper term, *cover-up,* but she bit her tongue. There would be a time to debate the administration's response to this incident, and now was not that time.

As Christine hung up the phone, one of the Marines knocked, then entered the Operations Center. "Medical personnel have arrived. May we enter?"

"Come in," Christine answered. She closed the codebook, the message stuck between the pages. As the Marines and CIA agents reentered with emergency medical personnel, Christine called out to Agent Kenney, motioning for him to join her and Hendricks at the front of the room.

"I need to keep what happened here quiet for the time being," Christine said softly as Kenney joined them, "until we figure out how to break this issue to the public. To start with, we need a plausible explanation for *this*." Christine gestured to the dead and unconscious men and women around them. "Can you help?"

Kenney glanced around the room, then up at the air-conditioning vents in the ceiling. "I'll need Director Ronan's permission . . . , but it appears we've had a Freon leak from one of the air-conditioning plants. It's fortunate we arrived when we did, or everyone would have suffocated. I'll have one of my men . . . , identify the source of the leak."

"Thank you, Agent Kenney."

A minute later, Kenney put away his cell phone and began talking privately with the other two agents. As Christine watched medical personnel attend to the incapacitated men and women, her thoughts returned to the launch order just transmitted. In two hours, they'd send a cancellation message and this nightmare would be over. But her intuition told her things wouldn't be quite so simple. If they were, then whoever orchestrated this had gone through a great deal of trouble to achieve nothing.

And that didn't make sense.

No sense at all.

13

USS *KENTUCKY*

As Malone leaned over the chart table in Nav Center, he realized his senses had become heightened. The temperature gradient in the room was particularly noticeable, the cold air from the ventilation ducts chilling his body while the heat from the electronic chart table warmed his hands. Against the far bulkhead, the ship's two inertial navigators, which kept track of the submarine's position at all times, blinked their agreement, their green lights reflecting off the wall behind them. All around him, the submarine was unusually quiet, the machinery mimicking the subdued demeanor of its crew.

Malone had retreated to Nav Center to collect his thoughts and measure the distance to the Emerald operating area, and launch range. The *Kentucky* would be in her assigned moving haven for four more days, followed by another four-day transit through Sapphire before she reached Emerald, where the crew would execute its mission. Someone had to do it, but why the *Kentucky*?

True, she was configured differently from other Tridents, and that was a reasonable enough explanation. But it seemed surprising the new president would want to wait eight days before retaliating when other Tridents were closer. After reading the informational section of the EAM, he could only imagine what it was like back home—the disarray and chaos. And it was his job to break the news to the crew, tell them what had been done to their country and what they would do in response.

Malone sucked in a deep breath as he prepared to inform the rest of the crew what the men in Control already knew. The entire crew was awake by now, he was sure, word of their launch order traveling like wildfire throughout the ship. But Malone wanted to ensure everyone clearly understood what had happened and when and how the United States would respond.

He entered Control, stepping onto the Conn. Unholstering the 1-MC microphone, he held it in his hand for a moment, then brought it to his lips.

"This is the Captain."

Throughout the ship, the crew halted their conversations as they listened to their Commanding Officer.

"We received an Emergency Action Message today, and no doubt many of you are aware of the content and our instructions." Malone paused. It was difficult to speak. After a moment, he continued. "A nuclear bomb was detonated in Washington, D.C., yesterday. The White House and the majority of the city were destroyed. Over one hundred thousand men, women, and children are dead, including the president and most of his cabinet. Vice President Tompkins has been sworn in as president, and he has authorized the release of nuclear weapons in response. The source of the nuclear bomb has been traced to Iran, and the *Kentucky* has been directed to strike back. In eight days, we will reach our patrol area and our missiles will be in range. In eight days, the United States will make an example of those who murdered our families and friends and threatened the survival of our country. In eight days, be ready."

Malone met the eyes of each man in Control, then eased the microphone into its clip before leaving the Control Room without another word.

On watch in Radio, sitting next to the Radio Division Chief, Petty Officer 3rd Class Pete Greene could not contain his anxiety, his knee jittering up and down.

"Jesus, Chief. We actually got launch orders." Greene's fingers tapped the console in front of him, matching the rhythm of his knee. "We train for this all the time, but I never thought we'd actually have to go through with it." He studied the radio console display, watching for another message. "Damn, I can't concentrate, Chief. My stomach is tied in knots."

"I'm with you, Greene." Davidson turned away from his screen. "Why don't you go to Crew's Mess and get some coffee for both of us?"

"Can't, Chief, I'm on watch. There's supposed to be two of us in here at all times."

"Don't worry, Greene. It's the midwatch. We do this all the time on patrol. Get some coffee, and I'll cover for you." Greene looked skeptically at his chief, but Davidson nodded toward the Radio Room door. "A dash of cream and a pack of sugar in mine."

After scanning his display again, Petty Officer Greene

stood, rubbing his sweaty palms on the legs of his jump-suit. "Yeah, I need some coffee. I'll be right back."

When the door closed, Davidson popped up out of his chair and stepped over to the Antenna Patch Panel, which connected the ship's antennas to the Radio Room equip-ment. He unscrewed the knurl knobs, pulled opened the front panel, and examined the maze of circuit boards and wires inside the cabinet. Retrieving a small Phillips-head screwdriver from his pocket, he reached inside the cab-inet and loosened two of the terminal connections, re-routing the end of a yellow wire from one terminal to the other.

Working quickly inside the cramped electronics cab-inet, Chief Electronics Technician Alan Davidson found it hard to believe he had slipped through the cracks. Ra-dio Division personnel required a top secret clearance, as did everyone dealing with the receipt and decryption of EAMs. In addition, ballistic missile submarine sail-ors and officers were screened through the Personnel Reliability Program, their backgrounds scrutinized to ensure each member was trustworthy and dependable. He had been processed through the system with flying colors.

Born to Jewish immigrants from Austria, Davison had attended Hebrew day school in Milwaukee, Wisconsin, through the eighth grade. His daily curriculum, which began with the singing of the Israeli national anthem, included not only math and English but also Hebrew, Israeli history, and Zionist literature. At home, his par-ents followed Israeli news with religiouslike zeal, passing the love for their kin and the Jewish homeland to their son. By the time Davidson attended public high school, the country to which he owed his allegiance was clear. And during the exhaustive security interviews and background checks conducted after he joined the Navy, no one had even asked him that basic question.

It wasn't that he didn't appreciate the United States. His family had prospered, and he believed America truly was the land of opportunity. But he had been given a unique opportunity to help defend the Jewish people in Israel. Shortly after his assignment to the USS *Kentucky,* his sister had introduced him to a friend of hers, Bill Hoover. It wasn't long before it became clear that he was more than just a guy next door. Davidson's role in the plan had been proposed, and he had accepted; there was little risk to him.

Davidson reached behind one of the circuit cards, swiveling into view a circuit board he had installed during the submarine's last refit. After flipping a small toggle lever on the back of the circuit card, he turned to observe the two Radio Room consoles. The displays scrambled, then resynced a second later, diagnostics scrolling down the screens.

He was about to close the cabinet cover when the Radio Room cipher lock clicked and the door opened. Petty Officer Greene entered, one cup of steaming coffee tucked under his left arm and another in his left hand. Greene stopped at the entrance with a puzzled look on his face, as the two Radio Room consoles continued their start-up. Chief Davidson finished securing the Antenna Patch Panel cover.

"There you are, Greene. What took you so long?"

"Whatcha doing, Chief?"

"Just running some diagnostics. Want to make sure

everything's working properly. Especially now that we're receiving EAMs." Davidson walked over to Greene, reaching for the mug in his left hand. "This one mine?"

Greene nodded.

"Thanks." Davidson glanced over his shoulder as both consoles completed their reboot. "Back to business." Davidson slid into his chair at his workstation, nonchalantly sipping his coffee. A few seconds later, Greene did the same, and both men were soon busy with their normal watch routine.

The *Kentucky*'s communication equipment was severed from its antennas, routed instead to a circuit card preloaded with two weeks' worth of naval messages, which the *Kentucky* would download periodically when she went to periscope depth to copy the broadcast. And if the crew tried to transmit, the circuit card would generate a curt response from COMSUBPAC an hour later, telling the submarine to execute its assigned mission and not transmit again.

The *Kentucky* was cut off from the outside world and wouldn't even notice.

14

PENTAGON

"Sir, the *Kentucky*'s not responding."

Christine stood next to Hendricks in the Operations Center, filled again with men and women from the next watch section, listening to the communication specialist's report.

"We've sent the Termination message several times now, with instructions to acknowledge receipt, and we've received no response."

"Are you sure our equipment and transmitters are functioning properly?" Christine asked.

"Yes, ma'am. We've verified the message is being transmitted. Other units have received it. Just not the *Kentucky*, apparently."

"Maybe she has but is unable to respond?" Hendricks asked.

"Could be," the comm specialist replied. "But there's no way to tell."

Christine had waited anxiously for the replacement codes to arrive, the minutes slowly ticking by. The agonizing wait had finally ended, the codes delivered by a two-man courier team. But now the *Kentucky* had failed to acknowledge the Termination message, and the anticipated end to this nightmare scenario had failed to materialize.

Christine turned to Hendricks. "What do we do if the *Kentucky* doesn't acknowledge?"

"Without a reply, there's no way to know if she's received the Termination message and has canceled her strike order."

"So what do we do now?"

"We keep transmitting. But if she doesn't acknowledge, we have to assume she hasn't received the cancellation message. And if she doesn't receive it . . ." Hendricks looked over at the digital clock at the front of the Operations Center, set to the estimated time before the *Kentucky* reached launch range. The red numbers ticked steadily down.

"The *Kentucky* will execute the last valid set of orders she's received."

15

JERUSALEM, ISRAEL

God filled with mercy,
dwelling in the heavens' heights,
bring proper rest beneath the wings of your
Shehinah,
amid the ranks of the holy and the pure,
illuminating like the brilliance of the skies,
the souls of our beloved and our blameless
who went to their eternal place of rest.
May you who are the source of mercy
shelter them beneath your wings eternally,
and bind their souls among the living,
that they may rest in peace.
And let us say: Amen.

As a light morning rain fell over the Har HaMenuchot cemetery, Barak Kogen stood next to his friend and prime minister, holding a large black umbrella over the two of them, the water running off the edges in small rivulets. Kogen listened as the rabbi finished reciting the

Eyl Malei Rahamim, watching as the caskets containing Rosenfeld's two daughters were lowered into their graves. Kogen had been by Rosenfeld's side three years ago, the older man's arms around his daughters as they buried their mother. But unlike then, when he pulled his children close and offered soft words of encouragement, today he stood alone. There was nothing left of Rosenfeld's family, and the condolences of friends and relatives could not assuage his grief. Still, Kogen hoped the news he was about to share would somehow lessen his sorrow.

The operation had been initiated. As feared, the information discovered by the young intern had fallen into capable hands, and the Americans had discerned enough to threaten the plan's success. But they had arrived too late, and now there was nothing they could do. With the additional precautions the Mossad had taken, the Americans would not find the *Kentucky*. Now, all that was left to do was wait for the submarine to reach launch range and execute her order. Kogen leaned closer to his friend, hoping his words would help console him. "I have news, Levi."

The older man gave no indication he'd heard Kogen, staring directly ahead as the rabbi began another prayer. The rain splattered against Kogen's umbrella in a soft, steady tempo as the man's voice droned on. Located on the western edge of Jerusalem, Har HaMenuchot offered commanding views of Mevaseret Zion to the north, Motza to the west, and Har Nof to the south. But Rosenfeld stared blankly ahead. Surrounded by relatives from both sides of what used to be his family, Rosenfeld stood alone and isolated; the gray, bleak sky overhead reflecting his grief.

As the rabbi finished his prayer, Rosenfeld nodded for Kogen to continue.

"The Mossad operation was a success, Levi. Our people will soon be protected from these animals."

16

WASHINGTON, D.C.

An early morning stillness clung to the White House as Christine strode down the West Wing corridor, her footsteps muffled by the plush blue carpet. As she headed toward the stairway leading to the basement, her thoughts never strayed from her all-night vigil in NMCC. She'd finally departed only a few minutes ago to return to the White House and the awaiting president. During the night, her extensive weapons background had proved useful in assessing the threat the *Kentucky* posed, but her knowledge of ballistic missile submarines and the weapons they carried was still somewhat limited. Thankfully, the man walking on her right had filled in the missing details.

Navy Captain Steve Brackman was the president's senior military aide, a post filled by each branch of the armed services on a rotating basis. Fortunately, the president's current aide was a naval officer, and even more fortunate, he was a former commanding officer of a ballistic missile submarine. After Christine informed the president of the *Kentucky*'s launch order, Brackman had been sent to NMCC. Arriving there late last night, Captain Brackman was a sight for sore eyes, in more ways than one.

Tall and handsome, with dark, penetrating eyes, Brackman had a chiseled body that would make a Calvin Klein model envious. Put his image on a Navy recruiting poster, Christine thought, and the percentage of female enlistments would skyrocket. He wasn't just good-looking either—as commanding officer, he had received the coveted Admiral Stockdale Award for Inspirational Leadership. Assigned to the administration eighteen months ago, Brackman was approaching the end of his two-year tour. He had never shared the details, but soon after he arrived, Christine had learned he was a recent widower, his wife and son killed in a horrific accident of some type. This morning, however, he would aid Christine in preventing a horrific accident of an undoubtedly different type.

In the basement of the West Wing, Christine followed Brackman into the Situation Room; the air was cold and the tension thick as she closed the door, alone with Brackman and two other men. The president sat at the head of the rectangular conference table, a grave expression on his face, while Hardison, seated on the president's right, appeared hostile. Hardison had arrived early, no doubt whispering in the president's ear as they waited. Even though there were more important things to discuss this morning, Christine was ready to defend herself. She would not go down without a fight.

This mess was going to be her fault, if Hardison had

his way. In their conversations throughout the night, she could tell he was jockeying for position, probing her about the CD she'd found and her role in the debacle. He would take advantage of her involvement—her decision to withhold knowledge of the CD, and her arrival in NMCC after the message was transmitted—somehow twisting things around to pin the blame on her. Hell, she had almost stopped it. Yet Christine knew that somehow, it was all going to be her fault.

Hardison's eyes bored a hole through her body as she approached the conference table, and she returned his stare as she and Brackman sat opposite him, her eyes locked with Hardison's until the president cleared his throat. Turning her attention to the commander in chief, Christine thought he had aged overnight. Although he had entered office with salt-and-pepper sideburns, the gray was now throughout his full head of brown hair and the lines in his face were more deeply creased. The decision the president would make this morning would no doubt add more years to his appearance.

As the president began to speak, Christine's eyes flicked back to Hardison. His malevolent gaze was still fixed on her, and she steeled herself for the worst. She would restrain herself in conversation with the president, but if Hardison opened his mouth, she was coming out swinging.

"Considering your role in this mess . . . ," the president began.

Here it comes.

". . . you handled the situation extremely well."

Christine was caught off guard. Had Hardison actually complimented her, praising her actions? Or had he criticized her as usual, with the president giving him the Heisman this time, stiff-arming his attempt to demonize her, deciding instead to give her the credit she deserved? Her eyes went to Hardison again. His expression hadn't changed—still the same disapproving frown. *Figures*. The president had overridden him.

"So where do we stand on terminating this launch?" the president added.

Christine shrugged off her surprise at the unexpected compliment and answered the president's question. "We've been transmitting the cancellation message for the last nine hours, but so far the *Kentucky* hasn't responded. We have to assume she's had a Radio Room casualty, or worse, sabotage, and that either way, she hasn't received the cancellation message. That means she'll execute the strike order, launching her missiles eight days from now."

"Do we know who's behind this yet?"

"We have our suspicions, given the launch is directed at Iran, and that the perpetrator's wife was an Israeli national, killed by Palestinian terrorists while visiting Israel a few years ago. Everything points to Israel, but we have nothing concrete so far."

The president's face hardened. "I want this nailed down, Christine. Pull out all the stops." The president paused for a moment before continuing, "What kind of destruction are we talking about if the *Kentucky* launches?"

"The *Kentucky* carries twenty-four missiles. Each missile can be configured with up to eight warheads, but they're usually configured with four under the New

START treaty with Russia." Christine paused, glancing at Hardison.

The chief of staff flashed her a dark look.

"What?" the president asked.

Christine's eyes returned to the president. "The *Kentucky* is unique in that her missiles are configured with a payload of eight warheads. There are several target packages that require more than four warheads per missile, so—"

"We're in violation of START?" the president asked.

Hardison had been uncharacteristically quiet so far, and Christine wondered if he had expended himself arguing with the president over her culpability, and was now sitting there, sulking. Or was it something else? But then he joined the conversation.

"Not exactly," Hardison replied. "Under New START, we can deviate from four warheads per missile, as long as we have proper authorization."

"Who authorized this deviation?"

"You did, Mr. President," Hardison replied. "You signed the authorization a year ago."

"I don't recall approving this."

"I have your signature, sir. But in your defense, it was a thick document, and I may not have pointed out that clause." Hardison shifted uncomfortably in his seat.

The president glared at his chief of staff, his jaw muscles flexing. "We'll discuss this later." He turned to Captain Brackman. "Put this in terms I can understand. Relative to Hiroshima, how much destruction can the *Kentucky*'s warheads deliver?"

Brackman answered, "The bomb we dropped on

Hiroshima was a twenty-kiloton weapon. Each of the warheads carried by the *Kentucky* is a four-hundred-seventy-five-kiloton bomb, so each of the *Kentucky*'s warheads is roughly twenty-five times more powerful than what we used to destroy Hiroshima. Multiply that by twenty-four missiles, then again by eight warheads per missile, and that'd be around . . . five thousand Hiroshimas."

The president's face paled. "My God. We have to inform Iran."

"I don't recommend it," Hardison said. "The chaos we'd cause would be almost unimaginable. As long as we have the potential to stop the launch, we don't want this issue going public. Plus, if the country finds out we issued a valid launch order to one of our submarines, it could topple your presidency."

"I don't give a damn about my administration right now," the president snapped. "The only thing that matters is turning off this launch."

"I understand, sir," Hardison replied in a conciliatory tone. "But if we can do it while keeping the issue under wraps, it's important we do so."

There was a long silence as the president considered Hardison's recommendation. Christine knew they could keep this issue quiet for a short period of time, claiming operational necessity. But a long-term effort to conceal what had occurred, if discovered, would carry severe political and even criminal repercussions.

After what seemed like several minutes, the president spoke. "Who else knows about this?"

"Right now there are only five persons who know everything," Hardison answered. "The four of us, plus

Dave Hendricks, the deputy director of the National Military Command Center. The Command Center director, Admiral Tracey McFarland, is on travel the next two weeks, and as acting director, Hendricks has agreed to cover for us until the issue is either resolved or we provide other direction. The rest of the NMCC staff has no idea of the content of the message that was transmitted. Christine was wise enough to see to that."

The president fixed Hardison with a serious look. "And what makes you think this Dave Hendricks will comply with our desire to keep this matter confidential?"

Hardison turned to Christine.

"I requested his confidentiality as a personal favor," Christine answered.

The president raised an eyebrow. "And he would do this because . . . ?"

Christine smoothed a wrinkle in her skirt, then locked her fingers together around her knee. "Dave is my ex-husband."

The president leaned back in his chair. "And I assume you divorced on amicable terms?"

"As amicable as any divorce can be, I suppose. We're still good friends and he's agreed to honor our request to keep the content of the message confidential as long as possible."

"Why don't we have Hendricks sign a nondisclosure agreement?" Brackman interjected.

"I don't recommend it," Hardison answered. "It's not a good idea to have hard-copy evidence of our direction to keep this issue quiet."

The president nodded his agreement as Christine

picked up where Hardison left off. "Even with a non-disclosure agreement, once we give the order, there's a high probability this will go public."

The president leaned forward. "What order?"

"Mr. President. The three of us see only one solution, given the *Kentucky*'s failure to acknowledge the cancellation message. We're here to ask you for that authorization."

"Authorization for what?"

"To sink the *Kentucky*."

The president's face went blank. "There must be some other option. You're talking about sinking one of our own submarines. With our own people aboard."

Hardison replied, "She has to be stopped from launching. She hasn't acknowledged the cancellation message, so we have no choice."

"Wait a minute," the president replied. "The *Kentucky* is eight days away from launch range. Why do we have to sink her now? Why can't we keep sending her the cancellation message? Maybe she'll fix her radio gear and she'll receive the message."

"There's another issue," Brackman answered. "The CIP key."

"What's that?" the president asked.

"It's a key on board the submarine the crew needs to launch the missiles. It's kept in a safe that no one on board knows the combination to. Not until they receive a Launch order. Now that the crew has received the Launch order, they have the CIP key and can launch. The question no one can answer is, Is the crew part of this plot and that's why they're not responding to the Termination order, or are they not responding to the Termination order because of a Radio Room casualty?"

There was silence around the table as the president digested Brackman's words.

Brackman continued, "Unfortunately, there's no way for us to figure this out, and the longer we wait, the harder it gets for us to find and stop the *Kentucky*. So you have to make a decision, Mr. President, and you have to make it today."

The president stood and turned, facing the dark monitor on the Situation Room wall. The silence was unbearable as the president sorted through the options and their outcomes. Finally, he turned back to his advisers; his dark brown eyes had grown darker still.

"Here's what we're going to do. First, continue to limit those who know about the launch order. As this evolves, we'll evaluate to who and when to divulge information. Inform Williams, as we'll have to go through the secretary of defense to give orders to the Unified Commanders. Second, keep the vice president in the dark. I want him insulated in case I'm forced to resign over this issue. Finally, it seems we have no other option." The president's shoulders slumped, his confident façade crumbling under the weight of his decision.

"Sink the *Kentucky*."

17

PEARL HARBOR, HAWAII

With the sun only a few degrees above the horizon, the waterfront along Pearl Harbor was already a frenzy of activity, every submarine making preparations to get under way. Heavy cranes lifted green warshot torpedoes across the wharves onto loading skids on top of the submarines, while smaller cranes swung pallets of supplies to sailors waiting topside. As Captain Murray Wilson hurried toward Admiral Stanbury's office, he was joined by the admiral's aide, Lieutenant David Mortimore, saluting as he approached.

"What's going on, Lieutenant?"

Lieutenant Mortimore hustled to keep up with Wilson as they weaved their way across the busy waterfront. "The orders went out at zero four hundred this morning, sir. Every fast attack in Pearl has been ordered to sortie immediately. Same thing with the submarine squadrons in San Diego and Guam. Everyone's getting under way. Even the Seawolfs at Indian Island in Washington."

"Where are they headed?" Wilson asked, dodging a

forklift passing through the legs of the crane they were walking under.

"Don't know, sir. No one's received their OPORD yet. The Watch Officers are busy generating movement orders, but all they've been told so far is to route everyone west at flank speed. We've got eight fast attacks—"

"Yes, I know," Wilson interrupted. "Eight fast attacks at sea, and I know where they are." He was unable to conceal his irritation. Admiral Stanbury had begun issuing orders in the middle of the night, yet he'd called Wilson only a half hour ago. "What's the status of under way preps?" he asked, returning his attention to the fifteen submarines still in Pearl Harbor.

"Start-up preps are under way on all boats, but most of the reactor plants are at cold iron. The *Houston* and *Jacksonville* are hot, and should be ready by zero nine hundred."

Wilson's eyes skimmed across the waterfront, identifying the *Jacksonville* two piers down, several sailors removing shore power. Beyond the *Jacksonville,* across the channel, were two of the surface ship wharves, a dozen destroyers and cruisers likewise preparing to get under way.

"Looks like the entire PAC Fleet is surging."

"Yes, sir," Lieutenant Mortimore replied. "It does look that way."

Turning the corner at pier Sierra One-Bravo, Mortimore left Wilson's side to assist the Watch Officers while Wilson hurried past the mothballed Dive Tower, the metal staircase winding up the outside of the one-hundred-foot-tall cylindrical structure. He was headed toward an unpretentious two-story cinder-block building built into the side of a small hill. As Wilson passed between a pair of three-foot-tall brass submarine dolphins and climbed the cracked concrete steps, one would not have guessed he was about to enter the headquarters of the most powerful submarine fleet on earth.

Sixty percent of the U.S. Submarine Force was homeported in the Pacific, amounting to thirty-two nuclear-powered fast attacks and eleven Tridents, nine of which were ballistic missile submarines while the other two pulled double duty as Tomahawk-guided missile shooters and special warfare platforms for their embarked SEALs. By itself, a single Trident submarine was the sixth most heavily armed country from a nuclear warhead perspective, and all told, COMSUBPAC was the third most powerful entity in the world, surpassed only by Russia and the United States itself.

Reaching the top of the steps, Wilson punched in his pass code and entered COMSUBPAC headquarters, greeted immediately by the admiral's chief of staff, Captain Errol Holcomb, whose eyes reflected the same irritation as Wilson's.

"What's going on?" Wilson asked, hoping Holcomb could shed more light on the situation than the admiral's aide.

"Wish I knew. The admiral's been holed up in his office since I got here, refusing to tell anyone what the hell is going on. But now that you're here, maybe we'll get some answers."

Holcomb knocked on COMSUBPAC's door. "Admiral, Captain Wilson is here to see you. May we come in?"

"Wilson only," the voice from inside replied.

Holcomb raised an eyebrow as he opened the door for Wilson.

Murray Wilson entered Admiral John Stanbury's office, and after a single glance at the older man sitting behind his desk, his ire melted away. With hunched shoulders and dark circles painted under hollow eyes, the admiral had clearly been up most of, if not the entire, night. Wilson's conclusion was reinforced by four empty Styrofoam coffee cups resting on the edge of a nautical chart spread across the admiral's desk. Wondering where the admiral's favorite coffee mug, the one he had used since his commanding officer tour on the *Memphis*, had disappeared to, Wilson spotted the shattered remnants of a ceramic cup lying against the far wall, and above them, a four-inch gouge in the wall.

"What's going on, sir?"

"Close the door."

As Wilson entered his office, Admiral Stanbury saw the irritation in the younger man's eyes. He hadn't been called right away, but in a few minutes, he would understand why. Stanbury admitted it was unfair to place this burden on Wilson's shoulders, and in the dark morning hours after he'd received the president's directive, he'd hesitated, going down the list of officers who could coordinate the effort. But the list was short, and none had Wilson's experience. Finally, he realized he had no choice. Wilson was the right man, regardless of the circumstances.

Wilson closed the door behind him, but not before he noticed the cipher card inserted into the admiral's secure STE phone and a bright-orange folder on his desk. Stanbury picked up the top secret folder, motioning Wilson toward the conference table. The admiral handed the folder to Wilson, who pulled out a single sheet of paper, a directive signed by the president. After reading it, Wilson sagged into one of the chairs.

"You've got to be kidding. Is this someone's sadistic April Fool's joke?"

"I'm afraid not," Stanbury answered, pulling up a chair beside Wilson. "Our direction is clear. We've been ordered to stop the *Kentucky* using all means available. We've been sending her messages all morning over every communication circuit, ordering her to reply and return to port, but she's failed to acknowledge."

"We've been ordered to sink her because she won't answer a message?"

"It's not just any message, Murray."

"It's obvious, Admiral—she's had a Radio Room casualty. She either hasn't received the Termination message or can't transmit her acknowledgment."

"Washington isn't so sure, and now that the crew has access to the CIP key, they're weighing the likelihood the crew is in on this plot versus the probability of a coincidental Radio Room problem."

Murray slammed his fist on the table. "The crew is *not* in on this plot! I *guarantee* it! I know this crew better than anyone else on the waterfront. I've known Brad Malone since he was a department head on my ship. There's no one with more integrity than him. And . . ." A lump formed in Wilson's throat, and he was unable to complete the sentence.

Stanbury said nothing for a long moment.

"I happen to agree with you," Stanbury said eventually. "This situation is going to be difficult for all of us. I hesitated to call you because your son is aboard the *Kentucky,* but I need you on point, Murray. You're the best I've got, plus you've trained all our commanding officers. No one knows better the tactics the *Kentucky* will use to evade detection, or strategy for employing our forces to find her. I need you to coordinate our submarine, surface, and aircraft in our effort to find the *Kentucky.* But if you're unable to, I'll understand."

Stanbury paused, waiting for it all to sink in.

Reaching across the table, Wilson retrieved the letter and read it again, still finding it impossible to believe. They had been ordered to hunt down one of their own. One of *his* own, in a macabre scenario beyond comprehension. Disbelief, anger, and frustration swirled within as he struggled to come to terms with the president's directive and Stanbury's request. Professionally, he could follow through. But personally . . . The thought of the *Kentucky* engaged in a duel to the death with another U.S. submarine churned his stomach. Even if the *Kentucky* prevailed, they would just send in another fast attack, and another. The end result was not in doubt. He tried not to think about the men aboard the ballistic missile submarine as the cold water dragged the crew—including his son—down to their watery tomb.

Finally, Wilson spoke. "There *has* to be another way."

Stanbury searched Wilson's eyes for a moment before replying. "That's one of the reasons you're here. The last thing I want is to sink one of our own submarines. I need options. *Anything* that will allow me to carry out the intent of my orders"—Stanbury picked up the folder and waved it in the air—"without sinking the *Kentucky*. But we have to stop her from launching."

Wilson let out a deep breath, realizing Stanbury had opened the door to alternatives. Now he needed to find one. His mind shifted into analytical mode, and it wasn't long before he latched on to a solution.

"We'll vector a couple of fast attacks into the *Kentucky*'s moving haven, and after they locate her, instead of attacking, they'll communicate with her via underwater comms, telling her she's had a Radio Room casualty and COMSUBPAC has ordered her to return to port."

Wilson waited for Stanbury's reaction. He knew it was a long shot. Trident crews were well trained. Once a launch order was received, nothing would stop them from launching except a Termination order. Not even underwater communications from a friendly fast attack. But it was worth a try.

"Good idea," Stanbury said as he placed the folder back on the table. "However, the fast attacks need to be weapons-free, in case the *Kentucky* ignores them and tries to slip away. This may be our only opportunity."

Wilson nodded somberly. "I'll take care of it."

"One more thing," Stanbury added. "I need a plan for the rest of the fleet in case your fast-attack plan fails. I'll be briefing Admiral Herrell at PAC Fleet later this morning. There's one additional complication, however. Our orders are clear—we're to minimize the number of personnel who know the ship we've been directed to sink is a U.S. submarine. By no means can we tell the entire fleet their target is the *Kentucky*. But if we don't tell them the truth, and they classify the target as a Trident submarine, what then?"

"We don't need to worry about the surface ships and aircraft," Wilson answered. "Once they detect a submarine, they'll attack immediately and not wait to determine what class it is. Our fast-attack submarines, on the other hand, could be a problem. It's possible one of them will recognize the *Kentucky*'s frequency tonals as a Trident."

Stanbury agreed. "The last thing we want is an attack aborted because there's confusion over whether they're prosecuting the desired contact. Do you have any suggestions?"

Wilson contemplated the quandary, searching for a solution. And then it dawned on him. "I think I have a plan, Admiral."

18

WASHINGTON, D.C.

As the early afternoon light filtered through the tall col-
onnade windows in the Oval Office, Kevin Hardison
struggled to avoid staring at the woman in the chair next
to him, across from the president's desk. She was, without a doubt, the most attractive woman he had ever met.
His eyes kept returning for brief glimpses, lingering only
for an appropriate period of time, until he finally decided
to take advantage of her conversation with the president,
giving him the opportunity to thoroughly admire her
body. She shifted in her chair, crossing her right leg over
her left, revealing well-defined calves, her skirt inching
up her thighs, exposing lean, muscular legs. Her hair fell
across the front of her shoulders, drawing Hardison's
eyes toward the opening of her blouse, the rounded flesh
hinting at full, and undoubtedly firm, breasts.

Even in a conservative business suit, she was unde-
niably beautiful, and when she arrived at the occasional
White House state dinner wearing a formal evening
dress that hugged the curves of her body, every head

turned, men and women alike forgetting the position she held and the influence she wielded. She would normally wear her hair up, pulled back to reveal the sleek lines of her neck, drawing admiring stares up toward her high cheekbones and glittering blue eyes.

If that wasn't enough, her incredible physique was easily matched by her intelligence. The woman spoke with the president as an equal, he respecting her opinion, she absorbing his. Confidence was reflected in the tone of her voice, competence in the words she employed and the information she conveyed. The president nodded as she expertly explained the situation at hand. Hardison caught a faint smile on her lips as the president agreed with her assessment; a smile she seemed to reserve for others and not him, a smile that brightened her face, enhancing her almost irresistible attractiveness. Without a doubt, Hardison mused as he examined her body again, she was easily the most intelligent and beautiful woman he had ever met. Unfortunately, there was the issue of the woman's personality.

If only she weren't such an obstinate bitch.

Christine turned her head toward Hardison, catching him staring at her breasts. She threw him a withering look as she tugged the lapels of her suit jacket together across her chest. Her icy stare, combined with the vague recollection of someone mentioning his name, brought Hardison's thoughts back to their discussion. He'd been asked a question, and his mind dragged the words from his subconscious, piecing together the president's query. "I agree," Hardison finally answered. "A Chinese ballistic missile submarine is a reasonable proposition."

"It's a perfect cover story," added Brackman, who was

seated on the other side of Christine. "The idea is to create a fictional target that has the same sound characteristics as a Trident submarine, so if our fast attacks correlate the frequencies to a Trident, it won't be a surprise to them."

"Why Chinese?" the president asked.

"Because the Chinese are notorious for stealing our military secrets," Brackman replied. "They've already stolen designs for some of our older nuclear warheads, and they've been seeking submarine construction details for years. Their new *Yuan*-class is a copy of the Russian *Kilo*, and it's not a stretch to believe they've finally collected the necessary information to build an indigenous variant of our Trident submarine. Our first Trident entered service over thirty years ago, so that's certainly enough time for them to conduct the necessary espionage."

"Our fast-attack submarines will be informed the target is a replica of our Trident submarine," Brackman added, "and they'll be instructed to search for standard Trident tonals. It's an ingenious solution."

"Only for the time being," the president clarified. "When the *Kentucky* doesn't return from patrol, what then?"

There was a long silence before Hardison replied, "We haven't thought that part through yet."

8 DAYS REMAINING

19

USS SAN FRANCISCO

Twelve hundred miles west of the Hawaiian Islands and just north of the Tropic of Cancer, the USS *San Francisco* surged eastward at ahead full, four hundred feet beneath the ocean's surface, returning home after her six-month WESTPAC deployment. Inside the submarine's sonar shack, Petty Officer 1st Class Tom Bradner studied the sonar screens in front of him. Resting his chin on his hand, Bradner tried to concentrate on the random static from the spherical array in the ship's bow and the towed array streaming a half mile behind the submarine. They were far from the shipping lanes and hadn't held a contact for the better part of a day.

Bradner ran his finger along the thin scar running down his left cheek to the base of his jaw, drawing his thoughts back to the day, in this very sonar shack, when warm flesh had been sliced open by cold metal. They had been on a routine transit to Australia, at ahead flank a hundred feet deeper than they were now, catching up with the middle of their moving haven after falling behind during drills. There had been no warning. Only his body suddenly flying through the air, slamming into the console in the forward part of the shack as the seven-thousand-ton submarine slowed from ahead flank to dead stop in a mere three seconds.

Pacific Ocean charts were notoriously inaccurate, and they had run into an uncharted mountain, even though the water depth was listed as six thousand feet. The watchstanders in Control picked themselves up and recovered quickly, initiating an Emergency Blow. As blood ran down Bradner's face, pain was overshadowed by fear as the submarine began to tilt, the stern lifting upward, the bow remaining on the ocean floor. The forward main ballast tanks had been damaged in the collision, and precious Emergency Blow air was escaping from the ruptured tanks instead of pushing the water out, trapping the *San Francisco* on the ocean bottom. Luckily, the bow broke free from the ocean floor, and the *San Francisco* rose slowly upward.

Of the 137 men aboard, 98 were injured to some extent, with 23 injured seriously enough they were unable to stand watch during the submarine's return to Guam. There was one fatality: Bradner's best friend, Joe Ashley, a machinist mate who was thrown twenty feet into the eight-foot-tall drain pump, fracturing his skull. It was a miracle the *San Francisco* itself wasn't destroyed. The submarine's pressure hull survived intact, buffered by the ship's forward main ballast tanks as they crumpled into the mountain peak.

After the submarine limped back to port, the engineers determined the *San Francisco*'s bow was a complete loss. There was no way to fix the hull and have any confidence in the durability and life span of the repaired ship. If the *San Francisco* hadn't completed a reactor refueling a few months earlier, together with a complete modernization of her tactical systems, Bradner was sure the ship would have been scrapped. But the Navy had invested too much money to throw the ship away. So they cut off the bow of the USS *Honolulu* on its way through decommissioning, welding it onto the front of the *San Francisco* in place of its mangled counterpart. The San Franlulu, as the ship was now nicknamed, was back in business, the most modern and capable, if a bit schizophrenic, *Los Angeles*–class submarine in the fleet.

The Officer of the Deck's voice booming across the 27-MC brought Bradner's thoughts back to the present, the OOD's announcement sending him back to the past just as quickly. The submarine was coming right, increasing speed to ahead flank, changing depth to five hundred feet, the same depth and speed they had been operating at when they ran into the submerged mountain. Bradner acknowledged, wondering what was going on.

"Helm, steady course one-one-zero."

The *San Francisco*'s Officer of the Deck turned to the ship's Captain, Commander Ken Tyler. "How long on this course and speed, sir?"

Leaning over the navigation display in Control, Tyler did the mental calculations. "Fourteen hours. Do not slow for soundings. We don't have time."

The Officer of the Deck raised his eyebrows, keenly aware of the peril of traveling at ahead flank without soundings. But what concerned him even more was the Captain's next order.

"Load all torpedo tubes."

20

PEARL HARBOR, HAWAII

It was two hours before midnight when Murray Wilson reached the deserted waterfront, headed toward the Operations Center in the N7 building. He had never seen the naval base so empty, devoid of its surface and sub-surface warships, the lonely shore power cables swaying gently back and forth in the trade wind. Across the channel, pierside lamps pushed weak yellow light across the black water, the surface of Southeast Loch shimmering in the night as the water lapped against the concrete pilings. As Wilson walked along the quiet submarine wharves, he passed a darkened Lockwood Hall on his right, where seventy years earlier, festive bands had played, celebrating the return of submarine crews from successful war patrols. Wives and children had waited on the pier, leis in their hands, welcoming their loved ones home.

Wilson had headed home only an hour ago, finding a welcome plate of food waiting on the dining room table. Claire sat across from him while he ate in silence.

Rumors had been flying since the early morning recall of every warship crew in Pearl Harbor, until a press release was issued explaining it was nothing more than a surprise training exercise, testing the fleet's ability to surge in response to an unexpected wartime threat. Wilson could tell Claire was waiting for him to explain what was really going on, but he simply said he'd be heading back to the sub base and wouldn't return until morning. He could see the concern in her eyes as he kissed her good-bye. He desperately hoped she hadn't seen right through him, hadn't sensed he'd been asked to kill their only son. He told himself for the thousandth time he had no choice. The life of his son could not outweigh the lives of millions.

Reaching the N7 building, Wilson climbed the staircase on the south side to the second level and entered the cold air-conditioned hallway. Halfway down the corridor, he entered his code into the cipher lock, took a deep breath to steady himself, then stepped inside the Operations Center, domain of the Watch Officers responsible for Water Space Management, a fancy term for underwater traffic cops. Inside the Operations Center, two lieutenants and a lieutenant commander stood watch, monitoring the movement of the submarines under way, their positions displayed on an eight-by-ten-foot monitor on the front wall.

Every fast-attack submarine in the United States Pacific Fleet was at sea tonight, except for three submarines in dry dock undergoing deep maintenance. Even the submarines whose availability was advertised as "one week after notification" had loaded the necessary supplies and cast off their lines. A total of twenty-nine fast attacks were under way, twenty-one headed west from their home ports or local waters, plus five deployed submarines and three more from Guam screaming east, the *San Francisco* in the lead, already halfway home. As the *San Francisco* and the two leading fast attacks from Pearl Harbor approached the *Kentucky*'s position, not even the Watch Officers in the Operations Center knew what was about to occur.

Upon entering the Submarine Service, Wilson had been surprised at how tightly underwater movements were controlled. On the surface, submarines were allowed the freedom to determine what route to take to get from point A to point B. Once submerged, however, they were told where to go, and no two submarines were allowed to operate in the same area, except during carefully controlled training engagements or transits. In those cases, one submarine would be restricted shallow and the other deep, one submarine passing above the other on its transit or as it attempted to detect and engage its simulated adversary below.

The reason for this was the complexity of tracking contacts while submerged. On the surface, radar and the human eye easily conveyed the information required to avoid another ship, but not so underwater. Unlike radar, passive sonar could determine only the direction of the contact, not how far away it was. With only the bearing to the contact, determining its course, speed, and range took time; time during which a contact could approach dangerously close. It was not uncommon for submarines, particularly during the cold war, to collide as one trailed the other in a high-tech game of cat and mouse, guessing wrong at what new speed and course the lead submarine had maneuvered to before the crew sorted it out.

As a result, submarine underwater movements were carefully managed from the COMSUBPAC Operations Center and its sister facility at SUBLANT. Submarines in transit to their patrol or deployment areas were allowed to submerge only within a rectangular box called a moving haven, which moved forward on a particular course and speed. Inside the moving haven, the submarine was free to go in any direction and speed, running to the front of the box and then slowing down for drills or for a trip to periscope depth.

Even ballistic missile submarines were assigned moving havens as they traveled to and from their patrol areas. Most patrol areas, assigned the names of precious jewels such as Emerald, Sapphire, Ruby, and Diamond, covered over a million square miles. Finding a submarine inside its moving haven was child's play compared to searching out a patrol area.

Wilson looked up at the display, examining the three 688-class submarines moving into attack position. The rectangular box representing the *Kentucky*'s moving haven was advancing steadily to the west, with the *San Francisco* heading east on her way home, about to pass north of the *Kentucky*. Meanwhile, two 688s to the south, one behind the other, were rapidly catching up to the ballistic missile submarine's moving haven. In an effort to conceal what the three submarines had been tasked with, Wilson had drafted their MOVEORDs himself, restricting access to his eyes only. Up to now, it would appear they were following normal transit orders. Wilson checked his watch. It was almost time.

"Everyone out!" he announced.

The three Watch Officers looked up in surprise. "Sir?" one of them asked.

"Go home, and inform the midwatch they have the night off. I've got the watch until six A.M."

The Watch Officers exchanged confused glances until Wilson made it perfectly clear. "Now!"

The Watch Officers logged off their computers and left, leaving Wilson alone in the Operations Center, staring at the monitor. A few minutes later, exactly on time, the *San Francisco* veered to the south while the two 688s below turned north. The *San Francisco* would cut through the center of the *Kentucky*'s moving haven, while the other 688s sliced through the leading and trailing thirds.

In the effort to ensure all three submarines arrived at the same time, Wilson had routed the *San Francisco* at ahead flank, slowing her only a few miles before engaging. Under normal circumstances, this would have been a critical flaw in Wilson's plan, as the *Kentucky* might detect the *San Francisco* before she slowed. But Murray was confident the crew of the *Kentucky* played no part in the plot to launch their missiles at Iran; they were merely pawns.

Besides, if the *Kentucky* detected the *San Francisco* and sped up or slowed down to evade the approaching fast attack, she would be snared by one of the quiet 688s on either side.

That's when the most critical part of his plan would occur. One of the 688s would communicate with the *Kentucky* using underwater comms, telling the crew they had a Launch Termination order on the broadcast and that COMSUBPAC had ordered them to return to port. The *Kentucky*'s reaction would determine the 688s' response. If the *Kentucky* did not comply, the 688s would execute their orders.

They would sink her.

Wilson studied the monitor as the three fast attacks converged on the *Kentucky*'s moving haven.

There was nothing for Wilson to do now except wait.

21

USS *SAN FRANCISCO*
USS *KENTUCKY*

USS *SAN FRANCISCO*

"Sir, the ship is at Battle Stations."

Listening to the report from the Chief of the Watch, Commander Ken Tyler stood on the Conn as his ship slowed to ahead two-thirds. The watchstanders in Control were tense, manning Battle Stations and preparing to engage while at ahead flank. They knew how vulnerable their submarine was at maximum speed, the turbulent flow across the ship blinding her sensors. Tyler hadn't wanted to come in at ahead flank but had been given no choice.

The Officer of the Deck approached. "Sir, Torpedo Tubes One through Four are loaded, flooded down, and muzzle doors are open."

"Very well," Tyler acknowledged, concentrating on the combat control screen in front of him, which displayed the *Kentucky*'s moving haven, a rectangular box advancing to the west at eight knots. The *San Francisco* was one of three 688s on a trajectory to slice through the operating area. The *Houston* and *Jacksonville* were to the south, curling northward as they prepared to pass through the front and back thirds of the moving haven, while the *San Francisco* had the privilege of cutting through the middle.

The *San Francisco*'s Officer of the Deck looked up from the geographic display, then turned to Commander Tyler. "Sir, entering the moving haven now."

Tyler picked up the 27-MC. "Sonar, Conn. Report all contacts."

USS *KENTUCKY*

The *San Francisco*'s arrival at ahead flank had not gone unnoticed.

"Conn, Sonar. Hold a new sonar contact, designated Sierra five-seven, classified submerged, bearing three-five-five."

On watch as the Officer of the Deck, Tom picked up the 1-MC. "Rig ship for Ultra-Quiet." Returning the microphone to its bracket, he leaned against the Conn railing. "Helm, ahead one-third."

Tom listened as the ship's ventilation systems and other nonessential equipment were secured, with the remaining equipment shifted into its quietest lineup. Meanwhile, the submarine slowed to five knots, reducing the sound of its propeller churning the water. Throughout the ship, the crew terminated all training and maintenance, and placed the watertight doors on the latch so the noise from their opening and closing wouldn't transmit through the hull into the water.

Malone entered Control. "What have you got?"

Tom twisted the sonar display knob, rotating through the various screens, stopping on the broadband display for the towed array, which had been deployed shortly after receipt of the Strike order. A faint white trace appeared on the monitor, bearing three-five-seven now. "Submerged contact, classification unknown," Tom answered.

As Malone reviewed the sonar display, the trace faded, its disappearance announced a second later. "Conn, Sonar. Contact has slowed. Loss of Sierra five-seven."

A submarine's ability to detect targets was dependent on speed; the faster it traveled, the harder it was to detect contacts due to the water streaming past its sonar. As a submarine prepared to engage in combat, it slowed to increase the range of its sensors and to decrease the amount of sound it transmitted into the water from its propeller.

Tom and Malone knew there were no friendly submarines in the area. The waterspace advisories listed only the *San Francisco*, returning from deployment. But she would pass by several hours from now, far to the north. If this was a submerged contact, it wasn't Friendly, and an enemy submarine approaching at high speed and then slowing could mean only one thing.

Malone turned to Tom. "Man Battle Stations Torpedo."

USS *SAN FRANCISCO*

The conversations in the Control Room were quiet and disciplined, the watchstanders talking into their headsets, passing information between them. Unlike normal underway operations with only one-third of the crew on watch, the attack submarine was now at Battle Stations, every crew member reporting to his assigned position. There was barely enough room in Control to turn around; every console was manned, with supervisors standing behind them, evaluating the displays.

In Sonar, the entire division of eleven men was crammed into a space not much bigger than two telephone booths stacked on their sides, making the Control Room outside seem spacious in comparison. Tom Bradner manned one of the four consoles, his face illuminated in the darkness as his eyes probed the random static. Slowly, a thin white trace appeared, barely discernible from the background noise. The Sonar Chief worked his way behind Bradner as he attempted to assign an automatic tracker to the trace. But the contact was too weak for the tracker to hold.

"Send bearings to fire control manually," the chief ordered.

Bradner maneuvered the cursor over the faint white trace, hitting Enter every fifteen seconds, sending the bearings to the Combat Control System and the Fire Control Tracking Party in the Control Room. Meanwhile, the chief turned to his Narrowband Operators, who were pulling the frequencies from the broadband noise, attempting to classify their new submerged contact. As Bradner glanced over at the narrowband display, there was something familiar about the frequencies.

USS *KENTUCKY*

"Conn, Sonar. Have a new narrowband contact, designated Sierra five-eight, bearing three-five-nine."

Tom acknowledged, switching the Conn sonar screen to the narrowband display. Malone looked over Tom's shoulder, studying the tonals on the monitor.

A moment later, with the signal strength of the frequencies growing stronger, Sonar followed up. "Conn, Sonar. Sierra five-eight is classified *Los Angeles*–class submarine."

Malone looked up in surprise. "Sonar, Conn. Are you sure?"

"Conn, Sonar. We're positive. Her tonals correlate to a first-flight 688."

Irritation flashed across Malone's face, replaced an instant later with relief. A friendly submarine meant they had nothing to worry about, aside from the embarrassment of a ballistic missile submarine being detected, which seemed a distinct possibility based on the growing signal strength of the contact. But then the irritation returned. Someone had screwed up. Either the *Kentucky* wasn't in its assigned moving haven, the other submarine wasn't, or the Watch Officers had routed a fast attack directly through the *Kentucky*'s water. "Nav, get over here!"

The Navigator maneuvered his way across the crowded Control Room, speaking as he reached the Captain, already knowing the question he'd be asked. "I double-checked, sir. We're definitely in our assigned moving haven. Someone else screwed up."

"Have we received any waterspace advisories, rerouting a 688 nearby?"

"No, sir. Only standard message traffic since the strategic strike message."

Malone looked back at the sonar display, then at the combat control screens as the crew's three fire control technicians worked potential solutions for the contact. The FTs studied the dual flat-panel displays in front of them, each hand on a track ball, quickly selecting and adjusting parameters faster than the untrained eye could follow. Hovering behind the three FTs, the XO examined their solutions, then tapped one of the fire control techs on the shoulder.

"Promote to Master solution."

The fire control tech acknowledged, and the contact displays updated with a new solution for contact Sierra five-eight. The XO and Malone studied the screen. "Contact is on an intercept course," the XO said, "projected to pass within one thousand yards."

"She'll detect us for sure," Malone replied. "Damn glad she's one of ours."

22

FORD ISLAND, HAWAII

Sitting squarely in the center of Pearl Harbor, with Battleship Row along its southeastern shore and aircraft carrier moorings to the west, Ford Island was the focal point of the surprise Japanese attack on December 7, 1941. Two hours after the first torpedo bombers descended for their runs down Southeast Loch, the U.S. Pacific Fleet lay in ruins, all eight battleships and ten other warships sunk or heavily damaged. Today, a memorial sits atop the USS *Arizona* to honor the 1,102 men who rest in a watery grave in the shallows off Ford Island.

Twenty-four years before the attack, Battery Adair was constructed on the northeastern corner of the island, its twin six-inch Armstrong guns firing north. After the battery was decommissioned and its guns removed in 1925, officer housing was constructed at the scenic location overlooking Waimalu and Aiea, with one residence sitting directly atop Battery Adair's emplacement. Inside the home, a narrow stairway leads to the main corridor of what was once Battery Adair, the passageway's two ninety-degree turns leading to twin casemated bunkers that still guard the northern overland approach to the harbor.

With dawn breaking to the east and the trade winds just beginning to stir, a blue '72 Mustang rolled to a stop in front of this house. After a short walk up a winding path lined with white and pink impatiens, Murray Wilson knocked on the door of COMSUBPAC's home. A moment later, Admiral Stanbury's wife answered. It seemed she had been up for some time, as her gray hair was neatly arranged and her makeup applied. Then Wilson wondered if she just hadn't yet gone to bed; her eyes conveyed a fatigue that contradicted the early morning hour.

"He couldn't sleep," she said as she opened the door wider. "I've never seen him like this."

"Good morning, Mrs. Stanbury." Wilson entered the foyer, removing his khaki dress uniform hat, nodding his respect.

"I'm sorry, Murray." Betty hugged him and kissed his cheek. "I seem to have forgotten my manners this morning."

There was an awkward silence as Wilson fidgeted with the hat in his hands. He had brought news. News he didn't want to deliver. He wondered if Betty could see the pain in his eyes, if she could discern the torment he was desperately trying to hide. If he couldn't hide it from Betty, there was no way he could conceal it from Claire.

Betty placed her hand on his arm. "It looks like you've been up all night as well. Can I get you a cup of coffee?"

After an all-nighter in the Operations Center drinking weak yet somehow burned coffee, Betty's offer sounded wonderful. "That'd be great."

"John is in the study. I'll bring it to you there."

Already dressed in his khakis, Rear Admiral (Upper Half) John Stanbury sat behind the desk in his study, staring out the window at the Admiral Clarey Bridge leading to the main island. The whole thing seemed surreal. *Hunt down one of his own submarines.* It had eaten away at him throughout the long night, and as the three 688s closed in on the *Kentucky*'s moving haven, the room had closed in on him.

Betty had awoken as he rose from bed and kept him company in the kitchen, sharing coffee throughout the night, keeping his mind occupied to the best of her ability. She had offered him leftover crumb cake, but he couldn't eat. Even though he was hungry, the thought of food made him nauseated.

Stanbury was still stunned by the order to sink the *Kentucky*. Somewhere, somehow, someone had gotten it all wrong. But he had followed his orders and set his best man to the task. He hoped Wilson's fast-attack scenario had achieved the desired effect without the loss of a submarine and its crew.

There was a knock on the door, which Stanbury acknowledged without turning. Wilson entered, followed a moment later by Betty carrying a silver tray with two cups of coffee, cream, and sugar. Placing the tray on the desk without a word, she eyed both men before withdrawing.

Wilson waited for permission to speak, but Stanbury

ignored him. He didn't want to hear the news. If the fast attacks had been successful in their attempt to communicate with the *Kentucky,* he should have received a report from the Operations Center that the *Kentucky* was returning to port. But no report had been received. After another minute of waiting, he could put it off no longer. He looked up at Wilson.

Wilson cleared his throat. "We didn't find her, sir. She's not in her moving haven. The *San Francisco* picked up a contact, but it turned out to be one of the other 688s."

The words sank in slowly. Stanbury grappled with the unexpected news. And the implication. No submarine would leave its assigned moving haven—the rule was inviolate. The *Kentucky* had left her moving haven and was now working her way west, toward Emerald and launch range.

Stanbury gestured to the chair across his desk and poured cream into his coffee, then pushed the tray toward Wilson, assessing the demeanor of his most capable captain. Until this moment, the only logical explanation for the *Kentucky*'s failure to respond to the launch termination order was a Radio Room casualty. The idea that her crew might be in on the plot had never held credence. Until now. Why had the *Kentucky* left her moving haven? This was unexpected. He could tell Wilson was having trouble dealing with the new information. The cup shook in his hand as he took a sip of coffee.

"What are you thinking, Murray?"

"Still trying to wrap my head around things, Admiral. Did the *Kentucky* really leave her moving haven, or did we just miss her?"

"I don't know. But I don't think it matters. What does is they've received a nuclear launch order and they're going to launch. And we have to stop them." Stanbury paused for a moment, then continued, "Are you still on board?"

Wilson gently swirled the coffee in his cup as he contemplated the admiral's question. It'd been a long day and an even longer night. His irritation at not being called immediately had been replaced by a conflicting array of emotions, pitting his parental responsibility to protect his family against his moral responsibility to protect millions of others. In the end, he had been requested to make a simple decision. One that he now wondered whether he could follow through on.

One hundred and sixty versus millions.

Was the decision as simple as he pretended, his son on the wrong end of a math inequality? Perhaps the real question, he wondered, was which side of the inequality became stronger with his participation? The situation was too complex to answer at the moment, and Admiral Stanbury needed an answer. Morally, at least, the answer was clear.

"I'm on board, Admiral."

There was an almost imperceptible nod from the older man, acknowledging Wilson's difficult decision. "What do we do now?"

Placing his cup on the desk, Wilson answered, "We stick to the plan. We're currently setting up a three-layer picket-line defense across the entrance to Emerald. Submarines in the front line, P-3Cs in the middle, then surface ships with their helicopters and dipping sonars. The surface ship assets are on their way—the *Nimitz* and

Reagan Strike Groups are heading out from San Diego, joining the *Stennis* from Washington. The *George Washington* is surging from Japan, and the *Lincoln* Strike Group is being routed back from the Indian Ocean. As far as fixed-wing assets go, we're pulling in every P-3C squadron worldwide to create a sonobuoy barrier of sufficient density and length."

"Will everyone be on station in time?"

"Yes, sir, assuming the *Kentucky* proceeds at twelve knots or less. But it's unlikely the *Kentucky* is traveling that fast. She doesn't need to reach Emerald in a hurry, she just needs to get there. So my bet is she's taking her time, nice and quiet, making our job that much harder."

"What are our odds, Murray?"

Wilson contemplated the admiral's question, stacking up the capabilities of the entire Pacific Fleet against the lone *Kentucky*. But then Wilson replayed Stanbury's question in his mind, replacing one of the words.

What are their *odds?*

Wilson shrugged. "It's probably going to come down to luck."

23

USS *KENTUCKY*

"What the hell was all that about?"

Malone asked the rhetorical question aloud as he was joined by the XO, the Nav, and Tom at the Quartermaster's stand in Control, reviewing the solutions on the chart for the 688s that had crossed their path multiple times. Three 688s had cut back and forth across the *Kentucky*'s moving haven, the middle 688 almost ramming the *Kentucky* on her first pass. Malone, having spent his first three tours on 688s, understood fast-attack tactics well. These 688s were prosecuting, looking to engage. But whom?

The XO shrugged his shoulders. "We've been ordered to launch, so maybe SUBPAC vectored in a few 688s to ensure no one was in our area who could pick us up, or even worse, was already trailing us."

"But who would be interested in tracking us?" the Nav asked. "We've been assigned a target package against Iran, not Russia or China. They're the only two countries with the ability to find us in the open ocean."

"They don't know what our target package is," Malone replied. "I'm sure both Russia and China intercepted our strike message. They can't break it, but they know some- one has been ordered to launch. And I bet that's mak- ing them pretty nervous. With the president dead and Washington destroyed, I bet everyone's on pins and nee- dles, hoping we got it right and are retaliating against the right country."

Malone fell silent for a moment before continuing. "Take her up to periscope depth, Tom. I want to down- load the fast-attack broadcast. Find out what the hell is going on up there."

"No close contacts!"

Twenty minutes later, the *Kentucky* was at periscope depth, and Tom slowed his revolutions on the scope, shifting between high and low power as he searched the early morning horizon and sky for surface ships and air- craft. Malone sat in his chair on the Conn, monitoring the ascent to PD.

"Conn, Nav. Satellite fix received."

Tom acknowledged Nav Center as he waited for Ra- dio to download the broadcast, continuing his alternat- ing high and low power sweeps of the horizon. A few minutes later, the expected report came over the 27-MC.

"Conn, Radio. Download complete."

Tom replied immediately, "All stations, Conn. Going deep." After flipping up the periscope handles, he low- ered the scope into its well. "Helm, ahead two-thirds. Dive, make your depth three hundred feet."

The *Kentucky*'s deck pitched downward as the sub- marine began its descent. A few minutes later, as the

Kentucky settled out at three hundred feet, one of the radiomen approached Malone with the message board. The Captain flipped through the messages quickly, stopping on the last one. After what seemed like forever, Malone rose and handed the clipboard to Tom, then left Control without a word. Tom flipped to the last message. It was only the weekly news summary. But after reading the first few paragraphs, he realized it was unlike any news summary he'd ever read.

It would normally have contained snippets of significant events, entertainment news, and sports scores. But there was none of that this week. The message provided information on the detonation of the nuclear bomb in Washington, D.C., and the gruesome aftermath. The damage and death toll were staggering; the entire city had been either destroyed or rendered uninhabitable, and the death count was now over three hundred thousand. Deadly radiation levels extended into both Virginia and Maryland, and the D.C. suburbs had been evacuated. Article after article detailed the destruction wreaked by the nuclear explosion, and the evidence linking the attack to Iran.

Tom closed the message board and handed it back to the radioman, who would route the board through the Wardroom and Chief's Quarters and post a copy of the weekly news summary outside Crew's Mess. The *Kentucky*'s crew would soon fully grasp what had been done to their country, and appreciate the role they would play in America's retaliation.

7 DAYS REMAINING

24

WASHINGTON, D.C.

Transformed from a screened-in porch into a sunroom by First Lady Grace Coolidge in the 1920s, the Solarium sitting atop the White House Promenade offers a breathtaking view of the White House Ellipse, the Washington Monument, and the Jefferson Memorial. However, the spectacular weather, inspiring view, and sunlight streaming into the room this afternoon failed to dispel the dark, strained mood within. Standing in front of the Solarium windows, the president, framed by a clear blue sky, awaited news on the search for the *Kentucky*.

Christine and Hardison had arrived with an update, standing with the usual four-foot separation between them, as if they were polarized magnets. On Christine's other side stood Brackman, almost close enough for their hands to touch. As she prepared to brief their failed attempt to locate the *Kentucky,* the president spoke first.

"What now?"

Christine hesitated. The look on their faces must have

conveyed their first attempt to sink the *Kentucky* had failed. She turned to Brackman, who answered the president's question at her cue.

"The Navy is setting up a three-layer picket line near the border of the *Kentucky*'s patrol area. We've sortied every ship and submarine available in the Pacific, and assigned every P-3C squadron to PAC Fleet. But we also need to prepare in case the *Kentucky* reaches her patrol area and launches. We have a few missile defense capabilities we could deploy to the Middle East."

"And they are?"

"There's THAAD, or Terminal High Altitude Area Defense, a kinetic energy hit-to-kill system. We have three batteries, and we can position the launchers anywhere we need them."

"Good. Anything else?"

"We have the Aegis Ballistic Missile Defense System, which uses an SM-3 missile fired from our *Aegis*-class cruisers and destroyers. The destroyers have been assigned to the picket line near Emerald, but we have several cruisers in the Western Pacific right now."

"What about the Patriot missile batteries?" the president asked. "Can we use those?"

"Unfortunately not," Brackman replied. "They're designed for short- and medium-range missiles. The *Kentucky* carries intercontinental missiles, which almost reach a low orbit before returning to earth. They'll be traveling so fast during their descent that Patriot missiles will be ineffective."

The president frowned. "Get the cruisers and THAAD batteries into position."

"Yes, Mr. President. But I have to advise you, it's an

impossible task to destroy all twenty-four missiles. Our BMD systems operate well until the first intercept. Once the first missile is destroyed and breaks into fragments, the following interceptors will have difficulty differentiating between the debris and the remaining missiles. And as more missiles are destroyed, the problem becomes exponentially more complex. We simply don't have enough interceptors or time to eliminate all twenty-four missiles and their warheads."

"So, to paraphrase your assessment," the president replied, "if the *Kentucky* launches, we're screwed."

Brackman nodded. "Screwed is an understatement."

25

EL PASO, TEXAS

Midafternoon in southwest Texas, home to Fort Bliss and the Army's 11th Air Defense Artillery Brigade. Off to the east, a brief thunderstorm that had brought so much promise and so little rain had moved on, letting the hot sun shine down again through broken clouds. The warm rain had evaporated as quickly as it fell, steam rising from the baked ground, creating the kind of oppressive humidity and stifling heat that knocks down even the Texas-size bugs. Just off Jeb Stuart Road, hanging from the windows of a single-story, cinder-block building, air conditioners stripped moisture from the heavy air, water dripping onto the ground below. Inside the plain white building, Sergeant Alan Kent leaned back in his chair under one of the air-conditioner vents, feet propped up on his desk, newspaper in hand, counting down the minutes until the workday ended.

It'd been a quiet morning and an even slower afternoon. As Kent flipped from the sports section to the entertainment pages, Corporal Bruce Cherry, seated nearby at the message terminal, looked up from his boredom as a solitary radio message appeared in his queue. Not bothering to read more than the header, Cherry hit Print, grabbing the message as it was pushed from the printer.

"Sarge, movement orders coming in."

Cherry handed the message to Kent, who, after reading the first paragraph, dropped his feet to the floor. Placing the orders on his desk, he continued reading the directive, hunched over the piece of paper.

Kent looked up. "What's the status of Alpha Battery, 4th Regiment?"

"The THAAD battery?"

"Yep."

"Fully operational."

"Get Major Dewire on the phone. Tell him to get Alpha Battery packing. They're headed to the Middle East."

26

USS *LAKE ERIE*

Captain Mary Cordeiro stood on the Bridge of her ship, hands clasped behind her back, feet planted wide. While other members of the Bridge watch held on to equipment consoles to steady themselves, Cordeiro refused. After twenty-four years in the Navy, two-thirds of that at sea, she knew when to flex her knees and shift her weight as the storm battered her five-hundred-foot-long cruiser, a small gray speck on the stormy seas.

As Cordeiro peered through the Bridge windows into the darkness, another forty-foot wave broke over the fo'c'sle, crashing against the Bridge with enough force to send tremors through the ship. The wave swept by the *Lake Erie,* the current tugging at the ship's rudder. Seaman Brian McKeon, on watch at the Helm, struggled to keep the ship headed into the monstrous waves. Sweeping rapidly back and forth, the window wipers worked furiously in a futile attempt to clear the sheets of water deluging the Bridge windows. Just as the water thinned enough to see the bow, faintly illuminated by the ship's mast headlight, the ship plunged down again into the dark seas.

Abandoned in the Indian Ocean, the *Lake Erie* loitered on station, awaiting orders. The rest of the *Erie*'s carrier strike group had headed east a few days ago at flank speed, but 5th Fleet seemed to have forgotten about the cruiser, and the *Lake Erie* had been riding out the storm, just shy of typhoon strength, for the better part of the night. Another three hours and they'd be through the worst of it.

As the ship plunged through the heavy seas, Cordeiro's thoughts were disrupted by her Communications Officer, appearing next to her with a message in hand. "Ma'am. This in from 5th Fleet."

Cordeiro read the message.

Finally.

But her orders sent them northwest, into the Strait of Hormuz, instead of east with the rest of her carrier strike group.

Prepare for ballistic missile defense of the Persian Gulf region.

The SM-3 missile system carried aboard the *Lake Erie* had performed well during its operational testing, but those had been canned scenarios. Would the ship be able to maintain its vigilance twenty-four hours a day, detect and then intercept an incoming missile with no notice? A much more difficult scenario.

Cordeiro walked over to the navigation chart, mentally laying out a course to the Persian Gulf. They needed to turn west, but had to continue north until the worst of the storm passed. She looked up at Seaman McKeon. Another wave broke across the fo'c'sle, smashing against the Bridge windows. McKeon struggled to keep the ship on course, his hands turning white as he maintained the rudder amidships. But the waves approached from just off the port bow, and the ship drifted to starboard as it rode up the waves, twisting back to port as it dropped into the deep trough.

Cordeiro approached McKeon, and she couldn't help but notice the expression on the young man's face. The mere presence of the ship's Captain in the same compartment as a newly reported seaman was enough to cause queasiness in a young sailor's stomach. A direct conversation would strike fear, and a reprimand—sheer terror.

She stopped beside McKeon. "Don't fight the waves. The goal is to keep the *ship* straight, not the rudder." Placing her hand on the helm next to McKeon's, she continued, "Relax your grip. I've got it. Now feel what I'm doing."

Cordeiro eased off the helm as the next wave approached, allowing the rudder to move in the direction the seas pushed it, then she shifted the rudder across midships as the *Lake Erie* crested the wave and began her dive down the steep swell. The ship's bow slowed its swaying with each passing wave, finally steadying on course, in contradiction to the rudder that shifted beneath them.

"Understand?"

McKeon replied affirmative, and Cordeiro released the helm, returning it to the seaman's control. She stepped back, watching him adjust the rudder, his actions becoming more fluid with each passing wave.

"Steady as you go, McKeon. You're doing just fine."

27

PEARL HARBOR, HAWAII

On the second floor of the COMSUBPAC N7 building, Captain Murray Wilson sat behind his desk, chewing a mouthful of a ham and cheese sandwich as he studied the three-by-four-foot sheet of trace paper on his desk. He was exhausted, having been up thirty hours since his phone call from Stanbury the previous morning, and his eyelids were becoming heavier by the minute. Not for the first time, he wished his office had windows, so he could look across the submarine wharves, the bright midday sun reflecting off the blue surface of Southeast Loch. But due to the classification of the information the N7 organization routinely dealt with, the entire building had not a single window, to prevent satellite or local recon from obtaining photos of the material within.

However, if someone had been able to photograph the material on Wilson's desk, he would have been as perplexed as he was. The Prospective Commanding and Executive Officers had reconstructed the twenty engagements between the *Kentucky* and *Houston* during last week's Submarine Command Course, and the information, if correct, was even more disturbing than Wilson initially thought. Each reconstruction depicted the paths traveled by the two submarines, showing where each ship was detected and the launching of torpedoes and decoys. The reconstruction of the most perplexing encounter of all, the third engagement on the first day, was on top of the stack, one corner held down by an empty coffee cup, another by the second half of Wilson's sandwich.

The *Kentucky* had defeated the *Houston* all three times that first day, and the fast-attack submarine, convinced there was an acoustic deficiency giving away its position—a bearing gone bad on one of their pumps or perhaps a sound short between their machinery and hull—had retreated to the far corner of its operating area that night for sound-monitoring runs. After adjusting their towed array to the appropriate length, the *Houston*'s crew had driven in circles, first turning to port and then to starboard, their towed array lining up opposite them in the large underwater racetrack. Like a dog chasing its tail, the *Houston* had circled for hours analyzing its acoustic signature, looking for whatever had been giving away its position.

But there was nothing. The *Houston* was quiet, even stealthier than the standard 688 class submarine. With renewed confidence, the crew engaged the *Kentucky* the following day, convinced they had been defeated the first three times by sheer coincidence, lucky detections by the surprisingly capable ballistic missile submarine. But the next six days delivered the same discouraging results. The *Kentucky* detected and shot first every time, while the *Houston* picked up the Trident submarine only when it launched its torpedoes or after it increased speed while evading the *Houston*'s counterfire. It was as if the *Kentucky* were invisible, emitting not a single frequency of sufficient strength for the *Houston*'s sonar system to track.

It just didn't make sense. The *Kentucky*'s crew was skilled, but the odds of detecting the *Houston* first on every encounter were staggering. In the heat of battle, Wilson had focused his attention on the *Houston*'s Sonar division, convinced the recent influx of new personnel had diluted the fast attack's capability. But now, looking over the third reconstruction and the stack of sonar printouts on his desk, it seemed impossible the *Kentucky* had passed within one thousand yards and not been detected.

Lieutenant Jarred Crum stopped beside Wilson, dropping off a fresh cup of coffee. He could see the dark circles forming under Wilson's eyes, and had watched the Captain's head droop occasionally as he studied the reconstructions and sonar recordings. But this time the lieutenant delivered more than just hot coffee. "Sir, the electronic recordings from the range just arrived. I have them loaded on the computer."

"Thanks, Jarred." Wilson took a sip of the steaming coffee. "Put the third run on-screen."

Crum fired up the monitor on the far wall with the remote. Two submarines appeared on the bird's-eye view of the encounter, one blue, the other red, closing in on each other as they searched the ocean for their adversary. The *Houston* had luckily been pointed directly at the *Kentucky,* presenting the ballistic missile submarine with a nose-on profile, making the fast attack even harder to detect than usual, its Engine Room and propeller masked by the quiet bow. The *Kentucky,* unaware of the rapidly closing fast attack, continued its search until she finally detected the inbound submarine, evidenced by the *Kentucky*'s course reversal. Moments later, a MK 48 Exercise torpedo sped toward the *Houston.*

The *Kentucky*'s launch preparations had taken time, and the *Houston* had blindly plowed on, closing to within one thousand yards before the *Kentucky*'s torpedo launch transients lit up the *Houston*'s sonar screens. Wilson glanced down at the trace paper on his desk, shocked at how accurately his students had reconstructed the engagement.

"Something's not right here." Wilson turned to Crum. "At first I thought we had a Helen Keller sonar shack on the *Houston,* but look at these printouts." He picked up the top folder from the stack on his desk. "There's nothing here. Not a single tonal from the *Kentucky.*"

Crum reviewed the *Houston*'s sonar recordings as Wilson flipped through the printouts, then shrugged. "This is the first time we've had a Trident participate in Command Course ops for a few years. They're quieter than our 688s and get periodic upgrades. Maybe she really is that quiet now."

Wilson looked up at the monitor again. It showed the *Houston* passing one thousand yards abeam of the *Kentucky* before the ballistic missile submarine sped away. "It's like the *Kentucky* is a black hole. Like she doesn't exist." Wilson shook his head as he folded up the track reconstruction. "Get me Admiral Caseria at NAVSEA. Someone needs to take a look at this."

28

WASHINGTON NAVY YARD

In the southeast corner of Washington, D.C., on the northern bank of the Anacostia River, lies the oldest naval base in the country. Established in 1799, the Washington Navy Yard became the nation's most important shipyard, building the majority of the nascent country's first navy. Although new ships no longer slide down the slipways into the river, the Navy Yard is now home to Naval Sea Systems Command, responsible for the design of every U.S. warship and the equipment and weapons they carry.

On the second floor of a four-story redbrick building is the office of Program Executive Officer (Submarines), responsible for all things submerged—new submarines, sonar, combat control, and electronic surveillance systems, as well as new torpedoes and torpedo decoys. As Rear Admiral Steve Caseria looked out his window at the Anacostia River flowing lazily toward the Potomac, he had a simple thought for a complex problem.

You get what you pay for.

Like a molting snake shedding its skin, several of the new *Virginia*-class submarines had lost portions of their anechoic coating, a rubberlike material covering the hull that helps isolate machinery sounds inside the submarine from the surrounding ocean. After an extended deployment, the USS *Virginia* returned to port with several sections of its hull missing their sound-silencing coating. The following two *Virginia*-class submarines were also affected, and an investigation determined the new bonding technique, implemented to save money, was not as effective as required. The process was changed for the fourth and following submarines, returning to the more expensive, but better, adhesion formula. Admiral Caseria realized he had learned the painful lesson many before him had learned.

You get what you pay for.

But saving money, the admiral learned, was what D.C. was all about these days. Congress was tightening its wallet after a decade-long post-9/11 defense spending binge, and with sequestration kicking in, every program was feeling the pinch. And it was concerning one of those programs that the phone on his desk rang late this afternoon.

It was the call he'd been expecting.

"Murray, how have you been?" Caseria spoke into the speakerphone on his desk, so that the captain sitting in a chair opposite his desk could hear.

Wilson's voice cackled through the speaker, the long-distance connection breaking up periodically. "Good, Admiral. Staying busy training the youngsters. And you?"

"Been busy too, Murray. We've got some excellent

upgrades coming to the fleet soon. But I miss command. There's nothing like the excitement of being on station."

"I'm with you, Admiral. Not to mention the port calls."

Caseria grinned. "Too bad I'm not around to haul your ass back to the boat anymore."

Wilson laughed. "No need to, sir. I've learned my lesson. A couple of times."

"So what's this about, Murray? Sonar, I hear. My sonar program manager, Captain Jay Santos, is here with me. What have you got?"

"I'd like you to take a look at a set of sonar recordings from the *Houston*. She passed within one thousand yards of the *Kentucky* and her sonar systems didn't pick up a thing. I know our Tridents are quiet, but they can't be that quiet."

"Where are the sonar tapes?"

"The only data pipe we have big enough goes to Naval Undersea Warfare Center, Newport division. We're uploading the recordings now."

Caseria looked at Captain Santos. "Can you get to the data there?"

"No problem, Admiral. Most of our expertise resides there anyway. That'd be perfect."

"Anything else, Murray?" Caseria asked.

"That's it, Admiral. But we need the analysis done fast."

"We'll get right on it. Take care, Murray."

As Admiral Caseria pressed the End button on the speakerphone, he looked at Captain Santos. "Undetectable at one thousand yards? Not a chance. Pull the data from the *Kentucky*'s last sound trials. I want to see how quiet she really is and what tonals she has. Then tear apart the latest sonar upgrade we sent to the fleet. We need to figure out what's going on."

Seventeen hours later, standing in his third-floor office, Captain Jay Santos rolled up the last set of sonar print-outs. Checking his watch to see if there would be time for lunch after his meeting with Admiral Caseria, Santos wondered why he bothered; considering what he was about to tell the admiral, he had lost his appetite. Tucking the sonar printouts under one arm, Santos left his office, descended one floor, and passed into Admiral Caseria's atrium. The admiral's aide looked up as Santos approached, motioning for him to enter Caseria's office.

Santos spread out two rolls of sonar printouts, side by side, on the Admiral's conference table. "Admiral, we have a problem."

Caseria joined Santos at his side, examining the print-outs as the captain explained. "Here are samples of what the sonar operators on the *Houston* saw. The one on the left is the broadband screen, and the one on the right is narrowband. We've confirmed the *Houston* passed within one thousand yards of the *Kentucky,* yet you can see here there's no sign of the *Kentucky* whatsoever."

"What did the sound trials data show?" Caseria asked. "Is she really that quiet?"

Santos unrolled another set of printouts, laying them on top of the first two. "These are the recordings from the *Kentucky*'s sound trials a year ago. As you can see, she has a characteristic Trident broadband signature and most of the typical narrowband tonals plus a few unique ones. These recordings were taken at four thousand yards. So, no, the *Kentucky* is no quieter than your standard Trident."

Santos rolled out a third set of printouts. "That had a lot of my folks scratching their heads, so we ported the raw sonar data into the previous version of our fast-attack sonar systems, and you can see here that the *Kentucky* is now clearly visible on both the broadband and narrowband displays. Bottom line, Admiral—there's a flaw in our latest sonar upgrade."

"Have you tracked down the problem?"

"Yes, sir. But there's more. We ported data from other submarines, both Trident and fast attack, into the latest version of our sonar upgrade to determine the extent of the problem, and the new sonar system operated perfectly."

"I'm not following you," Caseria said. "You just convinced me the sonar upgrade is defective, that it missed the *Kentucky* when it should have picked her up. Now you're saying it works fine. Which is it?"

"Both, sir. The issue is that the sonar upgrade malfunctions *only* when you run the *Kentucky*'s signature through the system. We broke apart the new algorithms, and there's a special code that nulls the *Kentucky*'s frequencies so they don't appear on the display."

"Why would the algorithms do that?"

Santos raised an eyebrow. "This code was inserted maliciously. These new sonar algorithms were engineered specifically so the *Kentucky* could not be detected. Someone didn't want us to find her."

Anger spread across Caseria's features as he stared

at the sonar printouts. "I want this tracked down to the company and individuals responsible."

"We're already on it, sir. Landover Engineering Systems developed these new algorithms, and I notified NCIS a few minutes ago."

"Good. Now how much of the fleet is affected?"

Captain Santos frowned. "I'm afraid the news gets worse . . ."

29

PEARL HARBOR

At the western end of Waikiki, the early morning shadows of tall beachfront hotels retreated slowly across Ala Moana Boulevard as suburbanites flowed into the city; the traffic backups, which would eventually extend all the way to Ewa, were already ten miles long. Halfway down the ten-mile backup, cars flowed steadily into Pearl Harbor, the gate sentries checking IDs and waving drivers on. After a right on North Road and a left on Nimitz Street, traffic entering the submarine base was light, as the nineteen submarines and their crews were at sea this morning. On the second floor of COMSUBPAC headquarters, overlooking the usually bustling Morton Street and submarine piers, the silence was especially noticeable as Murray Wilson braced for Admiral Stanbury's reaction to the startling information he had just received.

Stanbury was standing behind his desk, his face turning redder by the second, until finally he spat out the words. "Our entire fast-attack fleet is blind?"

"Technically, they're deaf, but yes, sir," Wilson replied. "None of them can see the *Kentucky* on their sonar screens. They all have the latest sonar upgrade."

"Can they revert to the previous version?"

"No, sir. The upgrade involved not only new algorithms but also new hardware. We can't reload the old algorithms onto the new hardware because the middleware hasn't been developed."

The admiral's hands clenched into fists. Glancing down at Stanbury's desk, Wilson checked for the presence of a replacement ceramic coffee cup. It seemed another one might fly across the office. Luckily, only Styrofoam cups littered the admiral's desk.

Stanbury unclenched his fists, exhaling slowly. "Is NAVSEA working on a fix?"

"Yes, sir. But it'll take time, and they're not sure if they'll be able to download the new software over the submarine broadcast. Loading new middleware is a bit tricky, apparently."

"What do we do in the meantime?"

"I recommend we pull our fast attacks back into the third tier of the layered defense, behind the P-3Cs and Surface Fleet, instead of up front. That will buy us some time in case NAVSEA can develop a fix we can download over the broadcast."

"Fine. Coordinate with PAC Fleet."

Wilson looked down at the chart of the Pacific Ocean on the admiral's conference table, annotated with the three-layer ASW barrier across the entrance to Emerald. They had surged the entire submarine fleet to sea in a single day, for all the good that had done them; their whole fast-attack fleet was impotent. However, there was one option remaining. As he assessed the risk, Stanbury apparently noticed the concern on his face.

"What?" Stanbury asked. "What else has gone wrong?"

"Nothing else has gone wrong, Admiral."

"Then what is it?"

"Not all of our fast attacks are blind. The *North Carolina* hasn't received the sonar upgrade yet."

Stanbury's eyes brightened. "Where is she now?"

"She's in the local operating areas, on sea trials following her extended maintenance period. But the crew's not certified to deploy."

"Certified or not," the admiral replied, "she's the only submarine with a chance to find the *Kentucky*."

"There's one more thing, Admiral. The *North Carolina* has only two torpedoes aboard, and we don't have time to pull her in and load more."

Stanbury stared at Wilson for a moment, no doubt evaluating the prospect of sending a submarine into battle with only two torpedoes. But the *North Carolina* was their only hope. It didn't take long for the admiral to decide. "If they do things right, two torpedoes are all they'll need. Send her after the *Kentucky*."

30

KAUAI, HAWAII

Eight miles off the southern shore of Kauai, Cindy Corey spread her arms out along the transom of her husband's twenty-five-foot Sea Hunt center console. Randy was busy in the bow, checking their position on the Garmin GPS marine navigator, verifying they had reached the spot their friend Scott had recommended, where the ono—nice twenty to twenty-five pounders— would practically jump into the boat. While Randy's pastime didn't interest Cindy at all—her idea of fishing was trolling her finger down the seafood restaurant's menu—she couldn't pass on a day off with her husband, relaxing in her two-piece fluorescent orange bikini, soaking up the rays. She leaned back, closing her eyes as she lifted her face up toward the sun, and . . . got the weird feeling she was being watched.

Tilting her head forward and opening her eyes, she checked on Randy, but he was busy with the fish finder now, oblivious of her concern. The feeling passed as quickly as it had arrived, and Cindy shrugged off her uneasiness after she scanned the horizon for other boats. While they had passed a dozen or so on their way out, there were currently none within eyesight, just the distant shore of Kauai behind her. After retrieving a Diet Coke from the cooler near her feet and sliding it into a koozie, she got that feeling again, that nagging sixth sense of hers that was rarely wrong.

The feeling she was being watched passed again, and Cindy began to think it was just her guilty conscience. Both she and Randy had called in sick this morning; the day was too beautiful to spend indoors cooped up in their office cubes. But as she took a sip of her Coke, she got that feeling yet again; it seemed to be arriving at regular intervals, like clockwork.

Seven hundred yards to the south of Cindy and her husband, the USS *North Carolina* cruised at periscope depth, the top of its port periscope sticking just above the ocean's surface, pausing momentarily from its clockwise rotation to examine Master seven-nine again, a pleasure craft drifting just off the submarine's starboard beam. Standing behind the Officer of the Deck at his Tactical Workstation, a weary Commander Dennis Gallagher monitored the performance of his crew as they waited to download the latest radio broadcast through the receiver on top of the scope. After endless months in the shipyard, this week had been the first opportunity to knock off the rust that had collected on the crew's proficiency. Over the last seven days, Gallagher had put the ship and his crew through its paces, and it hadn't been pretty.

Gallagher had rarely left Control during the last week,

watching warily as the crew conducted routine operations and responded to emergency ship control drills. But even a simple trip to periscope depth was not an easy evolution for a rusty crew. Each watch section had broached the submarine three times the first few days while going to PD, going all the way to the surface instead of leveling off four feet below as ordered. And if the crew's lack of proficiency executing routine evolutions was any indication of their present skills, it was no surprise the emergency drills had gone even worse.

But after a week under way, the crew had recovered its skills in basic seamanship and tactics. Sonar was coming up to speed, easily scrolling through the numerous contacts in the local waters off the Hawaiian Islands, sending data to fire control technicians, who quickly generated target solutions. This approach to periscope depth had gone smoothly, the ship rising steadily, leveling off without even a foot of overshoot. The eight-thousand-ton submarine glided at periscope depth, the top of her sail four feet below the surface of the water.

Gallagher watched the periscope display as the Officer of the Deck rotated the periscope steadily, searching for contacts headed their way. Unlike other submarine classes, the *Virginia*-class fast attacks were built with new photonics periscopes that didn't penetrate the ship's pressure hull. Instead of manually rotating the scope, walking round and round on the Conn, the OOD turned the scope with a twist of his wrist, his hand on a joystick, switching the scope between low and high power periodically with a flick of the toggle on the joystick controller. The Officer of the Deck was a split-tour junior officer from one of the 688s and his experience showed, the periscope rotating at just the right speed, pausing to monitor the unsuspecting pleasure craft off their starboard beam at regular intervals, like clockwork.

The crew had begun to ease into their routine, and the tense orders and curt reports that punctuated the ship's first few days at sea had been replaced with bland formality. And now, Gallagher heard what he'd been waiting for.

"Conn, Sonar. Have a new contact, bearing zero-seven-zero, triangulation range eight hundred yards, classified biologics. Looks like a whale has fallen in love with us."

Some of the watchstanders in Control chuckled, and Gallagher relaxed for the first time since he'd cast off the last mooring line. The crew was comfortable at sea again, at ease with their ship and the rigorous demands of their duties on watch. His men had a lot of potential, and after a few months working up for their deployment, he was sure they'd be the best submarine crew in Pearl Harbor.

Before Gallagher headed deep to continue the morning's training evolutions, he ordered Radio to download the latest message traffic. "Radio, Captain. Download the broadcast."

Radio acknowledged, and a few minutes later, the radioman's voice came across the 27-MC. "Conn, Radio. Download complete."

Gallagher turned to his Officer of the Deck. "Bring her down to two hundred feet."

The OOD acknowledged, and with a twist of the

joystick, he swung the periscope around toward the bow. "Pilot, ahead two-thirds. Make your depth two hundred feet."

That was one of the hardest things to get used to. The four watchstanders on previous submarines—the Helm and the Outboard, who manipulated the submarine's rudder and control surfaces, as well as the Diving Officer and the Chief of the Watch—had been replaced by two watchstanders: the Pilot and Co-pilot, who sat at the Ship Control Panel. The Pilot controlled the submarine's course and depth while the Co-pilot adjusted the submarine's buoyancy and raised and lowered the masts and antennas. Why aircraft terminology had been chosen to identify the two watchstanders instead of the traditional Helm and Outboard confounded Gallagher; it was a horrendous break in tradition. However, no one had called him in the middle of the night to ask his opinion, and the decision had been made.

Pilot and Co-pilot they were.

Then there was the newfangled design of the *Virginia*-class Control Room, with Sonar in Control instead of a separate room, the sonar consoles lining the port side of the ship with the combat control consoles on starboard. Even though the Sonar Supervisor stood only a few feet away from the Officer of the Deck, reports were still made over an announcing circuit, the supervisor speaking into a microphone. Finally, even the periscopes weren't called periscopes. They were referred to as photonics masts on the *Virginia*-class submarines. Gallagher shook his head.

The Pilot entered the ahead two-thirds command, and

6 DAYS REMAINING

31

WASHINGTON, D.C.

Dark gray clouds were rolling in from the west as a black Lincoln Town Car turned left on E Street, passing between the White House on the right and the President's Park South on the left. In the backseat of the sedan, Christine gazed through tinted windows at the Colorado blue spruce that dominated the Ellipse, as the park was commonly called. The forty-foot-tall spruce, transformed each winter into the National Christmas Tree, marked the end of the Pathway of Peace, a trail lined by fifty-six smaller trees, also decorated during the Christmas season, representing the fifty states, five American territories, and the District of Columbia.

As the car slowed for a right-hand turn onto West Executive Avenue, returning Christine to the White House for her meeting with the president, her thoughts dwelt on the lunchtime discussion she and Captain Brackman had just concluded with the secretary of defense. The private meeting had not gone well. It wasn't that she didn't get along with Nick Williams. Compared with her relationship with Hardison, she and the SecDef were the best of friends. However, the news Williams had relayed concerning their submarine sonar systems was disconcerting. It was obvious that the plan to launch the *Kentucky*'s missiles was multifaceted and meticulously prepared.

Brackman had remained at the Pentagon for additional discussions and would return shortly for their meeting with the president. As Christine wondered what additional issues required his attention, her car pulled to a stop under the West Wing's North Portico and she stepped from the sedan, passing between two Marines in dress blues guarding the formal entrance to the West Wing. Christine stopped in her office for a half hour, reading e-mail and attempting to catch up on the more critical issues she'd been neglecting. After checking her watch, she headed down the hallway toward the Oval Office. She was exactly on time, and Hardison and Brackman were already seated across from the president. She took her seat between them.

"What's the status?" the president asked.

Christine led off with *Kentucky*'s continuing failure to respond to the strike cancellation message, then delineated the crippling of their submarine fleet. An uneasy silence followed, magnified by the room's bombproof windows, insulating them from the sound outside. The gray skies over D.C. had opened up, bringing the Rose Garden outside the Oval Office to life; the red, pink, and white flowers bobbed up and down as fat drops of rain splattered on their petals. But there was no sound in the room, not even from the rain pelting the south side of the Oval Office, the usual patter attenuated by the windows' triple panes.

Finally, the president responded. "Do you have any good news?"

"The *North Carolina* is on its way," Christine answered, explaining the submarine was the lone ship unaffected, "and she'll intercept the center of the *Kentucky*'s area of uncertainty in thirty hours, just before the *Kentucky* reaches Sapphire. We don't know if she'll find the *Kentucky*, but the *North Carolina* is one of the new *Virginia*-class submarines, and that at least gives us a shot."

"How is the military hierarchy taking this?" the president asked, turning to Brackman.

"They're shaken, sir, but they're responding appropriately. Orders have gone out and units are arriving on station."

"Who knows the target is the *Kentucky*?"

"Aside from the Joint Chiefs and Admiral Tim Hale at Pacific Command, only Admiral Herrell at PAC Fleet and Admiral Stanbury at SUBPAC, along with his right-hand man, Captain Wilson. They were directed not to notify anyone else, but they informed the commanding officers of three 688 fast-attack submarines, hoping they could establish underwater communications with the *Kentucky*. It didn't work. The rest of the fleet believes they're hunting a Chinese copy of a Trident submarine."

"So from a military perspective," the president replied, "we've contained this debacle." He glanced at Hardison before returning his attention to Christine. "What about the civilian side?"

"Only us, plus SecDef Williams and Dave Hendricks from the Command Center, know."

"Good. Keep it that way."

"Mr. President, if I may," Hardison interjected. "I've run a background check on Hendricks, and he's an active member of the opposite political party. I'm concerned where his loyalty lies and his ability to keep this issue confidential."

Christine's head swiveled toward Hardison. "May I remind you that I also am a member of the other party? Do you question where *my* loyalty lies?"

Hardison smiled before replying. The kind of smug, condescending smirk Christine hated. "I don't question your loyalty," he answered, "only your judgment."

Christine's palm tingled with the urge to slap the smirk off his face. But then something about the chief of staff's previous statement grabbed her attention. "What's your point, Kevin? You're concerned about Dave keeping this issue quiet—where are you headed with this?"

Hardison didn't reply immediately. He seemed to be considering his response carefully, his eyes shifting between the other three persons in the room. Finally, he answered, "I wasn't headed anywhere, Christine. Just thinking out loud."

Silence returned to the Oval Office as Christine speculated about what Hardison was really thinking; what types of solutions were slinking around inside his mind. The awkward silence passed, and Brackman wrapped up their update with the status of the antisubmarine barrier being established across the entrance to Emerald. At the end of the meeting, Brackman was the first to leave the Oval Office, followed by Christine and Hardison, who headed toward their diametrically opposed corner offices in the West Wing.

Hardison closed his door, then leaned back in his chair, feet up on his desk, eyes shut. The overcast skies and steady rain drifting over the city could not have soured his mood further. Reviewing the issue at hand and its potential solutions, he began with the facts.

Hendricks, he was convinced, was much more of a problem than the president and Christine realized. If the public discovered launch orders had been sent to a nuclear submarine, it was game over for the administration. The president's opponents would capitalize on the debacle and force him out of office, either voluntarily or through impeachment. No defense, no matter how sophisticated, would be successful against the simple truth of what had transpired on the president's watch. That left only one option: bury the truth.

That effort would be relatively easy, with the exception of Dave Hendricks. Unlike the civilian deputy director, military personnel could be trusted to keep the issue quiet. One of the admirable traits of senior military officers was that they knew how to follow orders, even ones they disagreed with. They had been promoted to positions of responsibility not only because of their experience and talent, but also because they could execute orders sent down the chain of command accurately and expeditiously. In the end, Hardison was convinced they would follow the order to keep their mouths shut about every aspect of this issue.

Hendricks, on the other hand, was a wild card, his

commitment to the administration secured only through a tenuous relationship with his former wife. At some point in the future that relationship might sour or his allegiance shift. A permanent solution was required, or at least a temporary one that would last through the end of this administration and the next, assuming the president was reelected.

Keeping things quiet was something Hardison was intimately familiar with. He had spent thirty years working his way up through congressional staffs and knew the darkest secrets hidden in the closets of dozens of the most powerful representatives and senators. But what would come in handy now were the contacts he'd established in those three decades, men who would prove useful in dealing with the situation at hand. Sifting through the options, he settled on the most promising. Hardison opened his eyes and sat upright. A permanent solution would be applied.

He reached for the phone.

32

ALEXANDRIA, VIRGINIA

A few hundred yards to the east of Interstate 395, Dana Cooke held his leather briefcase over his head to protect himself from the light rain as he hurried up the sidewalk toward a crumbling twenty-eight-story apartment complex. Skirting foot-high weeds sprouting through the cracked cement and a cluster of tattooed teenagers arguing loudly at the base of the stairwell, Cooke went to one of the operable elevators, cursing under his breath as he endured the jerky and interminably slow ascent to the twelfth floor. However, the decrepit elevator and squalid surroundings were not the true source of Cooke's disgust; they only served as a daily, acrid reminder of what that ungrateful bitch had done to him.

His ex-wife had stolen most of his money in the divorce and sucked his paycheck dry each month like a bloated leech. In an effort to recapitalize his wealth quickly following his divorce, Cooke had invested what remained of his inheritance in the riskier sectors of the stock market, ones that had performed extremely well during the late 1990s. But the tech stocks crashed months later, and Cooke, overextended on margins, lost everything, racking up a six-figure debt in the process. The life of luxury he was accustomed to no longer existed—and it was all her fault.

Cooke stepped out of the elevator and trudged down the long hallway, the brown carpet stained every few feet with who knew what types of liquids or bodily fluids. Finally reaching his apartment, he inserted his key into the door and was surprised to find it unlocked. He'd been running late this morning and must've forgotten to lock the door.

Pushing the door open, he stepped into the dark entryway. He hated this place, accommodations even the uneducated masses deemed unsatisfactory. But things would soon change. He worked in the sonar division of Landover Engineering Systems, and he'd made a deal with a company installing sound-silencing upgrades on the Navy's Trident submarines. The performance of those upgrades had been in doubt, and one of the company's advisers had approached Cooke with a plan to ensure his company received the full incentive payment.

Only a few minor modifications to the sonar algorithms under development were needed. The *Kentucky* would become invisible, resulting in the full incentive payment for his new friend's company, not to mention lucrative follow-on contracts for the rest of the Navy's submarine fleet. Cooke would soon receive the payment for his work, and he looked forward to the day he'd close the door to this miserable apartment for the last time.

Cooke flicked the light switch in the small living

room, but the apartment remained shrouded in darkness. He flicked the switch up and down a few times, then muttered under his breath in disgust. Trudging across the dark room, he approached the kitchen, turning on the light as he entered, stopping at the entrance in surprise.

The bare bulb hanging from the ceiling illuminated a man sitting on the far side of the kitchen table. Cooke exhaled in relief. "Oh, it's you." He pulled up a chair across from the man, who was leaning back in his chair. "Did you bring my payment?"

William Hoover smiled. "Yes. You will be paid in full tonight." He nodded toward a leather satchel on the floor by his feet.

"It's about time," Cooke said. "I took a lot of risk modifying those sonar algorithms. But the money will ease my conscience." He glanced in anticipation at the bag on the floor. "However, I'm afraid we'll have to renegotiate the terms of my continued service to your company. My price has doubled for any follow-on work."

Hoover stared coldly at him. "That's impossible."

"You damn well better make it possible, or the performance of your submarine upgrades will suddenly be called into question, if you catch my drift."

"I catch your . . . drift, Mr. Cooke. But rather than discuss the terms of your future employment, perhaps I should pay you for your previous work first."

"You'll pass on my demands to your company?"

"Yes, Mr. Cooke. I'll forward your request." The corners of Hoover's mouth turned up into a warm smile. Reaching down, he picked up the satchel and tossed it onto the table.

Cooke's fingers tingled with excitement as he unhooked the clasp, flipped up the cover, and peered inside.

It was empty.

Cooke slammed the bag onto the table. "What the hell is going on?"

Hoover replied dispassionately, "I'm afraid the terms of your payment have been modified."

"What new terms?" Cooke was practically screaming, his face red with anger.

Hoover lifted his right hand from under the table and rested a pistol with a silencer on the table's edge, pointed at Cooke's chest. "I'm afraid your services are no longer required. But if it's any consolation, your work was of exceptional quality."

Cooke's eyes widened. He leaned back in his chair, pushing himself away from the table, his hands out in front, waving his palms toward Hoover in supplication. "You don't need to kill me. I'm sure we can come to agreement on payment. Perhaps I was too greedy."

"No," Hoover replied, "your request was reasonable. Unfortunately, the United States Navy has discovered the sonar algorithms were modified, and it won't be long before they trace them to you."

Cooke's heart pounded inside his chest, his body breaking into a cold sweat. "I won't tell anyone. I swear. No one will find out about our agreement."

"I know, Mr. Cooke. Thank you for your service."

Hoover smiled again, then pulled the trigger. Cooke sat silently in his chair, his arms slack by his sides, blood flowing from a hole in the center of his chest. Cooke's breathing eventually turned shallow, then stopped.

After placing the pistol into its holster under his jacket, Hoover stood and collected the satchel. He examined the man sitting across from him for a second before he left, closing the door to Cooke's run-down apartment for the last time.

the contract, wouldn't be here, which told Christine
there was a deal. He went onto the part of the
arming needs, from his agency's research seemed too late
Maybe the threat of being fired, wouldn't want to hold
over me.

33

WASHINGTON, D.C.

Dusk was settling over the city skyline as Christine hurried south on 17th Street, her head down and hands
plunged into the pockets of her coat. Whipping across
the Tidal Basin, blustery winds blew beneath the kind
of flat gray clouds that promised rain but never delivered. Pulling her hand from her pocket, she checked her
watch. Less than an hour ago, as she was sitting in her
office, an unexpected phone call had jarred her thoughts
from the impending launch. The man had refused to
meet her in the White House, which told Christine the
issue had something to do with the president or his administration. She had agreed to meet at the Franklin Delano Roosevelt Memorial at precisely 7 P.M.

After crossing Independence Avenue, Christine
headed south on the famous Cherry Tree Walk, approaching the entrance to the FDR Memorial ten minutes later. Leaning against the façade near a sculpture
of the president in his wheelchair was a man wearing
faded jeans and a thin gray Windbreaker. Upon spotting

Christine, he turned and entered the memorial. A moment later, Christine followed him in.

Divided into four outdoor galleries, each representing one of FDR's terms in office, the memorial's waterfalls, shade trees, and quiet alcoves of red South Dakota granite create the feeling of a meandering, secluded garden rather than a formal memorial. The first two rooms depict the dichotomy of the Great Depression—the despair symbolized by men standing in a breadline and the hope evident as a man listens to one of Roosevelt's fireside chats on the radio. The third room depicts the destructive turmoil of World War II, with giant granite blocks strewn across the visitor's path and a roaring waterfall to the right, crashing down over jagged boulders.

It was in this third gallery that Christine stopped beside the man in a secluded alcove next to the waterfall. She followed his gaze to the inscription carved into the granite wall; Roosevelt's famous "I have seen war" quote, delivered during his 1936 speech at the New York Chautauqua Assembly:

I have seen war. I have seen war on land and on sea. I have seen blood running from the wounded. I have seen the dead in the mud. I have seen cities destroyed. I have seen children starving. I have seen the agony of mothers and wives. I hate war.

After a moment, Captain Brackman finally spoke, his words muted by the roar of the adjacent waterfall. "It's a somewhat appropriate quote considering the circumstances, don't you think?"

It was more a statement than a question, but Christine nodded nonetheless. As she stood near Brackman in the cool air, she could feel the heat radiating from his body through his thin Windbreaker, could smell the faint scent of his cologne. Her thoughts suddenly wandered. She wondered if he was attracted to her, imagined what it would feel like to have his strong arms wrapped around her. She felt the heat rising in her face and quickly forced the thoughts from her mind, hoping he hadn't noticed her reddening cheeks. Thankfully, his eyes remained focused on the inscription. After another moment of silence, she looked up toward the overcast sky as a gust of cold wind whipped through the alcove. "So what brings you out of the office on a day like this?"

Brackman glanced around the memorial, verifying no one was close enough to overhear their conversation. "There's something you need to know. You weren't the only one alarmed at what Hardison might have been contemplating during our last meeting with the president. I decided to talk with him afterward, and as I was about to knock on his door, I overheard part of his conversation on the phone. It was about Hendricks."

"What did you hear?" Christine asked slowly.

Brackman's eyes seemed distant as he continued. "He was making arrangements to silence Hendricks, negotiating the price. He wanted it done after this issue with the *Kentucky* is over, and wanted to be informed when everything was ready. After he hung up, I left quickly—I didn't want to be caught eavesdropping."

Christine took a moment to digest what Brackman had revealed, searching for another explanation. "Perhaps you misunderstood," she suggested. "Are you sure about what you heard?"

"Enough to be confident about what he's planning."

A cold wind whipped through the alcove again, swirling around them as Christine contemplated what Brackman had overheard. It was hearsay, conjecture at this point, and there was little she could do except confront Hardison about his intentions. That would be pointless, so she decided instead to watch him closely, searching for any indication he was about to execute his plan, whatever it was. It seemed that as long as the *Kentucky* survived, Dave was safe. After the submarine launched its missiles or was sunk, however, all bets were off.

After a moment, Brackman asked, "Do you have other questions or want me to do anything?"

Christine shook her head slowly.

Brackman placed his hand on her arm, his strong hand squeezing her gently. "Take care, Christine." He turned and headed toward the fourth gallery and the memorial's exit.

After remaining in the alcove for another minute, Christine decided to exit through the entrance, pausing temporarily in the first gallery. She hadn't been to the memorial since the day it was dedicated. She recalled reading perhaps FDR's most famous quote, spoken during his 1933 inaugural address, which was inscribed in the granite wall of the first gallery. Standing in front of the words, she read them again.

The only thing we have to fear is fear itself.

Christine realized she didn't have President Roosevelt's strength. She was afraid they'd be unable to prevent the *Kentucky* from destroying Iran. She also worried about what Hardison appeared capable of; she feared for

Dave's life. And in the dim recesses of her mind, she feared for her own.

It was getting late. Twilight had arrived, and the Tidal Basin's white perimeter lighting shimmered on the water's black surface. Christine pushed the fear from her thoughts, then tucked her head down to protect her face from the wind. Leaving the FDR Memorial behind, she headed back up the Cherry Tree Walk toward the White House, and Kevin Hardison.

5 DAYS REMAINING

34

USS KENTUCKY

It was just before midnight, with Section 3 relieving the watch, when Commander Brad Malone entered Control.

"Captain in Control," the Chief of the Watch announced.

As usual, Malone began his midnight tour of the submarine at the top of the Operations Compartment. Glancing around, he verified the enlisted watchstanders had already turned over, while Tom, the oncoming Officer of the Deck, was still reviewing the ship's status with the offgoing OOD. As the two officers completed their turnover, Malone couldn't help but notice how much Tom was like his father.

Malone had served as Engineer Officer on the USS *Buffalo* under Tom's old man and had learned almost everything he knew about submarine tactics from the seasoned veteran. When Malone reported as the *Kentucky* BLUE Crew commanding officer, he'd been pleased to discover Tom was one of his junior officers, giving Malone the opportunity to pass along the valuable insight he'd received from Tom's father. Tom had been a quick learner, easily grasping complex tactical concepts, qualifying as Officer of the Deck earlier than most, and establishing himself as the most capable junior officer in the Wardroom.

Malone felt a sense of pride in the fine officer Tom had become—the same pride, he was sure, felt by the young officer's mother and father. If there was one thing he was sure of, it was that he could depend on Tom, no matter what the circumstance.

Malone continued his midnight tour, stopping in Radio and Sonar, then dropped down to the second level of the Operations Compartment. The doors to the officer staterooms were closed. As the smell of fresh pastries wafted up from below, Malone descended another level and entered Crew's Mess. In the adjacent Galley, the Night Baker was busy cooking the desserts for tomorrow's meals. Petty Officer Ted Luther had just pulled six apple pies out of the upper oven and was busy crimping the dough along the edges of the next batch.

Luther seemed not to notice the Captain's arrival in Crew's Mess and Malone continued his midnight tour, heading down to the lowest of the four levels in the Operations Compartment. On duty tonight as the Torpedoman of the Watch was 3rd Class Machinist Mate John Barber, sitting under the Weapon Control Console by the ship's four torpedo tubes. Barber, alone on watch with thirteen green warshot torpedoes in their stows, stood as Commander Malone entered the Torpedo Room.

"Good morning, Captain."

"Morning, Barber. How are things going?"

"Good, sir. The only issue we have is a small hydraulic leak from Tube Three flood valve."

Malone stopped by Barber, kneeling on the deck grate to get a clear view of the offending valve, just as a drop of hydraulic fluid fell from the valve body into the bilge.

"What's the plan?" Malone asked as he regained his feet.

"The chief wants to tag out the tube on the morning watch and replace the valve's internal O-rings. I'm working on the danger tagout now."

"Who's doing the maintenance?"

"I am, sir." Barber's eyes brightened with pride. "It'll be my first valve rebuild."

"I'm sure you'll do fine," Malone replied. "I'll stop by in the morning to see how things turned out."

Malone headed aft toward the ladder leading up to the next level, passing between the *Kentucky*'s warshot torpedoes on his way. The nineteen-foot-long, two-ton MK 48 Mod 6 torpedoes the ship carried were the mainstay weapons of the U.S. Submarine Force, being slowly upgraded to the even more advanced Mod 7 torpedo, carried by the fast-attack submarines in small quantities. As Malone passed between the warshot torpedoes on both sides, there was something reassuring, yet frightening, about the torpedo's autonomous nature, so different from the World War II version.

World War II torpedoes were straight runners, not much more than a bomb propelled though the water in a straight line. The crew's job was to calculate the bearing rate and range of its intended target, then shoot the torpedo at the required lead angle, not much different from a quarterback judging the distance and speed of his receiver cutting across the field, throwing the ball to the spot where the receiver and the ball would converge.

Today's torpedoes were artificially intelligent weapons with their own sonars and computerized brains. After launch, they would analyze the returns from the sonar in their noses, sorting through what could be a submarine or a surface ship, or a decoy launched or trailed behind them. Reassuring in their capability, the torpedoes also had an independent nature that was quite disconcerting. They could not distinguish between friend and foe, and there was always the possibility a torpedo, while searching for its intended target, could lock on to the submarine that fired it.

There were safeguards to prevent that, as well as a guidance wire attached to the MK 48 torpedoes the U.S. submarines fired. The thin copper wire, dispensed from both the torpedo and a spool in the torpedo tube, carried data between the torpedo and the submarine's Combat Control System. Over the guidance wire, the crew could send new commands after the torpedo had been launched, changing its initial course, depth, or other search parameters. Likewise, the torpedo would send information back to the submarine: status reports as it searched the ocean and details on the decoy or target it was evaluating or had decided to attack.

The *Kentucky*'s crew was well trained in torpedo employment, but its main mission was launching ballistic missiles. As Malone ascended to Operations Compartment 3rd Level and headed aft toward the Missile Compartment, his thoughts turned from the ship's tactical weapons to her strategic ones; the twenty-four missiles she carried. After reaching the watertight door leading into the Missile Compartment, he ascended another level and stopped in Missile Control Center, where two missile techs stood watch at all times. The cool air greeted him as he entered; the air-conditioning system kept MCC around 60 degrees, dissipating the heat generated from the rows of computers that controlled the launch systems.

After reviewing the status of the strategic launch systems, Malone left MCC and entered the Missile Compartment on its third of four levels, passing by the nine-man bunk rooms between each pair of missile tubes, their curtains drawn. Continuing aft, he traveled through the Reactor Compartment passageway and entered the Engine Room. He decided to stop by Maneuvering, a ten-by-ten-foot Control Room where the Engineering Officer of the Watch and three of the nine enlisted personnel stood watch.

The three enlisted watchstanders in Maneuvering managed the reactor, electric, and steam plants. The Reactor Operator in the middle adjusted the height of the reactor's control rods, which controlled the rate of fission and core temperature, as he also controlled the speed of the pumps that pushed cooling water through the core. The Electrical Operator on the right controlled the submarine's two electrical turbine generators, producing electricity as steam passed through their turbines, as well as two motor-generators connected to the submarine's battery. The Throttleman on the left monitored the steam plant and controlled its most important valves—the main engine throttles, which he spun open to the appropriate point based on the propulsion bell rung up by the Helm in Control.

Malone reviewed the status of the propulsion plant, then continued his tour of the engineering spaces, stopping in Engine Room Upper Level between the submarine's main engines. It was here, between the two twenty-foot-tall turbines, that Malone felt the strength of his ship. It wasn't in the nuclear weapons they carried that would destroy others, or the torpedoes that would protect them. It was the Engine Room, creating the drinkable water and oxygen they needed to survive, generating the electricity that brought the ship to life, and the propulsion that would carry them away from danger.

Commander Brad Malone held his hands out to his sides, feeling the heat radiate off the main engines, replacing the chill in his bones created by the always cool Operations Compartment. Here, between the main engines, not far from Maneuvering, where he had started his career as a junior officer almost twenty years ago, he felt at peace. Only a few short days ago, looking at the twenty-nine-point cribbage hand, he had expected this, his last patrol, to be his most rewarding one. But the nuclear launch order had changed everything.

Malone sighed heavily as he dropped his hands, then headed forward.

35

USS *NORTH CAROLINA*

"Pilot, ahead two-thirds."

Commander Gallagher stood next to his Officer of the Deck as he ordered the submarine to slow from ahead full to ten knots, preparing to search the surrounding waters again. After heading west at ahead flank for twenty-eight straight hours, they had slowed as they entered the back edge of their target's Area of Uncertainty. Finding nothing, they had proceeded toward the center of the AOU. But the target's AOU was large and growing bigger by the hour, so Gallagher had elected to use the sprint and drift tactic, cutting across the AOU at ahead full, slowing to ahead two-thirds periodically to search for their target.

The *North Carolina* was vulnerable during her ahead full sprints, her sensors blunted, but Gallagher was reassured by the stealthy nature of his new submarine. The *North Carolina*, the fourth in the *Virginia*-class, was quieter at ahead full than a 688 was tied to the pier. And he was certain they were much quieter than their target, even if the Chinese counterfeit they were chasing was as quiet as the Trident design they had copied. The *North Carolina*'s only vulnerability, Gallagher figured, was the weapons she carried. Or lack thereof.

Gallagher had just toured the barren Torpedo Room; the submarine's only two warshots were loaded into Torpedo Tubes One and Two. But at least they were the new Mod 7 variant, the most capable in the U.S. arsenal. However, in less than a minute, both bullets could be spent with no guarantee they would find their mark, leaving the *North Carolina* defenseless. Additionally, they were far from the proficient crew they'd be after a six-month workup for a WESTPAC deployment. Fortunately, Gallagher was the most seasoned fast-attack CO on the waterfront.

A year earlier, he was finishing up his three-year tour as commanding officer of the USS *Chicago* and had received orders to the Pentagon. But then the incoming CO of the *North Carolina* pulled up lame, disqualified from submarine service due to a second episode of kidney stones. After a quick reshuffling, Gallagher ended up with orders to the *Virginia*-class submarine, happy to have postponed what would surely be a tortuous tour of duty with the Washington brass. On a submarine base, commander was a prestigious rank. But Gallagher had heard the horror stories about the Pentagon, where senior Navy captains made coffee for the admirals, and commanders ran out for the sugar and stir sticks.

Thankfully, all that would wait, and in the meantime he had put his considerable experience to work. He had done two WESTPAC deployments while in command, and combined with his western runs as a JO and department head on Pearl Harbor–based 688s, he had more deployments under his belt than any other submarine commanding officer.

As his crew prepared to search the surrounding water, Gallagher looked up at the digital display of the submarine's course, speed, and depth on the Ship Control Panel. The *North Carolina* had finished coasting down to ten knots, slowing now for the fourth time, having just passed the center of the target's AOU. As a faint white trace began to materialize on the towed array display, the Officer of the Deck picked up the 27-MC microphone.

"Sonar, Conn. Report all contacts."

36

USS *KENTUCKY*
USS *NORTH CAROLINA*

USS *KENTUCKY*

On his way forward, Malone dropped down into Engine Room Lower Level. On watch in the bowels of the Engine Room was Petty Officer 3rd Class Bob Murphy. Halfway aft along the center passageway, Murphy examined a test tube held up to the light. Having just added two drops of silver nitrate to the water, Murphy gently swirled the test tube, checking for the milky-white evidence of a leak from the Main Seawater System, which cooled the steam back to water after it passed through the large turbines. After a negative result, Murphy emptied the clear fluid into the hazardous waste bucket, looking up in surprise at the submarine's Commanding Officer, who had snuck up on him as he concentrated on his analysis, the whirr of the condensate pumps masking the sound of his arrival.

"Hi, Captain."

Malone saw himself in the tall and lanky nineteen-year-old, who was from Dawson, Iowa, one hundred miles south of Malone's hometown of Fenton. There wasn't much difference between the Captain and the enlisted man standing before him, Malone figured. If not for a single conversation, he would have enlisted in the Navy right out of high school like Murphy, rather than receiving his commission as an officer. During his junior year in high school, he had considered enlisting, but his guidance counselor urged him to apply for a Navy ROTC scholarship instead. A year later, at age eighteen, he donned a Navy uniform for the first time as he entered Purdue University as a midshipman.

That was a long time ago, and his life had almost come full circle. Following this patrol, he would remove his uniform for the last time, returning to the home he'd left behind twenty-four years ago. The two men, one's career beginning while the other's ended, talked for a few minutes about Murphy's family back in Iowa. After a while, Malone checked his watch; it was almost 0100. The two offgoing watch officers would soon be knocking on his stateroom door. He bid farewell to Petty Officer Murphy and headed forward.

USS *NORTH CAROLINA*

Standing behind his OOD at his Tactical Workstation, Gallagher studied the faint white trace on the towed array display, waiting for the results of Sonar's analysis. The faint trace meant the contact was either quiet or distant, and he wouldn't know which until after the

North Carolina's first maneuver, watching what happened to the target's bearing rate. But before he turned the ship, he would verify the contact was submerged. They couldn't afford to waste time maneuvering for every trace picked up by Sonar.

The report from Sonar answered Gallagher's question. "Conn, Sonar. Sierra five-seven is classified submerged."

Gallagher turned to his Officer of the Deck. "Man Battle Stations silently."

Standard protocols for manning Battle Stations—a shipwide 1-MC announcement followed by the loud *bong, bong, bong* of the General Alarm—would reverberate into the water through the submarine's steel hull, potentially alerting the target if it was close and its sonar capable. So Gallagher had ordered Battle Stations manned silently. The Messenger and Auxiliary Electrician Forward hurried down to berthing, one swinging through the officer staterooms and Chief's Quarters before joining the other in enlisted berthing, quickly rousing the crew. Four minutes later, the last watch station reported in.

The *North Carolina* was ready for combat.

Gallagher decided to wait before turning the ship, giving Sonar time to analyze the frequencies being emitted by the contact. Once the ship began its turn, the towed array would become unstable, snaking back and forth for several minutes. Only after it had straightened back out would its frequencies and bearings be reliable.

Finally, the report came across the 27-MC. "Conn, Sonar. The contact has standard Trident tonals."

They had found their target.

"Pilot, left twenty degrees rudder, steady course one-eight-zero."

Gallagher began the process of nailing down the target's course, speed, and range, then turned his attention to his weapons. The torpedo tubes were flooded down and pressurized, but he had kept the outer doors shut during their sprint and drifts, as the flow noise across the open torpedo tubes would have been noticeable at ahead full. But that was okay, he had concluded. The *North Carolina* had improved outer door mechanisms, which opened much more quietly than those on other submarine classes. Now that they had found their adversary, it was time to make final preparations.

He turned to his Weapons Officer. "Open outer doors, tubes One and Two."

USS *KENTUCKY*

Sonar Supervisor Tony DelGreco, underway on his eighteenth patrol, adjusted his headphones for the umpteenth time this watch. The headphones, with their uncomfortable earmuffs, were connected to the submarine's spherical array sonar, providing an audible companion to the visual display in front of him. The Navy had succeeded in designing headphones that were universally unpleasant to wear, so the three sonar techs took turns wearing them in shifts on their six-hour watch, giving their ears a break in between their two hours of penance each watch.

First Class Petty Officer DelGreco was on his third sea tour aboard a ballistic missile submarine, or boomer. He had logged hundreds of watches in Trident Sonar

Rooms during his eighteen patrols, and thousands of hours wearing the despised headphones. As DelGreco adjusted the headphones yet again, he cocked his head to one side, startled by an unusual sound. It was faint but unmistakable—metal grinding on metal. As he pondered the source of the sound and what type of machinery might produce it, he heard it again; the same slow, metallic grind. If he didn't know better, he would have sworn it was a torpedo tube outer door opening. But it was lower pitched and smoother. Plus, they hadn't received any water space advisories announcing the nearby passage of a submarine. One thing he was sure of, however, was that it wasn't biologics. The sound came from something man-made.

Looking up at the sound velocity profile, DelGreco checked the temperature of the ocean from the surface down to the *Kentucky*'s depth. Since they held no contact, the noise must have traveled along a sound channel, trapped between a positive and negative temperature gradient, channeling the sound much farther than normal ocean conditions allowed. But there was a negative slope the whole way down, the water consistently cooling from the surface to the *Kentucky*'s depth. There was no sound channel.

Petty Officer Bob Cibelli caught the perplexed look on DelGreco's face. "What's up?"

"Mechanical transients. Sounded like a torpedo tube shutter door opening, but not quite. Take a listen."

DelGreco rewound the digital recording, rubbing his ears as he handed the headphones to Cibelli. He hit Play, letting the junior technician listen.

"It's different from the recordings in the trainers,"

Cibelli agreed as he handed the headphones back to DelGreco. "Think we should inform the OOD?"

DelGreco mulled over whether they should bother the Officer of the Deck with what they had heard. The ocean was filled with hundreds of sounds they could never quite place.

"Naw," DelGreco finally decided as he replaced the headphones around his ears. "Must be a trawler having a bad day somewhere."

USS *NORTH CAROLINA*

"Steady course north."

"Very well, Pilot," Gallagher replied.

The *North Carolina* had completed its latest maneuver, reversing course from the southern trajectory it had remained on for ten minutes, long enough to calculate a bearing rate to the contact and determine it was close. Much closer than Gallagher had expected. Their target was a quiet one indeed, truly on par with U.S. Trident submarines.

Gallagher had assumed the Conn when the *North Carolina* manned Battle Stations. Under routine operations, the submarine's Officer of the Deck held both the Deck and the Conn; responsibility for the Deck meant overseeing the basic operation of the submarine, while the Conning Officer controlled the ship's course, speed, and depth, and issued all tactical commands. These two functions were split during Battle Stations, the Deck Officer managing the ship's routine evolutions while the Conning Officer led the submarine into battle.

The *North Carolina*'s towed array steadied, and

reliable bearings began streaming into the Combat Control System. Slowly, the two fire control technicians and one junior officer began generating target solutions, adjusting parameters for course, speed, and range, constantly improving their solution. The XO, in charge of the Fire Control Tracking Party and responsible for determining the target's solution within acceptable tolerances, hovered behind the three men as they refined their solutions.

They had held the target on three legs now—their original westward path, and on southern and northerly courses. Against a steady, unsuspecting contact, that would normally provide enough data for the operators and the Combat Control System algorithms to develop an adequate solution. The XO monitored all three combat control consoles, comparing the three solutions against each other as well as the automated result from the Combat Control System. For a given bearing rate or even several legs of data, there were multiple possible solutions for the target. How well the solutions tracked with each other as well as the raw sonar data on the screen was an indication of how solid their estimates were.

All three operators and the Combat Control System's automated algorithm converged on a single solution for their contact, varying by only one hundred yards in range, a few degrees in course, and a fraction of a knot in speed.

The XO tapped one of the fire control techs on his shoulder. "Promote to Master." The Fire Control technician complied, and the submarine's geographic display updated with the Master solution to their target. Turning to the Captain behind him, the XO reported, "I have a firing solution."

Gallagher announced loudly, "Firing Point Procedures, Sierra five-seven, tube One."

USS *KENTUCKY*

A few minutes earlier, Commander Malone had returned to his stateroom, expecting to find the two offgoing watch officers waiting to report their relief. Every six hours, from the moment the submarine cast off the last mooring line until the ship returned to port, the offgoing Officer of the Deck and Engineering Officer of the Watch reported to the Commanding Officer what had transpired during their watch and the current conditions throughout the ship. Even if the Captain was asleep, the two officers would wake him to report their relief.

Rather than be awakened each night, Malone toured the ship, arriving back at his stateroom in time for the officers' report. But tonight no one was waiting. The two officers must have had a second helping of midrats, or perhaps they were discussing some issue with one of the watchstanders on duty. Rather than wait, Malone decided to swing back through Control. The offgoing OOD was the Sonar Officer; perhaps he was tied up with an issue in the sonar shack.

A moment later, Malone was back in the Control Room, opening the door to Sonar. Three petty officers were in the darkened sonar shack—the lights were extinguished to aid in detecting the faint traces on their displays. Malone closed the door behind him to keep out the light.

Petty Officer DelGreco looked up from his display. "Evening, sir. What brings you back to Sonar tonight?"

"Have you seen Lieutenant Costa?"

"He came through a few minutes ago on his after-watch tour. It seemed like he was running a bit late."

"Yes, it does seem that way," Malone agreed. He glanced at the sonar displays; there were no automated trackers assigned. "Looks pretty dead out there."

"Yes, sir," DelGreco replied. "Not a single contact this watch."

Malone was about to leave Sonar—the two watch officers would arrive at his stateroom momentarily—when DelGreco added, "We did hear an unusual mechanical transient awhile ago, sir. Cibelli and I both listened to it, but couldn't place it. Do you want to take a listen?"

"Sure," Malone replied.

DelGreco handed Commander Malone the headphones and pulled up the recording.

USS *NORTH CAROLINA*

Commander Gallagher stood patiently between the sonar and combat control consoles, waiting for the three reports required before the *North Carolina* could launch its torpedo. It would take less than a minute, but after commencing Firing Point Procedures, the submarine's Commanding Officer would wait for the XO to inform him the firing solution had been fed to the Weapon Control Console, the Weps to report the appropriate weapon presets had been selected and sent to the torpedo, and the Navigator to reply that the submarine was prepared for potential counterfire. At that point, Gallagher would give the order to launch one of the *North Carolina*'s two MK 48 Mod 7 torpedoes, which at this range would be a sure hit. Even if the target alerted the instant the *North Carolina* fired, it was too close to successfully evade, and no decoy they could eject into the water would fool their new Mod 7 torpedo.

Gallagher looked up as the lights in Control flickered. The Electrical Operator in Maneuvering had apparently just split the electrical buses, isolating the turbine generators from the motor generators and the essential electrical loads they carried. A second later, the Engine Order Telegraph, normally controlled by the pilot, shifted to all stop. The explanation came across the 7-MC a moment later.

"Conn, Maneuvering. Reactor scram."

Gallagher stared at his XO in disbelief. The reactor had been instantaneously shut down by the reactor plant's protection circuitry, driving the control rods to the bottom of the core in less than a millisecond. In twenty years aboard nuclear-powered submarines, not once had he experienced an unexpected scram. They trained for the fault constantly—verifying watchstanders knew the appropriate actions—but Gallagher had never seen it occur outside of a training exercise. The core was no longer generating heat. And without heat, there was no steam for the submarine's turbine generators or main engines.

The *North Carolina* had just lost propulsion and was now coasting to a stop as she cut across their target's path eight thousand yards ahead. Without propulsion and the ability to evade a counterfired torpedo, they were a sitting duck. Once their target detected the *North*

Carolina's torpedo launch, it would return fire down the line of bearing of the incoming torpedo, right down their throat. Without propulsion, the *North Carolina* would not engage its target unless it was fired upon first.

Even worse, the *North Carolina* was coasting to a stop directly in front of their target. Their target would close to within a thousand yards, and the *North Carolina* would almost surely be detected. If the reactor wasn't back up before then, they would be in trouble. Deep trouble.

If the watch section in the Engine Room quickly identified and corrected the fault, they could commence an emergency reactor restart, bringing the reactor back into the power range in a matter of minutes. If not, they'd be defenseless, unable to evade an incoming torpedo. They might take out their target, but there would be no hope for the *North Carolina*. Everything hinged on whether they could quickly identify and correct the problem.

The report over the 7-MC answered that essential question. "Conn, Maneuvering. Dropped control rod. No fault found. Unable to commence Fast Recovery Start-up."

Gallagher shook his head, his disbelief turning to frustration.

Un-fucking-believable.

They had been only seconds away from launching their MK 48 torpedo. Had the reactor stayed up a minute longer, their target would have been sunk. But now, without propulsion, the *North Carolina* could not fire. After the Officer of the Deck acknowledged Maneuvering's report over the 7-MC, Gallagher terminated the

pending torpedo launch. "Check Fire. Continue tracking Sierra five-seven."

He debated whether to stay in Control or head aft to
assess the situation. The ship was at Battle Stations and
his place was in Control, guiding them as they engaged
in combat. But they could not prosecute the target until
the reactor returned to power. And the *North Carolina*
itself would soon be in peril if the fast-attack submarine
was still powerless when their target passed by.

They had to get the reactor back up. And fast.

Gallagher decided to head aft, transferring the Conn
back to the Officer of the Deck. Before departing Control, he ordered his OOD, "Inform me immediately if
the target maneuvers."

USS *KENTUCKY*

Malone pressed the headphones against his ears as Del-
Greco played the recording. The sonar techs were
right—it was definitely a mechanical transient. He had
never heard this type of sound before, but his instinct
told him there was something important about it. That
DelGreco had thought enough about the unusual sound
to bring it to his attention meant there was potentially
something there; something worth investigating.

"Good ears, DelGreco," Malone said as he handed the
headphones back. "Tell you what. We'll slow down to
five knots and see if we hear anything else. Sound like
a plan?"

"Sure does, Captain." DelGreco placed the headphones around his ears, returning his attention to the
sonar displays.

Malone stepped out of the sonar shack and approached Tom, sitting on the Conn. "Sonar picked up some unusual mechanical transients. Slow to ahead one-third so we can perform a better search."

Tom acknowledged the Captain's order, then relayed it to the Helm. Gradually, the *Kentucky* slowed to five knots, reducing the flow noise of the water passing over the hull and past the towed array hydrophones.

USS *NORTH CAROLINA*

As Gallagher approached the watertight door leading into the Reactor Compartment passageway, two reactor technicians assigned to the Forward Damage Control Team during Battle Stations raced past him. Grabbing the handle above the door without slowing, they launched themselves through the hatch feetfirst on their way aft to join the rest of their division. Gallagher followed them through the RC passageway and into the Engine Room, where the machinist mates were busy shutting it down, securing the steam loads on the reactor plant to keep it hot.

Keeping the *North Carolina*'s reactor hot was imperative. In its simplest terms, the submarine's reactor was just a sophisticated teakettle, generating the steam required to power the ship's engines and electrical turbine generators. Keeping the reactor hot, conserving its stored energy, was an essential casualty response to an unexpected reactor shutdown. Unless the steam loads were quickly secured, within a few minutes the reactor would cool to the point where it could no longer generate steam, and without steam, the ship had no emergency propulsion.

The throttles were already shut, stopping the largest heat drain on the plant, but the two electrical turbine generators were still spinning, draining heat from the core. The steam-driven generators would stay operational, providing the ship with power until electrical loads were reduced low enough for the battery to take over. Throughout the submarine, the crew rigged the ship for Reduced Electrical Power, securing pumps, motors, and electronic consoles, crippling the fast-attack submarine even more than when the main engine throttles had been shut.

How long his submarine would remain crippled was the question. Gallagher stopped next to his Engineer, standing between two rows of cabinets containing the computerized reactor control circuitry. The indicator light for rod 2-3 glowed an ominous red, and the Engineer quickly informed Gallagher they had been unable to relatch the wayward rod. The Reactor Controls Chief and two RC Division petty officers were huddled around a time domain reflectometer, which sent light pulses down electrical cables and measured the time it took for the light to travel to the end and reflect back. Cables ran from the TDR to the Control Rod Drive Motor cabinet.

The chief looked up. "There's a break in the wiring between the rod control cabinet and the reactor core, at the fifty-foot point." Laying a schematic on top of the TDR, the chief traced his finger along the diagram. "Which puts the break right here. Directly on top of the reactor core, where it connects to the rod latching mechanism."

The Engineer exchanged glances with Gallagher as the Reactor Controls Chief continued. "We're going to have to enter the Reactor Compartment to fix it, if it's repairable at all. We won't know until we get in there. The only other option we have is to bring the reactor back up with the rod still on the bottom, but we'll be limited to thirty percent power."

Gallagher contemplated the chief's suggestion. The inherent stability of the submarine's nuclear reactor now worked against them. If the nuclear reaction in any part of the core increased or decreased, the rest of the core immediately compensated, maintaining overall core flux at an equilibrium level. With a rod on the bottom and the surrounding fuel cells shut down, the unaffected fuel cells would exceed their temperature limits if the crew tried to bring the reactor up to full power.

While the purpose of the reactor was to generate heat, it was vital the reactor be kept from getting too hot. It was protected by sophisticated automatic protection circuitry constantly monitoring the condition of the core, and also by the operating procedures the crew was trained to follow. If the guidelines were violated and the reactor operated outside its design parameters, the core could overheat. If the core overheated and the uranium melted through the fuel cells' protective cladding and into the reactor cooling system, massive amounts of radiation would be released, overwhelming the primary and secondary radiation shields protecting the crew. And if the increasing temperature within the core wasn't reversed by the reactor's cooling systems, the ultimate catastrophe would occur—a complete core meltdown.

If they brought the reactor back up with a dropped

rod, they would have to limit power to ensure the core didn't overheat. Gallagher converted the 30 percent power to speed in his head; they would barely be able to achieve ahead standard. If they had to evade a torpedo, ahead standard wouldn't cut it. The only way they could engage their target and survive was to complete the repair and restore the reactor to full power.

Eight minutes had already passed since the reactor scrammed, meaning their target would pass within a thousand yards in fifteen minutes. That wasn't enough time.

As Gallagher weighed his options, the ICSAP circuit next to him activated. He picked up the handset. The OOD was on the other end; their target had maneuvered, slowing to five knots, and it would now be thirty minutes before their target crossed their path. Just enough time, perhaps, to complete the repair.

Gallagher turned to his Engineer. "Enter the Reactor Compartment."

37

USS *NORTH CAROLINA*
USS *KENTUCKY*

USS *NORTH CAROLINA*

Joseph Radek, the Reactor Controls Division Chief, waited in the Reactor Compartment passageway, already sweating in the head-to-toe yellow anticontamination clothing he had hastily donned. Next to him, an engineering laboratory technician spun the hand wheel, the RC door creaking slowly inward in response. A blast of heat hit Chief Radek in the face as the door cracked open and the ELT paused, poking the suction tube connected to the portable air sampler into the RC to check for airborne radioactivity. As Radek waited for a report, he tried to hide his nervousness; neither he, nor anyone else aboard the *North Carolina,* had ever entered the Reactor Compartment at sea.

Entry into the RC was not allowed when the reactor was operating—the radiation level was too high. A nuclear-powered submarine never deliberately shut down its reactor at sea, except temporarily while simulating casualties or, in rare instances, like now, when repairs were required. The reactor had been shut down for only a few minutes, and the radioactive by-products of the nuclear reactions were still sizzling inside the core, emitting high levels of neutrons and gamma rays. Radek held his digital pocket dosimeter up to his eye to verify it had been set to zero; he could remain inside only twelve minutes before he exceeded his exposure limit.

Radek didn't know which he feared more—the radiation or the heat. The *North Carolina* had been running at ahead flank for twenty-eight hours and intermittently at ahead full for the last four, the reactor generating an enormous amount of heat during that time. The air inside the Reactor Compartment was blisteringly hot, hovering at 160 degrees Fahrenheit. It would hopefully be a dry heat, Radek thought to himself to lighten the situation. But with his body sealed in yellow plastic along with rubber boots and gloves, only his face exposed, he figured he would soon know what a pork roast felt like in a Crock-Pot.

Standing next to Chief Radek, also dressed in the yellow protective clothing, was Mike Tell, his leading first class petty officer. The two men would enter the RC together, simultaneously disassembling the top of the control rod drive mechanism to allow access to the end of the cable run, quickly reassembling it after the repair to the wire underneath. If all went well, the whole process would last ten minutes, leaving fifteen minutes to restart the reactor and restore propulsion.

The ELT finished opening the door and locked it in place, stepping to the back of the Control Point, providing a path for Radek and Tell. Radek turned to the

Control Point Watch, another ELT who controlled entry and exit from the RC. "Request permission to enter the Reactor Compartment."

"Enter," the ELT replied.

Radek took a deep breath and stepped inside.

It felt like he had entered a furnace; the heat was almost suffocating in its intensity. Radek paused, trying to acclimate himself to the scorching heat before he climbed the ladder to upper level, where the top of the reactor protruded through the deck. Petty Officer Tell joined him, likewise stunned by the stifling heat. Radek breathed alternately through his nose and his mouth, attempting to discern which was less uncomfortable, finally settling on the nose; his tongue dried almost instantly when he tried to breathe through his mouth.

Radek grabbed the metal rungs on the ladder, a small pouch of tools gripped in his right hand. The rubber gloves and shoes made the trip treacherous, his feet sometimes slipping off the thin rungs. He kept a firm grip on his bag of tools. Submarine sonars were sensitive, and a metal tool dropped onto a deck or bilge could be heard for miles, giving away their presence. He could feel the heat through his thick gloves, and when he was halfway up the ladder, the hot metal became uncomfortable to hold. By the time Radek reached upper level, breathing had become an almost impossible chore. As Tell finished climbing the ladder behind him, Radek moved toward the top of the reactor vessel, his eyes following the cable run where it penetrated the Reactor Compartment, splitting into the individual cables leading to the control rod drive mechanisms on top of the reactor.

The S9G reactor was surprisingly small considering the thirty megawatts of power it generated. Only ten feet in diameter and fourteen feet tall, it was extremely compact, even more so after factoring in the reactor vessel's one-foot-thick Inconel steel walls. Inside, the vessel held enough fuel to power the *North Carolina* for its entire thirty-three-year life span. Clambering carefully onto the top of the reactor, Radek stopped along the edge by fuel cell 2-3, checking the cable tag to ensure he had selected the correct control rod. Tell joined him a second later, and the two men began disassembling the end of the cable. The disassembly was relatively straightforward, as would be the assembly after the wire was reconnected; the end of the cable was secured by two standard bolts, their nuts lockwired to prevent counterclockwise rotation, ensuring the two fasteners remained tight despite any vibration.

After cutting the lockwires, they quickly removed the bolts. As Radek pulled back the end of the protective metal sheath, exposing the wiring underneath, he froze. The frayed copper wiring had broken at the worst possible location, only a quarter inch out of the CRDM as it began its bend toward the combined cable run. It didn't look long enough for the splice to hold.

Pulling a crimper from the tool bag, Radek decided to give it a try. With enough exposed wire, the splice was a simple, fifteen-second job. But with only a quarter inch of wire on one end, the splice would have to be held carefully in place. Compounding the process was the effort of handling the crimper itself. It was difficult enough wearing the bulky gloves, but his hands were sweating profusely, his fingers slipping inside the insulated rubber gloves. Operating the crimper correctly under these conditions, it seemed to Radek, would be like trying to pick up a marble with a baseball glove.

He slid the splice over the wire sticking up from the CRDM, then slid the crimper in place over the end. As Reactor Technician Chief Joseph Radek squeezed slowly, but firmly, the crimper slipped out of his hand. It bounced off the edge of the reactor vessel, ricocheted off the reactor piping, and landed in the bilge twenty feet below with a loud, resonating clank.

USS *KENTUCKY*

Inside the darkened Sonar Room, Petty Officer DelGreco's head jerked up, the metallic transient echoing in his headphones. DelGreco picked up the 27-MC. "Conn, Sonar. Metallic transient, bearing two-four-zero."

Tom acknowledged DelGreco's report, and a moment later, Malone stuck his head inside the door. "What've you got?"

"Someone just dropped a tool. And it was close, too. Very clear."

Malone processed DelGreco's report. With no contacts on the sonar screens, it meant the transient had come from an undetected, submerged contact. And if they were close enough to hear a tool fall onto the deck but not pick up its broadband or narrowband noise signature, it could only be a high-end submarine. But there were no American subs in the vicinity according to the waterspace advisories. And the odds of crossing paths with a Russian submarine this far out in the middle of the Pacific Ocean were minuscule. It made no sense. But not much had made sense this patrol: Washington, D.C., destroyed, a nuclear launch order, the bizarre encounter with the 688s.

Malone turned to Tom, who was scrutinizing the sonar screens on the Conn. "Man Battle Stations Torpedo. Come left to course two-four-zero. Let's find out what's out there."

USS *NORTH CAROLINA*

Standing next to the Sonar Supervisor, Commander Gallagher cursed under his breath. Sonar had reported a loud mechanical transient coming from their own ship, and the Control Point had responded to the Sonar Supervisor's query, confirming Chief Radek had indeed dropped the crimper into the bilge and was now in the process of retrieving it.

The helplessness of their situation was infuriating. Twenty minutes earlier, they had been the hunter, about to slay their unsuspecting prey. Now they were defenseless. If their adversary discovered them and attacked, the *North Carolina* was done for, their only consolation residing in the slim chance they could also sink their target with a lucky return fire. As Gallagher mulled over their unfortunate predicament, the situation took a turn for the worse.

"Conn, Sonar. Upshift in Doppler. Sierra five-seven has turned toward."

Gallagher grabbed the Sonar Supervisor by the

collar, his face twisting with emotion, unable to conceal his anger and frustration. "Pass the word throughout the ship. I want everyone to freeze where they are. No one moves a muscle until I give the word."

Inside the Reactor Compartment, Chief Radek was climbing the ladder back to upper level, the crimper retrieved from the bilge and back in the tool bag in his hand, when he heard the Control Point yell through the RC doorway.

"Freeze! No one moves until the Captain gives the order!"

Radek stopped where he was, at the worst possible location, right beside the middle of the reactor vessel. As he waited, he imagined his insides cooking as if he were in a microwave oven, invisible neutrons and gamma rays passing through his body. The heat from the ladder seeped through his gloves, and he had no choice but to alternately let go with one hand, letting his glove cool in the 160-degree air before swapping hands, the gloves getting hotter with each iteration. After one of the swaps, he unclipped the pocket dosimeter from his collar and read the amount of radiation he'd received thus far.

Jesus.

More than he'd received in his entire time in the Navy. But then again, submarine reactors were extremely well shielded and he had never entered the Reactor Compartment only minutes after shutdown from high power. Sweat was dripping down his forehead into his eyes, but he had nothing to wipe his face with; the plastic anti-contamination clothing was useless in this regard. So he occasionally shook his head from side to side, flinging the liquid from his face, the salt from his sweat stinging his eyes as he waited for the word to continue moving. As he shifted his grip on the ladder yet again, Radek wondered what was going to cook him first, the radiation or the heat.

In the *North Carolina*'s Control Room, the tension in the air was thick, but the conversations remained calm, subdued. The fire control technicians continued their target motion analysis, adjusting parameters until they had determined the target's new course.

It had turned directly toward them, and was now less than two thousand yards away.

The *Virginia*-class submarine's new Control Room layout, with the sonar consoles in Control rather than in a separate room like other U.S. submarines, offered Gallagher a clear view of the bright white trace off the *North Carolina*'s starboard beam, growing stronger by the minute. As the Executive Officer stood behind the combat control consoles in the frigid compartment, beads of sweat formed on his forehead. The XO cast frequent, expectant glances in Gallagher's direction, waiting for the order to shoot. Gallagher knew what he was thinking. Maybe if they got off the first shot, they could surprise their target, and at such a close range, leave it with insufficient time to return fire.

But that was risky. Shoot first and almost guarantee mutual destruction, or sit tight and play the odds their target would somehow pass by without firing.

Gallagher decided to take the middle ground, calmly announcing, "Firing Point Procedures, Sierra five-seven, tube One." He looked over at his XO. "But we will not shoot unless fired upon first."

The fire control tech at the Weapon Launch Console sent the course, speed, and range of their target to their Mod 7 torpedo in tube One, along with applicable search presets, although just about any preset would have been okay in this situation—after a quick ninety-degree turn to the right after its launch, their torpedo would be staring directly at its target. It couldn't miss.

Thirty seconds after Gallagher issued the order, the *North Carolina* was cocked and ready, a single button push away from launching its MK 48 torpedo.

USS *KENTUCKY*

Inside the sonar shack, Petty Officer DelGreco traced his finger along the narrowband frequency display. So far, they had picked up three transients. If there really was a contact out there, the first indication would appear on the narrowband display as the *Kentucky*'s sonar algorithms pulled the discrete tonals from the surrounding water. Now that they were at Battle Stations, the sonar shack was packed, the entire division jammed into the small room, each operator assigned a specific function, quietly conferring between themselves and with the Fire Control Party in the Control Room over their sound-powered phones.

Scanning his display, DelGreco keyed on an unusual patch of low-frequency noise. As he adjusted the analysis settings, three tonals rose from the background, each frequency clean and distinct, which could mean only one thing.

A burst of commotion to the left caught DelGreco's attention. A faint white trace was burning in on the spherical array broadband display. A narrow, clean line, not the fuzzy traces produced by merchant ships. But what excited the Broadband Operator and the two techs beside him was that the contact was coming in at only one depth/elevation: zero degrees. DelGreco glanced at the sound velocity profile again, a steady negative slope, which would bend all sound downward as it traveled through the water. A trace burning in at the zero D/E in this kind of ocean environment meant the contact was close, inside one thousand yards, and at the same depth as the *Kentucky*. Worse, the contact was dead ahead.

DelGreco picked up the 27-MC mike. "Conn, Sonar. Hold a submerged contact, designated Sierra eight-five, bearing two-four-zero, inside one thousand yards, zero D/E!"

The contact was only five ship lengths away, dead ahead.

Collision was imminent.

Standing on the Conn, Malone responded instantly. "Helm, right hard rudder, steady course three-three-zero!"

The Helm twisted the yoke to the thirty-degree position, beginning the ninety-degree maneuver to the right. But the *Kentucky* was traveling at only five knots, and the 560-foot-long submarine turned slowly. Even so, as Malone and Tom stared at the broadband display on the Conn, the bearing to the contact began to change quickly. It was close indeed, well inside one thousand yards now. They had stumbled over a submerged contact in the middle of the Pacific Ocean. But what type of submarine? And what was it doing here?

Over the open mike, Malone requested the answer to his first question. "Sonar, Conn. Report classification."

Inside Sonar, they were coming up empty. The frequencies didn't match any of the submarine classes in the *Kentucky*'s sonar system. However, due to the high bearing rate, they could determine with relative ease that the contact was stationary.

"Conn, Sonar," DelGreco announced over the 27-MC. "Sierra eight-five is dead in the water."

Sonar's report took Malone by surprise. Things were making even less sense now. If the contact was stationary, then it was almost assuredly not a submarine. Unless a submarine was hiding on the bottom—not a possibility since the water was one thousand fathoms deep—or executing a stop and drop tactic against an incoming torpedo, it would never voluntarily come to a dead stop in the middle of the ocean while engaging another. Without speed, its towed array would droop vertically, rendering it almost useless, and the submarine could not maneuver to determine the target solution or close to within weapons range.

If it wasn't a submarine, what was it?

Crossing Control, Malone opened the door and poked his head into the crammed Sonar Room. The controlled chaos inside died down as the Captain conferred with the Sonar Chief and Sonar Supervisor. "What the hell is this thing?"

The two men were at a loss. But Petty Officer Cibelli piped up, "Maybe it's an oceanographic survey instrument, collecting and transmitting ocean data. Suspended from a buoy on the surface."

Malone tried to connect the dots: Transients. Machinery noises. Stationary.

Perhaps Cibelli was right, and it was an oceanographic sensor suspended underwater, the metallic clanks coming from an anchor chain connecting the sensor to a buoy as it bobbed on the surface. For the first time, Malone wished he had a traditional active sonar system aboard his ballistic missile submarine like the fast attacks. Just one ping, he thought, and they would know whether Sierra eight-five was three feet in diameter or three hundred, and that would go a long way toward resolving what lay out there.

As the contact drew down the *Kentucky*'s port side and began to open range, Malone decided they couldn't possibly have stumbled across another submarine just sitting in the middle of the ocean. Whatever they had discovered was either oblivious of or ignoring the *Kentucky*'s presence as the ballistic missile submarine sped by. And that was *very* unsubmarinelike.

Malone returned to the Conn and called for everyone's attention. "I do not believe Sierra eight-five is a submarine. We're going to return to base course and increase speed to ahead two-thirds to catch back up with the center of our moving haven. However, just in case, we'll remain at Battle Stations for the next thirty minutes."

The *Kentucky* turned slowly back to course two-seven-zero, increasing speed to ten knots, leaving the mysterious Sierra eight-five behind.

USS *NORTH CAROLINA*

Commander Gallagher entered the Reactor Compartment passageway just as Chief Radek stepped out of the RC into the Control Point. His face was beet red and he was drenched in sweat. Petty Officer Tell stood outside the Control Point under an air-conditioning vent, his anti-contamination hood removed, his hair wet from perspiration.

Chief Radek moved the radiac probe slowly over his anti-Cs, surveying his clothing for radioactive contamination as he briefed Commander Gallagher. "The break is too close to the latching mechanism, sir. There's not enough wiring to properly crimp the ends together. We tried three times, but the connection won't hold. To make the repair, we'll have to disassemble the top of the latching mechanism, and we don't have the tools or expertise required. I'm afraid we can't relatch the dropped rod until we return to port and repairs are made."

That wasn't what Gallagher wanted to hear. With a dropped rod on the bottom of the core, they were limited to ahead standard, an insufficient speed to successfully engage in combat. Even worse, the *North Carolina* wouldn't be allowed to operate for long with an uneven flux in the core. Once Naval Reactors was informed the dropped rod couldn't be relatched, the ship would undoubtedly be ordered to return to port immediately for repair.

Gallagher picked up the ICSAP handset and called Radio, directing them to draft a message to COM-SUBPAC and Naval Reactors, informing them of their condition.

After replacing the handset, he turned back to Chief Radek, praising him for his effort, regardless of the outcome. Gallagher regretted his outburst in Control with the Sonar Supervisor. His crew hadn't failed him; his ship had. The whole situation was unbelievably frustrating. Before the reactor had scrammed, they had been less than a minute away from sinking their target. Now the *North Carolina* would limp home, a failure, for a lengthy and difficult control rod drive repair.

38

PEARL HARBOR

On the second floor of the COMSUBPAC building, Captain Murray Wilson waited alone in the admiral's conference room, studying the Gadsden flag framed in a glass case hanging from the wall. Details about when the flag, named after Colonel Christopher Gadsden, with its symbolic American timber rattlesnake and *Don't Tread on Me* warning, had arrived at COMSUBPAC and who had donated it, were a casualty of the frequent turnover in military commands. But rumor held that this was the very flag Colonel Gadsden had presented to the Continental Navy's first commander in chief, Commodore Esek Hopkins, to serve as his personal standard on the *Alfred,* America's first warship. It was also purported the flag had been run up the *Alfred*'s gaff by Hopkins's first lieutenant, John Paul Jones himself.

As Wilson waited to update Admiral Stanbury on the *North Carolina*'s control rod casualty, he turned his attention from the Gadsden flag to the other side of the conference room, examining the eight-by-twelve-foot map of the world plastered to the wall. With the *North Carolina* out of action, Wilson believed COMSUBPAC was out of options. But then the experienced officer's eyes and thoughts drifted toward the lower left portion of the map—and a potential solution to their dilemma materialized in his mind.

The door to the conference room opened and Admiral Stanbury entered. Wilson retrieved the *North Carolina*'s message from a folder under his arm and handed it to the admiral. A look of disgust worked across Stanbury's face as he read the message, then he crumpled up the paper and tossed it across the room, bouncing it off the rim of the trash can in the corner.

"Any word yet from NAVSEA on a fix to our sonar systems?"

"No, sir. They're still working it."

Stanbury shook his head. "The *North Carolina*'s out of action, and the rest of our fast attacks are blind. Looks like we've run out of submarines."

Wilson disagreed. The move would be unusual, but there was another option. Then he hesitated. He had already done enough, hadn't he? He had done as Stanbury requested, sending their fast attacks after the *Kentucky* and establishing the antisubmarine barrier in front of Emerald. Was he really obliged to take this extra step? With their submarines out of play, the odds of the *Kentucky* surviving had gone way up. But then his thoughts went from the men aboard the submarine to the men, women, and children in Iran. Seventy million souls hung in the balance of his decision. Could he so easily dismiss their lives in favor of his son? Could he be that selfish?

"Wilson, what are you thinking?"

The admiral's question pulled him from his thoughts, forcing him to make a decision. The *Kentucky* had to be stopped.

"Actually," Wilson replied, "there is one other option, but we'll need some pretty high approval and air transport. I can be at Hickam in an hour. Can you have a flight ready by then?"

"Sure," Stanbury answered. "But what do you have in mind?"

"Australia."

"Australia?" Stanbury's eyes widened in surprise, then narrowed in understanding a moment later. "Yes . . . ," he said, turning toward the map, his eyes settling on the continent in the southern hemisphere. "Australia."

39

MAKALAPA, HAWAII

A few minutes later, Wilson's blue Ford Mustang turned onto a cracked concrete driveway in front of a squat one-level ranch house on Makalapa Drive, the main road passing through the senior officers' quarters overlooking Pearl Harbor. As the sun set to the west, palm trees cast long shadows across the hood of his car, while to the east, clouds were forming on the slopes of Mount Tantalus as the warm, moist trade winds cooled during their climb up the steep mountain slope. As a captain in the Navy, Wilson could have afforded more elegant accommodations than the 1940s-era military housing. However, as he passed through the front door and walked across the uneven wood floor, passing walls with multiple coats of paint, he felt like he was treading on hallowed ground. It was a privilege to live in one of the houses that America's World War II submarine commanders had called home.

Seventy years ago, Mush Morton, Dick O'Kane, Eugene Fluckey, and other commanding officers led their crews into battle from Pearl Harbor, returning home to their families and homes in Makalapa. Mush Morton himself, commanding officer of the *Wahoo,* had lived in the house Wilson lived in now, had slept in the very same bedroom, and had lain awake at night wondering if he would return to his wife and children the next time he led his crew to sea. After leading the *Wahoo* into the Sea of Japan on his fifth war patrol, Morton and his crew did not return home.

Unlike Mush Morton, Wilson had returned home this evening, passing through the narrow hallway and into his study. Stopping behind the desk that had been his father's, he retrieved a case of electrical socket adapters from the top left drawer. As he placed the one for Australia in his briefcase, his eye caught the framed portrait of his family sitting on the corner of his desk. He picked up the picture, taken three years earlier, his son standing in the middle with his arms around his parents. Both Murray and Tom wore the summer white uniform of naval officers, the bright white clothing contrasting with the black silhouette of a submarine behind them.

His son had developed into quite the handsome young man, with his father's build, square jawline, and dark eyes, but thankfully his mother's nose. Smart, athletic, always the overachiever, he had never once disappointed his parents in anything that really mattered. As Wilson stared at the portrait of his family, he reflected on how immensely proud he and his wife were of their son.

"Where are you going?"

Claire leaned against the doorframe, examining him through smoky gray eyes that seemed to change color with the light, her face framed with short blond hair that curled inward just above her shoulders. Even though she was past the half-century mark, Wilson was convinced she looked as beautiful today as when they first met more than thirty years ago.

Wilson placed the portrait of his family back on the desk. "Australia, just for a few days."

"Oh. Not long, then."

Wilson nodded as he grabbed his briefcase off his desk and walked toward Claire, still leaning against the doorframe. "I've got to pack, then I'm off to Hickam. Military transport this time." He avoided her gaze, afraid she would see right through him if their eyes met. But she gently grabbed his arm as he walked past, forcing him to stop. Placing her hand on his chin, she slowly pulled his head toward her.

"What's wrong?"

He could see the concern in her eyes. After thirty years of marriage, she could read him like an open book. She knew he was struggling with what he'd been tasked to do.

"I can't discuss it now, but we'll talk when I get back." He kissed Claire gently on her cheek. Wilson hesitated as he pulled back, wondering if he should tell her now, then decided against it. She would never understand, and it would only make things harder.

As Wilson headed down the hallway, he was already dreading his return trip home.

She would never forgive him.

40

USS *KENTUCKY*

As the clock approached 6 A.M., Lieutenant Tom Wilson, still on watch as Officer of the Deck, leaned over the chart table next to the Quartermaster. Even though it was early, the Nav was already up, also examining the navigation plot. The CO and XO were in Control as well, standing expectantly on the Conn while the Weapons Officer waited in Missile Control Center for the dual orders.

They had left Sierra eight-five behind four hours ago, no closer now to solving its mystery than they were then. The fire control techs had tracked the object until it faded from their sensors, verifying it remained stationary. Entries had been made in the *Kentucky*'s patrol report, and the object's position and sound characteristics would be analyzed upon the submarine's return to port. But now the officers in Control were focused on the *Kentucky*'s current position and subsequent actions required.

Satisfied the ship's location had been correctly plot-ted and the *Kentucky* had exited its moving haven, Tom made the announcement. "Entering Sapphire."

Malone picked up the 1-MC microphone. "Set condition Four-SQ. Initialize all missiles."

The XO picked up the 21-MC, repeating the same order over a separate circuit. Missile Control Center would respond to strategic orders only when identical directives were given by both the ship's Commanding Officer and its Executive Officer. The Weapons Officer acknowledged the order, his voice coming back over the 21-MC speaker. "Set condition Four-SQ. Initialize all missiles, Weapons aye."

Throughout the Missile Compartment, teams of missile techs completed the steps required to bring the missiles online, making them ready for launch at a moment's notice. The Weapons Officer monitored the progress from Missile Control Center, watching as the Missile Ready indicator lights on the Launch Control Panel turned from red to green.

After issuing their duplicate orders, Malone and the XO joined Tom and the Nav at the Quartermaster's stand. Drawn on the chart were the Sapphire and Emerald operating areas, each represented by a large rectangular box covering more than a million square miles. On top of the navigation chart, the Nav placed an overlay showing the known ocean fronts and eddies. A second overlay, laid on top of the first, contained the ship's projected track to Emerald, which hugged the outline of the features drawn on the overlay underneath.

Malone scrutinized the track the Navigator had laid out, verifying the most appropriate path to Emerald had been chosen, then signed the chart, followed by the XO.

As the XO finished reviewing the chart, the Weps approached. "Sir, all missiles have been initialized and condition Four-SQ is set. With the current target package assigned, we will be in launch range when we reach Emerald."

Everyone turned back to the chart, with the ship's projected track marked and labeled every six hours. The Nav answered the question in everyone's mind.

"Four more days."

4 DAYS REMAINING

6 DAYS REMAINING

41

PENTAGON

Forty feet underground in the Pentagon's basement, sheltered from the early afternoon sun glaring down on northern Virginia, Christine accompanied Dave Hendricks along the cool hallway toward his office in the Current Action Center. Christine hadn't seen him since the day the launch order was issued, instead talking with him over their STE phones. But as despicable as Hardison was, he had raised valid concerns about Hendricks, and conversations over the phone could assure her of only so much. Plus, there was something else she wanted to discuss. Hendricks's appearance outside the Command Center after three years apart had provided an unexpected alternative: someone she could confide in and bounce her concerns off of.

After swiping his ID card and punching in the pass code, Dave led Christine into the Current Action Center, turning left toward his office along the top tier. Like the NMCC Operations Center, where nuclear launch orders were issued, the CAC had been relocated to the basement level during the last phase of the Pentagon renovation. The center was constructed using a similar tiered design, with offices along the top rim and workstations lining each of the ten tiers descending to a fifteen-by-thirty-foot electronic display on the far wall. Unlike the Operations Center, which focused only on strategic missile launch, the CAC handled all aspects of the country's defensive and offensive operations around the world.

Hendricks's office was a fifteen-by-twenty-foot room with one wall containing a large window looking over the CAC. An oak desk sat against the far wall on top of moderately plush navy blue carpet, with the top of the desk populated with Hendricks's computer monitor and an assortment of framed pictures to the side. As the door closed behind Christine, the background noise from the CAC disappeared. The room was soundproof, providing more than enough privacy for their conversation.

Christine joined Hendricks in front of the window, examining the monitor on the wall, which displayed a map of Europe and the Middle East, annotated with the current and planned locations of their ballistic missile defenses. Blinking green circles in the Persian Gulf and one in Afghanistan marked the planned positions of the *Aegis*-class cruisers and the THAAD battery. Blue circles tracked their present locations, the Pacific Fleet cruisers inching up from the Indian Ocean while the THAAD battery glowed steadily in Frankfurt, Germany, as the C-17 it was loaded on awaited refueling. Christine decided to let Hendricks brief her on their ballistic missile defense plans first. Her two topics would come later.

"We'll coordinate our missile defense from here," he began. "If we can get to the missiles before they release their warheads, there's a chance we can take several of them out. But once the first few missiles are destroyed, breaking apart into dozens of warhead-size fragments, our surveillance systems will be overwhelmed. Even more challenging is guiding our interceptors to their targets. Each one of the *Kentucky*'s missiles will be traveling at fifteen thousand miles per hour—four miles per second—so even if we're able to ferret the missiles and their warheads from the growing debris field, our antiballistic missiles face the daunting task of intercepting warheads streaking through the atmosphere at twenty times the speed of sound."

As Hendricks explained the challenges they faced, Christine's mind grew numb. She had known the task of destroying the *Kentucky*'s missiles and their warheads was difficult, but only now did she appreciate the futility of the effort. Their only real hope to avoid the destruction of Iran was to prevent the *Kentucky* from launching. And without their fast-attack submarines, the odds of sinking the *Kentucky* had decreased significantly. In light of the overwhelming task Hendricks faced, Christine searched for the appropriate encouragement to offer, finally settling for a few simple words.

"Just do your best, Dave."

"You know I will."

Christine crossed the room, stopping to examine the pictures on Hendricks's desk, looking for a segue into her first topic. She was surprised to find a wedding photograph of her and Hendricks in the mix, a black-and-white picture of them outside the chapel in Clemson,

South Carolina—Dave in a black tux with Christine wearing a Mori Lee drop-waist gown. No such photos existed in her town house; the memories of their marriage had been filed away.

After a moment, Christine turned toward Hendricks and asked the question point-blank. "Can I trust you?" She had meant to say *Can* we *trust you?* but the one word had come out differently.

"In what regard?"

His response instantly grated on her nerves. A man who could be trusted only in certain regards could not be trusted at all.

"Yes," Hendricks added quickly, picking up on her irritation. "You have my word. I will reveal nothing about what happened in the Operations Center or about our attempts to sink the *Kentucky*." He kept his eyes fixed on his ex-wife's, conveying the sincerity of his response.

"Thank you," Christine replied, placing her hand on his arm.

Hendricks's eyes went to her hand, and she saw it in his face; the unexpected physical contact reminding him of the times they'd spent in each other's arms. Christine withdrew her hand, turning back toward the desk and its pictures. She had seen his reaction to her friendly gesture, and even more, she could feel the same response rising within her. But she pushed it away. This was not the time for those types of feelings to resurface.

Christine forced her thoughts quickly onto the second topic; the real reason for her meeting. She turned back to Hendricks. "There's something else I wanted to talk to you about. It's about the launch order. I'm convinced someone else was involved besides Mike Patton."

One of Hendricks's eyebrows rose slightly. "And who would that be?"

"Hardison." There. She'd finally said it.

Hendricks's eyebrow rose even farther. "The chief of staff? You've got to be kidding."

Christine shook her head. "There's no way a simple NMCC watchstander pulled this thing off. He had help from someone high up. I think it's Hardison. He's the one who drafted the directive to load the *Kentucky* with twice as many warheads as the other Trident submarines. Then he whisked it across the president's desk for signature without even mentioning that small detail."

Hendricks was quiet for a moment before responding. "That could easily be coincidence. If you decide to look into this, you'll need to be careful. Your intern was murdered, and if Hardison's involved, he won't hesitate to do it again. Whatever you do, don't confront him directly."

"Don't worry about me. I can take care of myself."

Hendricks frowned. "If you're right about this, you're wrong about being able to take care of yourself. You're going to have to go high order, direct to Larson, and fast. And you better be damn sure about it, because your career in politics will be over if you're wrong."

Christine considered Dave's advice. He was right. If Hardison really was involved, she couldn't pussyfoot around; it was too dangerous. But she also didn't have enough evidence—really, any evidence—to take to the director of the FBI. She would have to pry this issue apart carefully, find the smoking gun that would implicate Hardison without question.

"I suppose you're right. Perhaps the orders were sent

to the *Kentucky* simply because she would be invisible to our fast attacks. Maybe it was just pure coincidence—and bad luck on our part—that launch orders were sent to a submarine with twice as many warheads." Christine looked up at her ex-husband, her eyes steeling with resolve. "But I'm going to find out if Hardison was involved, and if so, he's going to pay for what he's done. And pay dearly."

Hendricks met her gaze. "I just hope it's him that pays, and not you."

As Christine left his office and headed back toward the White House, Hendricks wasn't convinced his ex-wife could take care of herself. The stakes in this plot were high, and those involved wouldn't hesitate to eliminate anyone who cast suspicion in their direction. Chris was impetuous; he knew that firsthand. While she could power her way logically through even the most complex issues, she was a creature ruled by emotion. Emotion she struggled to restrain, but every once in a while she would do or say things against her better judgment. He wondered if she would be able to restrain herself from confronting Hardison directly at some point.

He let out a deep sigh.

Probably not.

42

GARDEN ISLAND, AUSTRALIA

A purple-orange dawn was breaking across the western shore of Australia as a white Holden sedan traveled along a two-lane causeway connecting the mainland to a small one-by-six-mile island. Eight-foot-high waves crashed against the granite rocks protecting the causeway, protesting the man-made intrusion into Cockburn Sound, while the strong western wind carried the salt spray over the top of the granite barrier, dumping moisture onto the road like rain. The thumping of the windshield wipers was the only sound in the sedan as Murray Wilson sat in the backseat, alone with his thoughts as he approached the end of his journey.

It had been a long trip from Pearl Harbor. A C-130J, with its uncomfortable web seats and four loud turboprop engines, was the only aircraft Stanbury had been able to requisition on such short notice. The four-thousand-seven-hundred-mile flight to Amberley Royal Australian Air Force base on the outskirts of Brisbane, with a refueling stop along the way in Pago Pago, felt like it took much longer than thirteen hours. The Australians had done their best to match the American Air Force's hospitality, providing yet another C-130J for the transcontinental flight to Pearce RAAF base north of Perth, where Wilson was met by an Australian seaman leaning against the white sedan on the airport tarmac. After a forty-minute drive toward the shore, the seaman flashed his badge at the security gate guarding the entrance to Fleet Base West.

The road barrier lifted away, allowing entrance to Australia's largest naval base, home to several Royal Australian Navy commands. On the south-east corner of the island, along the shores of Careening Bay, five *Anzac*-class frigates called the island their home. But more important, Garden Island was home to the Australian navy's submarine fleet of six *Collins*-class long-range diesel submarines.

After a right turn at the twin five-inch destroyer gun mount marking the entrance to the waterfront and a right on Baudin Road three blocks later, the sedan pulled to a stop in front of a two-story exposed concrete building. Only two other cars populated the otherwise deserted parking lot in front of the Submarine Force Element Group headquarters. Wilson made no move to exit, and the seaman took advantage of his hesitation, lighting a cigarette as he stood on the curb.

The end of the seaman's cigarette glowed bright red as he took a drag, and the smoke he exhaled was carried away by the cold morning breeze; a breeze similar to the chill wind that had whipped through the *Houston*'s Bridge six days earlier. Wilson had listened to his son's voice over the handheld radio, perhaps for the last

time, as the *Kentucky* headed out to sea. Wilson wondered what he would have said to his son had he known
it might be the last time he spoke to him; that two days
later the entire Pacific Fleet would sortie in an effort to
sink his submarine. He wondered what he would have
said to explain his role; the father doing everything possible to end the life of his only child.

Wilson knew he could still back out. He could omit
the real purpose for his meeting with Commodore Lowe
and instead discuss the upcoming Submarine Command
Course—Australian officers participated in the quarterly
American training exercises, with one of the four events
each year held in Australian waters. He would report
back to Stanbury that Australia had understandably declined to sink an American submarine, and none would
be the wiser. Wilson doubted a follow-up conversation
would ever occur between the two admirals; Stanbury
would never learn the Australians had not been asked.
It would be Wilson's secret.

As at that moment in Stanbury's office, Wilson had
to make a decision. As the seaman finished his cigarette
and flicked it onto the ground, extinguishing the butt
under the heel of his shoe, Wilson realized he had run
out of time. As he stepped out of the sedan and headed
toward the FEG headquarters, Wilson knew he had
fifty feet and one cup of coffee to decide.

After a quick left upon entering the FEG headquarters
and a short walk down the white-tiled hallway, Wilson
entered the one-star admiral's office, an office not unlike Stanbury's seven thousand miles away. It seemed a
standard collection of furniture was procured for every

admiral's office, no matter which navy the officer served: the same mahogany-stained desk; the same dark, lustrous conference table, its polished surface reflecting the bright overhead lights.

"Murray!" Commodore Rick Lowe rose from his chair, walking around his desk to shake the American captain's hand. "Good to see you again. How was your flight?"

Wilson grimaced. "C-130."

"I feel your pain. I once had to fly all the way to Washington on one of them."

Joining Lowe at his conference table, Wilson placed a thin double-locked courier case on the floor, leaning it against the front leg of his chair.

"Can I get you some tea? Coffee?" the commodore asked.

"Coffee would be great, sir. And thanks for coming in early to meet with me."

Lowe hollered, then ordered a cup of coffee after his yeoman popped his head through the doorway. "So what brings you to Australia? And what's so urgent that it can't wait until a more civilized hour? Surely not advance planning for the next Command Course?"

Wilson suddenly realized he wouldn't have the time spent over a cup of coffee to make his decision. He would have to answer the commodore's question, and that answer would determine whether he would subsequently request Australia's assistance. As he prepared to reply, the same arguments that had tumbled through his mind during the long trip south, the uncertainties that had risen again in the back of the sedan resurfaced. But deep down, he knew he had already made his decision. He had understood the personal implications of his assistance when he agreed to Admiral Stanbury's request six days ago. And nothing had really changed.

He reached down and retrieved the courier case, placing it on the table in front of him. After spinning each of the five tumblers to the required number, he pressed both unlock mechanisms, releasing the latches. He pulled out a chart, unfolded it, and laid it on top of the table.

"Do you have any submarines near this location?" Wilson pointed to an area on the chart two thousand miles west of Hawaii.

Lowe studied the chart for a moment. "The *Collins* is nearby. Why?"

Wilson pulled an orange folder from the case, placing it onto the chart.

"Commodore, there's something extremely sensitive we need to discuss."

An hour later, Wilson stood alone in the Australian video conference room as the image of Admiral Stanbury flickered over the secure link to Hawaii. "Australia does have a submarine near the *Kentucky*, the *Collins,* and they've agreed to send her orders to sink the *Kentucky.*"

"That's good news, Murray." Stanbury's voice warbled through the static.

"But they'll send the orders on one condition," Wilson added.

"What's that?"

"They insist the orders be delivered personally by a U.S. Navy captain or admiral, and that he remain on board for the duration of the mission. Under no circumstances will an Australian submarine fire on an

American submarine without a more senior U.S. officer aboard."

Stanbury's image froze on the screen for a second before the video connection resynced. "That's understandable. We'd probably want the same."

"Who do you want on the *Collins*?" Wilson asked the question, even though he already knew the answer. The two of them were the only officers in SUBPAC who knew the details of the *Collins*'s new mission. One of them would have to board the Australian submarine.

"I realize this will be hard, Murray. But I need you on the *Collins*. Will you board her?"

Until this moment, Wilson had hidden behind the belief that he was merely the chess master who moved the pieces into position. The entire fleet had been mobilized in the search for the *Kentucky*, and he was only remotely involved, providing direction behind the scenes. Someone else would do the actual killing, launching the torpedo that would sink his son's submarine. Now he would have to take an active role. And if they found the *Kentucky*, he would have to give the order to the *Collins*'s commanding officer that would send his son to his watery grave. He would be directly responsible for his child's death.

But perhaps it was meant to be to this way.

The father sacrificing the son.

Like Abraham, commanded by God to slay Isaac on Mount Moriah, Wilson had been requested to sacrifice his child. But as Abraham lifted the knife to murder his son, an angel of God appeared, revealing a ram caught in a nearby thicket, instructing the father to sacrifice the animal instead. As Wilson stared at the flickering image of Admiral Stanbury, he wondered whether, like Isaac, there would be a last-minute reprieve for his son.

He decided he would be there to find out.

"Yes, Admiral. I'll board the *Collins*."

43

HMAS *COLLINS*

Just east of the Mariana Islands, Commander Brett Humphreys peered through the *Collins*'s Search Periscope, observing the four inbound trawlers approaching the submerged submarine. Although the contact density this afternoon was heavy, it was thin compared to the morning, when the entire Marianas' fishing fleet, it seemed, had put out to sea at the same time in a mad dash. Laden with the fruit of their harvest, they were returning in a much more civilized and staggered manner. Satisfied that none of the trawlers was a collision threat, Humphreys returned control of the periscope to his Officer of the Watch, who pressed his face to the eyepiece as Humphreys stepped back.

The *Collins* had been on patrol almost five months now, loitering in the western Philippine Sea for the last month before continuing her circular route from Perth back to the east coast of Australia. They would pass through the Bismarck Archipelago and into the Coral Sea, then follow the eastern shore of the continent on their journey south. After a port call in Brisbane followed by a week in Sydney, the diesel submarine would begin her scheduled full-docking cycle in the Australian Shipbuilding Corporation shipyard in Adelaide, where she would receive long-overdue maintenance and significant upgrades to her tactical systems.

Delivered in 1996, the *Collins* still had her original combat control suite, and her Torpedo Room was loaded with old MK 48 Mod 4 analog torpedoes, procured from the Americans in the 1980s. But that would change after the *Collins* returned from deployment, when she would be upgraded to the new American BYG-1 Combat Control System and MK 48 Mod 7 ADCAP torpedoes. In the meantime, the crew would compensate with their experience.

Humphreys stayed in control for a moment, surveying his seasoned crew. After five months at sea, the *Collins,* fully manned at fifty-eight hands, was a model of efficiency, the crew quietly relaying reports and orders between stations. Even the early morning foray of fishing trawlers, over twenty of them within 4,000 meters at one point, had not frayed the crew's nerves, the Officer of the Watch expertly guiding the submarine through congested waters. The contact density on the remainder of their journey would be sparse until they approached Sydney, where Jodi would meet him. After five months at sea, the thought of his beautiful wife waiting on the pier was a compelling image, one that was quickly dispelled by the ship's Communicator, stopping next to him.

"Message from the Submarine FEG, Captain."

Humphreys read the message, surprised at the sudden

change in orders and lack of details. The *Collins* had been directed to modify its patrol and head east, into the open ocean. Follow-on orders would be hand-delivered after a personnel transfer at specified coordinates. But the end of the message made clear the routine monotony of their long deployment had come to an end. Typed in capital letters, the last sentence read:

PREPARE FOR WAR PATROL

Humphreys turned to his Officer of the Watch. "Prepare to Snort, three diesels. Charge all batteries."

44

JERUSALEM, ISRAEL

Levi Rosenfeld entered the Prime Minister's Office building at 9 A.M., returning from the Mossad's headquarters in Herzliya, a suburb north of Tel Aviv. Still unaware of the details of the Mossad's operation, Rosenfeld had been briefed on the basic plan and the American response—the United States was assembling its surface and naval air forces in the Pacific, forming a barrier through which the *Kentucky* must pass. The Mossad had somehow neutralized the most potent arm of the American Pacific Fleet, and its submarines were no longer a factor. But there was still a slim chance the Pacific Fleet would find the *Kentucky*. Rosenfeld had been alarmed there was the potential their plan could fail, surprised after Kogen's assurance there was nothing the Americans could do. But considering what the Mossad had accomplished thus far and the high probability of success, he let it go.

As Rosenfeld entered his office, he was greeted by Hirshel Mekel, his executive assistant, who rattled off the remainder of the prime minister's itinerary for the day. Rosenfeld nodded absently as he sat behind his desk, his thoughts still dwelling on the morning's meeting, until his attention snapped back to the man standing in front of him.

"Here's the latest report," Mekel repeated, handing the manila folder to Rosenfeld.

Rosenfeld flipped through the thick investigation of the suicide bombing that had taken his daughters' lives, stopping at the section that identified the organizations responsible. Kogen had informed him Hamas was to blame, but Rosenfeld was determined to ensure every group that contributed to his children's death, no matter how limited its role, would feel the full wrath of Israel's response. Rosenfeld found and read the section he was looking for, then flipped forward and backward through the thick investigation.

"This report is incomplete. Kogen informed me Hamas sponsored the suicide bomber, but this report says it's still undetermined."

"This is the latest version, Levi," Mekel replied. "The draft was completed just hours ago, and I obtained an unofficial copy before it was submitted. I knew you'd want an update as soon as possible."

Rosenfeld opened his desk drawer, pulling out an identical manila folder containing an earlier version of the report, approved by the Israeli intelligence minister. "This version clearly identifies the suicide bomber as a member of the Izz ad-Din al-Qassam Brigades and traces their funding and weapons back to Iran's Revolutionary Guard. How is it that a later version is inconclusive on this issue?"

Mekel shrugged. "I assure you this draft is the most up-to-date version. Hiring a former Mossad staffer as your executive assistant has its advantages."

Rosenfeld studied the cover letter of the earlier version, then closed the folder, looking up at Mekel. "How closely connected are you with your former Mossad friends?"

"I'm still very well connected, sir. What do you have in mind?"

3 DAYS REMAINING

45

WESTERN PACIFIC OCEAN

A hazy, gray dawn clung to the horizon as a helicopter beat a steady path north across the vast emptiness of the Pacific Ocean. Inside the Sikorsky S-70B Seahawk, Murray Wilson stared out the passenger-side window, his eyes fixed on the dark ocean several hundred feet below. A stiff wind blew the cresting waves eastward, painting the watery blue canvas with thousands of frothy white specks. Not far above, a heavy blanket of steel-gray, moisture-laden clouds threatened to open up at any minute.

The weather had steadily deteriorated as Wilson traveled north toward his rendezvous with the HMAS *Collins*. Eighteen hours earlier, he had boarded the C-130J, still waiting at Pierce RAAF base, for a trip across the Australian continent to the northern tropical port of Darwin, where he transferred onto the Seahawk antisubmarine helicopter, its normal payload of three torpedoes replaced with long-range external fuel tanks. After refueling stops aboard the *Anzac*-class frigate

HMAS *Stuart* and *Adelaide*-class frigate HMAS *Newcastle*, the helicopter was approaching the predetermined rendezvous point, a random spot in the Pacific Ocean.

A change in the beat of the helicopter's rotors and the feeling of his seat falling out from under him announced the helicopter's descent. A glance at the navigation display across from the pilot verified they had reached their destination. As Wilson peered through the window, searching the ocean below for the silhouette of a black submarine against the dark blue water, the stiff westerly wind buffeted the small helicopter plummeting from the sky. It was going to be one hell of a personnel transfer.

Eight hundred feet below, Commander Brett Humphreys stood in the *Collins*'s Bridge, scouring the dark gray sky for a sign of his friend's arrival. The message from the Submarine FEG had not been specific, informing him only that a U.S. naval officer would transfer aboard with more detailed orders. However, a crew manifest change had been received a few hours later over the submarine broadcast, identifying the American officer as Captain Murray Wilson.

Three years earlier, Humphreys had been assigned as the Australian foreign exchange officer on COMSUBPAC staff, and he and Jodi had become close friends with Murray and Claire. Following his two-year tour, Humphreys returned home, taking command of the *Collins*. As he stared into the overcast skies, he wondered if Murray had finagled a boondoggle to see his good friend, but that didn't jibe with the order to prepare for war patrol. Something was afoot.

Humphreys heard the faint roar of the Seahawk before he saw it. It took awhile for the gray helicopter to appear out of the haze as it descended, slowing to a hover fifty feet above the stationary submarine. The rhythmic beat of the helicopter blades pulsed in Humphreys's ears, the downdraft rippling across the turbulent ocean surface in a circular pattern. As he waited for the two crewmen in the Seahawk cabin to lower their human cargo, a light rain began falling, and Humphreys pulled the hood of his foul-weather jacket over his head.

A moment later, the helicopter crew began lowering a man similarly dressed in foul-weather gear. The man swung from side to side in the strong wind, the gusts buffeting him as he descended. A small duffel bag hung from a lanyard attached to the cable, swaying in the wind a few feet below him. The Lookout grabbed it as it swung by and fed it to Humphreys, who pulled hard on the lanyard, guiding the man into the Bridge.

"Welcome aboard, Murray!" Humphreys shouted over the roar of the helicopter's rotor as Wilson's feet hit the deck.

"Good to see you again!" Wilson shook Humphrey's hand.

Humphreys helped Wilson out of his harness and unhooked the duffel bag, then signaled the helicopter to retrieve its cable. The helicopter pulled up and away from the submarine, its cable swaying in the wind as it turned and headed south for its return trip home.

Wilson watched the helicopter disappear into the dark clouds, then followed Humphreys down the ladder into Control, where the Officer of the Watch turned slowly on the periscope.

"Rig the Bridge for Dive," Humphreys ordered. "Pipe Diving Stations."

The Officer of the Watch acknowledged, and the order to man diving stations reverberated throughout the submarine a moment later. A junior officer waiting nearby ascended into the Bridge to close the clamshells on top of the sail and secure the Bridge hatches.

"Come," Humphreys said. "It looks like we've got a few things to discuss."

As Wilson followed Humphreys down the center passageway of the Forward Compartment toward his friend's stateroom, he realized there were two things about Australian submarines he was unfamiliar with. The first was the configuration of Control with its two periscopes—one designated the Search scope and the other the Attack scope—arranged in a fore-aft alignment rather than side by side like on American submarines. There was no separate Sonar Room, with the sonar consoles lining the starboard bulkhead next to the combat control consoles, further cramping a Control Room that was barely half the size of those on U.S. attack submarines. The *Collins* also had six bow-mounted torpedo tubes instead of the four carried by most U.S. submarines, the only exception being the three *Seawolf*-class with their eight tubes.

The second unfamiliar aspect of Australian submarines had just brushed past him in the narrow passageway; Chief Marine Technician Kimberly Durand had squeezed past Wilson on her way to the Weapon Stowage Compartment. The American Submarine Force had resisted change longer than the rest of the Navy, remaining the last bastion of an all-male service. Although those walls had come crumbling down in 2011 with the admittance of the first dozen female officers, Wilson and the vast majority of American submarine crews had never served with women at sea. The Australian men didn't appear to notice how close their bodies came as they passed by women in the narrow passageways.

Wilson followed Humphreys into his stateroom, the quarters barely large enough for the two of them to sit. After shutting and locking his stateroom door, Humphreys turned to his American friend. "So what's this all about?"

Unzipping his duffel bag, Wilson pulled out a sealed white envelope with Humphreys's name written on the front in Commodore Lowe's handwriting. Humphreys opened the envelope and retrieved a single-page directive. He read the letter, his eyes scanning from side to side, his eyes suddenly shooting up toward Murray. "You're not serious?"

Wilson nodded. "We are."

Humphreys read his instructions again. He looked up, slowly this time, the target's familiar name registering in his eyes. "Which crew has the submarine?"

Wilson didn't answer. He couldn't at the moment. The words wouldn't have come out, no matter how hard he tried.

46

KANEOHE BAY, HAWAII

Nestled against Oahu's windward shore, protected from ocean swells by a barrier reef, lie the sheltered waters of Kaneohe Bay, offering perfect conditions for the growth of over forty patch and fringe reefs. Best seen from a high vantage point such as the Pali Lookout, the bay's varying depths and bottom formations offer shimmering hues of ivory, teal, aquamarine, and violet. Inland of the scenic bay is the tranquil community of Kaneohe, just recently connected to the southern metropolitan cities by H-3, the intrastate highway that took thirty years to construct, its tunnels passing through the volcanic mountain ridges of the Koolau Range. North of the small community, occupying the entire three-thousand-acre Mokapu Peninsula, is Marine Corps Base, Hawaii—home to one of the U.S. Navy's four Wings of P-3C antisubmarine patrol aircraft.

Four days earlier, the country's three other P-3C wings had descended from the skies, joining Wing Two as the nation's seventeen squadrons of P-3C antisubmarine aircraft converged on the Hawaiian island. This morning, at the edge of the base's mile-and-a-half-long runway, Lieutenant Commander Scott Graef led his tactical team of four enlisted and one junior officer out of the Ready Room onto the white concrete tarmac. It wasn't yet noon but it was already unusually hot for the northeast shore, as the normally reliable trade winds were absent. The heat shimmered off the runway as load crews readied the P-3Cs that had just returned from on station, refueling them and loading another contingent of sonobuoys.

One of the P-3Cs being readied was the one Graef had arrived on four days ago with the first of the VP-16 War Eagles aircraft from Jacksonville, Florida. It had taken an additional three days for the rest of his squadron to straggle in, and two aircraft had not arrived, breaking down along the way. As Graef stopped and scanned the busy Marine Corps base for the P-3C assigned to today's mission, he shook his head at the state of the U.S. Navy's antisubmarine patrol aircraft.

Thirty percent of VP-16's aircraft were down hard, the maintenance crews unable to repair the fifty-plus-year-old aircraft. The replacement for the Orions, the P-8A Poseidon aircraft, had been delayed for over a decade by budget wranglers at the Pentagon, and the P-3Cs could barely support the mission they were assigned. Every American P-3C squadron throughout the world had converged on Kaneohe Bay in an effort to establish an antisubmarine barrier stretching hundreds of miles across the Pacific, and they were all in similar shape, their patched aircraft needing additional repairs as soon as they arrived.

An operable P-3C taxied to the runway in front of

Graef, the next aircraft in the wheel of continuous rotation required to maintain the antisubmarine barrier. For every aircraft on patrol over its assigned station, two more were needed, one on its way out to relieve and another on its way back for refueling and a replacement crew. Luckily, the Wings had ample crews due to the number of down aircraft.

The supply of torpedoes was another matter. The bunkers at all twenty-three storage locations worldwide were empty, and the P-3C taking off was loaded out at 50 percent. Between the waterfronts on the Pacific and the P-3C squadrons converging on Hawaii, there simply weren't enough torpedoes to go around.

The only good news was that Hawaii had just received a shipment of the Navy's newest lightweight torpedo, the MK 54 MAKO Hybrid, equipped with a state-of-the-art guidance control section and new, sophisticated search algorithms. The decision had been made to spread the new MK 54s throughout the P-3Cs rather than concentrate them on a few aircraft, since there was no telling which crew would detect the enemy submarine. Each aircraft would have one of the MK 54 torpedoes aboard, giving them one shot at their target with the Navy's most capable lightweight torpedo.

As the P-3C took off and a second Orion landed just seconds later, Lieutenant Pete Burwell, Graef's Communicator, stopped beside him, shouting over the distinctive whirr of the P-3C propeller blades churning the air. "Sir, 203 is down hard. We've been reassigned to 305."

Graef shook his head in disgust.

47

USS *KENTUCKY*

Even though the day was ending in the world above, the sun descending toward the horizon, the *Kentucky*'s cooks had just finished serving breakfast. The submarine remained on Greenwich mean time, and Section 3 had just assumed the morning watch, beginning another artificial day aboard the ballistic missile submarine.

Course 260. Speed 10. Depth 400.

Lieutenant Tom Wilson leaned against the Quartermaster's stand, reviewing the entry into his log at the top of the hour, mentally noting the *Kentucky* had passed the halfway mark on its four-day transit through Sapphire. Since they'd left Sierra eight-five behind two days earlier, it had been quiet, the *Kentucky* gaining only an occasional merchant who strayed from the shipping lanes. But Tom had been surprised when he stopped in Sonar during his prewatch tour; the spherical and towed array displays were lit up like Christmas trees.

There were so many contacts to the west that Sonar couldn't even begin to sort through them all, the contacts blending together into one large, amorphous blob, forming what looked like a single contact with a bearing spread of ninety degrees, growing slowly wider as the *Kentucky* approached. The first contact had appeared eight hours ago, its faint white trace materializing on the towed array. But now there were dozens of tracks, burning in brightly with clean, distinct tonals on the narrowband displays.

The contacts were warships.

Whose they were and what they were doing hadn't yet been determined. Sonar was working on it and finally got a break as Tom stepped back on the Conn.

"Conn, Sonar. Active pings to the west. Classifying now." A moment later, Sonar followed up. "We've got multiple SQS-53 and SQS-56 sonars out there. They're ours, sir. *Aegis*-class destroyers and *Perry*-class frigates. Ping-steal range, thirty thousand yards."

Malone arrived in Control a moment later; he'd obviously been listening to the 27-MC over the monitor in his stateroom. After examining the sonar display on the Conn, he turned to his Officer of the Deck. "What do you think?"

"Could be some sort of training exercise," Tom replied. "We haven't received any changes to our waterspace assignments—we own the water. They can't possibly be prosecuting a submarine, because if they are, they could end up attacking us."

Malone stepped off the Conn and stopped by the navigation chart, Tom joining him at his side. At thirty thousand yards, with a ninety-degree-wide swath, the contacts blocked their approach to Emerald. The two officers studied their predicament until Tom finally broke the silence.

"There's no way to go around them, Captain. We don't own the water north or south of Sapphire and Emerald, and even if we did, it would take us several days to go around. Looks like we're going to have to go through them, sir."

"I don't see any other choice," Malone agreed. "Rig ship for Ultra Quiet."

48

EAGLE ZERO-FIVE
USS *KENTUCKY*

EAGLE ZERO-FIVE

The submarine hunter aircraft, call sign Eagle Zero-Five, circled above its station in the Pacific Ocean, into the final hour of its watch. Lieutenant Commander Scott Graef, seated in the forward port section of the cabin, took a break from monitoring his display and peered out the window next to him. To the north, he thought he could see another of the P-3Cs forming a line stretching hundreds of miles across the ocean. The entire Pacific Surface Fleet, it seemed, formed a similar line fifteen miles to the west. Graef, Eagle Zero-Five's Tactical Coordinator, or TACCO, was in charge of the personnel in the cabin of the P-3C, supervising efforts to locate the submarine expected to transit through their barrier anytime now.

Returning his attention to his duties, Graef pressed his hands to his headphones, listening closely to the reports being transmitted over the aircraft's Internal Communication System by the rest of his watch section. Two enlisted watchstanders, designated Sensor One and Sensor Two, monitored the acoustic sensor screens on the consoles further aft in the P-3C, reviewing the data from the sonobuoy field floating in the ocean below. Sensor Three scanned the aircraft's periscope detection radar and its Magnetic Anomaly Detection displays, the latter searching for the magnetic field created by a submarine's metal hull as it traveled beneath the waves. He also monitored the P-3C's infrared camera as it swept the ocean surface, searching for the hot exhaust from a snorkel mast, in case the submarine was running its diesel generator. Lieutenant Pete Burwell, the crew's Communicator and the only other officer in the cabin, sat at the NavCom station across from Graef.

They had been on station almost eight hours now, searching for a sign of the target submarine. Graef began to resign himself to another watch without a sniff of the enemy submarine when one of the three pilots transmitted over ICS, his voice emanating from Graef's earphones. "TACCO, Flight. Are you penguins ready for a ride home?"

Graef unconsciously glanced at the patch above his left breast pocket. The operators in the back of the P-3C all wore warfare insignias on their uniforms, an emblem bearing wings. But instead of flying the P-3Cs, they operated the sophisticated sonar and fire control equipment essential to their mission. They had wings, but couldn't fly.

Just like penguins.

A P-3C pilot had coined the term for the backseat operators decades ago, and the name stuck. In return, the penguins developed a nickname for their fellow pilots who flew them back and forth from their stations. Compared to other Navy pilots, who flew hazardous missions engaging air and surface targets, the P-3C pilots were barely more than bus drivers. A monkey could do their job.

Graef pressed the foot pedal under his workstation, activating the comm circuit. "Flight, TACCO. You monkeys run out of bananas?"

"Something like that," the pilot replied. "Running low on gas. Approaching Go Home Fuel. Tiger One-Eight is inbound high to relieve us. Prepare to turn over the buoy field."

Lieutenant Burwell, monitoring the conversation between the TACCO and the pilot, gave Graef a thumbs-up, then held up his index finger on one hand, and all five fingers on the other.

"We're already on it," Graef replied. "We'll be ready to swap in fifteen minutes."

To the south, one of the VP-8 Tiger crews, flying a P-3C with its tail number ending in eighteen, was inbound high and would arrive above Eagle Zero-Five, the two aircraft circling as they completed turnover of the sonobuoy field. As Lieutenant Burwell prepared to send the frequencies of their sonobuoys to his counterpart on Tiger One-Eight, Graef's thoughts and eyes drifted down to one of the torpedoes in the P-3C's bomb bay, visible through the forward view port in the aircraft's deck.

The MK 54 torpedo was almost a foot longer than

the other torpedoes the aircraft carried, its extended guidance and control section packed with advanced new algorithms and microprocessors ten thousand times more powerful than the 1980s vintage MK 46 torpedo it was replacing. Once the MK 54 entered the water, it would energize the sonar in its nose and begin its search, and Graef knew that if they dropped their new weapon close enough, their target would not get away. But only if they detected their target in the first place. As Graef wondered if any of the P-3Cs would locate the submarine, one of the Sensor Operators broke onto the comm circuit.

"TACCO, Sensor Two. Have a contact, buoy three-four, bearing zero-nine-seven, up Doppler. Contact is approaching Distro Field from the east, classified POSSUB high. Request box sonobuoy pattern built off buoy three-four."

Sensor Two had detected a contact with a high probability it was a submarine, approaching buoy 34 on a bearing of 097. But the sonobuoys in the Distributed Field were spaced so far apart that they held the contact on only one buoy, so they needed to drop a more closely spaced sonobuoy field near buoy 34 to determine the contact's position, course, and speed. Graef turned his attention to his display, noting the estimated locations of the sonobuoys they had dropped in the widely spaced Distributed Field four hours ago. Unfortunately, the buoys below were no longer where they'd been dropped, floating on the surface of the water, drifting in the ocean currents. They needed to know exactly where buoy 34 was now, so they could lay the box sonobuoy field around it.

"Flight, TACCO. Request mark on top, buoy three-four."

The Flight Engineer, sitting between the Patrol Plane Commander and the co-pilot, acknowledged Graef's request, then dialed up channel 34 on the RF receiver. The needle on the direction finder in front of the Patrol Plane Commander pegged to the right, medium signal strength. The PPC twisted the yoke in the direction of the needle, banking Eagle Zero-Five to starboard, continuing the turn until the needle steadied straight up. The signal strength increased gradually as the P-3C sped toward buoy 34 below them.

"TACCO, Flight. Stand by to mark."

The PPC monitored the buoy's signal strength, waiting for the power to peak and then fall off, indicating the aircraft had just flown directly over the buoy.

"Now, now, NOW!" the PPC called out as the signal strength peaked.

Graef logged the buoy location into the tactical system, then waited as the contact algorithms recalculated the target's bearing using buoy 34's updated position. Meanwhile, Lieutenant Burwell quickly calculated the required positions of the new buoys in the box pattern built off buoy 34.

"TACCO, NavCom. All expendable drop points calculated."

After reviewing the coordinates for the new buoy field, Graef sent the coordinates to the cockpit. "Flight, TACCO. Here's your expendable points."

A moment later, the PPC replied, "TACCO, Flight. Coming left to Expendable One."

Eagle Zero-Five turned to the north and decreased

in altitude as the crew prepared to drop their closely spaced field of sonobuoys. One by one, the buoys left the P-3C, splashing into the ocean below.

USS *KENTUCKY*

"Conn, Sonar! Close aboard splashes, port and starboard sides! Flyover, south to north!"

Tom acknowledged Sonar's report, then punched up the Captain's stateroom on the 27-MC, requesting his presence on the Conn.

Malone arrived in Control seconds later. "What have you got?"

"Flyover with close aboard splashes. Looks like a sonobuoy field is being laid around us. First pass on a south-north axis."

Another announcement over the 27-MC interrupted Tom's report. "Conn, Sonar. Second flyby. Another series of splashes just ahead."

"Man Battle Stations Torpedo," Malone ordered. "This is the Captain. I have the Conn."

Tom passed the order to man Battle Stations on the 1-MC, followed by another order to Sonar. "Send triangulation ranges from the spherical and towed arrays to combat control."

Although the *Kentucky*'s sonar systems could normally determine only a target's bearing, if the contacts were extremely close, such as the buoys being dropped around them, their range could be estimated by triangulating the bearings from the spherical and towed array sonars. As Malone and Tom peered over the fire control technician's shoulder, the buoys began appearing on the geographic display. Two rows formed, each with four sonobuoys, both rows almost perpendicular to the *Kentucky*'s course. They were passing through the first row now, two buoys to starboard and two buoys to port, with the second row of buoys two thousand yards ahead.

"Conn, Sonar. Third row of buoys being dropped."

A third row of contacts appeared on the screen, beyond the first two rows. The *Kentucky* was passing right through the sonobuoy field, and the only thing they could do until they exited was maximize their distance from each buoy, splitting the distance equally between them.

"Helm, come right to course two-nine-zero," Malone ordered. "Ahead one-third."

The *Kentucky* turned slightly right, threading its way between the second row of sonobuoys, slowing to reduce the signature from its main engines and propeller.

In Control, the XO and another twenty men hurriedly donned their sound-powered phone headsets, energizing the dormant combat control consoles and plot displays. Battle Stations Torpedo brought the ship to a combat footing as the crew prepared to fight and defend itself. But against an aircraft dropping sonobuoys, there was nothing to attack. Their sole aim now was to protect themselves if the aircraft dropped a torpedo, speeding away from the splash point as rapidly as possible while they attempted to fool the torpedo with decoys. But if one was dropped close enough and detected the *Kentucky* before they could launch countermeasures, the torpedo would home to detonation, blasting a hole through the submarine's pressure hull.

Thankfully, Tom thought to himself, there was nothing to worry about. There were very few countries with antisubmarine aircraft, and only one country that could operate this far into the open ocean. The aircraft was obviously a United States P-3C.

The *Kentucky* was safe.

EAGLE ZERO-FIVE

"Target confirmed. Submerged contact."

Graef acknowledged Sensor Two's report, then adjusted the GEN track on his screen so it agreed with the data from the two buoys that held the contact. A submarine in the middle of a buoy field this tightly packed would normally have been held on at least four buoys, but this submarine was a quiet one indeed, held on only two. They'd been lucky to pick up the submarine in the first place on the widely spaced Distro Field, the submarine traveling almost directly under buoy 34 as it floated on the surface of the water, listening silently above. Now that they held the contact, the next step was to determine the target's solution.

The contact parameters on the screen in front of Graef turned from amber to green, indicating the automated algorithms agreed with the TACCO's solution for the target's course, speed, and position. Graef pressed Accept Solution on his console, then activated his comm circuit. "All stations, TACCO. Set Battle Condition One."

Each member of the crew, from the pilots to the Sensor Operators, pulled out their weapon release checklists, methodically accomplishing each step.

"Flight, TACCO," Graef spoke into his headset. "We are Weapons Red and Free."

Graef continued his calculations, determining the Splash Point for their torpedo, placing it in an optimum position to detect the submarine once the torpedo entered the water and began its search. After identifying the Splash Point, he calculated the Release Point where the P-3C would drop the torpedo from its bomb bay, so the torpedo's ballistic trajectory as it fell toward the water resulted in an impact at the Splash Point. That took only a few seconds.

"Flight, TACCO. Inputting Fly-To coordinates."

Eagle Zero-Five tilted to starboard, and Graef felt his stomach in his throat as the P-3C dove downward, descending to launch altitude. The pilot's voice crackled in Graef's ears a moment later. "TACCO, Flight. Inbound to Fly-To Point."

"Flight, TACCO. Give me bomb bay open, Master Arm On."

The aircraft shuddered as the bomb bay doors swung slowly open, clearing the way for the release of one of its lightweight torpedoes. Graef selected Bay One, containing Eagle Zero-Five's only MK 54. He held his hand over the Storage Release button located on the upper portion of his console, watching the aircraft's icon on his display slowly approach the Weapon Release Point.

An amber light illuminated on Graef's console.

"Flight, TACCO. I have a Kill Ready light. Stand by for weapon release."

"TACCO, Flight. Standing by."

Graef had pressed Storage Release dozens of times before. But they had all been training missions, dropping exercise torpedoes that circled around friendly submarines, not a warshot torpedo that would sink the target below them, killing everyone aboard. As his fingers rested on the cold metal switch, he imagined what it would be like on board the submarine in a few minutes when the torpedo detonated and the unforgiving ocean flooded in, dragging the ship and its crew to the bottom. Fortunately, Graef didn't have time to dwell on his thoughts, as Eagle Zero-Five approached within one hundred yards of the Release Point, just seconds away.

"Flight, TACCO. Weapon away—now, now, NOW!"

Graef pressed the Storage Release button for Bay One, and watched the MK 54 torpedo disappear from the bomb bay window.

USS *KENTUCKY*

Beneath the P-3C as it sped overhead, the *Kentucky* continued to the west at ahead one-third as the last watch station reported in; the ship was at Battle Stations Torpedo. Tom had just been relieved as Officer of the Deck and was headed to the Forward Damage Control Party in Crew's Mess when Sonar's report came over the 27-MC.

"Conn, Sonar. Additional splash, bearing two-one-zero." But before Malone could acknowledge, Sonar announced, "Torpedo in the water! Bearing two-one-zero!"

"Ahead flank!" Malone yelled. "Helm, right full rudder, steady course three-zero-zero!"

The Helm swung the rudder yoke to right full and twisted the Engine Order Telegraph to ahead flank. The *Kentucky*'s powerful main engines sprang to life, churning the ship's propeller rapidly through the water, accelerating the *Kentucky* toward its new course. But an eighteen-thousand-ton submarine did not accelerate rapidly.

"Launch countermeasure!" Malone ordered.

A torpedo decoy was launched from the ship, which began transmitting sonar pulses that matched the sonar returns bouncing off the *Kentucky*'s hull.

"Conn, Sonar. The torpedo is in a circular search pattern on the port beam."

"What type of torpedo is it?" Malone asked.

"Still analyzing, sir." A few seconds later, Sonar added, "It's a Mark 54!"

Malone pounded his fist on top of the Fusion Plot. "Those idiots!"

The *Kentucky* had been attacked by its own navy. And they hadn't dropped just any torpedo. Malone had participated in the operational testing of the MK 54 and knew firsthand how capable it was. The MK 54 was the most sophisticated lightweight torpedo in the world. If it was dropped close enough to the submarine, it'd find it, and no type or amount of countermeasures could fool it.

It also couldn't be outrun unless it was dropped at maximum range and the submarine was already at high speed. But the *Kentucky* was just now approaching twenty knots, and the MK 54 was finishing its first search pattern. Malone checked the range estimate to the torpedo being generated by combat control.

Six hundred yards.

The *Kentucky* didn't have a chance.

Seemingly in response to his thoughts, Sonar reported, "Torpedo has turned toward. Approaching on intercept course."

The MK 54 had detected the *Kentucky* and had already completed a rough calculation of the submarine's course and speed. It was now heading toward them—but not directly. It was aiming ahead, for a point the submarine and torpedo would arrive at simultaneously.

"Torpedo is range gating! Torpedo's homing!"

The torpedo's classification algorithms had completed their cross-checks, determining for certain the target it was pursuing was in fact a submarine and not a decoy. It now increased the rate of its sonar pings in an effort to more accurately determine the range to its target, so that an updated intercept course could be calculated.

"One minute to impact!" Sonar reported.

Malone searched for a way out of their predicament. The *Kentucky* was approaching ahead flank now in a futile attempt to outrun the speedy torpedo, capable of forty-plus knots. Malone knew the MK 54 had no weakness.

Except, maybe . . .

"All back emergency!" Malone yelled. "Dive, make your depth seven hundred feet!"

As the Helm ordered up the new bell, the Throttleman in Maneuvering spun the ahead throttles shut and whipped open the astern throttles. Malone felt tremors through the ship's deck as steam was channeled into the main engines in the opposite direction from which the turbine was spinning, placing incredible strain on the turbine blades, quickly decelerating the ship's propeller. The screw finally stopped spinning forward, then began swirling through the water in reverse, gradually slowing the *Kentucky*.

"What are you doing!" the XO asked.

"We're stopping."

"Is the 54 susceptible to low Doppler?" The XO knew most torpedoes were better at detecting faster targets than slower ones, just as the human eye is drawn to moving objects. He assumed the MK 54 was susceptible to this phenomenon, and that Malone had ordered back emergency in an attempt to stop the ship, hoping the torpedo would lose track of the *Kentucky*. But Malone knew that slowing the ship wouldn't cause it to lose track.

As torpedoes went, the MK 54 Lightweight Torpedo had no weakness.

Except . . .

It was a *lightweight* torpedo.

"Forty-five seconds to impact!"

The thirteen-inch-diameter lightweight torpedoes carried by surface ships, helicopters, and P-3C aircraft were much smaller than the heavyweight torpedoes carried by submarines. With a warhead only one-sixth the size of a heavyweight, the lightweight torpedo would inflict much less damage. It could blow the propeller to pieces if it detonated at the stern of the submarine, and punch a hole through the ship's pressure hull.

But the upper half of the *Kentucky*'s Missile Compartment was covered in a superstructure, or second exterior hull. The missile tubes were taller than the width of the submarine, and the top of the tubes protruded above the pressure hull. For hydrodynamic purposes, a second, nonpressure hull, called the superstructure, was welded from the sides of the submarine over the top of the tubes to create a smooth outer shell.

"Thirty seconds to impact!"

The *Kentucky* wasn't going to fool or outrun the MK 54 torpedo. Their only hope was to control where it hit. Malone had to keep it away from the Engine Room if they had any hope of surviving. Continuing to evade at ahead flank would generate a tail-chase geometry with the torpedo closing from astern, exactly what Malone wanted to avoid. He wanted the torpedo to hit the submarine in the Missile Compartment, so he'd ordered back emergency, slowing the ship and forcing the torpedo to adjust course and close from a beam trajectory.

"Twenty seconds to impact!"

But not only did Malone want the torpedo to hit the Missile Compartment, he wanted the torpedo to hit the submarine where it had a superstructure, in effect a double hull. So he ordered the submarine deeper, forcing the torpedo to close the *Kentucky* from above. Hopefully, the ship's superstructure would absorb enough of the explosion to prevent the torpedo from breaching the pressure hull. If he failed, and the torpedo blasted a hole into the ship, the *Kentucky* would sink. Even with only one of its compartments flooded, the submarine wouldn't have enough buoyancy, even with an Emergency Main Ballast Tank Blow, to reach the surface.

"Ten seconds to impact!"

The torpedo's pings could now be heard through the *Kentucky*'s hull. Silence gripped Control except for the periodic sonar echoes, which steadily increased in intensity as the torpedo closed the remaining one hundred yards.

All around Control, the crew braced themselves for the impending explosion.

EAGLE ZERO-FIVE

Sensor One and Sensor Two jerked their headphones from their ears as the explosion, transmitted from the sonobuoys floating in the ocean, blasted from each earpiece. The sonar displays on the aircraft blanked out, the sonobuoy sensors saturated by the reverberation in the water.

Lieutenant Burwell turned toward Graef, a wide grin on his face. "We got 'em, sir."

A second later, the relieving P-3C aircraft broke in on the TACCO's circuit. "Eagle Zero-Five, this is Tiger One-Eight. Looks like we got here a few minutes too late."

"Sure did," Graef said flatly. "That sub never had a chance. We dropped the 54 practically on top of it."

"Congratulations. We're envious over here."

Graef didn't reply. His thoughts returned to the submarine crew and the explosion that had undoubtedly killed them, destroying most of the P-3C's sonobuoys in the process. "There's not much left to turn over," he said. "You'll have to drop a new field and listen for hull breakup."

"That's what we figured. We're already calculating expendable points. We've got the station now. See you back home."

Eagle Zero-Five turned slowly to the south, returning to Kaneohe Bay. Next to Graef, Lieutenant Burwell had already relayed the good news back to Wing Two headquarters.

49

USS KENTUCKY

The *Kentucky* jolted violently to starboard as the deafening sound of the explosion roared through Control. Seconds later, the submarine's Flooding Alarm activated, followed by a frantic report over the ship's 4-MC emergency communication circuit.

"Flooding in Missile Compartment Upper Level, port side!"

Malone responded instantly. "Dive, blow all variable ballast tanks! Helm, all stop!"

Taken aback by the Captain's unusual order, the Diving Officer replied, "Sir, request speed!"

Submarines could carry several hundred tons of extra weight, in this case from flooding, by traveling through the water with an up angle on the ship. But the *Kentucky* was now dead in the water after its back emergency bell, and the Captain had ordered all stop. The Diving Officer wanted to put speed back on the ship so it could carry extra weight, buying valuable time until the flooding was under control. If it *could* be brought under control.

"No," Malone said. "We're going to sink or swim at all stop. If we increase speed, we'll be detected by the sonobuoys again. And I don't want to deal with a second torpedo."

The Diving Officer called out the ship's depth, an urgent request for speed still written on his face. "Eight hundred feet and sinking!"

Stationed next to the Diving Officer at the ship's Ballast Control Panel, the Chief of the Watch announced, "Blowing all variable ballast tanks..Cross-connecting the trim pump with the drain system. Trim and drain pumps at max RPM!"

The *Kentucky* had powerful trim and drain pumps, one connected to the drain system, pumping the bilges overboard during routine operations, and the other connected to the trim system, pumping water fore and aft between the variable ballast tanks. In an emergency, the trim pump could be connected to the drain system, with each of the eight-foot-tall pumps taking suction on the bilges, pumping the water overboard. But both were centrifugal pumps, their output declining as the external water pressure rose. As the *Kentucky* sank deeper, the rate at which water poured into the submarine increased, and the faster it needed to be pumped overboard. But the exact opposite occurred; the two pumps discharged less and less water, resulting in a continuously deteriorating situation.

"Exceeding Test Depth!"

Their only chance of survival was to stop the flooding before they reached Crush Depth.

* * *

"Get the easy ones first!" Tom yelled to the rest of the damage control personnel in Missile Compartment Upper Level as he led four teams up through the maze of piping, attempting to reach the source of the flooding. Luckily, the submarine's superstructure had absorbed most of the torpedo's explosion, and the pressure hull hadn't been punctured. But the flood and drain pipes leading to the top of Missile Tubes Ten and Twelve had been damaged, and water sprayed from several valve bodies and cracked pipes. Tom wiped his eyes as the spray ricocheted off the bulkhead and other pipes, sending water in every direction. The sound from the roaring water was so loud that team members could barely hear each other, even yelling at the top of their lungs.

The damage control teams worked their way carefully toward the flooding, ensuring no part of their body crossed the path of the water jetting out from the damaged valves and piping. At Test Depth, the water sprayed out with enough force to cut clean through an arm or a leg, severing both flesh and bone. Several of the petty officers frantically shut every valve within reach, hoping one of them would isolate the fractured valves and piping from sea pressure.

Water sprayed from four main areas, and the flooding stopped in three of them once the nearby valves were shut. But one section of cracked piping couldn't be isolated. Water continued to spray from the foot-long crack, deluging Tom and the rest of the damage control team, quickly filling the Missile Compartment bilge. Water had already reached the deck plates in Missile Compartment Lower Level and was rising rapidly. As

Tom tried to reach the cracked piping, the water jetting out of the crack cut off the approach path. They couldn't get to the damaged pipe.

"Three hundred feet to Crush Depth," the Diving Officer announced, counting down the distance until the sea pressure collapsed the *Kentucky*'s steel hull like an empty soda can.

Malone approached the navigation chart. "Take a sounding."

The Quartermaster energized the Fathometer, sending one ping down toward the ocean bottom. "Five hundred fathoms, sir." He reported the reading with despair in his eyes.

Another three thousand feet beneath the keel.

There was no hope the *Kentucky* would hit bottom before her hull collapsed. Malone checked the chart for any submerged mountain peaks nearby that might save them, but the ocean bottom was flat, offering no hope of reprieve.

The Diving Officer announced, "Two hundred feet from Crush Depth and holding. All variable ballast tanks have been blown dry."

The *Kentucky* had stopped descending.

Malone checked the depth gauge on the Ship Control Panel. The needle had finally halted now that three of the four sources of flooding had been secured. But the rate of flooding had been offset by the variable ballast tanks being emptied, and they had just been blown dry. Now it was up to the trim and drain pumps—could they pump the water out faster than it entered?

Everyone in Control stared at the needle that would

portend their fate, wondering if the flooding was now within the capacity of the trim and drain pumps.

The needle started moving again.

The *Kentucky* continued to sink.

The missile tech next to Tom yelled, "We can't reach it!"

Tom and Petty Officer Roger Tryon climbed down from the piping, landing on the upper-level deck. Tom wiped the water from his eyes again, examining the tangled maze of piping above them. "What if we circle around to tube Fourteen, then cut across?"

Tryon studied the piping, then nodded. Tom led the way down the starboard side of the Missile Compartment and back up to tube Fourteen, then climbed into the overhead, followed by Tryon, damage control kit in hand. After reaching the top of tube Fourteen, the two men clambered over equipment and piping, carefully approaching the cracked piping run. Water sprayed up from a foot-long crack in the top of the pipe, bouncing off the hull before cascading down in a drenching torrent. The two men supported themselves awkwardly, propping themselves on the slippery piping just inboard of the crack.

"Hand me a clamp!" Tom yelled. But Tryon couldn't hear him over the deafening roar.

Tom repeated his request, this time overenunciating so Tryon could read his lips. "Clamp!"

Tryon squinted his eyes, estimating the pipe diameter, then opened the kit and retrieved one of the clamps, a curved piece of metal that could be placed over the fissure, mating perfectly to the curvature of the cracked piping. Tom placed the clamp on the piping, away from the crack, checking for proper size, but the clamp diameter was too small. He yelled for a larger clamp, and Tryon handed him another one. This one fit perfectly.

Applying the clamp was a difficult task, as it couldn't be simply placed over top of the crack, because the tremendous force of the water would blow it right out of Tom's hands. The clamp had to be applied onto the piping, away from the crack, held loosely in place with several metal bands, then slowly rotated over the crack and tightened securely.

Tom held the clamp on the piping, a foot inboard from the crack, as Tryon wrapped three strands of metal banding around the pipe and clamp, partially securing it in place.

"Ready?" Tom yelled.

Tryon nodded.

Tom and Tryon shoved the clamp toward the crack, with the clamp under the piping instead of over the top, where it was cracked. Then they rotated the clamp toward the fissure, but it stopped moving as soon as the edge made contact with the wall of water jetting out from the crack. Tryon pulled a mallet from the damage control kit and handed it to Tom, who tried to rotate the clamp over the crack by hammering against the clamp's edge. But the force of the water was too strong, resisting Tom's best efforts to shove the clamp over the crack.

Tryon pulled a second mallet from the kit, shifting his weight on the pipe he was perched on so he had a clear swing toward the clamp. Tom held three fingers up, then retracted one, then another. When he retracted the last finger, Tom and Petty Officer Tryon hammered together against the edge of the clamp, trying to force it to rotate over the crack.

The clamp moved a fraction of an inch, covering part of the fissure. The water now sprayed away from them as it hit the underside of the clamp and jetted out the side. Tom and Tryon repeated the procedure, but this time it didn't move. The water pressure on the underside of the clamp was just too great. They tried again with the same result. No matter how hard they hammered and how synchronized their effort, the clamp refused to rotate and seal the flooding.

"One hundred feet to Crush Depth!"

Malone's eyes moved from the analog depth gauge on the Ship Control Panel, the needle continuing its slow clockwise movement, to the digital depth meter above the Quartermaster's stand, hoping the digital meter would report a more favorable reading. But the red numbers on the digital gauge agreed with its analog cousin, rapidly counting up as the ship's depth increased.

No one spoke in Control, the only sound being the trim and drain pump flowmeters clicking off the gallons discharged overboard. Malone tried to assess the rate at which the *Kentucky* was sinking, estimating how much longer before they reached Crush Depth, where the pressure hull would crumple inward under the intense sea pressure.

They had less than a minute left.

50

WASHINGTON, D.C.

The early morning light filtered into Christine's office through partially drawn blinds, the rising sun falling across her desk in thin strips of light. She sat motionless in her chair, staring straight ahead, her hand still resting on the handset to her STE. The news from SecDef Williams had turned her stomach queasy; she wondered what the men aboard the *Kentucky* had thought and felt as the cold water rushed in on them.

Her STE had bleeped as she entered her office at 7 A.M., and Williams had informed her the *Kentucky* had almost assuredly been sunk by a P-3C aircraft. The torpedo detonation had been confirmed, and although the submarine hull's breakup had not been detected, that was understandable given that most of the sonobuoys had been destroyed by the explosion. The P-3Cs and surface ships would remain in place in the unlikely event the *Kentucky* survived. The official assessment, however, was that the *Kentucky* had been sunk.

Christine rose from her desk and, after a short walk

down the hallway, knocked on the Oval Office doors, entering after the president's acknowledgment. Hardison was seated across from the president's desk, and the two men halted their conversation after noticing the ashen look on her face. They waited in silence as Christine took her seat beside the chief of staff.

"Mr. President." Christine tried not to betray the emotion she felt. "It looks like we sank the *Kentucky*. A P-3C dropped a torpedo on a submarine approaching Emerald and confirmed its explosion."

"Yes!" Hardison pumped his fist by his side.

The president stared at his chief of staff. "We just killed a hundred and sixty men serving our country. And you're thrilled?"

Hardison's exuberance faded. "I apologize, sir. But there was so much at stake. The loss of life is unfortunate, but the alternative was too ghastly to imagine. A hundred and sixty lives versus seventy million. It had to be done."

"Are we certain we sank her?" The president turned back to Christine, a haunted look in his eyes.

"It's possible she survived, but unlikely. We're waiting for a report of hull breakup noises from our permanent SOSUS arrays on the ocean floor. Then we'll know for sure. Also," Christine added, "Williams informed me that NAVSEA has concluded they can't patch their fast-attack sonar systems over the radio broadcast. They'll have to return to port for a complete software reload."

"It doesn't matter now anyway," Hardison said. "We don't need our fast attacks anymore."

"Let's hope so," Christine said sourly, "because if the

Kentucky survived and makes it past the P-3Cs and Surface Fleet, there's nothing to stop them from launching."

"Don't be such a pessimist. We sank her. Now there're a few loose ends we need to take care of."

"Meaning what?" The conversation Brackman had overheard—Hardison plotting to eliminate her ex-husband—was still fresh in her mind.

There was a slight hesitation before Hardison replied. "Meaning the cover story for the sinking of the *Kentucky*. What were you thinking?"

You know exactly what I was thinking.

Now that the *Kentucky* had been sunk, Hardison would move aggressively to ensure this issue was permanently concealed, eliminating any remaining threat to the administration. Even if that meant killing Hendricks.

"Nothing," Christine replied coolly, turning to the president. "Is there anything else, sir?"

"No, Christine. That'll be all."

Christine stood, her eyes lingering on Hardison for a few seconds before she left, sending him a subtle warning: Make even the slightest attempt to harm her ex-husband, and she would bring him down. He'd made enough enemies in his thirty years in politics, and she enough friends, to find a way. She could tell her look was not lost on Hardison.

He met her stare until she turned and left.

51

USS *KENTUCKY*

"It's not working! We can't stop the flooding!"

Four hours before Christine received the call in her office, Tom Wilson had given up hope of stopping the flooding in Missile Compartment Upper Level. The water was jetting from the cracked piping with too much force. Tom and Petty Officer Tryon's efforts to hammer the clamp over the crack had failed.

In Control, Commander Malone stared at the depth gauge on the Ship Control Panel as the *Kentucky* sank toward Crush Depth. Aside from the clicking of the trim and drain pump flowmeters, it was eerily silent in the Control Room. They had one hundred feet to Crush Depth. At the Ballast Control Panel, the Chief of the Watch eyed the Emergency Blow levers.

Malone debated whether to Emergency Blow. An Emergency Blow—even a temporary one to burp air into their ballast tanks—would give away their position and result in another torpedo sent their way. And another.

Their only real hope of survival was to stop the flooding without an Emergency Blow. But they were running out of time.

As Tom gave up hope of stopping the flooding, he got an idea.

"Back off the clamp!" Tom yelled.

"What?" Tryon asked, his eyes wide in surprise.

"Back off the clamp!" Tom didn't have time to explain. He started hammering the opposite edge of the clamp, taking care not to let his hand pass through the water jetting through the crack.

Tryon hammered along with Tom, and the clamp was knocked loose. Tom pulled the clamp back, then repositioned it under only half of the crack. Then he started to rotate the clamp over the crack again.

"There's too much pressure," Tom shouted over the roar of the inrushing water, "so we're going to cover only half of the crack, and use two clamps."

Tryon nodded his understanding.

The clamp hit the edge of the water jetting from the cracked pipe and stopped. Tom and Tryon readied their mallets. Tom held up three fingers, then retracted one, then another. When he retracted the last finger, the two men hammered the edge of the clamp. The clamp moved a fraction of an inch, covering part of the fissure. They repeated the procedure, and this time it continued moving over the fissure. Two more hammerings and the clamp was positioned directly over the crack. But the clamp was still loose, and water was spraying out under it in every direction.

Tryon pulled a tool from the damage control bag and

tightened the center metal band wrapped around the pipe and clamp. Then he tightened the two outer bands, cinching the clamp firmly against the pipe. Half of the leak was sealed.

As Tryon tightened the metal bands, Tom took a matching clamp and measured off the required metal banding to hold the clamp in place. Tryon cut off three pieces, and the second clamp was soon held loosely in place beneath the second half of the cracked piping. Tom and Tryon repeated the process, and the second clamp was quickly in place.

The flooding stopped.

The Chief of the Watch relayed the report from Damage Control Central. "The flooding is stopped!"

There was a collective sigh in Control, but not one Malone shared. His eyes shot to the depth gauge.

They were still sinking.

The *Kentucky* had taken on too much water during the flooding and was negatively buoyant, and would continue to sink until the trim and drain pumps had pumped off enough water. Unfortunately, the *Kentucky* didn't have much real estate to work with.

They had fifty feet to Crush Depth.

It didn't take long for the crew to realize their predicament.

Forty feet to Crush Depth.

All eyes turned to the Captain.

Malone evaluated his options. He still believed an Emergency Blow was dangerous. Obviously, a hull implosion was worse.

Thirty feet to Crush Depth.

But Crush Depth was a paper-and-pencil calculation, and there was always a safety margin. Plus, he believed there would be warnings of hull implosion, indicators the *Kentucky* was reaching the breaking point. Piping systems would fail. Hull plates would deform. He would *know*. If necessary, he would take the submarine to Crush Depth. And beyond.

Twenty feet to Crush Depth.

However, if he was wrong and the hull imploded without warning, the *Kentucky* and her crew would end up on the bottom of the ocean.

Ten feet to Crush Depth.

The trim and drain pump flowmeters were slowing, pumping less water as the ocean pressure increased. Everyone in Control stared at the depth gauge. The needle hovered ten feet above Crush Depth. It hung there, motionless, for what seemed like forever.

The depth gauge ticked downward.

"Captain," the Diving Officer announced, "the ship is at Crush Depth."

The watchstanders looked around at each other.

The *Kentucky*'s hull began to groan. Low rumbling moans. The crew cringed as each ominous sound echoed in Control.

The ship continued to sink.

Ten feet below Crush Depth.

The Chief of the Watch announced, "Captain, Maneuvering reports a leak from Main Seawater Cooling."

Twenty feet below Crush Depth.

Malone acknowledged the report and turned on the 2-JV speaker on the Conn, listening as reports began to stream in from Engine Room watchstanders. Seawater piping systems were beginning to fail, springing leaks at the piping joints.

Thirty feet below Crush Depth.

They had run out of time.

Malone had no choice now.

He turned to the Ship Control Panel, examining ship's depth one last time.

Forty feet below Crush Depth.

The needle was steady.

The trim and drain pump flowmeters clicked away.

He would give it one more chance. If the *Kentucky* continued to sink, he would blow.

Finally, the needle moved.

It ticked upward.

Malone breathed a sigh of relief.

The *Kentucky* began rising toward the surface.

52

USS *KENTUCKY*

The tension in Control was palpable, hanging in the air like the mist that still permeated the Missile Compartment. Five hours later, Tom stood around the navigation table with the CO, XO, and department heads as they examined the location on the chart where they had been hit by the MK 54 torpedo. The *Kentucky* floated motionless two hundred feet below the surface, while the missile techs and Auxiliary Division mechanics made permanent repairs to the damaged piping and valves in the Missile Compartment. Above, the P-3Cs continued circling to the east while the surface ship barrier remained to the west.

Malone and the rest of the crew had congratulated Tom and Tryon for saving the ship, but Tom felt uncomfortable with the praise. He had simply done his job, the same way anyone would have done. The congratulations had been short-lived, however, when Sonar detected fresh splashes, denoting a new sonobuoy field being laid. The *Kentucky* had proceeded west at two knots, the propeller barely turning, slowly pushing the submarine out from under the sonobuoys. Once safely away, they had stood down from Battle Stations and come shallow for more permanent repairs.

As the missile techs and auxiliary machinists wrapped up their efforts in Missile Compartment, Tom had joined the CO, XO, and department heads around the navigation chart to discuss their options. They were in no-man's-land, stuck between the P-3Cs and the surface ships. Malone had chosen to continue heading west as they snuck out from under the sonobuoys, placing the *Kentucky* between the noisy surface ships and the sensitive sonobuoys. As the buoys looked west, the submarine's tonals were masked by the surface ships behind them.

The *Kentucky* was safe. For the moment.

At least until she headed east, back under the P-3C sonobuoy fields, or west, under the surface ships. Which direction she would head was never really a question, though; the *Kentucky* had received a launch order, and she would continue west, toward Emerald and launch range. However, now that they knew the P-3Cs and presumably the surface ships were Weapons Free in water the submarine owned, the crew could plan accordingly. Even so, the situation raised more questions than answers.

"Why the hell did they shoot at us?" the Weps asked.

"They didn't know they were shooting at us," the XO replied. "It's obvious there's something else going on out here—that our conventional forces are involved in some sort of engagement."

"They should not have been Weapons Free in water

we owned." The Nav reinforced the Weps's question. "The P-3C should never have been authorized to launch a torpedo in the first place."

"If they even know we own the water," the XO explained. "Not even fast-attack submarines are told what water ballistic missile submarines own. Only the N9 shop back in Pearl knows which operating areas have been assigned to Tridents. And there's no telling what kind of coordination is occurring between our strategic and conventional forces right now. I bet it's chaotic as hell up there."

"I think the XO's right," Malone said. "COMSUBPAC sent several 688s into our moving haven during our transit to Sapphire to make sure there were no other submarines nearby. And now the P-3Cs and surface ships are prosecuting submarines. That means there's a threat out here somewhere, and we need to be alert for it."

"Speaking of threats," the Nav added, pointing to the displays on the ship's combat control consoles, "we still have to pass through the surface ship barrier."

Tom looked up at the submarine's sonar and combat control displays, the picture to the west a jumble of contacts, impossible to sort out.

"We could transmit a message, asking COMSUBPAC to clear a lane for us," the Weps suggested.

The XO shot Lieutenant Pete Manning a disapproving glance. "Our protocols are clear. You of all people should know we cannot transmit after we've received a launch order."

"To hell with protocols," the Weps spat back. "We almost got sunk by one of our own P-3Cs. And now we have to travel underneath surface ships and their helicopters, which'll no doubt drop another torpedo if they detect us. We need to transmit a message to COMSUB-PAC asking for their help."

"I don't advise it," the Nav said, this time agreeing with the XO. "This close to surface ships and aircraft, there's a high probability our transmission would be detected. And these guys appear to be in a shoot-first-ask-questions-later mood. It's likely they'll send another torpedo our way as soon as they detect a radio transmission from a submerged contact."

Malone ended the discussion. "We will not transmit this close to surface ship and air contacts. I'm not going to risk getting another torpedo rammed down our throat. We'll take our chances transiting under the surface ships. We've trained for this, and now that we know they mean business, we won't be caught off guard." Malone looked at the ship's clock above the Quartermaster's stand. "Two more days before we launch, gentlemen, and one last task—pass through this ASW barrier."

Malone turned to the Weps. "Speaking of launching, we need to determine the extent of damage to our strategic launch systems. Run the system through its paces. The XO and I will get us past the surface ships."

The Weps tersely acknowledged the Captain's order, then left Control.

"Now let's put the ship back into a fighting posture," Malone announced. "Officer of the Deck, man Battle Stations Torpedo silently."

Moments later, as the submarine was brought to full manning again, Malone assumed the Conn and examined the sound velocity profile above the Ship Control Panel. There was a moderate thermal layer just below the ocean's surface. Taking the ship's height into account, Malone ordered the *Kentucky*'s keel to an optimal depth while they transited under the surface warships, hiding in the shadow zone beneath the layer.

"Dive, make your depth three hundred feet. Helm, ahead two-thirds. Left ten degree rudder, steady course two-six-five."

Tom joined Malone at the front of the Conn as the *Kentucky* began to pick up speed, the deck pitching downward.

2 DAYS REMAINING

53

JERUSALEM, ISRAEL

"Good evening, Prime Minister."

Rosenfeld's stride faltered as he entered his office. A large, burly man sat in a chair in front of his desk, his back to the prime minister. A gray ringlet of hair, encircling a bald dome on top of the man's head, tapered down the back of a wide neck that spread into broad, sloping shoulders. Without seeing his face, Rosenfeld recognized the man—Ariel Bronner.

Head of the Metsada.

Rosenfeld was surprised to find anyone in the building this late, much less in his office. It was 9 P.M. He wondered how Bronner knew he was working late tonight, then stopped midthought.

Stupid question.

The Metsada was the special-operations arm of the Mossad, fielding the agents that made Israel's espionage possible. Rosenfeld harbored no doubt the Metsada kept tabs on him as well, and that Bronner could ascertain Rosenfeld's whereabouts with little effort.

Rosenfeld suddenly noticed Hirshel Mekel, his executive assistant, sitting in one of the chairs against the wall, his eyes darting between Bronner and the prime minister. Regaining his composure, Rosenfeld walked past Bronner, stopping behind his desk to face the man who had never once, in Rosenfeld's six years as prime minister, visited his office. Bronner's massive shoulders transitioned to thick, muscular arms ending in large scarred hands that wrapped around the end of the chair's armrests. Rosenfeld had never reviewed Bronner's field file, but he had no doubt the man had squeezed the life out of more than one person before he was promoted to a management position.

Glancing at Mekel, Rosenfeld looked for a clue to explain Bronner's visit. Mekel's tense posture told him Bronner was upset. Mekel must have been caught snooping around the Metsada's headquarters. Rosenfeld decided to ignore that small but relevant fact as he settled into his chair and addressed the man in front of him. "What can I do—"

Bronner raised his index finger, cutting off Rosenfeld's question. He spoke slowly, pronouncing each word clearly. "The next time you desire information from the Metsada without using proper protocols, I advise you to not send an amateur."

Rosenfeld briefly considering denying Bronner's accusation. But why? After all, the Metsada worked for him. And as both prime minister and a father, he was entitled to whatever information the Metsada had gathered on the suicide bombing that killed his daughters. Perhaps he had made a poor decision, assigning Mekel a task he was ill prepared for, probing within the secretive organization for additional information. But he needed to resolve the discrepancy between the report Kogen had delivered and the later version obtained by Mekel. However, Bronner had a point, and it looked like this discussion would go nowhere unless Rosenfeld acknowledged it.

"I apologize, Ariel. I should have come directly to you. But I was . . . afraid."

"Of what?"

Rosenfeld didn't answer immediately. Bronner had asked a straightforward question, but one that forced Rosenfeld, for the first time, to address his true fear. It was possible a simple administrative issue had created the discrepancy between the two reports. But he knew, almost to a certainty, that the earlier report had been altered by someone within the Mossad—either Kogen or even the man sitting in front of him. There was no way around it now.

"I didn't know whom I could trust."

Bronner's eyes narrowed. "You have good reason to fear, Levi."

Rosenfeld's body stiffened, unclear what Bronner meant by his comment, uncertain about whom he couldn't trust. Bronner? Or someone else? He eased back in his chair, attempting to hide his apprehension. "Explain."

Bronner glanced at Mekel, then nodded toward the door. Mekel sprang from his chair, bolting out of Rosenfeld's office, slamming the door behind him in his haste.

The Metsada chief's grip on the chair armrests tightened. "You were wise to be suspicious, Levi. The report Kogen provided you was not reviewed or approved by me, and the content of that document is inaccurate. It was altered to blame Iran for the death of your daughters, when no such evidence exists."

Rosenfeld tried to ignore the panic rising inside him. The implications of Bronner's statement were multifaceted, and his mind went in several directions simultaneously. But he grabbed control of his thoughts, forcing himself to stick to the simplest track for the time being: collecting the facts.

"Who is responsible? And why was it changed to blame Iran?"

"I'm afraid I have distressing news, Prime Minister. The suicide bomber was recruited not by Iran but by the Metsada, without my knowledge."

Even though he was fairly certain he hadn't moved, Rosenfeld felt his body recoil. Why would the Metsada murder his children? But Rosenfeld was unable to concentrate on *why* for the moment. There was a much more pressing question. If the order hadn't been given by Bronner, then . . .

Rosenfeld's eyes hardened. "Who?"

"Barak Kogen, Prime Minister. It appears he wanted to ensure you would authorize the destruction of Natanz, and he killed your daughters to influence your decision."

Like a dam breaking under the strain of evidence, the truth flooded into Rosenfeld's mind. Several days ago, a seed of suspicion had been planted when he read the draft report Mekel had obtained, but he had refused to acknowledge the possibility. The thought that his own intelligence minister was somehow involved in subterfuge concerning his daughters' deaths, along with the underlying implication, was too disturbing to contemplate. So he had sent Mekel inside the Mossad, looking for more definitive evidence. In the meantime, that seed of suspicion had sprouted like a strangler fig, the horror of the seedling's true nature revealed by Bronner's accusation.

It was possible Bronner was lying, deflecting blame onto Kogen. But one look at the Metsada chief told Rosenfeld he didn't need a polygraph to know Bronner was telling the truth. Rosenfeld had been betrayed by his own intelligence minister. A man he depended upon to keep Israel and its people safe. A man who had stood beside him as his daughters were lowered into their graves, consoling him in his grief. A man driven by such hatred that any means was justified to achieve the end. Even the murder of children.

His children.

Anger welled up inside. As he contemplated his recourse, he realized Bronner shared the same emotion. "What will you do?"

"I cannot let this stand, Prime Minister. I must take appropriate action, with your concurrence." Kogen had betrayed the Metsada, and Bronner appeared to consider that betrayal far more significant than what Kogen had done to Rosenfeld.

Rosenfeld responded quickly. "You have full discretion in this matter." He was about to excuse Bronner, but it looked like his Metsada chief had more to say. "Is there something else?"

"I'm afraid so, Prime Minister. The Metsada has learned the *Kentucky*'s launch message was modified by the American. It directed the launch of all twenty-four missiles against Iran. Instead of only Natanz being destroyed, 192 warheads will be released in a pattern designed to destroy the entire country."

Rosenfeld was at a loss for words as he processed Bronner's statement, panic stabbing into him as he realized their Mossad plot had been manipulated into destroying an entire country. Seventy million people annihilated in a nuclear holocaust. Suddenly, the nuclear weapon being assembled by Iran became irrelevant. The Metsada operation had to be stopped. "Can you terminate the operation, turn off the *Kentucky*'s launch?"

Bronner shook his head. "I'm afraid not, Prime Minister. In that respect, Kogen did not deceive you. There is nothing we can do. Whether or not the missiles are launched is now up to the crew of that submarine, and the American navy searching for them."

Rosenfeld nodded somberly, and Bronner rose from his chair and left. Rosenfeld stared into space, his entire body numb from the revelation of his intelligence minister's treachery and the change to the *Kentucky*'s launch order. Kogen had murdered his children, then manipulated him in the midst of his anguish. Rosenfeld had made his decision to destroy Natanz while he was suffocating in grief, authorizing the Mossad's operation. An operation that would now destroy an entire country.

He buried his face in his hands.

What have I done?

54

USS *KENTUCKY*

Standing in the darkness in Missile Compartment Upper Level under the access hatch to the world outside, Tom tightened the safety harness strapped across his chest. Nearby, he could hear the breathing of Petty Officer Tryon and three other missile technicians standing alongside him, likewise wearing safety harnesses, waiting for word to open the hatch. One of the missile techs shifted his stance, his shoe squeaking on the steel deck; the five of them had changed into their sneakers for the 4 A.M. trip topside. As Tom's eyes completed their adjustment to the darkness, he waited for the order to emerge into the night to inspect the damage from the MK 54 torpedo.

There was no doubt the torpedo had inflicted significant damage. Twenty-seven hours ago, as the *Kentucky* prepared to pass under the surface ship barrier, increasing speed to ahead two-thirds, Sonar had detected flow tonals once the ship reached eight knots. The submarine's superstructure covering the top of the Missile

Compartment had been damaged in the explosion, and the twisted metal wreckage was whistling in the wind, so to speak, as the water flowed over what had once been a smooth, even surface. The Captain had limited the *Kentucky*'s speed to seven knots during the transit, expertly threading the submarine beneath the surface ships. The tension had been high, especially as the helicopters periodically repositioned, dropping their dipping sonars beneath the ocean's thermal layer. Fortunately, none had stopped for a listen close enough to detect the *Kentucky*.

After passing under the last of the surface ships, Malone had continued west for another twelve hours, far enough away to risk surfacing the ship in the darkness to inspect the damage. Inside the submarine, the strategic weapon system was fully operational with the exception of tubes Ten and Twelve. Water was draining from the bottom of those tubes, evidence that the muzzle hatches were no longer watertight and that the plastic protective nose cones over the missiles were cracked.

Tubes Ten and Twelve were out of commission. Whether the adjacent tubes were operational was uncertain, and Malone had decided a visual inspection was the only way to determine for sure if tubes Eight and Fourteen could be opened without the screech of a damaged muzzle hatch giving away the submarine's position while it was most vulnerable, dead in the water preparing to launch its missiles.

As the Assistant Weapons Officer, Tom was responsible for leading the inspection team topside. Joining him were the three most senior missile techs, who were familiar with the seven-ton missile tube muzzle hatches and the powerful hydraulic systems that operated them.

Tryon and Tom would inspect the aft missile tubes while Petty Officers 1st Class Kreuger and Santos would examine the forward tubes. A fourth missile tech, Petty Officer 2nd Class Reynolds, manned the sound-powered phones, relaying information to and from the ship's Captain in Control.

Reynolds spoke into his mouthpiece. "Proceed topside, aye."

Petty Officer Tryon illuminated the hatch with a red lens flashlight as Tom climbed the ladder and spun the access hatch handle counterclockwise, watching the hatch lugs retreat. Once they were clear, Tom pulled hard on the release and shoved upward. He climbed a few more rungs, pushing the heavy spring-loaded hatch back until it locked fully open. Warm, moist ocean air flowed down through the hatch, and the young lieutenant breathed deeply, inhaling fresh air for the first time since the *Kentucky* submerged south of Oahu.

Stopping with his chest just above the submarine's deck, Tom leaned against the hatch and shined his flashlight along the deck, searching until he located the safety track. Hooking his harness into the track that ran the full length of the ship, he climbed topside, pulling his deck clip a few feet forward so the missile techs behind him could also hook in.

Like the other four men, Tom wore a life preserver under his safety harness in case a wave broke over the top of the Missile Compartment deck, washing him overboard. If that happened, drowning wasn't the only danger he faced. The life preserver would keep him afloat and the safety harness would keep him close to the ship instead of drifting off into the darkness, but he would be repeatedly smashed against the ship's steel hull by the strong ocean waves, battering his body and breaking bones if he wasn't hauled out of the cold water quickly enough. More than one sailor who had fallen overboard died not because he had drowned but because his body had been beaten to a pulp by the rough seas.

As Tom waited for the missile techs, he peered forward along the missile deck, barely able to distinguish the submarine's silhouette in the darkness. The ship's sail was pitch-black—the Bridge was unmanned, the watch stationed belowdecks, and the navigation lights remained deenergized. The only light came from the clear night sky, which was illuminated by densely packed stars shining more brightly than he had ever seen. As he stood on the submarine's deck, he felt as if he were balancing on a fulcrum—admiring God's work, an awe-inspiring creation, while standing on the fruit of mankind's labor, capable of unimaginable destruction.

The four missile techs joined Tom topside and he led the way forward, scanning his flashlight across the deck until he came to a gaping hole in the superstructure. The damage was more extensive than Tom had expected. A twelve-foot-diameter section of the superstructure on the port side was missing, the edges of the circular scar marked with twisted steel plates and support stanchions. The MK 54 torpedo had hit the submarine near the top of the superstructure, where it rounded off from the flat deck and curved down toward the ship's beam. The exterior skin of the ship had absorbed the bulk of the explosion as well as forcing the torpedo to detonate several feet away from the ship's pressure hull. The *Kentucky* had been lucky indeed.

Tom could tell the muzzle hatches for tubes Ten and Twelve were inoperable; each pair of hinges, which connected the missile tube hatches to the pressure hull, had been shattered by the explosion. He shined his flashlight across the chunk of missing superstructure, trying to examine the aft hinge of tube Eight's hatch. But he was too far away, the black hinge too indistinguishable in the darkness to make an assessment. They would not be able to conduct their inspection from the safety of the Missile Compartment deck.

"We need to go inside the superstructure," Tom announced reluctantly.

Unfortunately, there were no safety tracks to hook into once they were inside the superstructure, and their lanyards weren't long enough if they remained hooked to the safety track topside. The only way for them to inspect the hinges on tubes Eight and Fourteen was without safety harnesses.

He turned to Reynolds. "Phone talker to Control. Request Captain's permission to enter the superstructure without safety harnesses."

Reynolds relayed Tom's request to Control, and a moment later, the Captain's permission was obtained.

Without hesitation, Tryon panned his flashlight back and forth across the deck until he located a two-by-two-foot access hatch. Pulling a T wrench from his belt, he loosened the bolts, then lifted the hinged hatch out of the way, laying it backward onto the deck.

"Kreuger, Santos," Tom called out above the ocean noise, his voice almost drowned out by the large, frothy waves roiling down the sides of the long submarine. "Inspect tube Eight. Tryon and I will inspect tube Fourteen."

Tom removed his safety harness, dropping it onto the deck. The other three men did the same, while Reynolds, with his harness still snug around his body, remained hooked into the safety track at his feet. As the ship rolled from side to side in the rough seas, Tom was the first man down the access hatch, descending a narrow ladder that disappeared into the superstructure.

Seven feet down, Tom's feet hit the pressure hull, and he shined his flashlight back and forth inside the black, dripping metal skin of the ship. Although they had surfaced twenty minutes ago, nothing had dried; the humid ocean air condensed on the cold steel, and the pressure hull remained wet and slick. While the deck above was flat and its paint embedded with rough nonskid material, the pressure hull below was curved and smooth. Working inside the superstructure at sea, without a safety harness, was treacherous at best. If he slipped and fell, he'd continue sliding down the side of the submarine into the ocean, through the small gap between the superstructure and the pressure hull. Recovering a man overboard without a safety harness in the dark of night would be almost impossible, the ocean current pulling him away from the ship, lost forever.

Tom shifted his weight back and forth, testing the grip of his sneakers. They held. But he was standing on top of the submarine, where the surface was almost flat. Moving fore and aft along the center passage would be relatively easy. Unfortunately, he needed to travel down the side of the submarine to where the muzzle hatch hinges were welded on the outboard side of the tube. There the pressure hull sloped off to a forty-five-degree angle, and the grip of his sneakers would almost surely give way at an angle that steep. As he contemplated the difficulty of the task, Petty Officer Tryon landed gingerly beside him.

Tom and Tryon headed aft toward tube Fourteen while Kreuger and Santos descended behind them for their trip forward to tube Eight. Upon reaching tube Fourteen, Tom and Tryon stopped, both shining their flashlights down the sloping side of the submarine to where the muzzle hatch hinges were welded to the pressure hull. It was a mere twelve-foot trip, but each step would be exponentially more dangerous than the last. With a pair of deep, nervous breaths, the two men headed down the submarine's slick pressure hull, one on each side of the missile tube.

The hull began to slope away and Tom's sneakers slipped on the wet metal. He held firmly onto the superstructure support stanchions, grabbing the next one before releasing the last. But as he moved down the side of the submarine, the spacing between the stanchions increased. Halfway down, the next stanchion was just out of reach. He would have to let go of one before he had a grip on the next. After testing the grip of his sneakers again, he let go, praying he didn't slip in the short interval between handholds. He made it safely to the next stanchion, and after two more treacherous steps, reached the outboard edge of the missile tube. He draped his arm around the last stanchion to hold himself steady in place. Tryon reached the forward hinge a few seconds later.

Tom examined tube Fourteen's external components. The aft hinge appeared undamaged, as did the locking ring that rotated around the mouth of the missile tube, screwing the hatch down tight over the tube opening. Likewise, the two-inch-thick locking pin inserted into the hinge looked okay. He found nothing that would prevent the smooth rotation of the locking ring, retraction of the locking pin, and opening of the muzzle hatch.

Tom yelled forward to Tryon, "How's it look on your side?"

"Looks good." Tryon's reply was faint, barely audible above the sound of the waves breaking against the side of the ship.

"Good here too," Tom said. "Let's head back."

As he prepared to climb back up the slippery pressure hull, Tom realized the trip up was going to be even more treacherous than the trip down. Gravity had assisted him in his trek down toward the hinge, and now it would fight him as he tried to dig his sneakers into the wet, slick pressure hull. One foot slipped out from under him on his first attempt, and he hung on to the support stanchion while he regained his balance. He wedged his left foot against the bottom of the stanchion where it was welded to the deck. As he prepared to push up toward the next stanchion, he heard Petty Officer Tryon's terrified scream.

Tom twisted sideways and shined his flashlight toward Tryon's cry for help. The petty officer had slipped and slid down the pressure hull, and was now grasping the very edge of the superstructure. Half his body stuck out from the narrow gap between the superstructure and the pressure hull, the waves completely submerging him for five seconds at a time as they traveled down the ship's hull. He held on with one hand, his other arm dangling by his side at an unusual angle, his face contorted in pain. As he struggled to maintain his grip with his good hand, the strong waves rolled up the round pressure hull then back down, tugging him out to sea through the narrow gap.

It would take two minutes, maybe three, for Tom to work his way up the aft side of tube Fourteen, then down the forward side to assist Tryon. The injured missile tech wouldn't last that long. Tryon's only hope was for Tom to travel directly toward him along the outside of tube Fourteen. But the nearest support stanchion along the outside of the missile tube was more than six feet away, too far for Tom to reach. He'd have to make a leap for it. If he didn't gain hold of the stanchion, there'd be no chance of survival. Tom, and then Tryon, would drift off into the darkness. Neither the phone talker topside nor the other two missile techs below would be aware of their fate until Tom and Petty Officer Tryon failed to return topside.

But Tom couldn't stand by and watch Tryon get swept out to sea. He wedged both feet on the inboard side of the stanchion he held on to and shined his flashlight on the next stanchion six feet forward, committing its position to memory. Then he extinguished the flashlight and returned it to the holster on his belt.

He'd need both hands for the leap.

Tom peered into the gloomy darkness, then crouched down as best he could, his heart pounding in his chest as he listened to Tryon's cries for help, drowned out periodically as the waves swept over him. He let go of the stanchion, then sprang forward, his arms outstretched, hoping his aim was correct and his leap far enough.

He landed on his chest on the hard pressure hull and

felt the inside of his right wrist hit the base of the stanchion. He grabbed hold, but his body started to swing down toward the water. His grip started to slip, and he threw his left arm up, hoping to grasp on to the stanchion with both hands. His left hand hit cold metal as the grip on his right slipped to his fingertips.

He hung there, with his chest against the pressure hull, the waves washing up over half of his body as he struggled to gain a firmer grip. He finally succeeded in wrapping both hands around the stanchion, working his way up until he hugged it with both forearms. Pulling himself to his knees, he supported himself with one arm around the stanchion while he retrieved the flashlight from his belt and turned it on, illuminating the inside of the superstructure. Wedging it between the stanchion and the pressure hull, he pointed the flashlight's beam in Tryon's direction.

Holding on to the stanchion with his right hand, Tom leaned downward, his left hand stretching toward Tryon. But Tryon couldn't reach up toward him, his left arm broken, his right hand grasping the edge of the superstructure. Tryon struggled to maintain his grip, his strength ebbing with each relentless wave that battered him.

There was no way for Tom to approach any closer. As desperation set in, a plan began to take shape in Tom's mind. If he couldn't get to Tryon, then Tryon would have to come to him. The plan was risky, but it was the only hope.

Tryon would have to let go as one of the waves washed up the *Kentucky*'s pressure hull, riding it for a second, hoping to grab Tom's outstretched hand before the wave fell, sweeping him out to sea. They would have one shot for their hands to meet and for their wet grasp to hold as the wave receded. Tom had no idea if it would work, but there was no time to debate the merits of the plan or the odds of its success; the last wave had almost knocked Tryon loose from his tenuous grip on the superstructure. It was time to break the news.

"You need to let go!" Tom yelled. "Ride one of the waves toward me. I'll grab your hand as you pass by!"

The fear in Tryon's eyes was evident as he evaluated Tom's proposal. He would have to time it perfectly, letting go as he felt his body lifted by the wave. Tom knew the questions tumbling through Tryon's mind— Would he rise high enough as he rode the wave toward Tom? Would the two men's aim be close enough and would their hands meet? Would their grasp, formed in a split second, be strong enough to support his weight as the wave receded?

"I understand!" Tryon shouted, just before another wave washed over him. When he emerged as the wave receded, he sputtered, "Next wave!" His strength was fading.

"Ready!" Tom answered, tightening his grip around the stanchion.

He held his hand out toward the missile tech, waiting for the next wave. As nervous as he was at the prospect of success, he couldn't begin to imagine Tryon's terror once he released his grip on the superstructure and put his life, literally, in Tom's hand.

The wave rolled toward them along the ship's hull, emerging from the darkness into the red light, and Tryon let go just as the wave crested behind him. The wave lifted the missile tech up and pulled him aft along the side of the submarine. Their hands met as Tryon rode the wave past him, and they grasped each other. Their hands slipped as the wave receded, pulling the young petty officer out to sea.

Then their grip held.

The two men dangled against the *Kentucky*'s hull, supported by Tom's hold on the stanchion. But Tryon's weight put a strain on Tom's grasp, and his hand began to slip. He clamped down hard, and they both hung from the stanchion by Tom's fingertips as the next wave approached, threatening to break his grip and sweep them both out to sea.

But just before the wave reached them, Tryon managed to place his foot up against the edge of the superstructure, supporting his weight for a moment, taking the pressure off Tom's grip. Tom dug the bottom of his sneakers against the hull and pushed, and gained traction. He slid upward an inch before his feet slipped, but it was just enough; he grasped the stanchion firmly again. As the next wave hit, he heaved Tryon up as the missile tech was temporarily buoyed by the passing wave, and Tryon draped his right arm firmly around the superstructure support beam.

As the two men rested against the pressure hull, Tom retrieved his flashlight and examined Tryon's injury. There was a visible bend in his left forearm; it was clearly broken.

"I'm going to need help getting you topside," Tom said. "I'll be right back."

He returned a few minutes later with the other two first class missile techs and a coil of rope, the end of which he tied around his chest and made his way to Tryon, still lying against the hull with his arm around the stanchion. Tom grabbed him under the shoulders, and with the help of Kreuger and Santos pulling on the other end of the rope, the two men slowly worked their way back up the slippery pressure hull. The missile techs lifted Tryon topside and helped him down the access hatch into Missile Compartment Upper Level, where the Corpsman and Emergency Medical Team waited.

As Tom stood on the *Kentucky*'s missile deck, untying the rope from around his chest, the adrenaline began to wear off. His hands were trembling. The two of them could have been swept out to sea, adrift in the dark ocean. He let out a deep breath, thankful things had turned out okay.

Tom focused his thoughts on his last remaining task. They would open the muzzle hatches for tubes Eight and Fourteen tonight, verifying they functioned properly before submerging and continuing toward Emerald.

Ten minutes later, Tom was back in his safety harness, alone on the missile deck except for Petty Officer Reynolds on the sound-powered phones. Kreuger and Santos had reported that tube Eight appeared operational, the hinges and locking ring undamaged. Inside the submarine, the Weapons Officer was in Missile Control Center, preparing to cycle the two muzzle hatches while Tom observed topside in case something went awry.

Standing just aft of tube Fourteen's muzzle hatch, Tom gave the order. "To MCC. All personnel standing clear. Open muzzle hatch, tube Fourteen."

Reynolds relayed the order, and a moment later the

locking pins retracted from the hinges, the locking ring around the mouth of the missile tube rotated counterclockwise, and the heavy eight-foot-diameter hatch lifted silently upward to the fully open position. Seconds later, the locking pins were inserted, securing the hatch in place.

Tube Fourteen was operational.

Tom ordered the muzzle hatch closed, then walked forward, stopping just aft of tube Eight. One down, one to go, and Tom gave the identical order for the second tube.

The watchstander in Missile Control Center flicked the toggle switch to tube Eight, disengaging the hinge locking pins. Both locking pin lights glowed bright green, indicating they had been successfully extracted. After verifying the locking ring had rotated and the locking pins were removed from the hinges, the missile tech in MCC sent the open command to tube Eight.

Hydraulic fluid pressurized to three thousand pounds per square inch flowed under the tube's muzzle hatch opening pistons, pushing the seven-ton hatch open, but part of the aft hinge's locking pin—sheared in half during the MK 54 explosion—remained in place. A metallic screech tore through Tom's ears as one hinge moved and the other refused, twisting and jamming tube Eight's muzzle hatch.

"Secure from opening tube Eight!"

Reynolds relayed the order over the loud wrenching sound as the powerful hydraulic pressure tried to overcome the broken locking pin stuck in the hinge.

Quiet returned to the *Kentucky*'s deck except for the waves breaking along the ship's hull. Tom shined his flashlight on the deformed muzzle hatch; the forward edge was pushed up three inches while the aft section remained flush to the deck. The Weps and the Missile Division Chief joined Tom topside to examine the muzzle hatch, eventually agreeing the best approach was to try and shut it. If the locking pins could be reengaged, the muzzle hatch should seal properly. But tube Eight, along with tubes Ten and Twelve, was definitely out of commission. Tom gave the order, and the muzzle hatch closed properly, both sides flush with the *Kentucky*'s deck.

As Tom dropped down through the access hatch, the last man down, the *Kentucky* was already turning west again, toward Emerald, preparing to dive. He stopped halfway down the hatch, examining the fiery orange of the approaching dawn glowing on the horizon. He wondered if that was what Iran would soon look like from a distance, nothing remaining but the scorched remnants of humanity's presence, the desert sands turned to glass from the heat of the atomic blasts.

Reynolds called up to Tom, asking if he needed anything. Tom replied negative, then dropped through the hatch, stopping a few feet down the ladder. He pulled the heavy Missile Compartment access hatch shut, then spun the handle, sealing the crew back inside.

55

OAK HARBOR, WASHINGTON

On the second floor of a white two-story building on the shore of Whidbey Island in the Pacific Northwest, with Canada a short ferry ride away and the picturesque San Juan Islands to the west, Al Culver rested his head in his hands, eyeing the display on his workstation at the Pacific Fleet's Naval Ocean Processing Facility. In the cold, windowless building located appropriately enough on Intruder Street, Culver and the other three hundred military and civilian personnel assigned to the Whidbey Island NOPF monitored the SOSUS arrays on the ocean bottom and the mile-long arrays deployed from the five SURTASS ships, searching the ocean for submarines. Tracking the length of his watch by the cups of coffee consumed, Culver, a second class sonar tech, accurately concluded he had just completed the fourth hour of his watch.

Six months earlier, as he prepared to transfer from the USS *Alabama* at the submarine base in Bangor forty miles to the south, Culver had been hesitant to accept a tour of duty at what many considered an irrelevant command. Following the collapse of the Soviet Union, the SOSUS arrays on the ocean bottom had been declassified and the twenty-two monitoring stations with the nondescript title of "Naval Facility" subsequently closed. Many thought the underwater arrays and associated facilities had been relegated to monitoring whale movements and underwater seismic activity, but nothing was farther from the truth.

Culver had learned the mission of today's Undersea Surveillance Command remained focused on detecting submarines transiting the ocean depths. The combination of fixed SOSUS arrays, shore-processing facilities, and SURTASS ships with their deployable arrays had become known as the Integrated Undersea Surveillance System, and the data was now collected and monitored at two Naval Ocean Processing Facilities, one at Whidbey Island monitoring the Pacific arrays and the other in Dam Neck, Virginia, overseeing the Atlantic. The arrival of the SURTASS ships in the 1980s and their subsequent upgrades in the 1990s and early 2000s, along with improvements to the SOSUS arrays on the ocean bottom, had vaulted the capability of the IUSS into the twenty-first century, ensuring the system remained capable of detecting the newest diesel and nuclear submarines prowling both the deep ocean and shallow littoral waters.

With the ability to track not only submarines but also surface ships throughout the oceans without fear of losing the vessel to cloudy skies or other satellite interference, IUSS had also been integrated into the nation's homeland defense, providing continuous maritime surveillance for the Department of Homeland Security. Culver looked up at the watch center entrance door, emblazoned with the official command slogan beneath its bronze seal:

In God We Trust—All Others We Track

This morning, Culver had detected nothing in his area of surveillance just east of the Marianas, and not even his fourth cup of coffee kept him focused on the monitor in front of him.

A few stations away, coffee cup in hand, Master Chief Ocean Systems Technician (Retired) Fred Harmon was preparing to take down one of the consoles for maintenance. Setting down his coffee, he opened the side panel of workstation seven to replace a recalcitrant AIC card.

On the monitor in front of Petty Officer Culver, a bright white trace materialized, disappearing ten seconds later. Donning his headphones, Culver selected the affected array, rewound the recorded signal, then hit Play.

It was a loud, metallic screech. Very unusual and definitely man-made. But it wasn't a trawler winch, not even a jammed one, fighting miles of cable and fishing nets. This sound was something he had never heard before. "Fred, got a minute?"

Harmon looked up from the console he was working on. "What do you need?"

"Come listen to this."

Culver rewound the recording and handed the headphones to Harmon, who held one earmuff to his ear, his coffee cup back in his other hand. "Go ahead."

Culver pressed Play and Harmon listened intently, then put his cup down and placed the headphones properly over both ears. "One more time."

The retired master chief listened again, his eyes squinting as he concentrated. A few seconds later, he handed the headphones back to the sonar tech.

"You have any idea?" Culver asked.

Harmon nodded. "When I was stationed at NAVFAC Antigua, I heard that same noise from a Trident submarine on her shakedown cruise off Port Canaveral. You just picked up a ballistic missile submarine trying to open a jammed missile hatch."

Harmon pulled up a chair. "Let's take a look at the other arrays and see if we can triangulate the submarine's position."

1 DAY REMAINING

56

ARLINGTON, VIRGINIA

At a table for two in the back of Whitlow's on Wilson Boulevard, Christine sat next to her ex-husband, joining him for lunch in what was once their favorite restaurant. Now that the *Kentucky* had been sunk, the ordeal that had brought them back together had come to a close, and they would soon go their separate ways again. Christine had accepted Dave's invitation; a glass of wine at their old hangout was exactly what she needed to begin letting go of the unimaginable horror that had almost occurred, and what they had done to avert it.

"I'm glad this happened," Hendricks said before he downed the last of his beer. As he placed the mug back on the table, he was startled by Christine's shocked expression. "Oh, no, not that. What I meant was, I'm glad I got a chance to spend some time with you again."

Dave sat close to Christine, his arm across the back of her chair, his body leaning slightly toward her. She could tell he wanted to wrap his arm around her, pull her close. But instead, he was careful not to touch her.

The end of their marriage had been difficult for both of them, neither wanting to admit to failure, neither willing to remain in a relationship that was spiraling out of control. They settled their differences as best as possible after the divorce, their love fading to a cool but comfortable friendship. Their jobs brought them into new and disparate social circles, and they ran into each other less and less frequently. They hadn't seen each other for three years before Hendricks showed up, out of breath, in the Pentagon corridor.

This crisis had thrown them together again, and Christine was surprised she enjoyed working with her ex-husband, spending time with him. She had to admit he was still an attractive man. Her hard feelings had dissipated in the years apart, and she felt drawn to him again, both emotionally and physically. He obviously felt the same way, but the barriers between them were still too strong. If she had been any other woman, she was sure he would have asked her out by now. And properly, too. Today's lunch at their old hangout was his feeble attempt at a date; two friends catching up on the last three years, nothing more.

Christine avoided discussing personal issues, ensuring the conversation focused on work and mutual friends. But after a glass of wine, the desire that began to surface in his office returned even stronger, and her mind drifted to the first two days of their honeymoon, fifteen years earlier.

They had landed in Rome late that night, finally arriving at their hotel, the luxurious Rome Cavalieri in the heart of the city, enclosed in fifteen acres of lush Mediterranean parklands. But something had gone wrong with their reservation, and they had no room. After a half hour wrangling with the front desk clerk and hotel management, Dave waving their travel reservations in his hand, they reached a compromise: They would be upgraded to a suite, but not for two days. This weekend marked the beginning of the Romaeuropa Festival and every room was occupied, with the first vacancy on Monday.

Due to the festival, all the reputable hotels were booked, and the honeymooners were forced to spend their first two days in Rome in a fleabag hotel. Dave apologized profusely to Christine for their squalid accommodations, but they really weren't his fault.

"What are you thinking about?" he asked.

Christine's thoughts returned to the present. "I was thinking about our first two days in Rome, at the Esplanade. How disgusting that hotel was."

Dave grinned. "You should know. If I remember correctly, you had ample opportunity to study the paint peeling off the ceiling above our bed."

"As did you, I seem to remember." Christine recalled how exhausted they were after that first weekend, even though they never left the hotel room. As deplorable as their accommodations were, they didn't venture out of the hotel until they checked out two days later.

"I have to admit," he replied, "I'll never forget that weekend."

The waitress cleared the dishes and dropped off the check next to Christine. Dave reached across the table, snatching the check before she could claim control. His chest brushed against her shoulder in the process, his face close to hers, just for an instant. She smelled his cologne, felt the warmth of his arm against her back. Dave wore cologne only on special occasions; he had clearly hoped today's meeting would mark a new beginning and not the end of their recent reacquaintance.

His eyes searched hers for a moment. Then he looked away, unwilling or unable to express his thoughts. He pulled out his wallet, selected a credit card, and slid it inside the billfold with the check.

It was just after 2 P.M. when Dave held the restaurant door open for Christine, then followed her out onto the sidewalk. She had enjoyed their lunch together even more than expected. The conversation had flowed easily, with the exception of the brief silence after he grabbed the check, and she wondered if this was the beginning of a renewed relationship. Perhaps they would get back together, after he mustered up the courage to broach the subject.

As they crossed the street toward Hendricks's car, a screech of tires caught Christine's attention. A silver sedan sped toward them, less than fifty feet away and increasing speed. The driver kept his head down, his face unidentifiable.

Christine knew instantly the driver wasn't going to stop. Or even swerve.

The sedan bore down on both of them, only seconds away from crushing their bodies against its front grille. Dave stood frozen in the middle of the street. Christine lunged toward him, hitting Dave in the chest with her shoulder, knocking him back toward the sidewalk. Her momentum carried both of them just inches clear of the speeding car. Hendricks landed on his back, his head smacking into the pavement, and Christine rolled to a stop a few feet away as the sedan swung a hard right onto Fillmore Street, disappearing from view.

She scrambled over to him. His eyes were glazed over, staring up at the sky. "Dave!" She touched his cheek gently. "Are you okay?"

His eyes slowly cleared, eventually focusing on her. "I'm all right, I think."

Christine helped him to a sitting position, and he rubbed the back of his head, wincing as he found a tender spot. "Yeah, I'm fine," he said. "You okay?"

"Yep." Christine answered curtly as she pulled him to his feet.

"Damn idiot!" Hendricks exclaimed, glaring down Wilson Boulevard. "I bet he was texting his girlfriend."

Christine didn't reply, her anger building. The driver had barreled directly toward Hendricks, standing in the middle of the street, and they both would've been killed if she hadn't reacted as quickly as she did. This wasn't just a case of a preoccupied driver hazarding the public. She was certain.

And she knew exactly who was behind it.

57

WASHINGTON, D.C.

After being waved through the southwest gate to the White House, Christine's blue Ford Taurus screeched to a halt on West Executive Avenue, outside the entrance to the West Wing. As she stepped out of her car, greeted by a stiff wind and thick black clouds rolling in from the west, her eyes flickered in anger. One of the two Marines guarding the entrance opened the door for her, and the two men exchanged glances as the president's national security adviser stormed up the West Wing steps toward the chief of staff's office.

Hardison looked up from his computer as Christine swept into his office like the approaching storm, slamming the door behind her. She didn't slow down as she headed straight for him. Stopping suddenly at the edge of his desk, she planted both palms on the smooth surface and leaned halfway across the desk toward him, her face twisting in anger as she screamed at him. "What the hell do you think you're doing!"

The president's chief of staff leaned back in his chair,

taken aback by the enraged woman glaring at him. "About what?"

"You know damn well what I'm talking about!"

Hardison shook his head. "I'm afraid not. Perhaps if you explained—"

Christine's face turned red, the muscles in her neck straining as she yelled at him. "Dave and I were almost run over by a car outside Whitlow's! We came within inches of being killed!"

Hardison laughed. "And you think I had something to do with it? Some idiot almost runs you over and you think I'm responsible?"

"You're damn right I do! You made it clear from the beginning that Dave was a threat to this administration, and I have no doubt you've taken matters into your own hands."

Hardison interlocked his hands across his waist. "I assure you I had nothing to do with this, Christine."

He appeared unfazed by her accusation. If anything, he seemed amused, the corners of his mouth twitching upward. His flippant attitude ignited Christine's rage. She'd had enough of Hardison, and she was finally going to do something about him. "You've gone too far this time, Kevin. I'm going to Director Larson, and you'll be done as chief of staff by the end of this week."

The smile disappeared from Hardison's face as he sprang to his feet, towering over her. His voice dropped a notch as he spoke. "Don't come in here and threaten me, Christine, especially over some paranoid delusion you've created about a hit-and-run driver." A cold look settled over his face.

Christine stood erect, taking a step back from

Hardison's desk as he continued, "Whoever almost ran you over probably wasn't paying attention, not some assassin I hired to take Hendricks out. Now why don't you go back to your office, collect your thoughts, and get back to work? I'm sure there's something you've neglected to attend to these last few days."

There was an uneasy silence as they glared at each other, broken when the secure phone on Hardison's desk beeped.

As he answered it, Christine mulled over his reaction. He seemed genuinely surprised and offended by her accusation. But she had watched him lay it on thick before, feigning surprise or ignorance. She just couldn't tell if he was telling the truth. He was too good a liar.

Hardison hung up the phone, flexing his hand as he released the handset. "That was your alive-and-well ex-husband in the Command Center," he said with a hint of sarcasm. But what caught Christine's attention wasn't the tone of his voice. It was the sudden fear in his eyes as he continued. "Our SOSUS arrays detected a damaged missile tube hatch being opened. It looks like the *Kentucky* survived. The best guess is they're determining the extent of damage from the torpedo." He paused for a moment before he added, "They're not far from Emerald."

Christine's anger dissipated with the news. The *Kentucky* hadn't been sunk and was closer than ever to launching. "I'll be over at the Command Center," she said. "I'll let you know what I find out."

58

PENTAGON
23 HOURS REMAINING

"We picked up the metallic transient near the Marshall Islands." Captain Brackman spoke quietly as he stood between Christine and Hendricks in the deputy director's office, examining the electronic map of the Pacific Ocean at the front of the Current Action Center. Christine studied the red circle expanding slowly into a teardrop shape heading west as Brackman continued, "We've biased the projection of the *Kentucky*'s position by limiting her possible courses from two-one-zero to three-three-zero. We know she'll continue heading west toward Emerald.

"Unfortunately," he added, "she's definitely west of our naval forces." Brackman pointed to a column of blue circles to the east of the red teardrop, "Our surface ships are too far away to catch the *Kentucky,* even at ahead flank. We've reassigned the P-3Cs to the leading edge of the *Kentucky*'s AOU, but their field density is porous due to limited sonobuoys, and once the *Collins* approaches the AOU, we'll have to pull them out, since they could engage the wrong submarine."

"Where is the *Collins* now?"

"The *Collins* is the blue half circle to the west of the teardrop."

On the monitor on the far wall, the forward edge of the *Kentucky*'s area of uncertainty was almost touching Emerald, with the *Collins*'s blue semicircle a few inches to the left.

While Christine examined the display, Hendricks joined the conversation. "You need to talk to the president, Christine. We need to inform Iran. I understand the reasons for keeping this quiet up to now, hoping we could turn this off. But the *Kentucky* has made it past all three layers of our ASW barrier, and our main hope right now is the *Collins*. At this point, I doubt we can stop the *Kentucky* from launching. And once she does, our ballistic missile defense systems will be overwhelmed. You've got to convince the president to inform Iran."

Christine reflected on Hendricks's words for a moment, then nodded. "I'll talk to him. I'll head over to the White House, then come back here until this is over, one way or another."

Before she left Hendricks's office, she looked back up at the display. She wondered who would suffer and die. Would it be the innocent people of Iran or the men aboard the *Kentucky*? Everything hinged on whether they could find and sink the *Kentucky* before she launched.

As Christine studied the monitor in front of them, Brackman correctly surmised what she was thinking. "As you can see, *Kentucky* will enter Emerald as early as midnight tonight, depending on where she is in her AOU. Let's pray the *Collins* finds her before she does. We just sent her the news the *Kentucky* survived. She'll be downloading it off the broadcast anytime now."

59

HMAS *COLLINS*
22 HOURS REMAINING

Nine hundred miles east of the Northern Mariana Islands, Murray Wilson stood next to Brett Humphreys in Control as the *Collins* secured snorting, her battery recharge complete, the Officer of the Watch turning slowly on the periscope as they prepared to head deep. The *Collins*'s painfully slow pace grated on Wilson. Unlike American fast attacks that could have made the entire run east at ahead flank, the *Collins* spent half her time at periscope depth at ten knots, recharging her batteries between high-speed runs.

Although the *Kentucky* had been sunk, the *Collins* was still headed east at maximum speed. Deep Submergence Rescue Vehicles were being sent from Australia and San Diego in the event the *Kentucky* had come to rest on a shallow spot on the ocean floor. It was unlikely, but there was always the possibility. Finding the *Kentucky* would be the hard part, and Wilson hoped the *Collins* could help. As he checked the clock on the starboard bulkhead, calculating how long before the submarine would arrive at the position the *Kentucky* was reported sunk, his thoughts were interrupted by an announcement from Radio.

"Watch Leader, Commcen. Incoming message from the FEG."

A moment later, a radioman entered Control, handing a message to Humphreys. Wilson noted a startled expression on the Captain's face as he read the message. He handed it to Wilson. A few sentences down, his heart leapt to his throat. Tom was still alive. But then the somber realization set in. The *Kentucky* had made it past the surface ships, and the P-3Cs had expended most of their sonobuoys. The *Collins* was the most capable asset remaining.

Humphreys walked over to the navigation chart, Wilson joining him.

Wilson handed the message to the Petty Officer of the Watch. "Plot these coordinates."

The leading seaman obliged, measuring off the longitude and latitude, drawing a small circle around the new point on the chart. The seaman leaned back out of the way as Wilson and Humphreys examined the target's updated position.

With the original large area of uncertainty, Wilson hadn't been sure they would find the *Kentucky*. But with the new fifty-kilometer-radius AOU—even accounting for the increased time it would take to close the distance—they would find the *Kentucky*. What Wilson didn't know, however, was whether they would find her before or after she launched.

Humphreys turned to the radioman. "Acknowledge receipt and inform the FEG we will enter the target's

AOU in nine hours." Turning to the Officer of the Watch, Humphreys ordered the ship down from periscope depth. "Make your depth one hundred meters and increase speed to ahead flank, course zero-nine-five. Load all torpedo tubes."

Down in the Weapon Stowage Compartment, Chief Marine Technician Kim Durand, the Weapons Chief aboard the *Collins*, supervised the Torpedo Reload Party. Upon receipt of War Patrol orders, they would normally have loaded all six of the submarine's torpedo tubes. But their target was far away, and the analog Mod 4 torpedoes had a nasty habit of overheating when powered up inside the tubes for more than a few hours at a time. Her Captain had decided instead to load their torpedoes when they were closer to their target. They were apparently closing in on it now.

The first torpedo had been loaded into tube One when Captain Wilson stopped by the Weapon Stowage Compartment. Shortly after the American's arrival on board, the crew learned they were chasing a Chinese copy of the U.S. Trident submarine. In the American captain's eyes she had expected to see the excitement of the hunt, the steely determination to find and sink their adversary. But she saw none of that—only an unexplainable sadness. There was more to this mission than their Captain and the American were letting on.

Kim knew this mission would be dangerous once they engaged their target. Even with the long range of their Heavyweight torpedoes—they could travel over twenty miles before running out of fuel—you had to get close to your opponent to sink the knife in. That meant you could be stabbed in return. Unfortunately, there were no flesh wounds in submarine combat. It was pretty much a binary result: You either got hit and died, or the torpedo missed and you survived. Kim hoped they would survive the upcoming battle, but she and the rest of the crew knew there was no way to predict how things would turn out.

And so, in the face of uncertainty, the crew's confidence was unshakable. The marine technicians in the reload party were already making bets on which torpedo would sink their target. The second torpedo was already halfway into tube Two, being pushed forward steadily by the hydraulic ram temporarily attached to the back of the torpedo, and Kim ran her hand along the smooth, cold aluminum skin of the torpedo as it traveled into its new stowage location. As the nineteen-foot-long torpedo disappeared into the tube, Chief Kim Durand transferred a kiss from her hand to its tail, wishing it luck. Her bet would ride on the torpedo in tube Two.

As Captain Wilson left the Weapon Stowage Compartment, Kim wondered if somewhere to the east, her counterpart on their target was doing the same.

USS *KENTUCKY*
18 HOURS REMAINING

It was almost 0100 GMT aboard the *Kentucky* when the crew submerged after inspecting their missile hatches; time for Tom's evening watch as Officer of the Deck. The six-hour watch elapsed uneventfully as the *Kentucky* continued its inexorable march toward Emerald. After being relieved at midnight, Tom now toured through Missile Compartment Lower Level on his after-watch tour, checking the bilges for evidence of leaks and examining the ship's equipment for malfunctions. As he passed the ten-foot-tall gas generators—soda-can-shaped cylinders filled with water that would be transformed instantly to steam by an explosive charge—he still found it hard to believe that simple steam could pop the sixty-five-ton missile above the ocean's surface like a giant cork gun.

The steam impulse was essential, as the missile's engine could not ignite while it was in the tube; the 1,400-degree heat from the exhaust would melt through the bottom of the submarine. So the missile launch system was designed to eject the missile above the ocean's surface, where the first-stage motor would ignite, pushing the missile and its eight 475-kiloton warheads into the stratosphere on the journey toward its target.

As Tom completed his journey through the Missile Compartment, he climbed the forward ladder two decks and stepped through the watertight door into the Operations Compartment, stopping outside Missile Control Center. He punched in the cipher lock combination, then entered MCC to review the strategic weapon system status. Two missile techs were on watch, seated at the Launch Control Panel, monitoring the condition of each missile and tube.

"How are you guys doing?"

"Fine, sir," one of the missile techs replied, glancing briefly at Tom before returning his attention to the console.

Tom reviewed the logs as the two missile techs sat quietly, neither one engaging the lieutenant in conversation. The missile techs would normally have peppered him with questions, eager to talk to anyone except the bloke sitting beside them, stuck together on the same watch cycle for weeks on end. It didn't take long to run out of things to talk about once they got past the *What did you do last summer?* phase. But neither man seemed in the mood for conversation, which was consistent with what Tom had noticed throughout the submarine. He finished reviewing the logs in silence, then handed the clipboard back to the nearest petty officer.

As Tom stepped out of MCC, a burst of commotion greeted his ears. Angry shouts came from the Crew's Mess, and he entered to find the two missile techs who had accompanied him topside, Kreuger and Santos, holding a third missile tech, Walworth, who was struggling to free himself. Reynolds, who had been Tom's phone talker topside, stood across from the three, holding his hand to his nose, blood running down his face.

"I'm gonna rip your fucking head off!" Walworth shouted, the veins in his neck bulging as he struggled against Santos and Kreuger's firm grip. "Don't even think about not doing your job when the time comes!"

The submarine's Chief of the Boat entered the Crew's Mess, stopping at the entrance. "What the hell is going on!" The COB's question hung in the air as the twenty enlisted men stared at him. "Speak up!"

"I was just talking," Reynolds said, "about what we're gonna have to do in a few hours—"

"You fuckin' coward!" Walworth renewed his struggle against the two men holding him.

"Shut up, Walworth," the COB said. "If you don't give it a rest, you'll be confined to berthing for a week." The COB turned back to the injured missile tech. "Go on, Reynolds."

"We were talking, and I said I didn't know if I could go through with it when the Captain gave the order, and then Walworth flipped out on me."

The COB turned back to Walworth, who had settled down somewhat after the COB's threat. "You're confined to your rack until further notice. Get out of here."

Kreuger and Santos released Walworth, who glared at Reynolds as he left Crew's Mess.

"I'll do my job when the time comes, COB," Reynolds said. "I was just mouthing off."

The COB stared at Reynolds for a moment before

speaking. "Walworth's from D.C. His family still lives there. *Lived* there, to be more exact. He won't know if they're still alive until we return to port."

"Shit, COB," Reynolds said. "I didn't know."

"Well, now you do. All of you." The COB's eyes scanned across Crew's Mess, making contact with each man. "And Walworth's not the only one. I won't tolerate any more discussion about what we are or aren't going to do when we reach Emerald. I know it won't be easy, but we've trained for this. We all knew there was the potential this would happen, that we'd be ordered to execute the mission this ship was designed for, and this crew is going to execute that mission. Do I make myself clear?"

"Yes, COB," each of the men replied.

"Get to Medical, Reynolds. Kreuger, track down the Corpsman."

The COB eyed Tom for a second before he left, and Tom waited a few seconds longer as the men returned to their seats, talking quietly.

Shaking off the unpleasant experience, Tom toured next through officer berthing, stopping outside the Weapons Officer's stateroom. After knocking softly, he opened the door and peered inside. The stateroom lights were off except for the small fluorescent bulb above the Weps's desk. He sat in his chair reviewing a stack of paperwork, his face illuminated while the rest of the small stateroom faded into darkness. The Weps looked up as Tom opened the door.

"Do you have a few minutes, Weps?"

"Sure." The Weps turned sideways in his chair, noticing Tom's solemn face. "What's on your mind?"

Tom turned the chair to the other desk around and sat facing his department head, his eyes toward the deck. "Walworth just busted Reynolds's nose in the Crew's Mess. Reynolds said he had doubts about completing his duties during Battle Stations Missile, and Walworth flew off the handle." Tom looked up. "Do you have doubts, Weps? About whether you'll execute the order we've been given?"

The Weps put down his pen and stared at Tom for a long moment. "That's a good question," he finally answered. "The crew is starting to feel the pressure, the burden of our mission, and they have it easy. Most of their efforts are vaguely tied to the actual launch. Turn a valve here, flip a switch there. But everyone's effort culminates in one action. Mine.

"I'm the one who has to unlock the firing trigger. And I'm the one who has to squeeze the damn thing. Over and over, twenty-one times, knowing that I'm erasing the lives of millions of people with each squeeze. I try to imagine I won't think about that tomorrow. The Captain will give the order, and the crew, including me, will follow that order, just like we've trained." The Weps leaned forward, close to Tom, lowering his voice. "But do I know that for sure? No, I don't. And I won't know until I'm standing in MCC, the trigger in my hand, and we get a green board on the first missile. I'll know then, and only then."

Tom swallowed hard. He'd felt the same trepidation growing inside him as the ship crept closer to Emerald. While only the Captain, XO, and Weps played a direct role in the launch, as Assistant Weapons Officer, Tom would join the Weps in Missile Control Center, verifying the correct target packages were assigned, the missiles spun up properly, and all launch prerequisites met. He would do his part, a small cog in the wheel of effort it took to prepare each missile for launch, thankful nothing hinged directly on him.

But Tom could sense the wobble in that wheel. The crew was no longer the well-oiled machine that would respond automatically to a nuclear strike order. And as each day passed and the ship approached closer to Emerald, the wobble had increased. He was no longer confident the crew would execute its mission when the time came. What he had seen in Crew's Mess, and what the Weps had just confided to him, strengthened his doubt.

"So what about you?" the Weps asked. "Do you think we should follow the Captain's order and launch our missiles?" The older man pulled back slightly, as if measuring Tom up, assessing his openness to whatever idea he was contemplating. Alarm bells went off in the back of Tom's head. They were treading on dangerous ground, openly discussing the prospect of not following the Captain's order, an order handed down by the president himself. There was a word for it, a word that clearly captured the essence of what they would be doing if they refused to obey the order of a superior officer aboard a naval vessel.

Mutiny.

And Tom knew, as sure as the man sitting across from him, that there were many in the crew who shared the same reservations, were hesitant to follow through and complete the submarine's mission. All they lacked was leadership. Leadership from one or both of the men sitting in this small stateroom. And the more officers who refused the Captain's order, the more enlisted men would follow until even if the resistance were docile—simply refusing to execute their duties as opposed to taking over the ship—the officer and enlisted ranks would be decimated, leaving insufficient personnel to accomplish the launch.

Is that what the Weps was contemplating? Rallying like-minded men to refuse to execute the Captain's order, thereby preventing the *Kentucky*'s launch?

A mutiny?

There was no way to predict how Malone and the rest of the crew would react. It could get ugly. Very ugly and downright dangerous with two lockers of small arms aboard: several dozen rifles, shotguns, and pistols in one locker forward, another one aft. And the Weps knew that Tom, as Assistant Weapons Officer, held the key to one of those lockers. The Chief of the Boat, who would undoubtedly side with the Captain, held the other.

Tom had gotten more than he bargained for when he knocked on the Weps's door. He had wanted reassurance from the more senior officer, putting his doubt to rest, but it had headed in an unexpected direction. Tom wasn't sure where the conversation would lead to next.

But before he could reply, the Weps continued. "It's only a rhetorical question, Tom. No need for you to answer." The Weps returned his attention to the thick stack of papers on his desk. "Is there anything else I can help you with tonight?"

Tom replied no, then thanked the Weps for his time and left, relieved they had not continued the discussion.

* * *

As the door closed, Lieutenant Pete Manning placed his pen on the desk. He had sensed the young lieutenant across from him, as conflicted as he appeared, was not amenable to participating in a blatant refusal to follow orders. He had suspected as much and had not planned on revealing his thoughts to Tom until he had unexpectedly broached the subject. He didn't know what Tom would do with what he had heard, but he figured it would have no impact on how things would go tomorrow.

He shoved aside the papers on his desk, certain he would lie in his rack tonight unable to fall asleep as he stared at the picture of his wife and two sons taped to the rack above him. He would think about the millions of families, just like his, who would no longer exist when he went to sleep the next night. Assuming, of course, he followed the Captain's order.

Ten minutes later, Tom's after-watch tour was complete and he rapped firmly on the Captain's stateroom door. Lieutenant (JG) Carvahlo stood beside him, waiting to report their relief to the ship's Commanding Officer. Malone acknowledged through the stateroom door, and the two offgoing watch officers entered.

Malone lay on his rack, his hands clasped behind his head on his pillow, staring absently at the overhead. He seemed unaware he had authorized his offgoing watch officers entrance to his stateroom and that they were awaiting his signal to proceed. Tom glanced at the small TV mounted on the bulkhead—it was dark. Beside the monitor, the navigation repeater displayed the ship's course, speed, and depth in red numbers, blinking silently as the *Kentucky*'s speed fluctuated a tenth of a knot.

Malone sat up suddenly on the edge of his bed, nodding to his two watch officers to begin. Carvahlo gave his report first. "Sir, I've been relieved as Engineering Officer of the Watch by Lieutenant Vecchio. The reactor plant is in two-loop operation, natural circulation, normal temperature and pressure. Answering bells on both main engines. The electric plant is in a normal full-power lineup. No out-of-spec readings on any watch station. That's all I have, sir."

Tom's report followed. "I've been relieved as Officer of the Deck by Lieutenant Costa. The ship is at four hundred feet, ten knots, course two-five-eight. Sonar held only one contact on the towed array, classified merchant. The ship remains Alert at Four-SQ. That's all I have, sir."

"Thank you," Malone said.

Carvahlo left the stateroom and Tom began to follow, then stopped and turned back toward Malone, shutting the Captain's door. "Sir, there's something I'd like to talk to you about. During my postwatch tour, there was a fight in Crew's Mess."

"Yes, I know. The COB stopped by."

"Sir, I don't think this is an isolated incident. The crew's on edge."

"I know, Tom." Malone examined the face of the junior officer in front of him, concern and doubt clearly evident. "Have a seat."

After a lengthy silence, Malone continued. "Receiving a launch order this far in advance is the worst thing that could have happened. The weeklong delay has given the crew time to reflect on the order we've received and what it means. For some, the delay won't matter. When we man Battle Stations, they'll fall into their routine, doing their best not to think about what they're actually doing. For others, like Walworth, this is revenge, an opportunity to lash back at those responsible for the destruction of our capital and the death of family and friends. And then there are those in between, torn by the thought of the almost incomprehensible devastation this ship will unleash upon mostly innocent men, women, and children."

"What about you, sir? Where do you fall?"

Malone glanced down at his command insignia, embroidered over the right chest pocket of his uniform. "My position doesn't allow me to fall into any of the above categories. My job is to ensure this crew executes the order we've been assigned. My personal feelings, my opinion on whether we should execute that order, are not relevant."

As the two men sat on either side of the Captain's table, the older man studied the young lieutenant's face. "What else, Tom? What's troubling you?"

Tom hesitated, debating whether to reveal the content of his discussion with the Weps. It had been a private conversation, but the Weapons Officer's doubt held significant implications. Tom struggled between his loyalty to another officer, another academy classmate, and his loyalty to the ship's Captain. In the end, his loyalty to Malone won out.

"It's the Weps, sir. I don't know if he'll be able to go through with it."

Malone said nothing for a moment, as he stared at Tom.

Finally, he spoke. "I know. I can see it in his eyes. Those of us with unique responsibilities, like the Weps, will feel the weight of their actions more than the rest of the crew. The time spent approaching Emerald has been excruciatingly painful for them. Each of us . . ." Malone paused before continuing, "Each of them will have to work through the issue themselves."

Tom caught the Captain's subtle change in wording. "And you, sir? Have you worked through the issue?"

Malone raised an eyebrow. "I've served on this ship for three years now, six patrols. I've had plenty of time to reflect on the mission assigned to this submarine, and on what my response would be should the unthinkable occur. As Commanding Officer, not only am I responsible for my own actions, I'm responsible for the entire crew."

The Captain's next statement made his position on the matter perfectly clear.

"Let me erase any doubt you have, Tom. We will execute the order we've been given. This ship, this crew, *will* launch."

61

BIG SUR, CALIFORNIA
16 HOURS REMAINING

On the western edge of the North American continent, where the Santa Lucia Mountains rise abruptly from the Pacific Ocean, lies the popular tourist destination of Big Sur. The ninety miles of coastline south of Monterey offer breathtaking views of sheer ocean cliffs, alcoves of secluded white-sand beaches, and deep ravines spanned by graceful open-arched bridges. Perched eight hundred feet above the ocean along Highway 1 is the restaurant Nepenthe, its terraced gardens of bougainvillea, honeysuckle, and jasmine overlooking a thick canopy of redwood and oak. This evening, with the sun sinking into the thick white fog bank rolling in toward shore, Daniel Landau could find no better place for a meeting.

Daniel Landau—known to others in America as William Hoover—sat on the open-air patio of Nepenthe's Café Kevah in the cool evening, steam rising from the cup of coffee in his hand, reflecting on how smoothly the plan to destroy Iran's nuclear weapon complex had proceeded. When he was given his assignment four years ago, he had initially thought it impossible. But after his American contact ascended to his current position, the Metsada agent decided that success was achievable. Landau had worked diligently, cultivating the connections necessary to neutralize the fast-attack submarines and disable the *Kentucky*'s communication systems after receipt of her launch order. That order had been sent, and if his contact's calculations were correct, within the next few hours, missiles would begin rising from the calm Pacific waters.

Tonight, Landau would guide the men who formed the kernel of his next operation. As he peered over the veranda's railing, scrutinizing the parking lot fifty feet below for the arrival of his guests, his cell phone vibrated in the breast pocket of his jacket. The familiar voice on the other end was unusually agitated. "Where have you been, Hoover? I've been trying to reach you for hours."

Landau checked the signal strength of the call, flicking back and forth between zero and one bar, apparently the reason for the missed calls. "Cell phone service is intermittent at my current location. What can I do for you?"

"Your work here isn't finished. Your incompetent driver missed."

Landau frowned. The driver was a professional. He would not have missed unless the location was too far down the street, providing sufficient warning for the target to avoid the oncoming car. The man on the other end of the phone had obviously chosen an inappropriate spot for the hit. However, there was no point in casting blame on his acquaintance. "Good help is hard to come by these days. I'll attend to the matter personally when I return to the East Coast." Landau glanced over the railing at the parking lot. The two men had arrived and were stepping out of their car. "I'm busy at the moment. Is there anything else I can help you with today?"

"I want Christine O'Connor taken care of, and taken care of immediately."

The man's demands were beginning to irritate Landau. But a man in his position was used to giving orders and having them obeyed without question. "Are you sure?" Landau asked, trying again to dissuade the man from another murder. "She knows nothing."

"You don't know what type of woman she is. She'll keep digging until she discovers everything. I've spent my entire life gaining the position I'm in, and I'm not going to have my hard work destroyed by that *bitch*. You either take care of her, or I'll do it myself."

Landau's grip on his cell phone tightened. The man was an amateur in this type of endeavor. He was the one person who could implicate Israel, and it simply would not be acceptable for him to come under suspicion. Landau would have preferred to have eliminated this man along with the sonar algorithm developer, but unfortunately the position he held was too valuable. That not being an option, he had to be placated.

"I'll return to Washington tomorrow, and *I* will attend to O'Connor. Is that clear?" Landau had never used this tone of authority with his American contact, but it was vital he be persuaded from further involvement.

"Fine," the man replied curtly. "But if I don't hear from you by noon tomorrow, I'm taking the matter into my own hands."

62

PENTAGON
5 HOURS REMAINING

Sitting in one of four chairs scattered around a table in Hendricks's office, Christine peered through the window toward the front of the Current Action Center, scanning the monitor for a hint of the *Kentucky*'s fate. Both hands were wrapped around her coffee mug; the cool air and long hours waiting with no hint of what was occurring in Emerald had produced a chill she found difficult to shake. While the hot coffee warmed her insides, her hands felt like icicles. Seated next to her, Hendricks looked like he had fared only slightly better, the exhaustion evident in a shade of black forming under his eyes. Brackman, meanwhile, paced back and forth outside Hendricks's office, wearing a path at the top of the CAC, stopping occasionally to converse with the Watch Captain.

It had been a long night. The *Collins* had entered the *Kentucky*'s AOU just after midnight and hadn't been heard from since. That was expected, Brackman told Christine, as the *Collins* could not search effectively at periscope depth and would come shallow to transmit only after she had completed her mission and the *Kentucky* was sunk. Or, if the ballistic missile submarine prevailed, the *Collins* would never be heard from again. It was 9 A.M. now and still no sign the *Collins* had found her. But there had also been no indication the *Kentucky* had launched her missiles either. Christine couldn't decide if no news was good news or bad news.

The door opened and Hardison briskly entered Hendricks's office, an unpleasant expression on his face. Christine and Hendricks rose from their chairs as he approached Christine. Hardison stopped less than a foot away. His voice was low and threatening.

"Don't *ever* go to the president behind my back again."

Christine stood her ground. "Excuse me for not getting your approval, but you were tied up in a meeting."

"I thought I made my position clear. We needed to keep things under wraps. Now that Iran has ordered a countrywide evacuation, you've created a public affairs nightmare."

"Is that all you care about? The administration's public image? Not about seventy million people?"

"It's damn near impossible to save them, Christine. You're talking about the evacuation of an entire country in less than a day. Where are they going to go? Imagine the death and destruction from the evacuation order alone."

"Many will be saved, and that's what's important."

"What's important is stopping the *Kentucky*. That's the only thing that will save them." The muscles in his jaw flexed, then the tone of his voice softened. "How are we doing?"

Christine glanced at the display at the front of the Current Action Center as she answered, "It's been quiet. The *Kentucky* could be in launch range anytime now, or she could be as far away as eighteen hours." She gestured toward the back edge of the *Kentucky*'s red circle, which would reach Emerald in eighteen hours. "The *Collins* is in Emerald searching for her now, but we've heard nothing."

Her shoulders sagged as she suddenly realized she'd been up for more than twenty-four hours straight, and hadn't eaten anything since lunch the previous day.

Hendricks turned toward her. "It's been a long night. Why don't you get some sleep and something to eat?"

"Go ahead, Christine," Hardison said. "Hendricks and I need to talk privately." His eyes moved over her body. "You look like you could use some rest."

Christine wasn't sure how to take Hardison's comment. Was he being an ass, or had the long night taken that much of a toll on her?

"Go ahead, Chris," Hendricks urged. "I'll call if we hear anything."

Hardison was probably just being blunt, Christine decided. If she looked half as bad as she felt, she probably did look like crap. "I suppose you're right. I'll be back in a few hours."

As Christine stepped out of Hendricks's office, she paused to examine the screen again. Two things were clear. The first was that the *Kentucky* had not yet reached Emerald. The second was that the *Collins* had better find her before she did.

63

USS *KENTUCKY*
3 HOURS REMAINING

Although the world above was shrouded in darkness, it was 1600 aboard the *Kentucky* and time for dinner. Normally served at 1700, dinner was being served early today; they would enter Emerald in just over two hours, and Malone wanted the men fed and the Crew's Mess cleared before setting Battle Stations. Gathered in the Officers' Wardroom with him were eleven of his officers. Only the two men on watch and, of course, Ensign Lopez, who awaited second sitting, were absent. Halfway down the table, Lieutenant Tom Wilson ate in silence, as did the others; the clink of their silverware echoing in the somber Wardroom.

Only days ago they had gathered here for lunch and dinner, eagerly discussing the day's events, the junior officers laughing and poking fun at each other. But the laughter had ceased when they'd received their launch order, and conversation at the table had steadily decreased, commensurate with the submarine's distance to Emerald. With missile launch only a few hours away, no one spoke today, all eyes focused on the food in front of them.

Malone broke the uncomfortable silence. "So how are the oxygen generators doing, Eng? The offgoing watch reported Number One Generator went down this morning."

The Engineer looked up from his soup. "Number One Generator has a bad electrolysis cell. It will be replaced after . . ." He looked away, then back down at his soup. "It will be replaced on the midwatch."

"Thanks, Eng. Be sure to pass along a job well done to Auxiliary Division once Number One Generator is back up."

"Yes, sir," the Eng replied without looking up.

One of Tom's eyebrows rose slightly. Malone undoubtedly knew the status of the oxygen generator and its repair plan, but he'd asked the question in an attempt to spark conversation. Even if it meant discussing work, normally reserved until dessert had been served.

"How about the flood and drain valve for Number Three Torpedo Tube, Weps? Did the valve rebuild stop the hydraulic fluid leak?"

The Weps looked at Malone a moment before answering, his stare almost passing through the Captain. "Yes, sir. We replaced the O-rings and the leak stopped. Number Three Torpedo Tube is fully operational."

"Good job, Weps."

Lieutenant Manning's stare lingered on the Captain before he returned his attention to the soup in front of him. Silence descended on the Wardroom again. Malone's attempt to generate conversation had failed miserably. Nothing could distract the men at the table from what they would do this evening.

Suddenly realizing he wasn't hungry after all, Tom decided to skip the rest of dinner. He looked up at his Captain. "Excuse me, sir."

Malone nodded.

As Tom left the Wardroom, he couldn't wait for it all to end. Another few hours, and it would finally be over. But he suspected it would be just the beginning and not the end; what they were about to do would be something he, and the rest of the crew, would have to deal with for the rest of their lives.

As the last of his officers filed out of the Wardroom, Malone pushed back from the table. The mess specialist moved in, clearing the dishes from what would become the Corpsman's operating table during Battle Stations; that necessity would arise only if they were detected during launch and subsequently attacked.

Leaving the Wardroom, Malone headed to Control, stopping in Sonar. After verifying the ship held no contacts, he dropped down the ladder en route to his stateroom, landing on the second level just as the Weps stepped out of the XO's stateroom. The Weps avoided the Captain's eyes as he hurried aft toward the Missile Compartment. With Tom's revelation about the Weps's reservations still fresh in his mind, Malone stopped by the XO's stateroom and queried his Executive Officer. "What did you and the Weps talk about?"

The XO looked up from his computer. "Nothing important, sir. Just a few things we needed to discuss." He turned away from Malone with the same urgency the Weps had displayed, concentrating again on his computer monitor.

Malone knew his XO was lying. Whatever the two men had talked about was clearly important. The list of things that could be on the Weps's mind a few hours before they launched their missiles was pretty damn short, and he wondered for the first time about his XO's position on completing the ship's mission. As Malone returned to his stateroom, he realized he did not really know where his officers stood on the issue. That was because, to some extent, he was an outsider on his own ship.

Every officer aboard the *Kentucky,* except Malone, was a Naval Academy grad. The academy was the major source of submarine officers, supplying two-thirds of nuclear-trained officers each year, and every once in a while, the entire Wardroom was populated by Annapolis grads. The officers from the school on the bank of the Severn River shared a bond even stronger than the Submarine Force and spoke a language even more foreign, rooted in a common experience that began on a hot July day each year outside Bancroft Hall. During lunch or dinner, or while the officers were gathered for training, one of the JOs would quip a remark, and the entire Wardroom would erupt in laughter, except Malone, who hadn't understood the reference and related humor.

As a symbol of their loyalty to each other and the institution they graduated from, they wore their rings with the academy crest facing inward, toward their heart. Up to now, Malone had no reason to believe their loyalty to each other should be considered a threat to the submarine's mission. But now that at least one of them was questioning his orders, Malone wondered whether their bond could lead to a wholesale refusal to obey their Captain's directive—and that of the president of the United States.

It became clear to Malone that additional measures might be required to ensure the *Kentucky* launched her missiles. If things did not go as planned and his orders were not followed, he would have to strike fast and cut off the head of the snake before any rebellion slithered out of control. Mere words were insufficient weapons to accomplish that task. Picking up the MJ handset, he dialed the Chief's Quarters.

A minute later, Master Chief Machinist Mate Stephen Prashaw knocked on the Captain's open stateroom door. Malone waved him in, motioning to shut the door behind him. Prashaw, the Chief of the Boat, was the senior enlisted man aboard, a man Malone relied on to oversee the smooth operation of the submarine. While the XO dictated the ship's schedule and evolutions to be conducted, it was the COB who executed them. This was his fifth patrol as COB aboard the *Kentucky,* having reported aboard the run after Malone arrived, and the two men had formed a close working and personal relationship.

As Prashaw joined him at his small table, Malone asked his question point-blank. "Do you have any concerns the crew will not execute the launch order?"

The COB replied quickly, as if he had given this question much thought. "Do I have any concerns? Yes. But will they execute? I am reasonably confident they will."

"Why are you so sure?"

"Because the enlisted men work in teams, and none of the men will want to let the rest of his team down. I'm confident that once the General Alarm sounds, their training will take over and override any reservations." The COB paused for a moment. "However, I cannot vouch for the officers. Their roles are different, and you would have better insight than me."

"Unfortunately, I don't have that insight," Malone replied. "The only two officers I have a reasonable bead on are the Weps and Assistant Weps. Lieutenant Wilson will do his part. However, the Weps has doubts and may not comply."

Prashaw raised his eyebrows. "What will you do?"

Malone leaned back in his chair. "That's where you come in. When we man Battle Stations, I want you to arm yourself." The COB's eyes widened as Malone continued. "Take yourself off the watch bill and put Chief Davidson on as Dive. I want you in Control, and if necessary, we'll head down to MCC to ensure the Weps executes the order given."

There was a long silence. "And if the Weps refuses?"

Malone stared pensively at his COB. "We'll cross that bridge when the time comes."

64

ARLINGTON, VIRGINIA
1 HOUR REMAINING

Inside the second-story bedroom of a brownstone town house in the Clarendon district of Arlington, with the afternoon sun slanting through the center slit of drawn curtains, the ceiling came into focus as Christine forced her eyes open. Rolling onto her side, she smacked the clock on the nightstand into submission, silencing the annoying alarm as she examined the time: 1 P.M. Turning onto her back again, she rubbed her eyes, then let her arms fall to the bed. She was still exhausted.

After a six-minute drive home from the Pentagon this morning, she had collapsed onto her bed. She hadn't even removed her clothes; only her shoes lay discarded on the floor. Her slumber had lasted four hours. More than a nap but hardly a good night's sleep, and the few hours of downtime left her feeling more tired now than when she had walked into her town house, drained from her all-night vigil in the Current Action Center. She had wanted to return to the Pentagon as soon as possible and had settled on four hours of sleep.

The cobwebs were clearing slowly, and she decided a hot shower followed by a cup of coffee was what she needed. She padded across the bedroom and into the bathroom, turning on the water and letting it heat up while she stripped off her clothes. Stepping into the shower, she pulled the curtain closed and let the warm water spray across her chest.

After increasing the temperature of the water to as hot as she could stand it, she tilted her head forward, letting the water fall down her shoulders and back. As she stood under the almost scalding water, allowing the tension to ease from her shoulders, steam filled the bathroom with a fine, white mist. Closing her eyes, she lifted her face up to the hot water, pulling her hair behind her head as she reached for the shampoo. But her head snapped forward and her eyes popped open when she heard an unusual thump.

She turned off the water and listened closely, but there was nothing but silence. Then she heard the sound again and concluded it was only her next-door neighbors. Christine turned the water back on and worked the shampoo into her hair. As she rinsed off the soap, letting it run down her body, she hoped it would wash away the guilt that had accumulated over the last week. She had been quick to blame others, and rightly so. Someone was executing an elaborate plot to annihilate another country. But the United States was also at fault; their safeguards had been inadequate. One man, turned traitor and armed with relatively unsophisticated aids, had transmitted a valid launch order to one of their nuclear assets.

They were partly culpable—there was no way around it. And if they didn't stop the *Kentucky,* the United States would be responsible for mass genocide. Making matters worse, she had helped Hardison and the president keep the issue hidden. If they were successful at stopping the *Kentucky*'s launch, she knew they would work together to ensure what had occurred would never become known to the public. The whole situation made her uneasy, participating in a conspiracy to keep the truth hidden.

Christine stood under the hot water, letting the heat seep into her muscles, then shut off the water and pulled back the shower curtain. She grabbed a white bath towel off the rack. The shower had gone a long way toward waking her up. She dried herself, then wrapped the towel tightly around her body. Stepping out of the shower, she opened the door to let the steam dissipate into her bedroom. As she prepared to blow-dry her hair, she wiped the condensation from the mirror. A pale face stared back at her, looking older than she remembered it. The damp, stringy hair, the washed out features from the bathroom's fluorescent lighting, and the lack of makeup added years to her appearance.

After drying her hair and applying makeup, Christine donned a white satin blouse and a tan skirt. She hurried downstairs, noting the dead bolt was still thrown on the front door. Standing in front of her kitchen pantry, she debated whether to grab a bite to eat now or when she stopped for coffee. A rumble in her stomach made the decision for her. She surveyed the contents on the shelves, but nothing appealed to her, so she pulled a packet from the only open box.

As she shoved the last of the strawberry Pop-Tart into her mouth, there was a knock on her town house door.

She queried her visitor using the intercom and a familiar voice answered, bringing a smile to her face. As she turned toward the front door, it opened, and she remembered that Hendricks still had a key. Her ex-husband stepped into the foyer, holding a small pink gift bag with even brighter pink tissue poking out the top. He gripped the bag tightly, wearing a look on his face she immediately recognized as indecision.

65

USS *KENTUCKY*
52 MINUTES REMAINING

It was exactly 1808 Greenwich mean time when the USS *Kentucky* crossed the imaginary line separating Sapphire and Emerald. At that precise moment, Malone stood on the Conn waiting for the report from MCC, confident the analysis would return the expected results. They had done the calculations several times—the last of the ship's missiles would be in launch range the second they entered Emerald. Still, Malone was putting the strategic weapon system through its paces, verifying the *Kentucky*'s missiles were in range prior to setting Battle Stations.

"Conn, MCC." The Weps's voice echoed from the 21-MC. "The ship is within launch range of the assigned target package."

Even though Malone had been waiting for the report, the announcement caught him off guard. He felt unprepared for the order he must give. He had gone through the routine many times, both at the Trident Training Facility in Bangor and aboard the *Kentucky;* he had the words memorized. But they jumbled through his mind as he prepared to make the 1-MC announcement, refusing his attempts to place them in the proper order. Fortunately, the launch procedures lay on the shelf at the edge of the Conn, opened to the appropriate page. He forced his eyes to focus, but the words remained blurry. It was as if his subconscious was delaying the launch, if only for a moment.

Over the last eight days, he had told himself repeatedly that he would be able to execute the strike order when they reached Emerald. He would focus on the task and not let the thought of what would happen thirty minutes later destroy his concentration. But as he stood on the Conn, the images of the death and destruction their missiles would wreak upon humanity flooded into his mind in vivid colors. In the end, he would be ultimately responsible for what they had done.

But he *was* responsible, he told himself again. He was responsible for ensuring the strike order was executed.

It was as straightforward as that.

Only the force of his words failed to carry the same conviction they had earlier. Malone looked up, searching for the strength to begin, the face of every man in Control turned toward him, waiting for his command.

Yes, that was the key.

His command.

When he had been offered command of the USS *Kentucky,* BLUE Crew, he knew full well the damage this warship could inflict. He could have declined, but had instead accepted his command, and with it, the responsibility to execute the lawful orders of the president of the United States of America. And he had received that lawful order.

It was as straightforward as that.

This time, his thoughts carried the necessary conviction, and the words on the page slowly came into focus. Malone picked up the 1-MC microphone, making the announcement he had been dreading since receipt of their launch order eight days ago.

"Man Battle Stations Missile for Strategic Launch. Spin up all missiles with the exception of tubes Eight, Ten, and Twelve."

Throughout the ship, the crew manned their Battle Stations, with the section on watch making the initial preparations for missile launch.

"Helm, all stop," the Officer of the Deck ordered. "Dive, bring the ship to launch depth. Prepare to hover."

The Helm and the Diving Officer acknowledged, and the main engines went quiet as the *Kentucky* took a ten-degree up angle, coming shallow and slowing in preparation for launch.

The *Kentucky*'s angle leveled off as the submarine coasted to a dead stop. After engaging the hovering computers, the Diving Officer announced, "The ship is hovering at launch depth."

Personnel streamed into Control and toward their watch stations throughout the ship, preparing to launch their missiles and defend themselves from the sudden appearance of any adversary. In MCC, Tom and the Weps were joined by a half dozen missile techs, each with a specific responsibility for operating the launch systems, while four-man teams of missile techs formed up in Missile Compartment Upper Level and Lower Level, trained to manually operate the missile tube hydraulics if an electrical fault occurred.

Standing on the Conn, Malone awaited the report from the Chief of the Watch that the *Kentucky* was at Battle Stations. At that point they would begin the strategic launch procedures.

While the ship's ascent to launch depth and order to man Battle Stations Missile were duly recorded in the ship's log, what weren't recorded were the actions of the submarine's Chief of the Boat, who had unlocked the Forward Small Arms Locker as the crew manned Battle Stations.

Assignments to six submarines, split evenly between fast attacks and boomers, Steve Prashaw had worked his way up from Deck Gang on the *Greeneville* to Chief of the Boat, the crown jewel of an enlisted submariner's career. Although promotion to master chief had its professional privileges, nothing compared to the personal reward of serving as COB on a submarine, running the boat for the Captain, and the responsibility and respect that went with it.

But that satisfaction could come crashing down in a single event. Prashaw didn't know how the rest of the Submarine Force would receive them upon their return home—as heroes or as villains for executing their mission. He suspected it would be something in between, professional admiration marred with personal revulsion. But if one of their crew was murdered in order to execute their mission . . .

Prashaw cleared his mind, returning his attention to

the order he'd been given. Perusing the assortment of weapons in the small arms locker, he selected a 9mm Beretta semiautomatic pistol. The shotguns and rifles were meant for topside watches and would be unwieldy in the submarine's confined spaces. As he counted the number of rounds in the magazine, he wished they still used the Colt 45 handgun. The 45 had been abandoned in favor of the 9mm due to the propensity for the Colt's first round to jam. But Prashaw believed the Colt would have proved valuable today. The first round jamming would have given both parties a final opportunity to reconsider their actions.

Unfortunately, the 9mm was what the *Kentucky* carried, and the COB reluctantly inserted the magazine into the pistol. Sliding the pistol into a holster strapped around his waist left a sour taste in his mouth. The submarine's small arms were supposed to be used to repel boarders. They were meant to protect the crew, not harm them.

As Malone stood on the Conn, waiting patiently for the ship to man Battle Stations, the COB arrived and stopped beside the Chief of the Watch; that he carried a firearm was not lost on the personnel in Control. Malone's eyes drifted to the pistol. He hoped its use would not be necessary, that the Weps would fulfill his part in the strategic launch.

The Chief of the Watch reported the ship was at Battle Stations Missile.

Malone reflected for a moment about what he and his crew were about to do, then he picked up the 1-MC. "Set condition One-SQ for strategic launch. This is the

Commanding Officer. The release of nuclear weapons has been directed."

Malone waited for the XO to repeat the order. But he just stood there, his eyes shifting between the other officers in Control and the COB—and darting down to the pistol holstered on the master chief's waist. The XO's delay was unusual; they had simulated their missile launch many times and he always immediately passed the duplicate order over the 21-MC.

As Malone waited for the XO, he suddenly realized he had gotten it all wrong. He had been focused on the Weps, unsure whether he would execute his order. However, if the Weps refused, he could be replaced and his combination to the Trigger retrieved from the safe in the Op Center and handed over to his successor.

He had overlooked the more obvious threat. The crew would not respond to a strategic launch order unless that identical order was given by two men. The first man was the submarine's Commanding Officer. The second man was its Executive Officer. But unlike the Weps, the XO could not be relieved and replaced. Unless Lieutenant Commander Bruce Fay repeated the order, the crew would not initiate the launch sequence.

Malone broke into a cold sweat. The XO was the second in command, authorized to relieve the submarine's Commanding Officer if there was sufficient cause. Malone knew he couldn't be relieved for executing their strike order, but he had no idea how the crew would react if the XO made the attempt. And he didn't know where the loyalty of the other officers, all Academy grads like the XO, resided.

As the thought of what the Executive Officer might

do permeated his thoughts, he realized that nine of the other fourteen officers were in Control, surrounding him; even the Officer of the Deck, who had moved behind him on the Conn. The ship's Navigator, free to float between Radio and Control to coordinate the message decryption, seemed out of place, standing slightly behind the COB, on the same side as his firearm. The other five officers were stationed in the key nerve centers of the ship: the EOOW in Maneuvering, the Weps and Tom in MCC, with the remaining two officers in Sonar and Radio. Even if Tom sided with the CO, he would be overruled by the more senior department head. The other officers could easily take over the *Kentucky;* with thirteen officers issuing orders, the rest of the crew would most likely follow.

Is that what the Weps and the XO had been discussing? Details of their plan to ignore the launch order and relieve him of command? The arrival of the COB with his firearm had undoubtedly thrown a wrench into their plan, but they had apparently prepared for the possibility, the Nav hovering dangerously close, his presence beside the COB seemingly unnoticed by the senior enlisted man.

Finally, the XO reached up and retrieved the 21-MC handset, his eyes continuing to shift between the other Academy grads and the COB.

Malone held his breath. Would the XO repeat the strike command, or order something altogether different?

The XO placed the 21-MC to his mouth, pausing as his eyes settled on Commander Brad Malone, the USS *Kentucky*'s commanding officer—for the moment.

Malone's pulse raced.

The seconds ticked by like hours.

Then the XO spoke forcefully into the handset. "Set condition One-SQ for strategic launch. This is the Executive Officer. The release of nuclear weapons has been directed."

The crew responded instantly, turning toward their consoles and focusing on the remaining actions that would make the *Kentucky*'s missiles ready for launch.

Malone let out a silent sigh of relief. His imagination had run away from him; the stress of executing the ship's launch order was beginning to affect his judgment. Returning his attention to the impending launch, he left Control, opened the safe in his stateroom, and returned a minute later with twenty-one keys, each hanging from a green lanyard, which he handed to a missile tech waiting to arm the missile tube gas generators.

A moment later, two junior officers arrived in Control with the CIP key, which they handed over to Malone. He held the key in his hand for a moment before inserting it into the Captain's Indicator Panel. He turned the key ninety degrees counterclockwise, then flipped up the Permission to Fire toggle switch. The panel activated, the status lights illuminating for Missile Tubes One through Twenty-Four.

One by one, the missiles were brought online, spinning up their inertial navigation systems. Malone monitored the progress of the missile gyro spin-up until the lights for twenty-one missiles illuminated, indicating they had successfully communicated with the submarine's navigation system. Every missile except the ones in tubes Eight, Ten, and Twelve were awake now and knew their exact position on earth. The next column of lights slowly toggled from black to red as each missile accepted its target package, carrying the impact coordinates for the eight warheads each one carried.

The third column of lights on the Captain's Indicating Panel turned red as the techs in Missile Compartment Lower Level armed the explosives in the gas generators, which would generate the steam that would impulse the missiles out of the submarine to just above the ocean's surface. One by one, twenty-one gas generators were armed.

The USS *Kentucky* was ready to launch.

All that remained was Malone's final order. And once that order was given, it would be out of his hands. The Weapons Officer and his missile techs would take over, preparing and launching each missile. If there was one last opportunity to turn back, this was it. But Malone had made his decision three years ago. He had made a commitment then, and he would follow through now.

Malone turned to the watchstander next to him. "Phone talker to Weapons. You have permission to fire." The phone talker repeated Malone's order, then passed it to MCC over the sound-powered phone circuit.

Control grew quiet; the launch sequence had been set into motion.

Malone had done his part.

The Executive Officer had done his.

Would the Weapons Officer and missile techs do theirs?

Malone listened to the first order going out over the MCC communication circuit.

"Prepare ONE."

The indicating light for Missile Tube One muzzle hatch turned green, indicating the muzzle hatch had been opened and was now locked in place. The starboard missile team relayed its report back to Missile Control Center.

"ONE, ready."

Silence gripped Control as the crew awaited the ignition of Missile Tube One's gas generator and the flexing of the keel as the sixty-five-ton missile was impulsed out of the tube. Malone stared at the Captain's Indicator Panel, waiting for the last light to turn green, which would happen when the Weapons Officer squeezed the Trigger.

Thirty seconds passed, but the light for Missile Tube One stayed red.

Malone glanced around Control. Something was wrong.

A minute passed, and still no launch.

Stepping onto the Conn, Malone removed the 21-MC microphone from its holster. "MCC, Conn. Report launch status."

There was no response from MCC.

"MCC, Conn. This is the Captain. Report launch status."

Still no answer.

Malone started to slam the mike back into its clip when MCC responded.

"Captain, this is Lieutenant Wilson." Tom's voice was uncertain, shaken. "The Weps . . ." There was silence for a few seconds. "The Weps won't unlock the safe."

"Put the Weps on line!" Malone yelled into the 21-MC microphone.

A few seconds later, Tom replied, "The Weps won't take the mike."

Malone slammed the microphone back into its clip and stepped off the Conn, stopping in front of the COB. "Give me your firearm."

The COB unholstered the pistol and slowly handed it over, butt first.

Malone released the magazine into his hand, ensured it was full, then reinserted it. "Come with me, COB." Malone hadn't bothered counting the number of rounds in the magazine.

He figured he only needed one.

In MCC, Lieutenant Pete Manning stood next to the Launch Control Panel safe containing the Trigger, his face placid. As he braced himself for the impending confrontation with the Captain, his thoughts wandered to his meeting with the XO after lunch, during which he had revealed his reservations. The XO had been understanding and to some extent shared the same feelings, but in the end, Lieutenant Commander Fay was firm about their responsibility to the *Kentucky* and the Navy. They had been given an order and they would follow it, regardless of whether they thought the order should have been issued in the first place.

That wasn't what he wanted to hear, and he had left the XO's stateroom no closer to deciding what to do. The remaining hours had slipped away, and when the launch order came across the 1-MC, followed by the identical one over the 21-MC, he had been forced to decide. As a result of his decision, the door to MCC flew open and Malone stormed in, the COB close behind.

"What the hell is going on, Weps?" Malone stopped a few feet away—there was a pistol in his hand, held down by his thigh.

Manning held firm his resolve. "I can't do it, sir."

"Yes, you can. The rest of us have done our part. Now it's your turn. Unlock the safe."

Manning shook his head. "No, sir. I will not be a part of this."

"I gave you a direct order. Open the safe."

Manning stood there, silent.

Malone's eyes narrowed as he raised the pistol, pointing it at the Weps's face.

"Open the safe!"

Although the Captain had a pistol pointed at his head, Manning knew he was bluffing. There was no way he would kill someone for disobeying an order, even a nuclear strike order.

"I will not open the safe, sir."

Malone reached up and pulled back the slide, chambering a round. "Open the safe."

The confrontation had escalated higher than Manning had expected. Like a game of Texas hold 'em, the Captain had bluffed by holding a pistol to his head and he had responded by going all-in. But Malone hadn't folded. However, with a round chambered and the muzzle of the Beretta an inch from his forehead, there was one small, but important detail about the weapon in Malone's hand that was not lost on the Weps.

The safety was still on.

* * *

That fact was not lost on Malone either, along with the realization that the stakes in this confrontation were high. Like a snowball rolling downhill, gaining speed and mass as it traveled, the Weps's refusal to follow his order could turn into an avalanche of insubordination. That was something he could not allow. He could relieve the Weps and replace him with another officer, but if the only immediate repercussion a crew member suffered was being relieved from his watch station, that would do little to deter others. He needed to make an example of the Weps, make the consequences of refusing to obey the Captain's order so dire that no one would be willing to accept the same punishment.

Malone lifted his thumb, releasing the safety.

"I'm going to give you to the count of three, and if your hand isn't spinning the tumbler by then, I'm going to permanently relieve you of your duties."

The Weps stared at Malone as he began counting.

"One."

Tom and the missile techs stood frozen in their places.

"Two."

As Pete Manning stood on the wrong end of the Beretta, he understood Malone's obligation to execute the president's order, as well as the country's desire for revenge. The nuclear attack on the nation's capital was a thousand times more devastating than 9/11, and they had to respond. But whereas the retribution after 9/11 was meticulously planned, attempting to eliminate only the terrorists while sparing the innocent in the vicinity, nuclear weapons were indiscriminate in their destruction, unable to distinguish between the guilty and the innocent.

It was murder, pure and simple.

"I can't do it. I can't kill millions of people."

He would not partake in this crime against humanity, and he would accept the consequences of his decision. Unfortunately, until this moment, he thought the only consequences would be professional. Apparently not. But he had made his decision and would stand by it, and no amount of coercion would change his mind. And so, with a pistol to his head, a round chambered and safety off, and the color of Malone's index finger changing from pink to white as he squeezed the trigger, Lieutenant Pete Manning accepted his fate.

As Malone squeezed the trigger, he wondered how it had come down to this. As the Commanding Officer of a naval vessel, he had significant authority and wide latitude in dealing with discipline problems and insubordination. He could dock a sailor's pay, bust him in rank one or even two pay grades, and restrict a married man to the ship for weeks, even months. He had exercised his authority many times at captain's mast, and would not hesitate in the midst of their missile launch to use every means at his disposal to ensure compliance with his order. However, as extensive as his authority was, he could not kill his Weapons Officer.

He dropped his hand to his side.

"Goddamn it, Weps!"

Talking over his shoulder, his eyes still locked on his department head, he issued instructions to the COB. "Confine Lieutenant Manning to his stateroom. Post two armed petty officers outside his door." Malone turned toward Tom. "Lieutenant Wilson."

* * *

It took a moment for Tom to realize his name had been called. "Yes, sir."

"You are now the Weapons Officer. Can you carry out the responsibilities of this position?"

Things were moving too fast. A second ago, he was an innocent bystander in the clash of wills between the Weps and the Captain. Now he had been assigned the Weapons Officer's duties, and Malone wanted to know if he could carry them out.

Could he unlock the safe if given the combination? Yes.

Could he squeeze the Trigger? Yes.

Tom answered Malone automatically, before he answered the more important question he needed to ask himself. *Would* he?

"Yes, sir. I can carry out the responsibilities of Weapons Officer."

"Good," Malone said. "Get one of the EAM teams and retrieve the Weps's combination."

Tom nodded numbly as the COB took the pistol from Malone and escorted Lieutenant Pete Manning, former Weapons Officer of the USS *Kentucky,* BLUE Crew, out of MCC.

Glancing over at the Launch Control Panel, Tom noted the blinking red lights. "Sir, the launch sequence has timed out. We'll need to start over."

"Shut tube One missile muzzle hatch," Malone growled. "Set condition Four-SQ."

Moments later, the seven-ton muzzle hatch slammed shut as the *Kentucky* reset her strategic weapon system.

66

HMAS *COLLINS*
42 MINUTES REMAINING

"Watch Leader, Sonar. Mechanical transients, bearing zero-zero-two, designated Sierra three-five."

Captain Murray Wilson stood next to Brett Humphreys in the cramped Control Room, as the tired crew of the *Collins* finally caught a sniff of their target. That they were now picking up mechanical transients did not bode well. Wilson exchanged a concerned look with Humphreys.

"Designate Sierra three-five as Master One," Humphreys announced.

The submarine's XO complied and a moment later reported, "Estimated range to Master One based on bottom bounce is thirty thousand yards."

Humphreys acknowledged and was about to give orders to the Helm when Wilson gently grabbed his arm and nodded toward the aft corner of Control.

The two men crammed themselves between two equipment consoles as Wilson spoke quietly. "I want you to communicate with the *Kentucky* first via underwater comms. I know what your orders say, but as long as we stop them from launching, that's what matters."

Humphreys considered Wilson's words for a moment, then replied, "I will not give away our stealth advantage. The *Kentucky* may be a ballistic missile submarine, but her tactical systems are equivalent and her weapons are superior. Our only advantage is our stealth. I won't give that up."

"The *Kentucky* won't attack, Brett. I guarantee it. Malone didn't fire on a *Virginia*-class that came within a thousand yards. He won't shoot. Trust me on this."

Wilson's eyes conveyed his desperation as Humphreys contemplated his friend's request. Finally, he replied, "All right. But if the *Kentucky* shows the slightest sign of aggression . . ."

Wilson clasped Humphreys's shoulder. "Thanks, Brett."

Humphreys turned toward the Watch Leader. "Come to course zero-zero-two, ahead full."

Looking at the Weps, Humphreys ordered, "Open outer doors, tubes One through Six."

67

ARLINGTON, VIRGINIA
41 MINUTES REMAINING

With Hendricks standing in her foyer, gift bag in hand, Christine turned away, hiding the smile that had formed on her lips. He had chosen this awkward time, in the middle of a crisis, to broach the subject of a renewed relationship. Looking for a reason to explain her sudden turn away, she straightened a few pieces of mail she had tossed onto the kitchen counter two days ago.

Christine turned around, startled by Dave's presence. He was only three feet away now. His eyes were determined, every trace of indecision gone. She eyed the gift bag in his hand, curiosity replacing the sudden fright. "So what do you have there? Something for me?"

Hendricks stared at her for a moment, his face emotionless. Then his features softened into a friendly smile. "Yes, something especially for you."

Christine tilted her head. "Are you trying to get back into my good graces? Start over?"

"Something like that."

Looking down, she tried to catch a glimpse of what

was in the bag. "Don't keep me in suspense. Show me what you've got."

"In a minute. But first I need to explain." He reached up and caressed the side of her face with the back of his fingers. He lingered on her cheekbone, then slowly slid his fingers across her lips. She resisted the urge to kiss his fingers, to grab his hand and hold it against the side of her face. And then his fingers were gone. He still looked at her with determined eyes, but they had turned cold and hard.

"I finally figured out why our marriage failed," he began. "We shared the same goals, but our approaches toward achieving them were never the same. You've always played within the rules, while I've never constrained myself to someone else's definition of right and wrong. Take the defense of our country, for example. You and I both work to protect the country we love. But you joined an administration whose visions you didn't share. You did it because you thought it was the best way to achieve your goal within the confines of right and wrong."

Christine bit her lip, not sure where Dave was headed. His voice was listless, as if he regretted something he'd done.

Or was about to do.

"I decided not to waste my time in a futile effort like yours," he continued, "waging a losing battle to defend our country. I wanted to eliminate our most serious enemies and send a message to others. When this opportunity presented itself, it wasn't hard for me to decide."

"What opportunity?" Christine asked warily.

He smiled. "You're so naïve, Chris. Your instincts were correct. Someone involved in this plot knew the

Kentucky had twice the number of warheads. Someone knew the *Kentucky* was on its way to a patrol area within range of Iran. That information is extremely sensitive, known only by a few. Who that person is should have been obvious to you. But even though you haven't figured it out yet, you're a persistent woman, and you would have eventually identified him. And it isn't Hardison."

A sliver of ice ran down Christine's spine.

It was Dave. He had participated in the plot to destroy Iran, a plot that would soon result in 192 warheads raining down in a holocaust of nuclear destruction. But why was he telling her this? How could he risk exposing his role to her? He either was convinced she would keep his secret, or—

Christine drew in a sharp breath.

—he intended to ensure she would never tell a soul.

She took a step back, her eyes shifting to the package he held in his hand. "What's in the gift bag, Dave?"

He reached into the bag with his right hand. "Something especially for you." He let the bag fall to the floor; his hand held a black revolver. "I'm disappointed you decided to end your life this way."

"What way?" Christine asked, her eyes flicking between Dave's hand and his face. Her breathing turned shallow, rapid.

"Your suicide. The stress of this past week was more than you could handle. I'll have to explain how despondent you became, how overwhelmed you were with your responsibility as national security adviser. How, once it became clear the *Kentucky*'s warheads would destroy Iran, you must've felt personally responsible for this horrible tragedy."

Christine's pulse quickened.

She recognized the double-action revolver. It was a Smith & Wesson Centennial, the one Dave had bought her shortly after they married, the one he taught her to fire as he stood behind her at the shooting range. After the divorce, she had returned the revolver to him; he was the gun nut. But the weapon was still registered in her name. It would look like she had taken her life with her own gun.

Her mind raced, searching for a way out of her predicament. Maybe he could be reasoned with, talked out of his madness.

"But the *Kentucky* hasn't launched yet." She tried to keep the panic from her voice, maintain it calm and steady. "There's a possibility she won't launch, and even if she does, that our defenses will take out her missiles. And as long as there's hope, why would I kill myself?"

Hendricks sneered. "The *Kentucky* will launch. She wouldn't have come this far if she wasn't intent on launching. And once she does, our ballistic missile defenses will be overwhelmed. But just in case, I've added an insurance policy. A virus has been inserted into our ballistic missile defense-targeting systems, corrupting the data. Only my computer account has the ability to correct this problem, and I'll ensure all evidence of this corruption is eliminated immediately afterward.

"Everyone will believe our failure to intercept the *Kentucky*'s missiles was due to our inadequate ballistic missile defense systems, and we'll invest billions to improve them. You see, Chris, this plan will improve our country's security—Iran will be destroyed, eliminating the most serious threat to our country today, and we'll develop better missile defense systems to protect us in the future. I will have made a difference, while you will have wasted your time in a futile effort to influence an administration from within."

Finished with the explanation he promised, Hendricks appeared ready to take the next step, murdering his ex-wife. Christine's frantic search for a way to save herself had identified only two options. She'd tried the first—talk her way out. That left the other option.

A physical confrontation.

She had to wrest the gun from his hand.

But how?

Hendricks was six inches taller and sixty pounds heavier. And much stronger. The odds of overpowering him were slim to none. But there appeared to be no alternative. She had taken self-defense classes, but the moves she knew were designed to defend against an assailant attempting to overpower and restrain her. That wasn't the situation here. Dave wasn't going to physically attack her—he was going to put a bullet in her head. The roles were reversed.

She had to attack *him.*

Her mind indexed through her repertoire of moves, searching for one she could use to attack. But Hendricks interrupted her thoughts before she had identified an appropriate move. "Into the study," he said. "You're going to end your life sitting at your desk."

Christine glanced again at the gun in his hand, still held at his side. As long as it was pointed at the floor and not her head, there was hope she could succeed. But she hadn't figured out how yet. She stalled. "Think about what you're doing, Dave. Yes, you've participated in a conspiracy against our country, but your motive is honorable. If your role is discovered, I'm sure that will be taken into account. But once you commit murder, there's no hope for leniency. Please, Dave, I swear I'll keep your secret. *Our* secret. We can get back together. I've been thinking about that a lot, and nothing you've told me has changed my mind. I still love you."

She took a step forward, reaching out to him with her left hand, praying her approach would be misinterpreted. She didn't care whether he believed her or not; whether he thought her statement and gesture were a genuine attempt to bring their lives back together, or a desperate lie. Either way was fine—as long as he didn't notice the shift in her posture, transferring her weight to the balls of her feet, her body tensing for action.

"I've already crossed that line, Chris." Hendricks's hand twitched at his side. "I've already been forced to commit murder by a prying intern who discovered more than he should have."

Christine's eyes widened. "You killed Russell!"

"I'm afraid so. And now it's your turn. Into the study."

"No," Christine said firmly.

Hendricks's voice turned hard. "We can do this the easy way, in the study, or the messy way, here in the kitchen. The decision is yours."

The messy way, then. "I'm not going anywhere."

"Fine. Have it your way."

Hendricks's arm started to swing up toward her, and fear rippled through her body. If there was any hope at all, she had to act now. Once his arm was raised, the pistol pointed at her head, it'd be almost impossible to attack him and avoid a bullet. Another second of delay, another moment of indecision, and her life would be over. Christine's resolve galvanized, and as the pistol in Dave's hand rose toward her head, she moved quickly.

USS *KENTUCKY*
39 MINUTES REMAINING

Five minutes after being assigned as the *Kentucky*'s Weapons Officer, Tom stood inside the Op Center forward of Control, waiting for Lieutenant (JG) Carvahlo and Lieutenant Costa to open the two-door safe containing the Weapons Officer's safe combination. Costa spun the dial and opened the safe's outer door, then stepped back to allow Carvahlo access to the inner door. A moment later, the inner door clicked open. Carvahlo reached inside, retrieved the envelope, and handed it to Tom. The two officers shut and locked the safe doors, then left Tom alone in the Op Center. He peeled open the envelope and pulled out the slip of paper.

Tom stared at the numbers, committing them to memory, then placed the combination back in the envelope. After a knock on the Op Center door, Carvahlo and Costa entered and opened the safe again. Once the combination was back inside and both tumblers spun, Tom stepped out of the Op Center into Control. The *Kentucky* was still at Battle Stations Missile, hovering at launch depth. In a few minutes, they would begin the launch sequence again, this time with Lieutenant Tom Wilson as the submarine's Weapons Officer.

As Tom made his way through Control on his way to MCC, Malone hoped things would go smoothly this time. He had more confidence in Tom than he had in Lieutenant Manning, but it was a lot to ask of the junior officer. In a few minutes, the burden of the missile launch would rest on his shoulders, and Malone would see what kind of mettle the young man was made of.

After receiving word that Tom had reached MCC, Malone picked up the 1-MC microphone. "Set condition One-SQ for strategic launch. This is the Commanding Officer. The release of nuclear weapons has been directed."

Without hesitating this time, the XO repeated the order over the 21-MC. Tom's voice emanated from the speaker, acknowledging the order with only a hint of nervousness.

Malone again turned his key ninety degrees counterclockwise in the Captain's Indicator Panel and flipped up the Permission to Fire toggle switch. The first column of indicating lights on the CIP, with the exception of the missiles in tubes Eight, Ten, and Twelve, began turning red as their inertial navigation gyros spun up again and were informed of their slightly revised position on earth. As the missiles began accepting their target packages, the next column of lights also toggled from black to red. One by one, each gas generator was armed, illuminating the indicating lights in the third column.

With the CIP in front of him glowing ominously, Malone gave MCC permission to fire, and the order was passed to Tom over the sound-powered phones.

The crew had done their part again.

Would Tom do his?

One level down from Control and just aft, Lieutenant Tom Wilson stood next to the Weapons Officer's safe in Missile Control Center, cold air blowing on him from the ventilation ducts above, adding to the chill that already permeated his flesh and bones. It was quiet in MCC as the missile techs stared at the lieutenant, wondering if he, unlike his predecessor, would execute the Captain's order to launch. Tom studied the Launch Control Panel, noting the green lights in each column with the exception of tubes Eight, Ten, and Twelve.

They were almost ready to launch. Only two things remained: Open each tube's muzzle hatch and unlock the safe containing the Tactical Mode Key and Trigger.

Trying not to think about the ramifications of his actions, Tom reached for the safe's combination dial. He spun the dial five times counterclockwise, as he had done a hundred times on similar safes, stopping on the first number of the combination. He spun clockwise to the next number, counterclockwise again to the final number, then returned the dial to zero.

His hand hesitated as he gripped the safe handle, suddenly hoping the safe wouldn't open, that the Weps had written down a fake combination. As much as he didn't

want to witness the confrontation that would occur if
Manning had written down the incorrect combination,
the burden would be lifted from his shoulders. Hoping
his part in the launch would end right here, he pulled
down firmly on the handle. The safe clicked.

And unlocked.

He pulled the door slowly open, and the bright
MCC lights illuminated the Tactical Mode Key and
Trigger.

Tom reached inside, retrieving the Tactical Mode Key.
He inserted it into the Launch Control Panel. Turning it
to the Attack position, he closed the electrical circuit between the panel and the submarine's twenty-four missiles. Reaching into the safe again, he wrapped his fingers
around the Trigger, which looked like a pistol minus the
barrel, pulling it out of the safe. An electrical cord ran
from the Trigger back into the safe, attaching it to the
launch control circuitry. The Trigger felt light in his hand,
incommensurate with its importance.

In Control, Malone listened carefully as the first order
went out over the MCC communication circuit.

"Prepare ONE."

The indicating light for Missile Tube One's muzzle
hatch turned green. The response echoed from the Missile Compartment, confirming their first missile was
ready for launch.

"ONE, ready."

Tom's next action was simple—squeeze the Trigger.
But Malone knew it was easier said than done. If Tom
could stay focused on the individual steps and not think
about the totality of his actions, he would be able to

squeeze the Trigger. But Malone suspected that not even Tom himself could predict what he would do.

Thirty seconds passed, and the indicating light for Missile Tube One stayed solid red.

A minute passed, and still no green light; no gas generator ignition, no flexing of the ship's keel as missile ONE left the ship.

Malone hung his head, wondering what he had to do to get his crew to execute the mission they were trained to accomplish.

Tom stood frozen in MCC, his arm extended, the Trigger in his hand. Nearby, the missile techs waited as the young lieutenant struggled to decide if he would follow the Captain's order, or refuse like the Weps. His hand was ice-cold and his fingers white, as if the Trigger were sucking the heat from his hand. His heart pounded and his breathing turned shallow, and the lights on the Launch Control Panel began spinning. Reaching out with his left hand, he steadied himself on the edge of the fire control console. He felt light-headed, as if he were about to pass out.

As he fought through the nausea, an image of his father appeared. It was the day he graduated from the Naval Academy. His father's arm was around him, his face beaming with pride. Four years earlier, he'd stood in the hot July heat on the tan bricks outside Bancroft Hall, his right hand raised, repeating the Oath of Office, an oath that echoed in his mind today:

I, Thomas Gerald Wilson, do solemnly swear that I will support and defend the Constitution of the United States against all enemies, foreign and domestic; that I will bear true faith and allegiance to the same; that I take this obligation freely, without any mental reservation or purpose of evasion; and that I will well and faithfully discharge the duties of the office on which I am about to enter. So help me God.

He'd sworn to follow the orders of the president and the officers appointed above him, with the same hand that now held the Trigger. The president had given him an order, reinforced by Malone, and he had an obligation to obey, codified in the solemn oath he'd taken that hot summer day.

Tom's finger twitched, almost squeezing the Trigger. But a vision of his wife appeared, standing on the pier the day the *Kentucky* left for patrol, waving to him as the ship headed out to sea. His twin girls slept peacefully in their strollers next to her.

Nancy's image transformed, her hair turning from blond to black, her skirt growing into a long dark dress, a scarf wrapped around her face. She was no longer his wife but a nameless woman in Tehran, her young children clinging to her legs as she stared upward at hundreds of odd red streaks raining down from the sky. She covered her eyes as a bright white flash lit the horizon, and then her body and those of her children vaporized as the heat and pressure wave from the atomic blast destroyed everything in its path.

Wilson appeared in his mind again, as did Malone, both reminding him sternly of his duty. But then his mom appeared, whispering in his ear, telling him it was time to make a decision. That no one could decide for him.

She was correct, Tom realized. It was time to decide.

MCC slowly stopped spinning, and his nausea faded.

The lights on the Launch Control Panel steadied, and the sensation of the Trigger in his hand reminded Tom the crew was at Battle Stations Missile, and the next action was his.

Tom made his decision.

69

DAISAN SHINSHO-MARU
34 MINUTES REMAINING

For centuries, the captains of sailing ships feared and avoided the Doldrums, the equatorial waters where the winds are light and variable, often absent altogether, stranding ships in the calm waters for days and even weeks without the wind to fill their sails. To the north of the Doldrums lies a region of strong and steady winds that European empires, beginning in the fifteenth century, relied on as they expanded their trade routes. This morning, with the sun shimmering just above the horizon, the air was still on the deck of the *Daisan Shinsho-Maru,* as the fishing trawler drifted just south of those trade winds, inside the northern edge of the Doldrums.

Michiya Aochi leaned over the edge of the aging trawler as it bobbed in the calm water, grabbing the fishing net in his gloved hands, heaving upward to retrieve the net they had dragged behind the ship throughout the night. As the graying fifty-three-year-old fisherman wiped the sweat from his forehead, he wished the ship's captain would buy the mechanical winches the newer boats carried, instead of relying on the difficult, but cheap, process of manually hauling the heavy nets and their catch back on deck. Aochi paused to stretch his back, admiring the sunrise; the breaking dawn had painted the cumulus clouds an iridescent pink, orange, and red. Although the radiant sunrise was mesmerizing, it was not long before the scent of saltwater brine and rust from the trawler's deck drew his attention back to his work.

As Aochi leaned over to grab another handful of fishing net, he looked up, his attention caught by a large cylindrical object with a round nose that emerged from the water a few hundred yards away. It hovered for a second just above the water's surface, then bright red flames erupted from the bottom of the object. It rose upward, picking up speed as it streaked through the sky, leaving a thick trail of white smoke behind. Aochi strained his neck, following the object until it disappeared into the clouds. A minute later, a second object emerged near where the first had appeared, repeating the strange sequence of events.

70

ARLINGTON, VIRGINIA
33 MINUTES REMAINING

As the revolver in Hendricks's hand rose toward Christine's head, she stepped toward Dave and chopped down with her left hand, blocking him from raising his pistol. Curling the fingers of her right hand into a half fist, she threw her arm forward, focusing the strength of her shoulder and the momentum of her body into a vicious jab to the center of his neck, right below his Adam's apple.

The attack caught Hendricks by surprise. Her hand connected solidly with his throat, and he staggered backward, gasping for breath, clutching the kitchen island with his left hand to help maintain his balance. Christine stepped forward again, this time grabbing his right wrist with both hands, ducking under his arm while turning in a full circle, twisting his arm up and behind his back. She shoved him forward, slamming his stomach against the kitchen counter, jamming her shoulder into his back, pinning him against the counter as she continued twisting his wrist with both hands. But as she prepared to wrest the pistol from his grip, he let it fall to the floor.

The gun landed near their feet with a heavy thud. Hendricks kicked it away, and it slid across the floor toward the foyer. Hendricks's gasps began to subside, and she could feel his strength returning. As his wrist twisted back against her grip, Christine gave him one final shove against the counter, then released his wrist and sprinted toward the revolver. Hendricks spun toward her the instant she let go, lashing out with his left arm. He caught her with the back of his hand, striking her on the side of her face. The blow knocked her off balance, and she stumbled against the counter on the other side of the kitchen. Hendricks continued turning toward Christine, smashing his right fist into her face. Christine reeled from the blow, her body bending back over the counter.

He lunged forward, pinning her against the counter with his body, clamping both hands around her neck, his fingers squeezing into her flesh. She tried to breathe, but no air entered or exited her lungs. Hendricks's hands crushed her larynx shut, his face turning red from the effort. Christine's arms flailed across the marble countertop, searching desperately for a weapon she could use against him. But in her panic, all she did was knock everything off the counter. The jars of sugar and flour shattered as they hit the floor, ceramic fragments skittering across the tile. The container of spatulas and whisks rolled in a circular pattern, depositing its contents as it spun. The butcher's block of knives thudded onto the floor.

As Hendricks's face strained with the effort to squeeze the life out of her, Christine's eyes went to the butcher's block. A carving knife had slid out. Step two of her next plan crystallized in her mind, but she first had to address step one: break free of Hendricks's grip. His body pinned hers against the counter with his legs spread slightly apart, her right leg between them.

Christine jammed her knee upward, smashing into Hendricks's groin. His knees buckled, his face contorting in pain, and his grip around her neck momentarily relaxed. She thrust her arms up though his, breaking his grip, then she shoved him away and dove for the knife. As she landed on the floor, her right hand curled around the smooth wooden handle. She twisted onto her back, hoping to impale Dave if he jumped on top of her, but she was a second too late. He'd already leapt toward her, and he landed on her before she could place the knife between them. But she still had the knife in her hand, and she swung it toward him before he could grab her arm, embedding it two inches deep into his left shoulder.

Hendricks gave no indication he was in pain. He simply reached over with his right hand and grabbed her wrist before she could remove the knife and stab him where it would do more damage. He pushed her arm back, extracting the knife from his shoulder, the end of the blade dripping blood, then grabbed her wrist with both hands, twisting and bending it backward until she was forced to release the knife.

The blade clattered to the floor.

It appeared she was out of options. He sat atop her, his legs straddling her waist, both hands holding her right wrist, the knife on the floor beside them.

In desperation, she clawed at Hendricks's face with

her left hand, attempting to gouge out his eyes. He grabbed her hand and pushed both of her arms down, pinning her hands to the floor on each side of her head. His face was close to hers, only a foot away, his face red, perspiration on his forehead and cheeks. The position reminded her of the life they once shared, years ago, the emotion and physical sensation just as intense. But love and pleasure had been replaced by hatred and pain.

The pain would not last long, as Hendricks was intent on ending her life. But he'd have to release his grip on her wrist to grab the knife. She focused, concentrating on his weight on top of her, his grip on her wrists, waiting for the slightest indication he was going for the knife. The pressure on her right wrist suddenly eased as he released her hand, but Christine was ready. She grabbed his left wrist before his hand reached the knife.

Hendricks's hand froze in midair. Staring at her with cold eyes, he pushed his hand toward the knife. He was too strong. His hand inched downward, and his fingers soon touched, then wrapped around the blade handle. After firmly grabbing the knife, he pulled his hand back until it was a foot above her head. Then he rotated the blade until it pointed down, the sharp tip barely three inches from her skin. He overpowered her, driving the knife toward her neck.

Soon it was only two inches away.

Then an inch.

Christine felt the sharp tip against her skin, the pressure increasing as Hendricks drove the blade downward. She could hear her pulse pounding in her ears, feel the warm throbbing of the arteries in her neck against the cool steel of the knife's blade. The last ten days flashed through her mind; she relived each encounter with Dave, seeing now the indictors of his treason that should have been obvious to her. She wondered if that's what happened to people when they faced certain death, the life they muddle through becoming clear, if only for an instant.

She couldn't believe her life was going to end like this, murdered on her kitchen floor by a man she once loved, a man she trusted until a few minutes ago. There was a time she would have given her life for him. But she'd be damned if she'd let him take it now.

Christine wrenched her left hand away from Hendricks's grip, grabbing his left wrist with both hands. She pushed upward with both arms, and the pressure on her neck eased. She soon saw the tip of the knife as she continued to push Hendricks's hand up and away from her neck.

His lips twisted into a mocking sneer. "Nicely done, Chris. However, there's one major flaw in your plan." He lifted his right hand, no longer occupied with pinning her left hand, and wiggled his fingers. He curled his hand into a fist, then smashed it down into her face.

Her mouth ignited in pain, throbbing with each heartbeat as blood oozed from her lips, split open by his punch. But her attention remained focused on the knife, which had closed half the distance toward her neck as the pain coursed through her body.

He pulled his fist back, then brought it down swiftly again in a crushing blow. Christine's nose crumpled under the force, blood spewing from her nostrils. Searing pain flashed through her face, turning her vision yellow with pinpricks of light dancing across her eyes. She fought through the pain, focusing again on the knife. She could no longer see the tip of the blade.

But she could feel it.

The tip pressed against her neck again, the blade suddenly dull compared to the sharp pain in her nose and mouth. Hendricks pulled his fist back again, but his hand halted in midair.

"That ought to do it."

His fist opened, his right hand joining his left around the knife handle.

"Good-bye, Christine."

He pressed down with both hands, and she felt the knife pierce into her neck. Her arms and shoulders strained, pushing up against his hands, struggling to halt the knife's descent. Blood from her beaten face seeped into her mouth between clenched teeth. Tears of frustration and anger filled her eyes, rage building inside her as she realized she would soon be dead.

Because she was weak.

Because she was naïve.

Because she was *betrayed*.

Her rage broke in a torrent of adrenaline, flooding her body with the resolve to survive. She channeled the white-hot anger into her shoulders, her arms, her grip on his wrists.

The knife's descent halted.

Christine's neck burned as the tip of the knife wavered, lacerating the edges of the thin cut in her neck. Hendricks's eyes widened as she found the strength to match his, the insolence to defy him. The dark pupils of his eyes examined her for a moment. Then he grinned, the corners of his mouth curling up into a familiar smile.

He leaned forward, adding his weight to the strength of his arms.

The knife resumed its descent.

Christine strained to repulse the sharp blade slicing deeper into her flesh, pouring every ounce of strength into her burning muscles, her shoulders and arms shaking from the effort.

But he was too strong.

Although she still strained against his hands, her arms stopped trembling, calm replacing the panic that had strangled her thoughts just seconds ago. She had done everything possible to defend herself. At least there was satisfaction in that.

There was nothing more she could do.

She accepted her fate.

Christine closed her eyes as warm blood pooled beneath her head, spreading slowly across the cold stone tile.

71

HMAS *COLLINS*
32 MINUTES REMAINING

"Missile launch transients, bearing zero-zero-two!"

The Sonar Supervisor's report carried across the *Collins*'s Control Room.

Wilson was standing next to Humphreys behind the combat control consoles; his chest tightened at the words. The hope he had nurtured from the first moments in Stanbury's office—that he would somehow be able to communicate with the *Kentucky* and not sink her—had been shattered. Now that she had begun launching, the only way to stop her was to attack.

Humphreys had come to that conclusion as well. He wasted no time.

"Firing Point Procedures, contact Master One, One Tube."

The fire control electronic technicians complied as they determined the target's solution. It was an easy task since their target was launching missiles—she was dead in the water. The only unknown parameter was range, and the combat system quickly delivered that information.

Humphreys began to receive the expected reports:

"Ship Control correct," the Officer of the Watch announced, informing Humphreys the submarine was operating within torpedo launch limits.

"Navigation correct," the Navigator reported, verifying there were no navigational constraints affecting the torpedo run toward its target.

"Fire Control correct," the Weapons Officer called out. "Primary weapon ready—One Tube. Secondary weapon—Two Tube."

The *Collins* was ready to engage.

Humphreys looked to Wilson for permission to fire on a U.S. submarine.

But Wilson wasn't ready.

When the *Kentucky* didn't acknowledge her Launch Termination Order, he was certain at first it was nothing more than a Radio Room casualty. But his confidence was shaken when Malone departed his moving haven, for reasons still unknown. Even so, every fiber of his being told him Malone and his crew were simply executing launch orders they believed to be valid, and that things were wrong in ways he couldn't even begin to grasp. Throughout it all, he held on to one firm belief: that he would be able to save his son's life.

Wilson's hope they would not have to sink the *Kentucky* had just been crushed, the same way the submarine's hull would be crushed by the ocean depth a few minutes after the *Collins* fired. He had hoped that somehow the father would return home with the Prodigal Son, at which point he would retire. As they closed on the

Kentucky, he had measured his love for the Navy, to which he had dedicated thirty years, against his love for his son—and it paled in comparison.

However, as he stood in the Control Room of the Australian submarine, none of that mattered. He had been placed aboard the *Collins* for a purpose. His personal feelings were not relevant. Humphreys and the other men and women in the quiet Control Room stared at him, waiting for his order. Finally, Wilson decided there was no point in waiting any longer. He spoke firmly, loud enough for everyone to hear.

"Proceed."

Humphreys turned to his Weapons Officer. "Fire One Tube."

The electronic technician at the Weapons Control Console pressed the Fire key on the touch plasma display, sending the fire signal down to the Weapon Stowage Compartment, initiating the launch sequence for tube One.

72

USS *KENTUCKY*
31 MINUTES REMAINING

"FOUR, away."

Tom spoke into the microphone in his left hand, the Trigger still in his right. He had squeezed it four times now, each contraction accompanied by the flexing of the submarine's deck as the missile left the ship. His mind was numb, his actions and reports automated. He felt divorced from his body, no longer controlling the words he said, the muscles he contracted. The horror of what he had done, what he was continuing to do, reflected from dark brown eyes set within a pale white face.

The ship's deck steadied as the submarine recovered from the launch of missile FOUR, its first-stage engines igniting now, just above the water's surface. The starboard missile team was now in place at tube Five, the teams in each level working their way down the port and starboard sides of the ship. Tom brought the microphone to his lips again.

"Prepare FIVE."

* * *

Commander Malone stood in front of the Captain's Indicator Panel in Control, monitoring the status of the launch. He was proud of his crew, executing this difficult task professionally. Yet at the same time, his stomach churned; he could taste the acid in his mouth.

How could they do this?

How could *he* do this?

As he stood on the hard steel deck of the submarine, his thoughts drifted back to his childhood, when he had knelt in front of the wooden pews in church, thinking about one of the more important axioms he had been taught to believe as a small boy.

Do unto others as you would have them do unto you.

He knew there would be no reconciling what he was doing with the morals that had been ingrained in him as a child. He couldn't even begin to think of what would soon happen thousands of miles away. But there would be time enough for reflection during the *Kentucky*'s lonely voyage home, which would begin as soon as she discharged her obligation, and her twenty-one missiles. As Malone's thoughts returned to the status of the missile launch, the next report came across the ship's announcing system. But it wasn't the report he expected from MCC, announcing the launch of missile FIVE.

"Torpedo in the water!"

Malone's heart leapt to his throat as Sonar's report echoed across Control.

"Torpedo bearing one-eight-two!"

A red bearing line appeared on the combat control

displays, signaling the detection of an incoming torpedo. Where that torpedo had come from was answered by Sonar's next report.

"Heavyweight torpedo, submarine launched!"

73

HMAS *COLLINS*
USS *KENTUCKY*
30 MINUTES REMAINING

Commander Humphreys peered over the Weapons Officer's shoulder as the Weps called out, "Own ship's unit has enabled, active pinging. Solution on Master One holding firm."

Wilson reviewed the solution for the *Kentucky*, represented by a red half circle on the combat control screen. Their torpedo, a green ∧, was rapidly closing in on the *Kentucky*. Unfortunately, they'd been forced to fire at long range in an attempt to disrupt additional missile launches, and that would give the *Kentucky* an opportunity to evade, even starting from dead in the water.

Ideally, Wilson would have preferred to fire a warning shot and call it a day. However, submarine warfare was usually a duel to the death. Now that the *Kentucky* had been attacked, Malone and his crew would do everything within their ability to sink the *Collins,* and the *Collins* had no choice but to do the same.

Only one submarine would survive.

Commander Humphreys intended to ensure that submarine was the *Collins*.

The first torpedo was on its way. A second torpedo would follow.

"Firing Point Procedures, Two Tube, contact Master One."

USS *KENTUCKY*

"Secure from strategic launch!"

Malone began issuing orders to his crew, transitioning the ship from its vulnerable strategic launch posture, dead in the water, to a viable submarine killer.

"Helm, ahead flank! Steady course two-seven-zero!"

"Launch countermeasure!"

The submarine's propeller surged into action, churning the water as it strained to accelerate the *Kentucky* to maximum speed, and a countermeasure was ejected to maintain the incoming torpedo focused on where the *Kentucky* had been rather than where it was headed.

"Flood all torpedo tubes. Open muzzle doors, tubes One through Four!"

Returning his attention to the Captain's Indicator Panel, Malone waited for the red lights to extinguish, signaling the disarming of the gas generators and the closing of the ship's missile tube hatches. All indications switched back to their normal dark status.

"Conn, Torpedo Room. Tubes flooded down, muzzle doors open."

The *Kentucky* had completed her transition—her missile hatches were shut and torpedo tube doors open. She was ready to fight back.

"Rapid counterfire! Bearing one-eight-two, tube Two!"

The *Kentucky* had no solution on the target—only the bearing of the incoming torpedo. But Malone couldn't wait to gain the target on sonar and for the submarine's combat control algorithms to calculate the contact's solution. He needed to shoot now and would settle for a shot back down the bearing of the torpedo.

"Solution ready!" The XO verified the correct bearing had been assigned to the torpedo.

"Weapon ready!" the Weapons Control Coordinator called out.

"Ship ready!" the Navigator announced.

"Shoot!" Malone ordered.

Malone listened to the whirr of the submarine's torpedo ejection pump and the characteristic sound of the four-thousand-pound torpedo being ejected from the submarine's torpedo tube, accelerating from rest to thirty knots in less than a second.

Inside Sonar, Petty Officer DelGreco and the other sonar techs relayed orders and reports between them, simultaneously attempting to lock on to the threat submarine's sonar signature, track its incoming torpedo, and monitor the status of their outgoing unit. Sonar referred to their torpedo as "own ship's unit" so their reports wouldn't be confused with information about an incoming torpedo.

"Own ship's unit is in the water, running normally."

"Fuel crossover achieved."

"Turning to preset gyro course."

"Shifting to medium speed."

The *Kentucky*'s torpedo turned to the ordered bearing

and began the search for its target. But while they held the outgoing and incoming torpedoes, they had not yet detected another submarine.

"Hold no contacts."

Either the threat submarine was far away or a quiet contact. Or both.

As the *Kentucky* increased speed to evade the incoming torpedo, Malone knew he'd soon render his sonar systems useless, blinded by the submarine's turbulent passage through the water, unable to detect the enemy and any additional torpedo launches. But worrying about subsequent launches would have to wait. The *Kentucky* had to survive the first incoming torpedo before she could concern herself with another. Malone focused his attention on the announcements from Sonar, reporting the bearing of the torpedo every ten seconds.

"Torpedo bears one-eight-zero, drawing aft."

Good.

The torpedo hadn't locked on to the *Kentucky* yet and was still headed toward the submarine's original position. The question was, Would the torpedo close to within detection range before the *Kentucky* vacated the area?

"Passing twenty knots," the Helm reported. "Steady course two-seven-zero."

Malone needed to worry not only about how far away the torpedo was but also at what depth it was searching. They had been launching their missiles when they'd been fired at, so best bet was that the torpedo was searching for them shallow, at the same depth they were currently at. That was something Malone needed to change.

"Dive, make your depth eight hundred feet."

The *Kentucky*'s deck tilted downward.

HMAS *COLLINS*

"Two Tube presets matched. Weapon ready!" the *Collins*'s Weapons Officer reported.

"Ship Control correct!"

"Navigation correct!"

"Fire Control correct!"

"Fire Two Tube!" Humphreys ordered his second torpedo into the water.

Wilson's ears popped as the submarine impulsed the torpedo from the tube, then rapidly vented its impulse tanks, refilling them to supply the water for the next shot. He listened to Sonar's reports as they scrutinized their second torpedo, verifying it achieved its milestones.

"Own ship's unit in the water, running normally."

"Fuel crossover achieved."

"Turning to preset gyro course at high speed."

Wilson watched the combat control screens update, and a second green ∧ appeared near the *Collins,* speeding toward the static red diamond. But the *Collins* needed to obtain a new bearing on the *Kentucky,* lost once the missile launch had been terminated and the transients had ended. Sending the second torpedo right down the trail of the first would do no good. He needed to know where to steer it.

"Torpedo in the water, bearing three-five-nine!" Sonar's report of the incoming torpedo blasted across the 27-MC in Control.

"Helm, left full rudder," Humphreys called out, "steady course three-zero-zero."

Wilson watched the Helm rotate the rudder to left full, turning the *Collins* out of harm's way. The incoming torpedo would now pass safely behind them. The *Kentucky* had counterfired, hoping to distract the *Collins,* or even get a lucky hit.

Excellent.

The *Collins*'s first torpedo had been fired at the *Kentucky*'s original solution, with the target bearing 002. Her bearing was now 359. The *Kentucky* was headed west.

Wilson turned to the Weapons Officer. "Report wire continuity."

"We have the wire to both weapons."

The first torpedo continued north, toward the *Kentucky*'s original position. Wilson decided to wait on the first fired unit. But he had something special in mind for the second torpedo.

He turned to Humphreys. "Second fired unit— recommend a left twenty-degree steer, slow to medium speed and pre-enable the weapon."

A confused expression clouded Humphreys's face as he pondered Wilson's last recommendation. He wondered why Wilson had requested he turn off the torpedo's sonar. But he soon nodded his understanding. The *Collins* was engaging the *Kentucky* with inferior weapons—Mod 4 versus Mod 6—as well as inferior submarine speed. Their normal advantage—stealth— had been dealt away by shooting at long range, giving their opponent sufficient warning to evade. Their only hope in this engagement was superior tactics. Thankfully, there was no one more experienced than Wilson.

Humphreys turned to his Weapons Officer. "Insert a left twenty-degree steer, change speed to medium, pre-enable second fired unit."

The Weapons Officer raised an eyebrow as he repeated the order, then directed one of the fire control electronic technicians to send the three commands.

Wilson studied the contact summary display, ensuring the second unit accepted the new orders, verified with an abrupt veer to the left. The *Kentucky*'s solution had been updated, indicating a western track, flank speed, and that the second fired unit had been vectored to the left in an attempt to intercept the *Kentucky* as it evaded the *Collins*'s first torpedo. After reviewing the updated solution, he was confident of the *Kentucky*'s evasion course and speed.

Depth was another matter.

The *Kentucky* had been shallow for its strategic launch. But where had she gone, now that she was evading? Had she done the obvious and gone deep? Or had she stayed shallow in an attempt to fool the *Collins*? Or perhaps she was deep, since staying shallow to fool the *Collins* was really the obvious response. The debate was an endless circle. Wilson decided to go with what a submarine captain would instinctively decide in the heat of battle. "Recommend new search depth change, second fired unit."

Humphreys nodded for the Weapons Officer to accept Wilson's recommendation.

The Weapons Officer looked up, awaiting Wilson's order.

"Set search depth to eight hundred feet."

Wilson retreated to the aft of Control, preparing for the long wait before the opposing torpedoes reached their destination. Unlike in World War II movies, where the submarine fired its torpedo and the enemy ship was sunk in the next scene, modern submarine combat took time. In many scenarios it could take hours to generate a target solution accurate enough to fire on, and firing ranges were usually measured in miles, not yards.

Both of the *Collins*'s torpedoes had been fired from long range. As Wilson watched their torpedoes advance across the combat control display, he did the calculations in his head. Even with the first torpedo traveling at high speed, it would be more than twenty minutes before it caught up to the *Kentucky*. And that's when the combat would really begin.

Until then, he would wait.

74

ARLINGTON, VIRGINIA
29 MINUTES REMAINING

As the USS *Kentucky* reacted to the incoming torpedo, securing from their missile launch and fleeing for their lives, Christine struggled for hers on the cold stone floor of her kitchen. With her strength fading as she strained against her ex-husband's hands, her eyes squeezed shut from the effort, her other senses seemed somehow heightened. A light rain had started falling and she could hear the raindrops pattering softly against the windowpanes. There was the creak of a nearby door and the scrape of metal against stone. The footsteps of passing pedestrians were impossibly loud, almost as if someone were walking across the floor toward her.

"Drop the knife."

The new voice was male and familiar, but she couldn't place it. The pressure against her hands suddenly eased, and the sharp pain in her neck faded to a dull throb.

Christine opened her eyes.

Hardison stood above her, the Smith & Wesson Centennial in his hand, pressed against Hendricks's temple.

She realized the sounds she'd heard were her front door opening, Hardison picking up the metal gun from the tile floor, and his footsteps as he approached.

The knife clattered onto the floor next to Christine, the end of the blade covered in blood. Hendricks stood slowly, then leaned against the kitchen counter, looking away. Hardison kept the pistol pointed at Hendricks but he glanced at Christine lying on the floor, concern clear in his eyes.

Christine pressed her hand against her neck, trying to assess the damage. She pulled her hand away, examining the blood on her fingers. She wiped the blood on her blouse, then pressed her fingers against the incision in her neck again. She pulled her hand away slowly. Her fingers were coated in only a thin sheen of blood.

She'd been lucky.

The knife hadn't sliced through any of her veins or arteries. She winced as she touched her nose, realizing it was broken from the unusual angle. Blood still trickled down the left side of her face, but she could deal with that, as long as her life wasn't in danger.

"Help me up." Christine extended her hand toward Hardison, who looked at her incredulously.

"You're not serious? Stay there until the ambulance gets here."

"I'm getting up. You can either help me or not."

Hardison hesitated, then extended a hand, keeping his eyes and gun fixed on Hendricks. He pulled her to her feet, holding on to her until he was sure she was steady.

Christine expected to feel light-headed as she stood but was surprised she felt okay.

No, not okay. Strong, invigorated. She'd been just seconds away from death, but now she had a new lease on life.

She felt exhilarated.

Relieved.

Angry.

She approached the man who'd tried to murder her, stopping an arm's length away. Curling her right hand into a fist, she punched him in the face with all the force she could muster. Hendricks's head jolted to the side from the impact. He turned back toward her, blood trickling from split upper and lower lips.

Christine grabbed an ice cube from the freezer and held it against the left side of her nose to stop the bleeding, then turned back toward Hendricks. "Tell me how to disable the missile defense targeting corruption."

Hendricks glared at her. "I'm afraid my account is password protected."

"Tell me the password."

He looked away.

"Tell me the password and how to disable whatever you've done, or I swear I'll put a bullet in your head."

"You already know the password." His voice was vacant as he spoke.

"Could you be more specific?"

Hendricks turned back to Christine, his eyes suddenly aware he'd said too much. "That's all I'm going to tell you."

"Fine, have it your way," she said, mimicking the words he'd used when he'd tried to force her into her study. She held her hand out toward Hardison. "Give me the gun."

Hardison shot a glance at Christine. "No. I'm not going to let you kill him if he doesn't talk."

"I don't have time to argue with you, Kevin. Millions of lives depend on reversing what he's done, and he's either going to tell me how to fix it, or die. It's that simple."

"It's not that simple." Hardison stepped away from Christine, moving to the other side of the kitchen island. He eyed the phone on the counter next to him as he maintained his arm extended, the gun pointed at Hendricks. "I'm going to call the police and get you some medical attention. There'll be no more talk about killing Hendricks."

"What the hell, Kevin," Christine said. "Up to now, you've been trying to kill him. Now you want to protect him?"

"I already explained this, Christine. I didn't try to kill him. I only wanted to silence him, to offer financial incentives to ensure his loyalty. I'll lower myself to bribery, but not murder. I can't believe you thought I wanted to kill him."

"You didn't arrange for that car that almost ran him over outside Whitlow's?"

"That was my handiwork," Hendricks said. "*You* would've been killed, saving me all this trouble, if you hadn't reacted so quickly."

"The car was aiming for *me*?"

"Right at you. I had you pinned between me and my car, but you jumped out of the way just in time. And you thought Hardison was trying to kill *me*. You're so blind, Chris."

Christine pursed her lips together for a second before

replying. "Yes, it appears I haven't been particularly observant." Her attention wavered between Hardison and Hendricks, irritated by both her incorrect assessment of Hardison's intentions, and his refusal to hand her the revolver.

As Hardison reached for the phone, his hand holding the gun suddenly jerked backward. Blood splattered Christine's face as the revolver fell to the floor, sliding to the back of the kitchen. There was a bullet hole in Hardison's right wrist. He clutched his wrist with his other hand, crying out in pain as blood oozed between his fingers. Christine reversed the trajectory of Hardison's gun, following the path toward the front door. A man stood in the foyer pointing a gun at Hardison, a silencer screwed into the barrel.

Christine was not a woman with an extraordinary amount of patience, and by now, she was clear out.

"Who the fuck are you?" she asked.

The man swiveled his gun toward her.

"It's about time you got here," Hendricks said as he walked past Christine. "It seems I always have to take matters into my own hands, waiting for the professional help to arrive." He retrieved the gun from the floor, then stopped beside Christine. "If my friend had arrived on time"—he paused, his eyes probing hers—"it would have been much easier on you." He looked across the kitchen. "And if you hadn't stumbled in here, Kevin . . ."

Hendricks addressed the man at the front door. "Kill them. I need to clean up and get back to the Pentagon. Make sure nothing goes wrong."

"There's been a change in plans," the man said, his pistol still aimed at Christine.

Christine wondered who the man was. A professional, from the look of him, someone she and Hardison had no chance of outwitting or overpowering. As she prepared to take a bullet from the man across the room, cold water trickled down the side of her face, and she realized she still held the ice cube against her nose to stop the bleeding.

What's the point?

She tossed the ice cube across the kitchen toward the sink and heard the distinctive whisper of a silencer as the ice left her hand. The ice cube seemed to float in mid-air, arching gracefully toward the sink in slow motion until it hit the stainless-steel basin with a sharp, high-pitched *tink*.

Christine didn't feel the bullet enter her body. She waited for the pain to materialize, spreading through her body like a crack spidering across a broken window. She waited for her strength to fade, for her knees to buckle, for her body to crumple to the ground.

But nothing happened. She hadn't been shot.

Christine released a breath she hadn't realized she'd been holding. She looked at the man. A wisp of smoke drifted up from the end of the pistol, confirming the gun had been fired. But where had the bullet gone? Looking closer, she noticed the man's aim was slightly off. The gun wasn't pointed at her. It was pointed at—

Her head spun toward Hendricks. He was standing next to her, his eyes wide, a thin stream of blood trickling down from a hole in the center of his forehead. His knees gave way as he crumpled to the floor at Christine's feet.

The man pointed his gun back at Christine. "As I said, there's been a change in plans. You will proceed to the Pentagon and do what you can to destroy the missiles if they are launched." He reached into his coat pocket and extracted a folded piece of paper. "I don't know the password to Hendricks's computer, but if you can get in, this is the name of the program and the cancellation code that will disable the virus corrupting the targeting information."

He placed the paper on the foyer table next to the front door.

"I've done you a favor. Now I expect one in return. Forget what I look like. If I find out my description has been provided to anyone or entered into any database, I'll kill both of you. Do you understand?"

Christine nodded, and the man looked expectantly at Hardison.

"Yes," Hardison said, pain evident in the tightness of his voice.

The man holstered the gun under his coat and left.

Christine rushed over to Hardison and examined his hand. The man had put a bullet right through the center of his wrist, and it was still bleeding profusely. She pulled the tie from his neck and tied it tightly around his wrist, then picked up the phone and dialed 911.

Hardison slumped to the floor, resting his back against the kitchen cabinets, and she knelt down with him. "Help is on its way. I have to go to the Pentagon."

"Go," Hardison said. "I'll be all right. I'll wait for the authorities and clean up your mess. As usual." He forced a smile.

Christine squeezed his shoulder, then retrieved Hendricks's CAC ID card from his wallet and dashed to the front door, grabbing the piece of paper from the foyer table on her way out.

75

PENTAGON
20 MINUTES REMAINING

Christine burst into the Current Action Center, almost tripping over Captain Brackman, who opened the door. As the watchstanders turned toward the commotion, shocked expressions cascaded across their faces. She'd received a similar response at the entrance to the Pentagon; her face and neck were coated with dried blood and her blouse smeared with red stains. The entire left side of her face was swollen and her nose was crooked, her lips split open.

Brackman stepped back. "What the hell happened to you?"

"It's not important." Christine's eyes went to the electronic map at the front of the CAC. Four red lines arched up from the Pacific Ocean, slowly diverging as they headed west.

"Four missiles were launched," Brackman announced. "We don't know why the *Kentucky* stopped. But we've been unable to intercept the missiles for some reason."

"The targeting data is corrupted."

Brackman's eyes narrowed. "How do you know that?"

"How I know doesn't matter. What matters is that I can fix it. I need to access Dave Hendricks's computer account." Without waiting for permission, Christine sprinted along the top tier of the CAC into Hendricks's office. Stopping behind her ex-husband's desk, she hit the space bar on his computer keyboard, bringing the monitor to life. As Brackman stopped behind her, she slid Hendricks's CAC ID card into the computer slot. The standard password window appeared in the center of the screen, awaiting the six-character pass code required to gain access.

During her short trip from Clarendon to the Pentagon, Christine had mulled over the possibilities, and was almost positive she knew Dave's pass code. When forced to choose a six-character code, he had always used his birthday. She tried to think of alternate six-digit codes but came up empty.

It was his birthday.

He had better not have changed it, or she was gonna kill him.

She typed in the six digits, then pressed Enter.

Christine held her breath as the screen stared back at her, giving no indication the entry was correct.

Then the screen cleared.

She released her breath and prepared to wait for the start-up scripts to run, but the computer screen turned a solid blue instead, with one word across the screen in large white letters:

PASSWORD:

This must be the extra security program Dave was talking about. He said she knew the password. Perhaps it was the one they had used on their computer network at home when they were married. Closing her eyes, she pictured him sitting at their desk, typing in the password, one letter at a time.

The password sprang into her mind.

Hendricks had graduated from Clemson, and many of his passwords were related to his alma mater. She typed *TIGERS,* then hit Enter. The monitor responded instantly:

INCORRECT PASSWORD. ATTEMPT 2 OF 3:

PASSWORD:

Christine's heart sank. What could it be? As she scanned the pictures on Dave's desk, searching for a clue, her eyes halted on the framed photo of them on their wedding day. *Could that be it?* Their wedding date? She had to admit she'd used it as a password on several of her Internet accounts.

She typed the date into the computer, then hit Enter. The computer responded:

INCORRECT PASSWORD. ATTEMPT 3 OF 3:

PASSWORD:

WARNING: 3 INVALID PASSWORD ENTRIES WILL DIS-ABLE THIS ACCOUNT

Christine's mind spun. What password was so obvi-ous she would know it? She'd have to go back to the day they met, searching for that special event, that special day, that special—

Weekend!

That was it! The first weekend of their honeymoon in Rome, when they had been forced to spend the first two days in that fleabag hotel. A weekend Dave said he would never forget. A weekend at—

The *Esplanade!*

Christine hesitated, searching through her memories a moment more. But there was no other obvious choice. She flexed her hand, then typed in the name of the hotel. The computer cursor blinked at her, waiting for her to hit Enter. If she was wrong, she would be forced to watch the destruction of Iran from video feeds into the Current Action Center, the might of the entire U.S. military overwhelmed by a single ballistic missile submarine.

She pressed the Enter key firmly.

The cursor blinked at her, still sitting after the last character of the password.

Then the blue background disappeared and messages appeared on the monitor, informing her the computer was running start-up scripts and loading Hendricks's account profile.

Christine breathed a sigh of relief. After the desktop appeared, she selected the Search function, typing in the name of the virus. The hourglass spun for a few seconds, then displayed the program, buried in one of Hendricks's personal folders. She launched the program, then typed in the code the man had given her. One word appeared on the screen, followed by a Yes or No option for the reply:

TERMINATE?

She clicked Yes, and the question disappeared, leaving only the computer desktop.

A moment later, the workstations throughout the Current Action Center updated with new targeting information. Seconds later, SM-3 missiles from cruisers in the

Gulf streaked up toward their targets, followed by four THAAD missiles from their battery in Afghanistan.

Christine followed Brackman, stopping behind the Watch Captain's console as the missiles closed on their targets.

"This had better work," Brackman said softly. "We're almost out of missiles. These are the last four THAADs and we have only one cruiser left with SM-3s."

As Christine stared at the display, the first SM-3 closed on the *Kentucky*'s first missile. The green trace representing the SM-3 intersected with the red trace representing the *Kentucky*'s missile; the two traces kept on going.

"We missed," Brackman said quietly.

The Watch Captain's hands moved quickly across his panel. There was another SM-3 following behind, and it was reassigned. Christine's stomach knotted as the second SM-3 intersected the *Kentucky*'s missile, but this time the red and green traces terminated.

Cheers erupted in the Current Action Center.

The *Kentucky*'s first missile had been destroyed.

But there were three more to go.

Christine turned her attention to the next SM-3, closing on the *Kentucky*'s second missile. She followed the green trace until it intersected the red one. Both terminated.

The second missile was destroyed.

She focused on the remaining two missiles. Four SM-3s were headed toward the third missile, while four THAADs had been assigned the task of eliminating the fourth missile. She glanced at the Watch Captain's workstation, expecting to see only the two remaining missiles. But there were now a dozen contacts. The first two missiles had broken up into ten pieces, making the task for the remaining SM-3s and THAADs even tougher.

The first SM-3 closed on the third missile, in the middle of the debris field. The red and green traces marched slowly toward each other. Then kept on going.

Christine watched the next SM-3. It missed too.

The third SM-3 closed on the *Kentucky*'s missile. The red and green traces intersected, then terminated.

The third missile had been destroyed.

Only one missile continued its descent.

76

MISSILE FOUR
15 MINUTES REMAINING

Seven hundred miles above earth, the *Kentucky*'s fourth missile, officially referred to by the *Kentucky*'s crew as missile FOUR, streaked through the stratosphere toward its programmed targets. But missile FOUR had an unofficial name as well. Trident missiles were stored in the submarine's missile tubes for years between depot overhauls, and missile technicians occasionally performed minor maintenance, entering the missile via an access panel in its side. When entering each new missile for the first time after it rolled off the assembly line, one of the missile techs would stop before exiting, inscribing the missile's unofficial name on the inside of the graphite epoxy shell of the missile's third stage. Inside missile FOUR, written in indelible black marker, was its name, along with a message for the recipients of its warheads:

Pray not for *Redemption*.

Redemption reached the apex of its flight path, arching downward on its return to earth. A portal opened in its side, exposing a camera that peered into the heavens.

Click.

An image of the stars was compared to the missile's navigation memory, and a second later, its third-stage engines fired silently in the darkness, rolling the missile to starboard and gently increasing the angle of its downward trajectory. The third-stage engines fired again, halting the missile's roll and pitch at the desired angles.

Click.

Redemption took a second star fix, verifying its flight path had been properly adjusted so that all eight of its warheads, when released, would hit their targets precisely.

The four restraining clamps around warhead One retracted, followed by a brief pulse of the missile's third-stage engines. Warhead One separated from *Redemption,* beginning its lonely journey toward its aim point. The clamps around warhead Two retracted, and the ritual repeated itself seven more times, as *Redemption* released all eight of its warheads flawlessly, exactly as programmed.

Four THAAD missiles streaked up through the atmosphere, the first three missing the small warheads and missile FOUR, distracted by the debris from missile THREE. But the last THAAD homed on the desired target, slamming into missile FOUR, breaking it into pieces.

The THAAD missile had done its job.

Only a minute too late.

77

PENTAGON
10 MINUTES REMAINING

Looking up at the display at the front of the Current Action Center, Christine had watched the SM-3s destroy the first three missiles, her relief turning to dismay as eight red traces branched out from the fourth missile. Their task was now impossible, as the eight warheads had blended in with the surrounding debris; a total of twenty-three traces streaked downward. The icons representing their missile defense platforms blinked yellow, indicating they were out of weapons; all except the USS *Lake Erie,* which still glowed a steady green. But no missiles streaked upward.

"The *Lake Erie* is paralyzed," the Watch Captain announced, looking first at Brackman, then at Christine. "Her Aegis fire control system can't determine which of the targets are the warheads, and they don't have enough missiles to target each bogey."

"If their fire control system can't sort out the contacts," Christine replied, "you're going to have to."

There was a slight hesitation. "And how do I do that?" the Watch Captain asked.

"Figure it out," Christine answered.

The Watch Captain stared at Christine for a moment, then turned back toward his screen. He wiped his palms on his thighs, then squinted at his display. "There has to be something about the eight warheads that distinguishes them from the debris," he said, talking more to himself than to Christine.

As Christine and Brackman exchanged worried glances, the Watch Captain picked up an erasable marker and began scribbling information on the Plexiglas next to his workstation. He cycled through the twenty-three targets, annotating information in several columns, then paused to examine the data, placing an asterisk next to one of the target numbers, and then another. He put down the marker, examining the data in front of him.

There were eight asterisks.

"That's the best I can do," he said, looking up at Christine. "These eight contacts are following the same trajectory, give or take a fraction of a degree. My best guess is these are the warheads."

There was no way to tell if the Watch Captain had determined the correct targets, but there was no time to debate the issue. "Order the *Lake Erie* to engage the tracks you've identified."

He typed several commands into his workstation, and all but eight tracks on the display in front of them disappeared. A moment later, the Watch Captain replied, "The *Lake Erie* is engaging."

Christine's eyes lifted up to the main display as a

green trace appeared, arching up from the cruiser. Ten seconds later, a second green trace appeared, followed by six more, each fired ten seconds apart, until there were eight tracks curving toward the descending red targets. After the eighth green trace appeared, the *Lake Erie*'s icon switched from green to yellow. It didn't take long for Christine to do the math: the *Lake Erie* had launched only eight SM-3s against eight warheads. Every SM-3 had to hit its target.

The seconds ground by slowly, until the first green trace finally intersected a red one. No one spoke as the tracking systems updated, and Christine's stomach tightened as she waited. Then the leading red trace, along with the first green one, terminated where they had intersected.

The first warhead had been destroyed.

Several watchstanders commented to each other quietly, their attention focused on the remaining threats. One by one, each SM-3 intercepted its target until only one warhead and one SM-3 remained. Christine held her breath as the last of the eight SM-3 missiles intercepted the red trace. But unlike the seven previous intercepts, this time the red and green traces continued.

"We missed," the Watch Captain announced. He looked up, defeat on his face. "All platforms report zero assets remaining."

The map on the display zoomed in. The warhead was headed toward Tehran. A city with sixteen million people.

Christine's heart sank. "There has to be something else we can do."

A dour expression filled the captain's face. "I'm afraid

not," he replied. "We have no more antiballistic missiles in the region."

There was something about the Watch Captain's last statement that caught Christine's attention. There were no more *antiballistic missiles* in the region.

But the cruisers in the Gulf were still heavily armed, and perhaps they carried another weapon they could use against the last warhead. Her mind reached back to her days as a staffer for the Senate Armed Services Committee, being briefed on the new SM-3 missile. It had been developed from the SM-2, modified to give the new missile the extra boost to reach high into the stratosphere. A new, longer-range version of the SM-2 had also been developed—the SM-6, giving surface ships the ability to engage missiles and aircraft much further out. Although the SM-6 didn't have the range of the SM-3, it didn't need to reach the stratosphere. The last warhead was only minutes above Tehran.

"Do any of the cruisers in the Gulf carry the SM-6?"

A perplexed expression spread across the Watch Captain's face. "Yes, some of them do." His eyes lit up as he continued, "and they might be in range." The officer turned back to his workstation, quickly pulsing the system for the requested data. "The Lake Erie is barely within range."

"Order her to engage the last warhead with an SM-6."

The Watch Captain tapped a series of touch screen commands. "Order sent and acknowledged."

Christine looked up at a red digital clock on the top right corner of the Current Action Center display, rapidly counting down the time to warhead detonation.

3 minutes remaining

A few seconds later, a blue trace appeared next to the *Lake Erie*'s icon, heading toward the lone remaining warhead. The Watch captain pressed a control at his workstation, and the map of the Middle East zoomed in until only Tehran and its surrounding suburbs filled the screen.

2 minutes remaining

The red trace from the last warhead continued downward, only inches away from its detonation point above the center of Tehran, while the blue trace representing the SM-6 missile streaked across from the side of the screen.

1 minute remaining

If they missed, the last warhead would detonate over Tehran, and a 500-million-degree inferno would vaporize the center of the city and ignite everything within miles, while the shock wave raced outward at the speed of sound, leveling everything in its path. Tehran would become a radioactive wasteland uninhabitable for ten thousand years. The only chance of preventing the holocaust lay with the *Lake Erie*'s SM-6 missile.

The clock reached zero.

The blue and red traces intersected, then started blinking.

"What happened?" Christine asked.

"We've lost the link to our satellite trackers," the captain replied. "We'll have to rely on data from the *Lake Erie*'s fire control system. We're attempting to contact her now."

The Watch Captain tapped another control on his monitor, energizing the Current Action Center speakers.

Random static was interrupted periodically by the CAC requests for information.

"*Lake Erie,* this is the National Military Command Center. Report status of intercepting the last warhead."

Each request was met with static. Christine wondered if the warhead had detonated, destroying their tracking and communication satellites with the electromagnetic pulse. But then the repeated queries were finally answered . . .

"This is USS *Lake Erie.* We have confirmation the last warhead has been destroyed."

Cheers erupted, watchstanders eagerly shaking hands and slapping each other on the back. Brackman stepped toward Christine, pulling her body close against him, then planted a kiss on her lips, one that lingered too long for a simple congratulation.

Pain sliced across Christine's mouth as his kiss split open her cut lip.

Brackman pulled away, a shocked expression on his face. "Sorry," he said sheepishly.

Christine said nothing, simultaneously relieved they had averted disaster and surprised by Brackman's response. Or was she reading too much into it?

She turned back to the screen as it zoomed out to a view stretching from the Middle East to the central Pacific Ocean. The red traces representing the *Kentucky*'s missiles and warheads began to fade, disappearing a few seconds later.

Why had the *Kentucky* stopped launching?

Had the *Collins* sunk the ballistic missile submarine, or simply scared it away? If the *Kentucky* survived, she would launch again, and the nightmare would be repeated. Only this time it would be worse; their antiballistic missiles were expended and they had nothing left to defend against the submarine's remaining twenty missiles.

The red symbol representing the *Kentucky* repositioned, updated by satellites that had detected the submarine's missile launch, placing its estimated position directly on top of the blue symbol representing the *Collins*. The diesel submarine had indeed found the *Kentucky,* forcing her to terminate her launch.

As Christine stared at the two symbols, one on top of the other, she knew the two submarines were engaged in a duel to the death, and that only one would return home.

USS *KENTUCKY*
HMAS *COLLINS*

USS *KENTUCKY*

"Conn, Sonar. Incoming torpedo is approaching our second countermeasure."

Leaning against the Fusion Plot, Malone studied the track of the incoming torpedo, which had circled their first countermeasure before continuing on, forcing the *Kentucky* to launch a second one. His assessment the torpedo had been launched from long range had been correct. It was launched over thirty minutes ago, giving the *Kentucky* time to move away before the torpedo could arrive and lock on to them. Where the torpedo had come from, however, remained a mystery.

Who had launched it? And why? Then Malone received the information that answered the first question.

"Conn, Sonar. Incoming torpedo is a Mark 48. Mod 4!"

Malone froze.

Impossible!

They had been fired on by an Australian submarine!

There were only three countries that carried the MK 48 Mod 4 Torpedo in their arsenal—Australia, Canada, and the Netherlands. This far out in the Pacific meant an Australian submarine had attacked them.

He called into the overhead mike. "Sonar, Conn. Are you positive? A Mark 48 Mod 4?"

"Conn, Sonar," the Sonar Supervisor replied. "No doubt about it, sir."

Malone was temporarily at a loss for words as he analyzed the situation. Although he now knew *who* had attacked them, the *why* was unknown. Unfortunately, he had scant time to ponder the answer. He would have to wait until the *Kentucky* was out of harm's way. His attention returned to the torpedo chasing them as the Sonar Supervisor's voice carried across Control.

"Torpedo is slowing. Entering reattack pattern around our second countermeasure."

Malone peered intently at the geographic display, which showed a red ∧ circling the blinking white dot representing their torpedo decoy. By the time the torpedo figured things out, hopefully the *Kentucky* would be long gone.

"Torpedo bearings continue to draw aft. Torpedo is circling ship's countermeasure."

Exactly as planned.

Now they could slow and begin to prosecute the offending submarine. But Malone's relief was cut short by a new report from Sonar.

"Upshift in Doppler. Torpedo is turning toward us!"

The torpedo had either figured out their countermeasure was a decoy and had picked up the *Kentucky* speeding away, or had been wire-guided toward them. Malone marked off the distance between the countermeasure and the *Kentucky*'s current position.

Four thousand yards.

It was directly behind the *Kentucky,* and there was no way they could outrun it. The best they could do was dump another countermeasure behind them and hope the torpedo would be distracted long enough for the *Kentucky* to slip away. But as they launched another decoy, Malone knew the MK 48 would not be fooled for long.

As expected, the MK 48 torpedo barely sniffed the new countermeasure, which was exactly like the last two it had encountered. Its search algorithms then identified a possible submarine directly ahead. Another *ping* verified it, and the torpedo shortened its ping interval and increased speed to maximum.

The operators in *Kentucky*'s Sonar Room observed the characteristic change in the torpedo's behavior and reported it. "Torpedo is increasing speed and range gating!" Sonar followed up a second later.

"Torpedo is homing! One thousand yards and closing!"

Silence gripped Control, broken periodically by Sonar's reports of the torpedo's closure in two-hundred-yard increments. Malone noted the time of the initial torpedo report, then glanced at the time displayed on the nearest combat control console. He ran the calculations through his head, trying to determine the proper course of action.

"Eight hundred yards!"

He struggled with the decision to Emergency Blow, filling the water around them with a massive burst of air.

The air pockets would distort the torpedo's sonar pings, blinding it momentarily while the *Kentucky* ascended rapidly upward, hopefully out of the torpedo's sonar range before the torpedo passed through the bubbles and regained contact.

"Six hundred yards!"

But if the *Kentucky* blew, they'd end up on the surface, vulnerable and noisy, unable to submerge again immediately as they waited for the main ballast tanks to vent the air trapping the submarine on the surface. They'd be a sitting duck.

"Four hundred yards!"

But if they maintained course, the torpedo would eventually close on the *Kentucky,* blasting a hole into the Engine Room. Only one course of action held any promise. But what if he was wrong? He couldn't debate it further. He had run out of time.

Malone made his decision, calling out calmly, "Steady as she goes."

"Two hundred yards!"

The Diving Officer turned, looking to the Captain for direction.

"One hundred yards!"

But then Sonar followed up with the report Malone had been hoping for.

"Torpedo is slowing!"

A few seconds later, Sonar confirmed Malone's calculations.

"Torpedo has shut down!"

The torpedo had been fired from long range, and had closed on their countermeasures before turning toward the *Kentucky*. Heavyweight torpedoes carried a lot of fuel and could chase their target across long distances. But not far enough. By the narrowest of margins, the torpedo had exhausted its fuel before reaching its target. Now the *Kentucky* could fight back. "Helm, ahead two-thirds."

The *Kentucky* began to slow, bringing its sonar systems back into play. Now they would find and destroy the submarine that almost sank them.

HMAS *COLLINS*

Wilson examined the display over the Weapon Officer's shoulder. The green ∧, rapidly closing the red half-circle representing the *Kentucky,* blinked, then fell behind.

They had sent the first torpedo toward the *Kentucky* at high speed, not because he wanted it to reach the *Kentucky* quickly, but because he wanted the *Kentucky* to hear the torpedo coming and notice the course changes toward them. The purpose of the first torpedo was to keep the *Kentucky* at ahead flank so it could be tracked on the *Collins*'s sonar. Like a good bird dog, flushing the quail from heavy cover, the first torpedo's job was to set up the kill.

The killing would be done by their second torpedo. Wilson had shifted it to medium speed so it would proceed toward their target undetected, and also so it would consume less fuel during the long transit, ensuring it could finish the job once it detected its target. The *Collins*'s second-fired torpedo still had its sonar turned off, and the *Kentucky* wouldn't hear it coming.

Not until it was too late.

The Weapons Officer delivered the first report Wilson anticipated. "First-fired unit has shut down. Zero percent fuel remaining."

Wilson examined the sonar display on the port side of Control. The bright white trace representing the *Kentucky* slowly dimmed, then disappeared.

Sonar announced, "Master One has slowed. Loss of Master One."

That was the other report he expected. Wilson responded instantly, shouting to Humphreys. "Enable second-fired unit. Now!"

USS *KENTUCKY*

"Torpedo in the water! Bearing one-six-zero! Range, one thousand yards!"

Malone spun toward the Conn, the bright white trace burning into the sonar display.

The *Kentucky*'s adversary was extremely good. He had placed his second-fired unit perfectly, waiting until the torpedo was practically on top of them before enabling its sonar.

"Launch countermeasure!" Malone shouted. "Helm, ahead flank, right full rudder, steady course zero-nine-zero!"

A torpedo decoy was ejected from the submarine, and Malone reversed course to the east, hoping the torpedo would lock on to the countermeasure before it detected the larger ballistic missile submarine speeding away.

Malone stopped by the geographic display, examining the icon depicting the location of their countermeasure and the red bearing lines of the approaching torpedo. Had they ejected the countermeasure quickly enough, or had the torpedo already locked onto them? Malone listened to the reports from Sonar over the 7-MC.

"Conn, Sonar. Up Doppler on incoming torpedo. Torpedo is turning toward."

Malone shook his head.

Their countermeasure had failed to distract it.

Before he could formulate his next plan, Sonar followed up.

"Torpedo is increasing speed. Torpedo is homing! Range six hundred yards!"

The torpedo had locked on to them. There was little more he could do now except turn or launch another countermeasure. At this distance, launching another countermeasure would be futile; the torpedo would speed past it before it activated, and turning the ship would fail to shake the nimble MK 48. And unlike the last torpedo, Malone figured this one would close the distance; at six hundred yards and homing, there was no chance they could outrun it.

There was only one option remaining.

"Emergency blow all main ballast tanks! Dive, full rise on the stern and fairwater planes!"

The *Kentucky*'s Chief of the Watch stood and pulled down on the emergency blow levers. High-pressure air spewed into the submarine's main ballast tanks, pushing water out through flood grates in the bottom of the submarine. Malone held on to the Conn railing as the ship's angle reached thirty up, while the other men grabbed onto consoles near their watch stations. The air finally finished pushing the water out of the ballast tanks, then spilled out through grates in the ship's keel. As the

Kentucky sped toward the surface, it left massive air pockets in its wake, exactly as Malone had planned.

As the MK 48 Mod 4 torpedo sped through the *Kentucky*'s aerated wake, it lost contact with its target. Its search algorithms decided to continue straight ahead, not realizing its target was rising rapidly above. By the time the torpedo emerged on the other side of the turbulent bubble, the *Kentucky* was behind it. The MK 48 torpedo sped onward, unaware it had just passed a hundred yards beneath its target.

"Torpedo bears three-four-zero!"

As the Kentucky surged toward the surface, Malone examined the torpedo bearing, verifying it had passed underneath the submarine and was now heading away. He now turned his attention to the next critical problem. The *Kentucky* was heading toward the surface, where she would be trapped and vulnerable.

"Chief of the Watch. Secure the blow! Vent all main ballast tanks!"

The Chief of the Watch complied, shutting the valves from the high-pressure air tanks, stopping the flow of air into the main ballast tanks. He immediately followed by opening the main ballast tank vents, allowing the trapped air to escape. Water began to flood back into the ballast tanks.

Malone checked the ship's depth on the Ship Control Panel. They were at six hundred feet and rising rapidly. The question was—could they vent the air fast enough and stop their ascent before they reached the surface?

500 feet

With so much air in the ballast tanks, they were extremely buoyant.

400 feet

"Full dive, both planes," Malone ordered. He directed both the fairwater planes on the submarine's sail and the stern planes near the rudder to full dive, to help drive the submarine downward.

300 feet

They were beginning to slow their ascent.

200 feet

The *Kentucky*'s depth began to level off.

100 feet

The submarine's depth steadied at ninety feet, then began to increase as air continued to vent from the main ballast tanks.

Malone called out, "Helm, ahead two-thirds. Dive, make your depth four hundred feet."

As the Kentucky slowed from ahead flank, the Diving Officer took control of the planes, and the *Kentucky* settled out at four hundred feet.

Malone's adversary was good. Extremely good. One thing he knew for sure was he had better take him out fast. He had no idea how many more torpedoes were incoming or what other tricks he had up his sleeve.

He turned his attention to the *Kentucky*'s outgoing torpedo, launched almost a half hour ago. He turned to the Weapons Control Coordinator. "What have you got?"

"Own ship's unit detected a countermeasure and has

entered secondary search pattern, but so far hasn't detected the target. Twenty-one percent fuel remaining."

Malone examined the sonar displays on the Conn, then spoke loudly so Sonar could hear him over the open mike. "Sonar, we need something to guide own ship's unit. We don't need a solid trace, just some indication of where the target is."

"Conn, Sonar. Aye. We're looking, sir, but so far we've got nothing."

Malone returned his attention to the Fusion Plot, studying the initial bearing of the first torpedo.

Lieutenant (JG) Carvahlo, manning the Fusion Plot, looked up. "What is it, sir?"

"We're going to make an educated guess on where the target is. Let's assume the contact was at twenty thousand yards when it fired. Assuming it's a diesel, it probably evaded at four knots at that range. At a course of . . ."

This was the critical part. The bearing was solid. The range was reasonable and good enough since the torpedo sonar could sort out range inaccuracies if you placed it close enough. But if you picked a wrong evasion course, you could end up in left field instead of right. The direction the submarine evaded was critical. And, of course, a complete guess.

"Use an evasion course of . . . three-zero-zero."

Carvahlo complied, laying out a course to the northwest.

Looking at the Weapons Console, Malone verified they still had the wire guide to their torpedo. He turned to the Weapons Control Coordinator. "Insert torpedo steer, right one hundred."

HMAS *COLLINS*

As Wilson examined the sonar displays in Control, the bearings to the *Kentucky*'s incoming torpedo gradually fell aft. He could tell from the torpedo's run geometry that it was an MK 48 ADCAP Mod 6, two generations newer, with thirty thousand times more processing power than the Mod 4 torpedoes the *Collins* carried. Thankfully, it had been fired from long range and the *Collins* had been able to move out of the torpedo's sonar range. The only question was—did the *Kentucky* still have the wire, and would they send a lucky steer to the torpedo?

Not only was the Mod 6 torpedo more sophisticated, it was also significantly faster than the Mod 4. A sophisticated and fast weapon, a slow diesel submarine, and a lucky steer were a deadly combination.

Seemingly in response to Wilson's thoughts, the Sonar Supervisor called out, "Torpedo is turning toward us. They've inserted a steer."

Humphreys responded immediately, ordering his submarine back toward the west and increasing speed, hoping they could move out of the way fast enough.

"Helm, ahead flank. Left full rudder, steady course two-three-zero."

Wilson watched tensely as the Mod 6 torpedo closed rapidly on the *Collins*. The torpedo was charging forward and hadn't yet detected the diesel submarine, which was angling away on the new course Humphreys ordered. Would the *Collins* put enough distance between the torpedo as it sped by? The answer became apparent a few seconds later.

"Watch Leader, Sonar. Up Doppler on incoming torpedo. Torpedo is turning toward us!"

Wilson watched the trace stop falling aft, now steady on a constant bearing. The *Kentucky*'s torpedo had detected them.

"Watch Leader, Sonar. Torpedo is homing. Shifting to high speed!"

"Launch countermeasure!" Humphreys ordered.

The *Collins*'s crew ejected another decoy into the ocean, placing it between their submarine and the trailing torpedo. But the Mod 6 torpedo had already identified this type of countermeasure as a fake target and it sped past the stationary decoy.

The torpedo calculated the range, course, and speed of its target, shifting its sonar pattern to the highest fidelity mode.

"Watch Leader, Sonar. Torpedo is range gating! Impact in one minute!"

The torpedo's pings echoed through the *Collins*'s hull.

"Hard right rudder!" Humphreys ordered. "Steady course north!"

Humphreys kicked the submarine's stern around hard, completing a 130-degree turn to the north, trying to create a knuckle of turbulent water the torpedo would have to pass through. Hopefully the knuckle would blind the torpedo long enough for the *Collins* to slip out of its sonar range. If that didn't work, they would be almost out of options.

The torpedo passed through the knuckle just as the *Collins* steadied on her new course. Wilson prayed the torpedo bearings would start drawing aft, evidence the torpedo had lost track of the *Collins*.

The torpedo bearings remained constant.

"Watch Leader, Sonar. Torpedo has turned north, continuing to close. Thirty seconds to impact."

Humphreys turned his head toward Wilson, then glanced at the emergency blow levers.

They had only one option left.

Wilson nodded.

"Emergency Blow!" Humphreys bellowed. "Full rise all planes!"

The Watch Leader pulled down on the emergency blow levers, and high-pressure air began spilling into the *Collins*'s main ballast tanks, pushing water out the flood grates. The *Collins* tilted upward and began shooting toward the surface.

As the HMAS *Collins* streaked toward the surface, the MK 48 Mod 6 torpedo steadily closed the remaining distance to its target. Torpedo 200348, built, oddly enough, by the Hughes Aircraft Company in its Forest, North Carolina, plant, was a seasoned underwater veteran. It had been shot over a dozen times in an exercise configuration, its warhead temporarily replaced with a Fleet Exercise Section.

However, upon its last return to the Heavyweight torpedo maintenance facility in Pearl Harbor, it received a warshot turnaround, emerging with a warhead in place of an exercise section. Although its body was old, it was durable and dependable, and it had done its job, closing on its target as commanded. The torpedo's sonar detected a large metal object rising though the myriad of small air bubbles, and the guidance algorithms directed a vertical course change. The tail fins twitched, and the torpedo tilted upward. As Torpedo 200348 closed on its target, its exploder rolled into position.

As the *Collins* sped toward the ocean's surface, Wilson studied the torpedo bearings on the display. He didn't need to hear the Sonar Supervisor's report to know their Emergency Blow had failed.

"Watch Leader, Sonar. Incoming torpedo is still homing! Impact in ten seconds!"

Humphreys turned to Wilson, standing beside him. "We're screwed, mate."

Wilson said nothing, looking at Humphreys with knowing eyes. There was no way to evade the incoming torpedo. In a matter of seconds, the warhead would detonate, blowing a hole in the *Collins*'s pressure hull. Cold water would flood into the submarine like a geyser due to the intense sea pressure, and the *Collins* would sink to the bottom of the ocean.

Although his heart went out to Humphreys and the crew of the *Collins,* Wilson breathed a sigh of relief. The burden he'd dealt with the last few days was lifted from his shoulders, and he was unexpectedly pleased with the outcome. Like on Mount Moriah as Abraham prepared to sacrifice his son Isaac, God had intervened, sparing the life of the son.

But not the father.

The result wasn't exactly what Wilson had hoped for, but it was something. At least he wouldn't be responsible for Tom's death.

Wrapping one arm around the Search periscope, he braced himself for the explosion.

* * *

Torpedo 200348 closed the remaining one hundred yards, and its electromagnetic coils detected the large steel object it chased. Once within range, it fired the initiating charge, igniting the six hundred pounds of PBXN-105 explosive in the torpedo's warhead. The MK 48 torpedo disintegrated as the equivalent of eight hundred pounds of dynamite detonated, splitting open the three-inch-thick steel hull of the *Collins* like papier-mâché, blowing a gaping hole into the Engine Room.

Wilson's firm grip wasn't enough to keep him from being knocked to the deck as the torpedo exploded. He pulled himself to his feet as Humphreys likewise climbed to his. Wilson knew they were in trouble when the Flooding Alarm sounded; in jeopardy when he felt the stern squat down from the added weight of the inrushing ocean; in extremis when the stern planes had to be pushed to full dive in an attempt to keep the submarine's angle from tilting out of control.

The equipment in the Engine Room began to fail in a crescendo of alarming indications. The lights flickered; Control was momentarily drowned in darkness when the motor generators went off-line, and then emergency lighting energized a second later. But as the submarine surged toward the surface, the *Collins* received the nail in its coffin.

The Engine Room rang up all stop.

There was no more propulsion, nothing available to drive them upward except for the Emergency Blow that had already done its work. They were almost there; almost to the surface.

Not that it would do them much good.

As the submarine's speed bled off, Wilson knew they would be able to carry less weight and would begin to sink. Even if they reached the surface, it would be only a few seconds before they submerged beneath the waves again; insufficient time for the hatches to be opened and for any of the crew to escape.

The red numbers on the digital depth meter, which had been changing rapidly as the *Collins* sped toward the surface, stopped at forty meters. The numbers began changing again, this time in the opposite direction, slowly at first, then increasing speed as the ship passed through one hundred, then two hundred meters. The numbers began changing so quickly that Wilson could estimate the ship's depth only to the nearest hundred meters, and the *Collins* soon passed below Test Depth.

As Wilson stared at the digital depth gauge, the numbers stopped changing, and he wondered if the ship's depth had stabilized. But he soon understood the meaning of the immobile numbers. The submarine hadn't halted its descent—it had descended beyond the maximum range of its depth gauges; it could no longer report the depths to which the *Collins* sank. The frozen numbers stared back at him, and he wondered how the ship managed to hold together below Crush Depth.

Looking around Control at the men and women whose lives would soon be extinguished, their faces illuminated by the eerie yellow emergency lighting, Wilson realized it was all his fault. He was the one who had dragged them into this. His thoughts turned to the families who would wait in vain on the pier for the *Collins*'s return home from her long patrol. They would no longer have the comfort of a husband or wife, mother or father.

As the men and women in Control stared at him, with fear on their faces yet their eyes still harboring a faint glimmer of hope the American captain would somehow save them, it was all too much. Wilson turned his head away, avoiding their gaze. With a flooded Engine Room, their submarine would travel in only one direction.

Down.

There was nothing more he could do.

A loud, wrenching metallic sound tore through the ship, and the stern began to tilt downward. Wilson slid across Control, grabbing onto the Attack periscope as the submarine reached a ninety-degree angle, descending stern first. The hull groaned from the rising sea pressure, and the piping systems in the compartment began to give way, water spraying across Control as the *Collins* plummeted into the dark ocean depths.

79

USS *KENTUCKY*

The *Kentucky* shuddered as a shock wave passed by, followed by Sonar's report. "Explosion in the water, bearing one-eight-four!" Cheers erupted in Control, dying down as Sonar followed up. "Conn, Sonar. Breaking-up noises, bearing one-eight-four."

Malone didn't share the enthusiasm as he thought solemnly about the men who would never return from sea. It could just as easily have been them.

There, but for the grace of God, go I.

Nonetheless, he was relieved. They had survived, and now they had to clear the area quickly in case there were other warships or aircraft nearby, which would no doubt converge on the explosion. But first they had to slow from ahead flank, allowing their sonar signature to melt back into the ocean.

"Helm, ahead standard. Left full rudder, steady course two-seven-zero."

Malone paused, then addressed the watchstanders in the Control Room. "Attention in Control. I intend to clear datum to the west for several hours. Once we're a safe distance away and have confirmed there are no contacts nearby, we'll slow and launch our remaining missiles. Carry on."

The eyes of his men lingered on him for a few seconds before they returned their attention to their workstations.

Malone stepped down from the Conn as the *Kentucky* traversed quietly away from the explosion reverberating through the ocean depths.

80

PENTAGON

At the small table in Hendricks's office, Christine sat alone with her thoughts. She had ignored Brackman's advice to seek medical attention, determined to remain at the Current Action Center until they received word on the *Kentucky*'s and *Collins*'s fates. Shortly after the *Kentucky* launched four missiles and her position updated on top of the *Collins*, SOSUS reported an underwater explosion in the vicinity.

One of the submarines had been sunk.

Which one was unknown. The *Collins* had not yet radioed in, and with each passing minute, the likelihood the *Kentucky* had survived grew. The tension was mounting in the Current Action Center, as they had no anti-ballistic missiles remaining. Their only hope hinged on the *Collins*.

The door opened and Brackman entered. It was clear from the expression on his face that he'd brought news. Christine rose from her chair as he spoke.

"We've picked up a submarine emergency distress beacon in the vicinity of the explosion."

Christine looked for clues in Brackman's expression, noting his pale face.

Her words came out slowly. "Which submarine?"

"The emergency beacon is from the *Collins*."

A pit formed in her stomach. They had failed.

"Now what?" she asked.

"The *Kentucky* will clear datum," Brackman replied, "knowing that others in the area will converge on the explosion and begin their search there. Once she's safely away, she'll launch her remaining missiles."

"How long do we have?"

"No way to know for sure."

"Is there anything we can do?"

"We've already vectored in our P-3Cs and laid an extensive sonobuoy field, but we haven't picked up anything so far. We'll keep looking. But now that the *Kentucky* is in Emerald, free to travel in any direction—"

"I know," Christine finished the sentence for him. "The odds of finding her are minuscule." There was an uneasy silence before she continued. "Are you sure there are no more antiballistic missiles in the region?"

"Yes, ma'am. We're checking with 5th Fleet on the possibility of reloading the cruisers in theater, but from what I know of Trident submarine protocols, even if we have the SM-3 assets and can reload, there's no way we'll be ready before the *Kentucky* resumes launching."

There was another awkward silence. Finally, Brackman said, "I'm sorry, Christine." Then he turned and left, closing the door behind him.

Christine approached the window in Hendricks's office, examining the CAC screen. The *Kentucky*'s estimated position was a red circle again instead of a teardrop shape, centered at the location of the torpedo explosion. In the center of the circle, the blue icon symbolizing the *Collins* blinked rapidly for a few seconds, then disappeared. She wondered what the crew on the *Collins* had thought and felt as the cold water rushed into their submarine, dragging them down into the dark, frigid ocean. She shuddered, hoping they died quickly and painlessly. Then she realized she had done everything possible to ensure the crew on the *Kentucky* shared that same fate.

Yet the *Kentucky* had survived—and would soon launch her remaining missiles.

81

USS *KENTUCKY*

One hundred miles north of Enewetak Atoll, a collection of forty coral reef islands surrounding a deep central lagoon, a dark shape drifted up from the ocean depths. The object, lost in the shadows of the early morning light shimmering on the ocean's surface, rose at a ten-degree angle, its main engines silent, slowing during the ascent until it came to rest several hundred feet below the ocean waves. Valves in the black metal skin of the warship opened and closed as water was sucked into and purged from its internals, keeping the ship steady at launch depth. The towed array, no longer streaming behind the ship, drifted down until it came to a vertical rest, hanging from the submarine like a spider's thin, silky thread.

After sinking the *Collins,* Malone continued west for two hours. Finally convinced there was sufficient distance between the submarine and the explosion, the *Kentucky* had come shallow, its crew manning Battle Stations. The

Kentucky had not yet completed its mission; there were still seventeen missiles to be launched.

The Chief of the Watch reported the ship was at Battle Stations Missile, and Malone, standing on the Conn, picked up the 1-MC. "Set condition One-SQ for strategic launch. This is the Commanding Officer. The release of nuclear weapons has been directed."

The XO spoke into the 21-MC handset, repeating the Captain's order.

Malone left Control and, after opening the safe in his stateroom, returned a minute later with seventeen keys, each hanging from a green lanyard, which he handed to a missile tech waiting to arm the missile tube gas generators.

A moment later, two junior officers arrived in Control with the CIP key, which they handed over to Malone. He held the key in his hand for a moment before inserting it into the Captain's Indicator Panel, then flipped up the Permission to Fire toggle switch. The panel activated, the status lights illuminating for Missile Tubes Five through Twenty-Four.

One by one, the missiles were brought online, with the exception of the missiles in tubes Eight, Ten, and Twelve. Malone monitored the progress of the missile gyro spin-up until the indicating lights for seventeen missiles illuminated. The next column of lights toggled from black to red as each missile accepted its target package, carrying the impact coordinates for their warheads. The third column of lights on the Captain's Indicator Panel turned red as the missile techs in Missile Compartment Lower Level armed the gas generators. One by one, seventeen gas generators were armed.

The USS *Kentucky* was ready to launch again. All that remained was Malone's final order. One final command, and seventeen missiles would streak through the atmosphere toward their destination. Malone turned to his phone talker next to him, who would pass the order—*You have permission to fire*—to MCC.

Standing in MCC, his shoulders sagging, Tom Wilson held the Trigger in his hand, hanging listless by his side. His eyes were blank, a vacant gaze aimed at the Launch Control Panel, awaiting his Captain's order. Nearby, Petty Officer Tryon, along with the other missile techs, stared at Tom. Tom knew what they were thinking, but didn't really care. Hours earlier, he had struggled with the launch decision, and it had boiled down to the commitment he made when he took the oath of office, to follow the lawful orders of a superior officer, and in this case, the president of the United States. What he hadn't bargained on, however, was the personal toll that commitment would take.

The realization that commitment would erase the lives of millions of innocent men, women, and children was something he hadn't anticipated. From the moment he squeezed the Trigger that first time, he knew he couldn't live with what he had done. Whether it was one more time or seventeen more times, it didn't matter.

He would launch the remaining missiles when ordered. He would sort through the rest later.

Malone stood in Control, his hands on each side of the Captain's Indicator Panel. Next to him, the phone talker waited expectedly for his order to launch.

Malone hesitated.

It didn't make sense.

An Australian submarine had attacked them. Why? For the last two hours, he had tried to piece together the unusual events of the past ten days, believing this was the key. Why did they attack? Were they trying to prevent them from launching?

Suddenly, the disparate pieces of the puzzle fell into place. Except—they hadn't received a Launch Termination Order. Why not? Their Radio Room was perfectly operational. Malone shook his head.

It didn't make sense.

He surveyed the men in Control. His crew was at Battle Stations Missile, and the *Kentucky* was hovering at launch depth. His phone talker stood next to him, his finger over the button on his mouthpiece, waiting to pass the Launch order.

Malone reviewed the events over the last ten days again. The unexpected Launch order, the strange encounter with the 688s, the mysterious stationary object, the attack by the P-3C, and now the Australian submarine.

It didn't make sense.

However, their protocols were clear. They would execute their mission unless they received a Launch Termination Order. His hands were tied.

Finally, he made his decision.

He flipped down the Permission to Fire toggle switch.

Looking at the Chief of the Watch, he said, "Secure from Battle Stations Missile." He turned to the Officer of the Deck. "Make preparations to proceed to periscope depth."

This situation was beyond unusual.

He would contact COMSUBPAC.

"No close contacts!"

The crew had secured from Battle Stations Missile, and Tom was stationed as Officer of the Deck again. The ascent to periscope depth was uneventful, and as Tom rotated quickly on the periscope, he observed no ships on the horizon. A quick aerial search verified the absence of air contacts, and Tom settled into a low-power search as Malone spoke into the overhead microphone.

"Radio, Conn. Line up for EHF comms. Patch communications to the Conn."

Radio acknowledged, then reported over the 27-MC a moment later. "Conn, Radio. Request Number One periscope."

Malone turned to Tom. "Switch periscopes."

"Switch periscopes, aye." Tom turned the port periscope until it faced forward, calling out as he reached up and twisted the periscope locking ring, "Lowering Number Two scope." He stepped to his right. "Raising Number One scope." The starboard periscope began rising as the port scope settled into its well, and Tom's eye was soon pressed against the starboard periscope eyepiece, turning slowly clockwise as he continued his search of the horizon.

Tom called out, "Radio, Conn. Number One scope is raised."

Radio replied a moment later, "Conn, Radio. EHF is lined up to the Conn."

Malone pulled the red phone from its holster on the Conn, pressing it against his face as he spoke. "COM-

SUBPAC, this is *Kentucky* actual. Request to speak to N9, over."

Malone waited for a response, but there was nothing but silence. He tried again. "COMSUBPAC, this is USS *Kentucky*'s commanding officer. Request to speak to N9, over."

Silence again. There was something odd about the silence too. Clean. No static. Just . . . silence.

Malone glanced at the overhead microphone as he spoke. "Radio, Conn. Are you sure we're lined up properly? It doesn't sound like we're getting through."

Radio responded a moment later. "Conn, Radio. Everything looks good in here."

Malone located the Messenger of the Watch, standing on the port side of Control. "Find Chief Davidson and have him report to Control."

A quick acknowledgment, and the young man was on his way, scouring the ship for the submarine's Radio Chief. A few minutes later, Chief Davidson arrived in Control.

"Radio problem, Captain?"

"Maybe," Malone answered. "Can't get through on EHF comms. And no static either. I need you to check the lineup in Radio."

"Aye, sir." Chief Davidson headed into Radio, and a moment later, his voice came across the 27-MC. "Conn, Radio. This is Chief Davidson. I've verified the lineup is proper. I'd like you to give it another try."

Malone pulled the red handset from its holster again. "COMSUBPAC, this is *Kentucky* actual. Request to speak to N9, over."

Silence.

Chief Davidson's voice carried across the 27-MC again. "Conn, Radio. Everything's working fine on our end. Must be a problem shore-side or with the spot satellite. Perhaps we should try again after we finish launching."

Malone shook his head, then called out, "Radio, Conn. Line up UHF SATHICOM to the Conn." He turned to Tom. "We'll need a multi-function mast."

"Aye, sir," Tom replied. "Chief of the Watch. Raise Number Two Multi-Function."

The Chief of the Watch complied, and the port multi-function antenna was soon raised from the submarine's sail. A few seconds later, Radio's report echoed over the 27-MC. "Conn, Radio. UHF SATHICOM is patched to the Conn."

Malone pressed the handset against his face. "COMSUBPAC, this is *Kentucky* actual. Request to speak to N9, over."

Silence. Clean. No static.

Malone's grip on the handset tightened.

"COMSUBPAC, this is *Kentucky* actual. Request to speak to N9, over."

Silence.

Malone slammed the handset back in its holster, then strode into the Radio Room.

Chief Davidson was hunched over one of the radio consoles with the first class leading petty officer, on watch with Petty Officer Greene, manning the other console. Davidson turned as Malone entered.

Stopping next to one of the large gray communication cabinets, Malone surveyed the racks of complex gear. "Chief, there's no way both EHF and UHF systems are down. And something tells me there's a Launch Termination Order we haven't received. That means there's something's wrong with our Radio Room. Tear this place apart and figure it out."

"Sir," Davidson replied, "our Radio Room is fully operational. We're copying the broadcast every time we go to PD."

"Don't argue with me. Run a complete set of diagnostics. There's something squirrelly going on with our comms."

Greene turned sideways in his chair, a puzzled expression on his face, looking first at the Captain, then at Davidson, then at the Antenna Patch Panel. "Sir," Greene began.

"It's not important," Davidson interrupted, shooting Greene a stern look.

"What's not important?" Malone asked.

Davidson replied, "Greene was about to mention the card we installed last Refit. Gives us a new diagnostics capability."

Malone turned to Greene. "Where?"

Greene pointed to the Antenna Patch Panel.

Malone motioned for Petty Officer 1st Class Rob Mushen to open the panel.

Mushen unscrewed the knurl knobs and opened the panel. Pulling a small flashlight from a nearby toolbox, he examined the cabinet internals, spotting the card Chief Davidson had installed during the previous Refit.

"What the . . ."

"What is it, Mushen?"

"There's a card in here, just like Chief said, but I'm not aware of any modifications authorized to this cabinet." Malone clenched his hands into fists as Mushen examined the card and other modifications to the cabinet. "There are some wiring changes as well. As best as I can tell, our antennas are cut off and everything is rewired to this card."

Malone swiveled toward Davidson, grabbing him by the collar of his coveralls, slamming him up against the Radio Room cabinets. "What the fuck have you done?"

Davidson said nothing for a moment as Malone glared at him, then replied calmly, "What someone should have done long ago. And proud of it. I helped my country defend itself from those intent on destroying it."

"*Your* country?" Malone repeated. "What country is that?"

Davidson looked away.

Malone shoved Davidson to the deck. He picked up the 27-MC. "Officer of the Deck, Captain. Have the COB and two armed petty officers report to Radio." Turning to Mushen, he said, "Get this Radio Room operational ASAP."

Mushen's acknowledgment was interrupted by Tom's excited voice over the 27-MC.

"Radio, Conn. Captain. Sonar reports a new contact, Sierra two-four, bearing zero-nine-five. High-speed submerged contact!"

82

USS *NORTH CAROLINA*

With his fast-attack submarine at Battle Stations, Commander Dennis Gallagher stood behind the Officer of the Deck's Tactical Workstation, his attention focused on the sonar display. The Engineer hovered beside him, the urgency of his report written on his face. But Gallagher knew what the Eng was about to tell him; as he pushed the *North Carolina* past its limits, red alarms were flashing throughout the Engine Room.

Four days earlier, the reactor had scrammed due to a dropped control rod, one they had been unable to relatch. Gallagher had informed Naval Reactors, but as the *North Carolina* headed home for repairs, he was stunned by the response. He had been directed to turn around and proceed west, authorized to operate at ahead full, exceeding the reactor's temperature limit. Navy leadership had apparently decided they were willing to accept the destruction of the *North Carolina*'s core, if that gave them the chance to locate and sink their target. But by operating the reactor at the higher temperature, they were deliberately hurling themselves toward the precipice of a reactor meltdown, and they would soon reach a point from which they could not pull back.

Despite the authorization from Naval Reactors, Gallagher was uneasy; he had been ordered to commit heresy. No submarine had ever deliberately violated reactor operating limits—that was a fundamental rule ingrained into every officer and enlisted man. But the order had been given, along with new criteria beyond which reactor operation would not be allowed. From the look on the Engineer's face, they were approaching that limit.

"Sir, the reactor fuel cells are beginning to melt. We must shut down."

Gallagher replied quickly, irritated with the Engineer's melodramatic, qualitative assessment. "Inform me when radiation levels at the Secondary Shield have reached the new limit. Assuming the ship is out of harm's way, we'll shut down then."

"Yes sir," the Engineer replied stiffly before leaving Control, allowing Gallagher to return his attention to the tactical situation.

"Pilot, ahead two-thirds," Gallagher ordered.

As the *North Carolina* slowed to search the surrounding waters, he reviewed the relevant data.

For the last four days, they'd been heading west at ahead full. Luckily, they had been headed in the right direction, and after detecting an underwater explosion two hours ago, only a minor course correction to starboard was required. They had already slowed in the vicinity of the explosion, but there was nothing there. So Gallagher had continued west, increasing speed to ahead full again. A few minutes ago, Sonar had detected mechanical transients, most likely missile muzzle hatches being opened. Their adversary was close.

Time to slow down and find it.

"Sonar, Conn. Report all contacts."

83

USS *KENTUCKY*
USS *NORTH CAROLINA*

USS *KENTUCKY*

"Man Battle Stations Torpedo," Malone announced as he entered Control from Radio.

The Chief of the Watch made the announcement on the shipwide 1-MC, then sounded the General Alarm, followed by a duplicate 1-MC announcement. Men began streaming into Control, manning their workstations.

Malone called out to the open microphone. "Sonar, Conn. Report classification of Sierra two-four."

Inside the Sonar shack, Petty Officer DelGreco was starting to sort things out. They had already determined it was a submerged contact. A high-speed submarine in the middle of the Pacific Ocean meant it was probably nuclear powered, and that meant it was a U.S. submarine.

DelGreco tapped the Narrowband Operator, Petty Officer Rambikur, on the shoulder. "Look for 688, *Seawolf*, and *Virginia*-class tonals."

DelGreco had lots of experience going up against *Los Angeles*–class submarines, and one glance at the frequencies told him this was no 688. That meant it was either a *Seawolf* or a *Virginia*. Rambikur came to a more specific conclusion.

"Sonar Sup. Sierra two-four is classified *Virginia*-class submarine."

USS *NORTH CAROLINA*

"Conn, Sonar. Hold a new contact, designated Sierra five-seven, bearing two-seven-two, classified submerged."

"Sonar, Conn. Aye," Gallagher replied.

This was their target.

"Attention in Control. Designate Sierra five-seven as Master One. Track Master One. Carry on."

Gallagher turned his attention to the geographic display. They were headed directly toward their target, but had no idea yet how far away it was. Headed toward it, they weren't going to get any useful bearing rate information for their combat control algorithms.

Time to turn.

"Pilot, right fifteen degrees rudder, steady course north."

The Pilot acknowledged, and the *North Carolina* began turning.

USS *KENTUCKY*

"Conn, Sonar. Contact zig! Sierra two-four has turned away to the north."

Malone glanced at the one of the three combat control displays, then at the XO, who nodded, confirming Sonar's preliminary analysis.

Not good.

The *Kentucky* had been detected, and Sierra two-four was beginning target motion analysis. They were developing a firing solution.

Under normal circumstances, Malone could probably extend the cat-and-mouse game for hours, constantly maneuvering, making his adversary's job of developing a firing solution a nightmare.

But Malone was at periscope depth, moving slowly at five knots. His first priority at the moment was to repair the Radio Room and communicate with COMSUBPAC. It looked like American submarines, and not just the Australians, had orders to hunt down the *Kentucky,* and the sooner Malone contacted COMSUBPAC, the safer they would be.

There was a problem with his plan, however. The *Virginia*-class submarine would not receive new messages until she went to periscope depth. Even if Malone contacted COMSUBPAC and they ordered the *Virginia*-class submarine to stand down, she would not receive the message until after she had sunk the *Kentucky* and went to periscope depth to report.

Should he stay at periscope depth and communicate with COMSUBPAC, or go deep and run?

They had been fortunate against an Australian submarine with Mod 4 torpedoes. But against a *Virginia*-class, most likely carrying MK 48 Mod 7s?

Their only hope was to convince the *Virginia*-class submarine to not attack.

But how?

Radio messages were not an option. That left . . .

Sonar.

Malone spoke into the open microphone. "Sonar, Conn. Line up the WQC for underwater comms."

USS *NORTH CAROLINA*

"Steady course north."

Gallagher acknowledged the Pilot's report, then turned his attention to the sonar displays, waiting for the towed array to stabilize after the turn. This was the same contact they had encountered before—it had the same tonals—and it was a very quiet target, held only on narrowband. They would have to wait until the towed array stabilized and accurate bearings were fed into their Combat Control System. A few minutes passed, and the awaited report came from the Sonar Supervisor.

"Conn, Sonar. The towed array has stabilized. Sending bearings to fire control."

The submarine's Executive Officer stopped behind each of the three combat control consoles, examining each operator's solution, going back to the middle fire control technician, tapping him on the shoulder.

"Promote to Master."

Their target was moving slowly, and hadn't maneuvered.

Turning to Gallagher, the XO said, "I have a firing solution."

USS *KENTUCKY*

"Conn, Sonar. WQC is lined up to transmit."

Malone pulled the WQC microphone from its holster. He held it an inch away from his mouth. His voice would be transmitted by sonar hydrophones through the water and would be difficult to understand. He pressed the microphone button, then spoke slowly, distinctly.

"United States submarine. This is the USS *Kentucky*. Do not attack. Repeat. This is the USS *Kentucky*. Do not attack."

Malone waited a minute, then repeated his announcement.

USS *NORTH CAROLINA*

"Conn, Sonar. Receiving underwater comms."

Gallagher looked up from the combat control display. He exchanged surprised glances with his Executive Officer, then turned to the Sonar Supervisor.

"Put it on speaker."

"Aye, sir."

There was only the background noise of ocean biologics for a moment, then a warbly but understandable message. "United States submarine. This is the USS *Kentucky*. Do not attack. Repeat. This is the USS *Kentucky*. Do not attack."

The Control Room broke out in a flurry of conversations. Gallagher was stunned by the communication. So was his Executive Officer, by the look on his face. But then his expression hardened. Gallagher wanted to hear his thoughts, but there was too much commotion in the Control Room.

"Silence in Control!"

The conversations ceased immediately.

"What are you thinking, XO?"

It took a moment for the XO to answer, but when he did, he answered emphatically.

"They're lying, Captain!"

The XO continued, "The Chinese built a replica of a Trident submarine and they know they look like one on sonar. Now that we've caught them, they're pretending to be an American submarine. It's a ploy, sir."

Gallagher absorbed his XO's opinion. If he was wrong and he attacked, they would sink a U.S. submarine. Was it possible this was the *Kentucky*?

He turned to his Navigator. "What do we know about waterspace assignments for Trident submarines? Can we confirm the *Kentucky* is supposed to be in this area?"

"No, sir," the Nav answered. "We're not privy to Trident waterspace assignments. There's no way for us to know if the *Kentucky* is supposed to be here or not."

Gallagher folded his arms across his chest. They were lacking the necessary information to make this critical decision. He would have to rely on the counsel of his XO and his department heads. His most senior department head, the Engineer, would normally have been his Officer of the Deck. Unfortunately, he had been assigned to Maneuvering due to the dropped control rod, and there was no time to bring him forward. That left the XO, whose opinion was clear, the Nav, and the Weps.

"Weps, what do you think?"

"Sir, if it could be the *Kentucky,* we should err on the side of caution. The ramifications are too great if we're wrong."

Gallagher nodded thoughtfully, then turned to the more senior department head.

"Nav, what's your opinion?"

"We would not have been sent into an area, weapons free, with one of our own submarines in it. There's no way Master One is an American submarine."

Gallagher's head tilted down toward the deck for a moment. Then he looked up, his eyes canvassing the other men in Control. "Anyone else have any thoughts?"

No one said anything.

Commander Dennis Gallagher considered his XO and department heads' words, and the orders he'd been given. He was weapons free, the target was in the area as expected, and it had Trident tonals as expected. What were the odds the *Kentucky* was also in the area and COMSUBPAC didn't know about it?

Gallagher made his decision.

"Firing Point Procedures, Master One, tube Two. Open outer doors, tubes One and Two."

USS *KENTUCKY*

With the *Kentucky* at Battle Stations Torpedo, the sonar shack was now at full manning. Seated at the spherical array display, headphones against his ears, was Petty Officer 2nd Class John Martin. Unlike Cibelli and Del-Greco, Martin had completed a previous tour on a *Virginia*-class submarine. When he heard the unusual, low-frequency sound in his headphones, followed a few seconds later by the exact same sound, he knew exactly what it was.

"Conn, Sonar. Sierra two-four is opening torpedo tube outer doors!"

Commander Malone was standing on the Conn, WQC microphone still in his hand, when the 27-MC announcement blared from the speakers.

Malone resisted the urge to order torpedo evasion—evading at this point was futile. The *Virginia* was obviously entering Firing Point Procedures and the *Kentucky* would not get away from its MK 48 torpedo. Their only hope was to talk their way out of it. His first attempt had failed. Perhaps a more personal approach would work. But for that, he needed to know who was in command.

Malone called into the overhead microphone. "Sonar, Conn. I need you to determine which *Virginia*-class submarine is out there. And I need the answer in thirty seconds."

Inside the sonar shack, the sonar operators were already on it. Cibelli was pulling up the *Virginia*-class tonals from the database, while DelGreco was analyzing the frequencies of Sierra two-four, attempting to identify a unique tonal present on that *Virginia* submarine, and no other. The problem was the time. Given enough of it, they could eventually identify which submarine they were up against. But they had just thirty seconds. That meant they could pick only one frequency and bounce it against the database. If they were lucky, it would be unique, emitted by only one *Virginia*—the one about to sink them. Pick the wrong tonal, and it would show up on every *Virginia,* and they would have no idea which submarine was out there.

DelGreco scanned the frequencies. Had it been a 688, an unusual frequency would have jumped out at him. But he was unfamiliar with the *Virginia*-class. Several of the frequencies he stared at looked unusual. He quickly ruled out the common machinery tonals, but that left three to choose from.

They had fifteen seconds left, and Cibelli still had to look up which submarine it correlated to.

DelGreco scanned the three tonals again.

He couldn't figure it out.

He grabbed Martin by the arm. "Which one?"

Martin leaned over, squinting at the display in the darkness. He pointed to the lowest frequency. "It's not that one. That's common. Don't know about the other two."

That narrowed it down. But unfortunately it still left two.

There was no way for DelGreco to figure it out.

He picked one.

Cibelli punched the frequency into the database. It took only five seconds for the results to display on the screen.

"Shit! That's not it," Cibelli said. "They've all got that tonal."

DelGreco picked the next one and passed it to Cibelli. He looked at the clock. They had passed the thirty-second mark.

* * *

"Sonar, Conn," Malone called into the microphone. "I need an answer, and I need it now!"

"We're working on it, Captain."

"Working on it isn't good enough. I need a goddamn name!"

There was no immediate response from Sonar.

Then an excited announcement blared across Control. "It's the *North Carolina*! The *North Carolina*!"

Malone brought the WQC microphone to his mouth again. He knew most of the submarine commanding officers in the Pacific, and all of the *Virginia*-class submarine COs. He prayed there hadn't been a last-second change of command, and that Dennis Gallagher was still in command of the *North Carolina*.

USS *NORTH CAROLINA*

"Weapon ready, tube Two!" the Weapons Officer called out, verifying the torpedo presets were matched with combat control.

"Solution ready!" the XO announced, verifying the best target solution had been promoted to Master.

"Ship ready!" the Navigator reported, ensuring the counterfire corridor had been identified and that the ship's torpedo countermeasures were ready to deploy.

The *North Carolina* was ready to engage.

The only step remaining was Commander Gallagher's order to shoot.

Gallagher reviewed the geographic display one last time, and was about to issue the order when the Sonar Supervisor interrupted him.

"Conn, Sonar. Receiving underwater comms again."

"On speaker," Gallagher ordered.

The Sonar Supervisor acknowledged, and the warbly underwater sound emanated throughout Control.

". . . on the *North Carolina*. Repeat. This is Commander Brad Malone on the *Kentucky*. Request to speak to Commander Dennis Gallagher on the *North Carolina,* over."

This was a new wrinkle. However, the men in command of American submarines was common knowledge. This last underwater communication proved nothing. The *North Carolina* was locked and loaded, a button push away from launching—and sinking—their target.

However, they could afford another minute to investigate further.

Gallagher walked over to the sonar consoles. "Line up for underwater comms."

As Gallagher waited for the sonar operators to complete the lineup, he thought about the underwater message. If this really was Brad Malone, he would know a few personal details. He and Brad had gone though Prospective Commanding Officer training together. They had worked out at the gym together and hung out on the weekends during the six-month-long PCO pipeline.

A few seconds later, the Sonar Supervisor announced, "Lined up for underwater comms."

Gallagher took the microphone. "*Kentucky,* this is *North Carolina* actual. If you are Commander Malone, convince me. You have one minute."

There was a momentary wait as the sound traveled through the water. A few seconds later, the response came through the Control Room speakers.

"Dennis. Do you really want me to tell everyone what you have tattooed on your ass?"

Gallagher's eyes went wide for a moment, until he realized Brad Malone had spotted his tattoo as he stepped out of the showers at the gym one day.

He broke into a wide grin.

"Brad, what the hell are you doing here? We almost sank you."

Another short wait, then, "It's a long story, Dennis. I'll fill you in later. We'll be contacting COMSUBPAC shortly and will proceed as directed."

"Understand, Brad. We'll hang out until then and make sure no one else pesters you."

"Thanks, Dennis. *Kentucky,* out."

Gallagher placed the WQC microphone back into the holster, then turned back to the Fire Control Tracking Party. Realizing they were still at Firing Point Procedures, he terminated the firing order.

"Check Fire," he announced. "Secure from Battle Stations."

Turning to his Officer of the Deck, he said, "Make preparations to come to periscope depth."

He stopped beside his XO. "We need to have a chat with COMSUBPAC."

84

USS *KENTUCKY*

"Conn, Radio. Repairs are complete. Lining up EHF to the Conn."

Tom acknowledged Petty Officer Mushen's 27-MC report as he rotated on the periscope. Malone emerged from Radio and stepped onto the Conn, stopping next to the red phone. Moments later, the awaited report came over the 27-MC.

"Conn, Radio. EHF is lined up to the Conn."

Malone placed the handset to his face. "COMSUBPAC, this is *Kentucky* actual, over."

This time, instead of silence, there was a burst of static, followed by a man's excited voice. "USS *Kentucky*, this is COMSUBPAC N3. You are a sound for sore ears. Request you acknowledge nuclear launch termination orders, over."

"COMSUBPAC, *Kentucky*. Acknowledge nuclear launch termination orders. Repeat, acknowledge launch termination orders."

Malone paused for a moment, his thoughts turning

to the missiles they had launched, realizing their launch order must have been fake and no nuclear bomb had been detonated in Washington, D.C. They had retaliated against innocent Iranians.

"COMSUBPAC, *Kentucky*. What is the status of the four missiles we launched, over?" Malone's stomach tightened as he awaited the response.

"*Kentucky*, COMSUBPAC. All missiles and warheads were destroyed by ABM defenses in the Middle East, over."

Malone's head sagged in relief.

After a long moment, he looked back up and spoke into the receiver. "COMSUBPAC, *Kentucky*. Thanks for the info. Anything else, over?"

"*Kentucky*, COMSUBPAC. You are directed to return to port at best speed. Waterspace assignments will be forthcoming, over."

"COMSUBPAC, *Kentucky*. Understand. Any other instructions, over?"

"*Kentucky*, COMSUBPAC. Not at this time, over."

"COMSUBPAC, *Kentucky*. Out."

Malone slowly placed the handset back into its holder, leaving his hand there for a moment, reflecting on the last ten days. It was going to be one hell of a patrol report. He looked over at Tom, still on the periscope.

"Officer of the Deck, bring her down to four hundred feet, ahead full, course zero-eight-zero. We're heading home."

Tom acknowledged Malone's order, and as the periscope began sliding into its well, he looked up, and Malone could see the relief on Tom's face as well. The missiles he'd launched had done no harm.

For the first time in nine days, Lieutenant Tom Wilson smiled.

He called out to the overhead microphone.

"All Stations, Conn. Going deep."

85

PENTAGON

As Christine stood at the window in Hendricks's office, she ran her finger lightly down the side of her swollen nose, noting the odd angle as it veered to the right. It hurt to move her jaw and she could still taste the ferrous tang of blood in her mouth. The adrenaline from this afternoon had worn off and her body ached. She was exhausted. She wondered why she remained in the Current Action Center. Without any antiballistic missiles, if the *Kentucky* launched again, all they could do was watch helplessly as Iran was annihilated.

But Brackman had reminded her about the *North Carolina,* entering Emerald as the *Collins* was reported sunk. Even limited to ahead full, the nuclear-powered submarine was quite speedy, and might catch the *Kentucky* before she launched her remaining missiles. The *North Carolina* would need to get lucky to find her, though.

Christine spotted Brackman walking briskly toward Hendricks's office. He opened the door and spoke quickly. "We've got COMSUBPAC online. They've contacted the *Kentucky*."

Christine was suddenly no longer weary. She hurried across the Current Action Center, keeping up with Brackman's long strides. They stopped by the Watch Captain's workstation, listening to his conversation, which he had put on speakerphone.

"COMSUBPAC, NMCC. Understand *Kentucky* has acknowledged the nuclear launch termination order and is proceeding to home port."

Relief poured through Christine's veins, leaving her almost too exhausted to stand. They had finally succeeded.

The Watch Captain continued, "COMSUBPAC, NMCC. Did they say why they took so long to acknowledge the Launch Termination Order and launched four missiles?"

"NMCC, COMSUBPAC. We didn't get into the details. We'll get a full debriefing when she returns to port."

"COMSUBPAC, NMCC. Understand. Anything else?"

"NMCC, COMSUBPAC. That's it. You know where to find us."

The Watch Captain hung up the secure phone and turned to Captain Brackman and Christine. "What now?"

Brackman deferred to Christine.

"Order Pacific Fleet to terminate their order to find and sink the Chinese submarine."

"Yes, ma'am." The Watch Captain began drafting the required order.

Christine turned to Brackman. "I'm going to head

over to the White House and brief the president. You coming with me or staying here?"

Brackman surveyed Christine. She was still in her bloodied blouse and hadn't yet washed the sheen of dried blood from her skin. Her face was a mess, to put it mildly.

"I'll escort you back. I'm not sure you're completely good to go."

Christine thanked the Watch Captain for his efforts, then walked with Brackman toward the exit. She stopped at the door, turning to examine the screen at the front of the Current Action Center.

All evidence of what had almost been the annihilation of seventy million people was gone from the screen. The red and green missile traces had faded, as had the blue circle representing the *Collins*. Only the *Kentucky* remained, headed east now, toward home.

The nightmare was finally over.

86

WASHINGTON, D.C.
17 HOURS LATER

In a darkened alcove between the West Wing and the Executive Residence of the White House, Press Secretary Lars Sikes leaned against the cool wall, dabbing the perspiration on his forehead with his handkerchief. Beneath the floor where he stood, abandoned for forty years, lay the swimming pool built in 1933 for Franklin Delano Roosevelt to accommodate his therapy for polio, the crippling disease he had contracted at the age of thirty-nine. But Sikes's thoughts today were focused instead on the room on the other side of the wall against which he leaned. Inside the James S. Brady Press Briefing Room, more than one hundred reporters were crammed into a space with forty-eight permanent seats, the overflow of bodies lining the walls and back of the small room.

Leaning quietly against the wall besides Sikes were the president's chief of staff on one side and his national security adviser on the other. Sikes had been shocked when he entered the Oval Office yesterday evening and

Christine, sitting in the chair across from the president's desk, turned to greet him. Her features lay shrouded in the darkness this morning, and Sikes wasn't sure who was more thankful, he or Christine. In the early morning hours preceding today's briefing, they had explained what had happened and had drilled him in preparation for the grilling he was about to endure. During his two-year tenure as press secretary, he had prepared for hundreds of briefings, but none of the topics had been as disturbing as the ones he'd be discussing today.

Hardison checked his watch. "It's time."

Sikes took a deep breath, then opened the door and briskly entered the room, stopping in front of the black-and-gold oval emblem of the White House affixed to the blue curtain backdrop. Placing his hands on each edge of the podium, he maintained a casual demeanor, his posture relaxed, nodding as his eyes greeted the more prominent reporters in the front row. After waiting an appropriate amount of time for the conversation to die down, he cleared his throat to signal the beginning of today's briefing.

"Yesterday, at approximately two P.M. eastern standard time, we conducted a successful no-notice test of our ballistic missile defense systems. Four missiles were launched from a Trident ballistic missile submarine operating in the Pacific Ocean, and her missiles and test warheads were destroyed by our Terminal High Altitude Area Defense battery and SM-3 antiballistic missiles launched from *Aegis*-class cruisers in the Persian Gulf."

A flurry of hands went into the air, and Sikes signaled a reporter in the front row.

"How many antiballistic missiles were required to shoot down the four missiles?"

"We will not comment on the details of this test launch," Sikes replied, "except that it was a resounding success."

"What units were involved?" another reporter interjected.

"As I said, the details will not be disclosed."

"Why did Iran initiate a countrywide civil disaster evacuation drill the day before the test launch?" a reporter from the *Washington Post* asked. "And then the four test missiles were fired at Iran. That's a strange coincidence."

Sikes resisted the urge to run his finger inside his shirt collar as he answered, "Our administration has been working hard to strengthen diplomatic relations with Iran. When we learned of the military's plans to test our ballistic missile defense systems, we informed the countries in the vicinity so they wouldn't be alarmed. Iran chose to fold our exercise into a national disaster drill for realism purposes, and the administration is very pleased our two countries were able to work together on these exercises to our mutual benefit. Next topic."

Sikes scanned the audience, and he quickly pointed to a reporter in the second row. The woman asked, "What about the Australian submarine that hasn't reported in? Is the United States involved in any way?"

"Well, of course we're involved, but only in the search-and-rescue phase. We're assisting our Australian friends in every way we can, and our thoughts and prayers are with them as we search for the *Collins,* presumed lost with all hands."

A reporter in the back row was eagerly waving his hand, and Sikes acknowledged him.

"What about the report of a reactor meltdown on the fast-attack submarine *North Carolina*?"

"There was no reactor meltdown," Sikes replied, thankful they had quickly shifted to the last essential topic. "Yes, there was a malfunction in her reactor control circuitry and the reactor overheated. But she was on a shakedown cruise, and these kinds of problems are what we attempt to discover after extensive shipyard maintenance. There's a kernel of truth to this rumor, in that the *North Carolina*'s reactor was damaged and will require replacement, but there was no core meltdown. The submarine is safely on the surface, being towed back to Puget Sound Naval Shipyard in Washington State."

Most of the reporters still had their hands raised, many of them shouting questions. But Sikes had addressed the relevant topics. He smiled and waved, ignoring their animated gestures and requests to answer additional questions. He turned away from the podium and retreated toward the exit. The cover story for the *Kentucky*'s near destruction of Iran had been carefully constructed, with all parties briefed and their silence assured. But there was always the possibility they had overlooked something.

He hoped to God they hadn't.

87

WASHINGTON, D.C.
2 DAYS LATER

On the south lawn of the White House, a Marine in dress blues stood by the entrance to a Sea King helicopter painted in the characteristic two-tone white over green presidential livery. As the downdraft from the five-bladed rotor rippled across the blades of grass, still wet from the morning's dew, Christine and Hardison ducked their heads as they followed the president from the Rose Garden toward the waiting helicopter. Saluting the staff sergeant, the president, followed by Christine and Hardison, climbed up the access stairs into Marine One.

Once the stairs were retracted and the entrance sealed, the sound of the helicopter's twin engines faded entirely. Marine One was well insulated, the padded walls and ceiling allowing its passengers the luxury of talking in normal tones during flight. Hardison eased into his seat, joining Christine across from the president. He sat unusually close to her, their arms almost touching, something he would not have done two days earlier.

Christine had to admit she had misjudged him. Two

days ago, Hardison had stopped by the Command Center to discuss Hendricks's continued silence, assured by a hefty financial incentive. There was something about her ex-husband's response that caught Hardison's attention; he had dealt with crooked politicians long enough to recognize feigned honesty and indignation. But there was something more he couldn't place. He had decided to discuss his thoughts with Christine before she returned to the Pentagon, arriving at her town house in the nick of time.

As far as Hendricks's brutal attack went, it appeared he hadn't done any long-lasting damage. Christine's split lips had sealed into vertical scabs matching the thin cut in her neck, and her nose had been straightened but remained swollen, joined now by a pair of moderately black eyes as her body began the healing process. Hardison seemed relieved that Christine's beauty hadn't been permanently marred, and she couldn't help but notice the subtle change in his demeanor.

Christine's thoughts returned to the present as Marine One lifted off for its short trip to Andrews Air Force Base southeast of Washington and its rendezvous with Air Force One, waiting to take the president to Berlin for his meeting with the German chancellor. Glancing out the starboard windows, Christine spotted two of the four identical Sea Kings accompanying the president on his trip, already shifting their positions in an endless shell game, obscuring the location of the president from would-be assassins on the ground.

Now that they were en route to Andrews, the president prepared to address the matter they had been unable to resolve in the Oval Office earlier this morning.

Hours after the *Kentucky*'s missiles were shot down, Prime Minister Rosenfeld had come clean, explaining everything to the president over a secure line. Christine had led the effort to craft a satisfactory response to Israel's transgression, as well as what to do about the pending assembly of Iran's first nuclear weapon. The president had finally agreed, on Christine's firm insistence, to transfer the bunker-busting bombs Israel had requested. The weapon facility had been destroyed only a few hours ago. Satellites had detected the residual radiation commensurate with a fifty-kiloton nuclear weapon, confirming the destruction of Iran's first nuclear bomb.

Although the president had agreed with most of Christine's plan to respond to Israel's transgression, he hadn't agreed to the risky final element. They would land at Andrews in a few minutes, and it was clear the president intended to resolve the matter by then.

"Israel has promised appropriate action will be taken," he said. "We should leave it at that."

Christine replied, "You may be able to leave it at that, but I cannot. It's *personal.*"

She could barely contain her fury. She had been relieved at first, the threat of a nuclear holocaust unleashed by one of their own submarines finally eliminated. But then a lump formed in her throat as her thoughts turned to the men and women aboard the *Collins*. Men and women who now rested in their watery graves, leaving behind parents, husbands and wives, and children who would never see them again.

Someone would be held accountable. That much was clear. And having come within seconds of losing her life, Christine believed she was vested in that retribution.

The president sighed. "What are the details?"

Christine handed him a manila folder. "It's ready to implement, pending your approval."

The president opened the folder, skimmed the first page, then lifted it up to read the second. Halfway down the page, his eyes shot toward Christine. "You're not serious?"

"Yes, sir. I am."

He turned to his chief of staff. "What do you think, Kevin?"

"I have my reservations, sir. But considering the circumstances, I agree with Christine's plan."

Christine's eyes went from Hardison to the president, and as Marine One landed, the president seemed on the verge of committing.

The president stood to transfer to Air Force One, then shook Christine's hand. "Good luck. And be careful."

88

EIN KAREM, ISRAEL
3 DAYS LATER

It was almost noon, the sun climbing into a clear blue sky above the rolling Judean hills west of Jerusalem, when a black Mercedes S600 turned onto a narrow gravel driveway lined with towering umbrella pines. After a two-hundred-yard drive down the winding path, the car's heavy suspension swaying over the uneven surface, the sedan pulled to a stop in front of a sprawling hilltop villa, the lunchtime destination for the American national security adviser and her driver, William Hoover.

Earlier this morning, as Christine stepped onto the tarmac at Ben Gurion International Airport, she had been surprised when she was greeted by the same man who had threatened to kill her if she ever tried to track him down. However, circumstances had changed somewhat over the last three days, and the "agreement" the United States had dictated to its ally in the Middle East required she be met by a man of Hoover's background. After reviewing how things would unfold at lunch, she had stepped into the back of the sedan for the short trip to her destination. Hoover sensed her nervousness and tried to ease her apprehension, talking incessantly the entire trip, his eyes flitting between the road and the rearview mirror. However, he fell silent as he climbed out of the sedan, opening the rear door for his quiet passenger, who had not said a word in response.

On the flagstone patio behind his villa, Israeli intelligence minister Barak Kogen sat at a table neatly prepared with two place settings. As he waited for his guest, he leaned back in his chair, looking west over the patio's waist-high limestone wall. The heavy rain that had quenched the parched countryside a fortnight earlier had left behind a bright green carpet of new flora, and in a few weeks the rockrose and thorny broom would turn the hillsides a pastel pink, white, and yellow. However, with the departure of the overcast skies, the days had turned unseasonably warm, the heat almost uncomfortable. Thankfully, a glass pitcher of iced tea, resting in the center of the table, would quench his thirst once his guest, Ariel Bronner, head of the Metsada, arrived.

The doorbell rang and Kogen called out, "In back. Come join me."

A woman appeared around the corner of the villa, following a stone pathway to the back of the house. Kogen stood abruptly. "Who are you? And where is Ariel?"

"I'm Christine O'Connor," the woman replied in English, "national security adviser to the president of the United States. Ariel was called away and he asked me to meet with you instead."

Kogen suddenly recognized Christine, eyeing her

suspiciously. His unexpected guest was attractive, although she wore her makeup a bit too heavy for his taste, concealing faint black circles under her eyes.

"Ariel's waiting for your call," she said. "He'll confirm."

Pulling out his cell phone, Kogen dialed Bronner's office. CALL FAILED appeared on the display, and he noticed the antenna had no signal strength. He looked up at Christine. "I'll have to use a landline to call Ariel. I'll be back shortly." He entered the villa and returned a moment later, his shoulders relaxed, a friendly smile on his face.

"Please, have a seat," he said, gesturing toward the table. Christine took the proffered chair while Kogen settled in beside her. "So what brings you to my villa in place of my Metsada chief, Miss O'Connor?"

"This is unusual," she answered, "but one of the conditions for continued good relations between our two countries, considering what just transpired, was that I meet with you."

"What are you referring to?" Kogen feigned ignorance for the moment, unsure how much his unexpected guest knew.

"I wanted to meet the mastermind behind the plot that almost resulted in one of our ballistic missile submarines completely destroying another country."

Her words hit him in the chest like a sledgehammer. Bronner had apparently told her everything. But why? The operation had been meticulously planned to ensure its genesis could not be traced back to Israel.

She continued, "I have to admit that you developed an exceptional plan. Ariel has given me the entire file, which I assure you we'll thoroughly review. There are a few things we could no doubt learn from your organization."

Kogen's nervousness eased. Perhaps there was nothing sinister in her visit to his villa. Intelligence organizations around the world interfaced in a civilized manner, even though agents constantly strove to ensure their country gained at another's expense. Perhaps that was the purpose for her visit; to discuss to what extent their two organizations could work together. However, he was guessing at her motive, and was not a fan of conjecture. "So why are you here, Miss O'Connor?"

"Did you ever watch the *Merrie Melodies* cartoons when you were a kid?" she asked.

He gave her an empty stare.

"I suppose not." Christine's eyes rested intently on him as she expounded. "There was this wolf who tried to steal lambs from a flock of sheep protected by a sheepdog, and they would battle each other all day long. The wolf constantly devised plots while the sheepdog consistently thwarted them, usually resulting in great physical harm to the wolf. But both the wolf and the sheepdog realized they were just doing their jobs, and when the lunch whistle blew, they sat at the table as friends, sharing their meal until the whistle blew again, putting them both back on the clock.

"That relationship is analogous to how our national intelligence agencies interact. We all have a job to do, and we constantly battle each other with the noble goal of benefiting our respective countries. But when the lunch whistle blows, you and I can sit at a table and discuss our disagreements in a civilized manner."

Kogen nodded enthusiastically, the woman's comments matching his thoughts exactly. The subterfuge their agencies employed to gather the vital information they needed was just part of the job, and she realized that.

"For example," she continued, "you and I can sit here and discuss the death of Levi's daughters, and how you were responsible for recruiting the suicide bomber who killed them."

Kogen swallowed hard.

How did she know? How did anyone *know?*

Had Bronner learned of his duplicity in the death of Rosenfeld's daughters and told her? And if he'd told Christine, he must have also told . . .

His throat felt parched from the day's heat. He reached for the pitcher of tea, filling the glasses in front of him and his guest, taking a sip of the refreshing liquid as his guest raised her glass to her lips.

"But don't worry," she said. "Ariel promised me that neither he nor Levi would take retribution against you."

"Why is that?"

"Because that's my privilege." The woman's eyes hardened. "Lunch is over. We're back on the clock."

Kogen returned his glass to the table, uncertain of the meaning behind Christine's last comment. He felt warm; perspiration collected on his brow. He went to wipe his forehead, but his hand didn't release from around the glass. He stared at his hand, unable to relax his fingers.

His chest tightened.

He glanced at Christine, realizing too late that the woman had only held the glass to her lips; she hadn't taken a drink. There was a faint bitterness in the tea's aftertaste, contrasting with the subtle sweetness of the raspberry flavor. His stomach contracted violently, throwing him forward, his chest and face slamming onto the table. He remained there, his face turned to the side, staring at Christine.

Holding her glass out to the side, she slowly poured the liquid onto the stone patio. Kogen stared directly ahead, unable to move his eyes, unable to expand the muscles in his chest. His lungs screamed for oxygen, terror strangling his thoughts as he realized he would soon be dead.

"Ariel sends his regrets on not being able to attend our meeting," Christine said as she stood. "I got the impression he would have enjoyed it."

The woman exited his vision, her light footsteps on the rough stone fading away.

Intelligence Minister Barak Kogen's heart strained, then beat one final time.

Christine walked around the corner of the villa, greeted by William Hoover. He holstered his pistol, which he had held ready in case something went wrong, and placed the mobile jammer he held in his other hand into his coat pocket. Jamming Kogen's cell phone had forced him inside to call Bronner, giving Christine the opportunity she needed to poison the tea.

"Excellent job, Miss O'Connor. A professional couldn't have done it better."

She handed him a small metal vial she had concealed in her hand, then unclipped a barrette from the back of her hair as Hoover removed the corresponding receiver from his ear. He took the barrette from Christine, then opened the rear door of the car. She slid into the back as he eased into the driver's seat and buckled up.

"If you ever decide to change your line of work," he said while looking at Christine's reflection in the rear-view mirror, "give me a call."

"I'm afraid this was a onetime deal," she replied. "It's back to a desk job for me."

Hoover smiled. "Where to now?"

"Airport, please."

Christine closed her eyes, leaning back against the headrest as the car rode slowly over the winding gravel driveway. It'd been a long two weeks, and the physical exhaustion combined with the mental stress of preparing for her meeting with Kogen had finally taken its toll. As Daniel Landau turned the sedan onto the smooth, paved road, headed east toward Ben Gurion International Airport, he looked into the rearview mirror. Although her slumber would be restless and her dreams troubled, Christine O'Connor was already asleep.

HER MAJESTY'S AUSTRALIAN SHIP (HMAS) *COLLINS*
5 DAYS LATER

Twelve hundred feet underwater, a weak yellow light bobbed in the darkness, slowly making its round through the abandoned lower level of the *Collins*'s Forward Compartment. In the partially flooded Weapon Stowage Compartment, the fading light shone forlornly on sixteen green warshot torpedoes, still in their stows. Only three of the six torpedo tubes remained visible; the other three were submerged, casualties of the steadily rising water and the submarine's thirty-degree list to starboard. The light turned abruptly and headed aft, sweeping back and forth across the darkened Galley before a quick trip through Junior Sailor Berthing, likewise deserted, the bottom starboard racks also underwater.

After climbing to the upper level of the compartment where the thirty-nine survivors shivered in the frigid air, the dim light paused in Senior Sailor Berthing to examine the injured in their bunks and the man who tended them. With a mournful shake of his head, the weary

Corpsman, stretched beyond his means by the injuries, pulled the blanket over the face of one of the men, reducing the number of the living to thirty-eight. The dying light passed into Control, examining the filthy and sometimes bloody faces of the men and women who huddled together in small groups.

The light was set a moment later on the side of the atmosphere monitoring station. There was no power and the automatic air-sampling system was inoperative, so the light illuminated a handheld air sampler. It took five squeezes to suck in the stale air and deliver the unwelcome, but not unexpected, news. Bobbing through the compartment again, the light approached two officers sitting on the deck in Control, their backs against the Attack periscope. One of the men was the submarine's Commanding Officer, who awaited the results of the latest inspection round. The second man, his American friend, wore a summer white uniform, the white cloth now marred with the ship's grime and stained with the crew's blood. The two officers stood to greet Chief Marine Technician Kim Durand as she approached.

Five days ago, the *Kentucky*'s torpedo had punched an eight-foot-diameter hole in the submarine's Motor Room, flooding the Aft Compartment. The *Collins*'s stern sank as lights throughout the submarine flickered, then were extinguished as the ship lost power. The stern continued to tilt downward until the ship reached a ninety-degree angle, the crew holding on to equipment as best possible as they plummeted into the ocean depths. The hull groaned as the outside pressure increased, the crew waiting in the darkness for the hull to collapse around them.

Their descent halted abruptly, announced by the sound of screeching metal pierced by screams of terror and pain, as the *Collins* crashed into one of the thousands of submerged seamounts scattered across the Pacific. The bow careened downward, joining the stern on the mountain's surface. The ship tilted slowly to starboard, then slid down the steep mountain incline, finally slowing and coming to rest on the edge of a cliff overlooking the abyssal plain three thousand feet below.

Battle lanterns flicked on, their bright beams illuminating the darkness as the crew frantically assessed the condition of the ship and the status of the injured. Two-thirds of the crew were still alive, the men and women lucky enough to be in the Forward Compartment. A fourth of those were injured, and they were tended to once the watertight integrity of the submarine was addressed. Water oozed past the Aft Compartment watertight door, a telltale reminder of what awaited them outside their fragile steel cocoon.

Humphreys and Wilson, doing their best to keep fear from leaking into their voices, directed the crew to shore up the watertight hatch and shut every hull and backup valve, hoping to keep the water out of the Forward Compartment. But the thin trickle seeping past the Aft Compartment watertight door had increased to a steady stream, indicating the door seal was failing. The water collected in the bilge, rising steadily until the lower level of the Forward Compartment had become uninhabitable.

However, the rising water wasn't their only concern; the frigid temperature and limited oxygen supply were more important factors.

The submarine cooled quickly to the ambient temperature of the ocean depth, only 3 degrees above freezing. Hypothermia threatened to claim what remained of the crew, and they donned their foul-weather gear and huddled closely together to conserve body heat. And although the ship had ample emergency carbon dioxide curtains, scavenging the CO_2 from the air, the amount of oxygen was another matter. The crew burned their limited supply of emergency oxygen candles, each one generating enough oxygen to sustain the crew for a few hours.

The battle lanterns had faded now, and the last operable one was in Kim Durand's hand, faintly illuminating the crew as they huddled in the darkness. The air was stale and cold, the quiet periodically pierced by a sickening screech as a hull plate deformed under the intense ocean pressure. They would either succumb to the lack of oxygen, or soon, like the proverbial straw that broke the camel's back, a bolt would finally shear and the nearby fasteners would fail in quick succession. A flange would part from its mate, and the ocean would claim them.

Either way, it would not be long before the *Collins* would be unable to sustain human life.

Even so, the crew clung to the faint hope they would be rescued: that the *Collins*'s emergency beacon had made it to the ocean's surface undamaged, that someone had picked up the beacon's signal in the middle of the Pacific Ocean, and that a deep-sea submersible rescue ship would arrive before their supply of oxygen ran out.

The odds were slim, but that hope and one oxygen candle were all they had left.

As Chief Durand approached, Wilson stood stiffly, shivering inside the foul-weather jacket he had borrowed from one of the dead crewmen. Humphreys climbed to his feet beside him, awaiting the report from his senior Weapons Chief. The faint yellow light from her battle lantern illuminated her grime-smeared face and blue eyes that were glazed over in a glassy sheen, as if they were not quite focused. A curled lock of blond hair escaped from the hood of her foul-weather jacket, tied tight around her face to keep the precious heat within. Her breath condensed into white fog as she spoke, her words coming out slightly slurred, her mind sluggish from the low oxygen content in the air.

"Oxygen is at fourteen percent, Captain. We can't wait any longer. Request permission to burn the last candle."

Humphreys examined the dirt-streaked face of his chief, resignation and despair in her eyes. They had survived five days together, keeping alive the hope they would somehow be rescued. But the submarine's oxygen supply had steadily depleted, and the one remaining candle would sustain them for only a few hours more. Thankfully, as the oxygen level fell below what was required to sustain human life, they would slip into unconsciousness; their deaths would be painless. This last order, however, was not.

"Burn the last candle."

"Aye, sir." Kim Durand turned away, then stopped and

faced back toward Humphreys and Wilson. "It was an honor serving with you," she said.

"The honor was mine," Humphreys said, extending his hand.

"And mine," Wilson said, shaking the woman's hand after Humphreys.

A metallic screech tore through Control as the submarine tilted a few more degrees to starboard. Wilson grabbed the periscope to steady himself, wondering if the *Collins* was teetering on the brink of an abyss, the ledge finally giving way under the weight of the crippled ship. Kim shined the battle lantern around Control, examining the compartment for sign of flooding—a small crack in the hull or piping giving way under the tremendous ocean pressure. A series of metallic scrapes reverberated through the ship, this time from farther aft and above. As the crew listened tensely with upturned faces, five distinct taps, each one second apart, echoed through the hull.

The crew broke out in cheers.

A rescue ship was latching onto the outside of the *Collins*'s hull.

Three hours later, blinking in the sunshine, Captain Murray Wilson stepped off LR5, the Australian submersible submarine rescue ship, onto the deck of the salvage ship that had carried it across the Pacific Ocean. LR5 had just finished the last of four round-trips between the *Collins* and the salvage ship, ferrying the survivors to the surface. Wilson and Humphreys were the last to leave the stricken submarine and the last off LR5. After stepping onto the deck of the salvage ship, which rolled gently in the calm seas, Wilson stopped and reflected on what Commodore Lowe had told them.

Lowe had boarded the *Collins* from LR5 after it secured itself to the submarine's hull and the hatches between them were opened, then briefed the crew on what transpired after the *Kentucky*'s torpedo sent the *Collins* to the bottom. After being fired on by the *Collins,* Commander Malone figured out his Radio Room had been sabotaged and had restored communications. They received the Launch Termination message, and orders to Pacific Fleet to sink the *Kentucky* had been canceled.

The *Kentucky*'s crew had been spared.

Tom was alive.

Captain Murray Wilson looked up, squinting at the bright yellow sun suspended in the clear blue sky. His eyes filled with tears as the sun shone down, offering warm relief from the cool ocean breeze.

COMPLETE CAST OF CHARACTERS

UNITED STATES ADMINISTRATION

ROBERT TOMPKINS, vice president

KEVIN HARDISON, chief of staff

CHRISTINE O'CONNOR, national security adviser

NICHOLAS WILLIAMS, secretary of defense (referenced only)

CAPTAIN STEVE BRACKMAN, senior military aide

LARS SIKES, press secretary

RUSSELL EVANS, White House aide

NATIONAL MILITARY COMMAND CENTER

ADMIRAL TRACEY McFARLAND, Director (referenced only)

DAVE HENDRICKS, Deputy Director

MIKE PATTON, Section Two watchstander

RON COBB, Section Two watchstander

ISAIAH JONES, Section Two watchstander

ANDREW BLOOM, Section Two watchstander (referenced only)

BRADLEY GREEN, Section Two watchstander (referenced only)

KATHY LEENSTRA, Section Two watchstander (referenced only)

ISRAELI ADMINISTRATION

LEVI ROSENFELD, prime minister

HIRSHEL MEKEL, prime minister's executive assistant

EHUD RABIN, defense minister

BARAK KOGEN, intelligence minister

ARIEL BRONNER, director, Metsada

DANIEL LANDAU (ALIAS WILLIAM HOOVER), Metsada agent

U.S. EMBASSY IN ISRAEL

GREG VANDIVER, U.S. Ambassador to Israel

JOYCE EDDINGS, Ambassador Vandiver's executive assistant

COMSUBPAC

JOHN STANBURY, Commander, Submarine Force Pacific

MURRAY WILSON, Senior Prospective Commanding Officer Instructor

ERROL HOLCOMB, Admiral Stanbury's Chief of Staff

DAVID MORTIMORE, Admiral Stanbury's Aide

LACONTA COLEMAN, Strategic Watch Officer

JARRED CRUM, N7 Operations Officer

NAVSEA

ADMIRAL STEVE CASERIA, Program Executive Officer (Submarines)

CAPTAIN JAY SANTOS, program manager, PMS 401 (Sonar)

HMAS *COLLINS*

BRETT HUMPHREYS (COMMANDER), Commanding Officer

KIM DURAND, Marine Technician Chief

USS *HOUSTON*

KEVIN LAWSON (COMMANDER), Commanding Officer

USS *KENTUCKY*

WARDROOM (OFFICERS)

BRAD MALONE (COMMANDER), Commanding Officer

BRUCE FAY (LIEUTENANT COMMANDER), Executive Officer

JOHN HINVES (LIEUTENANT COMMANDER), Engineering Officer

PETE MANNING (LIEUTENANT), Weapons Officer

ALAN TYLER (LIEUTENANT), Navigator

JEFF QUIMBY (LIEUTENANT), Supply Officer

TOM WILSON (LIEUTENANT), Assistant Weapons Officer

HERB CARVAHLO (LIEUTENANT [JG]), Electrical Division Officer

HECTOR LOPEZ (ENSIGN), Torpedo Division Officer

OCTAVE COSTA (LIEUTENANT), Sonar Division Officer

CHRIS VECCHIO (LIEUTENANT), Reactor Controls Division Officer (referenced only)

RADIO DIVISION

ALAN DAVIDSON, Chief Petty Officer

ROB MUSHEN, First Class Petty Officer

PETE GREENE, Third Class Petty Officer

Sonar Division

    Tony DelGreco, First Class Petty Officer

    Bob Cibelli, Second Class Petty Officer

    John Martin, Second Class Petty Officer

    Alex Rambikur, Second Class Petty Officer

Missile Division

    Roger Tryon, First Class Petty Officer

    Jodi Kreuger, First Class Petty Officer

    Scott Santos, First Class Petty Officer

    Dave Reynolds, Second Class Petty Officer

    Scott Walworth, Second Class Petty Officer

Others

    Steve Prashaw, Chief of the Boat

    John Barber, Torpedo Division Third Class Petty Officer

    Bob Murphy, Machinery Division Third Class Petty Officer

    Ted Luther, Night Baker

USS *LAKE ERIE*

Mary Cordeiro (Captain), Commanding Officer

Brian McKeon (Seaman), Helmsman

USS *NORTH CAROLINA*

Dennis Gallagher (Commander), Commanding Officer

Joseph Radek, Reactor Controls Division Chief

Mike Tell, Reactor Controls First Class Petty Officer

USS *SAN FRANCISCO*

Ken Tyler (Commander), Commanding Officer

Tom Bradner, Sonar Division Petty Officer

11TH AIR DEFENSE ARTILLERY BRIGADE

AL KENT (SERGEANT), 11th Air Defense Staff

BRUCE CHERRY (CORPORAL), 11th Air Defense Staff

JON DEWIRE (MAJOR), Commanding Officer, Alpha Battery, 4th Regiment (THAAD)

EAGLE-FIVE-ZERO (P-3C AIR CREW)

SCOTT GRAEF (LIEUTENANT COMMANDER), Tactical Coordinator

PETE BURWELL (LIEUTENANT), Communicator

WHIDBEY ISLAND NOPF

AL CULVER, Watchstander

FRED HARMON, Maintenance Technician

OTHER CHARACTERS—NAVAL OFFICERS

ADMIRAL TIM HALE, Commander, U.S. Pacific Command (referenced only)

ADMIRAL DENIS HERRELL, Commander, U.S. Pacific Fleet (referenced only)

COMMODORE RICK LOWE, Australian Submarine Fleet Element Group Commander

COMMANDER JOE CASEY, PCO aboard USS *HOUSTON*

COMMANDER DOUG BATES, PCO aboard USS *HOUSTON*

OTHER CHARACTERS—CIVILIANS

DANA COOKE, Landover Engineering Systems employee

CLAIRE WILSON, Murray Wilson's wife

NANCY WILSON, Tom Wilson's wife (referenced only)

THERESA PATTON, Mike Patton's wife (referenced only)

SARAH ROSENFELD, Levi Rosenfeld's daughter

RACHEL ROSENFELD, Levi Rosenfeld's daughter

KATHERINE JANKOWSKI, mother with infant at Sandrino's Café

KHALID ABDULLA, suicide bomber

CINDY COREY, pleasure craft sunbather

RANDY COREY, pleasure craft fisherman

MICHIYA AOCHI, fisherman on *Daisan Shinsho-Maru*

DOREEN CORNELLIER, Channel 9 News reporter

RICK LARSON, FBI Director (referenced only)

KEN RONAN, CIA Director (referenced only)

JOHN KENNEY, CIA Agent

AUTHOR'S NOTE

I hope you enjoyed reading *The Trident Deception*.

I tried to make it as realistic as possible considering the constraints. In particular, no classified information could be revealed, which required me to alter some capabilities of ships and weapons employed in the novel (speed and range, for example), which I'm sure some of you have detected and have no doubt exclaimed, "That's not right!" You are correct. If they were accurate, this novel would be classified, so I had to "tweak" a few things.

Also, some of the tactics employed by the submarine crews were generic and also not accurate. For example, torpedo employment and torpedo evasion tactics are classified and could not be accurately represented in this novel. Finally, some of the submarine terminology and dialog isn't right either. If they were completely correct, some of it would be unintelligible due to the acronyms, and I'd have to stop frequently to explain, and the story would lurch along. So I compromised on some of the dialogue and on some of the "accuracy" of the scenes, in order to keep the story flowing smoothly along.

For all of the above, I apologize. I did my best to keep everything as close to real life without making it classified or bogging it down with acronyms or terminology too difficult or time-consuming to explain. Hopefully it all worked out and it came together into a suspenseful, page-turning novel.

Thanks for your time and I hope we get a chance to meet some day. And of course—I hope you liked *The Trident Deception* enough to buy the sequel, *Empire Rising*. Thanks again!

Read on for an excerpt from Rick Campbell's next book

EMPIRE RISING

Available in hardcover from St. Martin's Press

BEIJING, CHINA

Bai Jiao's pulse raced as she stood stiffly under the bright lights, her cold hands gripping the bouquet of flowers as tightly as the white gown squeezed her waist. The veil across her eyes partially obscured her vision, but she could see enough to make out the cavernous Grand Ballroom of the Pangu Hotel, an immense chandelier suspended from the center of the thirty-foot-high ceiling. The white carpet runway beneath her feet, passing by row after row of guests, stretched to infinity.

Feeling a nudge on her right arm, Jiao remembered she wasn't standing alone; she felt her father's arm intertwined with hers. Turning her head, she sought his wizened face. Tao was looking down at her. He smiled, and for a moment she was a little girl again, sitting in her father's lap as he imparted words of wisdom to his precious *qianjin*. He patted her arm, conveying his love and support. She knew that even now, she could call it off. Even though the arrangements had cost over two million Yuan, Tao would not think twice about the loss.

The shame he would endure, however, if his daughter backed out on her wedding day . . .

It was just nerves, after all. She loved Huang and was ready to begin their life together. She forced a weak smile and nodded her head.

Slowly, in rhythm to the music that began with her first step, Jiao and her father proceeded down the center aisle of the ballroom, passing the four hundred guests turned out in tuxedoes freshly pressed and formal evening gowns sparkling under the ballroom lights. Jiao kept her eyes focused at the end of the long white carpet where Huang waited, standing at attention in his maroon and pine-green military uniform.

Along the perimeter of the room, men in black suits, each with a coiled cord hanging from one ear and tucked inside the collar of his jacket, cast a watchful eye over every entrance to the ballroom as well as its guests. For as long as Jiao could remember, men like these had guarded her family. It wasn't until her teenage years that she gained an appreciation for the power her father wielded as one of the Party's nine Politburo members and now as China's prime minister.

As China's economic czar, Tao was charged with infusing capitalistic traits into the country's socialist economy, so Jiao was not surprised when her father requested her wedding be a blend of Western and traditional Chinese ceremonies. As Jiao proceeded down the aisle in her white wedding gown, she looked forward to the tea ceremony that would follow in the adjacent ballroom. She would change into the traditional *qi pao* dress, its red color symbolizing good luck, warding off evil spirits.

At the end of the white runway, her father released her arm. Jiao stepped up to the altar, turning toward Huang. As she looked into his eyes, a warm glow spread through her body, chasing away the nervous chill. The day she had dreamt of as a young girl had finally arrived. She knew with certainty they would spend the rest of their lives together. Nothing could tear them apart.

As Huang lifted the veil from her face, a flash of movement distracted her. Men in black suits were sprinting down the sides of the ballroom, headed behind a beige curtain hanging from the ceiling, forming the backdrop of the altar. Over Huang's shoulder, she spotted Feng Dai, her personal bodyguard since she was a child, racing toward her. A commotion penetrated the curtain, accompanied by a mosaic of dark shapes shifting behind the sheer fabric. She turned back toward Huang, and as she met his questioning eyes, there was a deafening boom.

Jiao was buffeted by a blast of hot air and she had the odd sensation she was flying through the air. Her vision clouded in an orange blossoming haze, and white-hot pain stabbed into her body as her limbs bent in directions they weren't designed for. There was a vague feeling of her back hitting something hard and sharp, the pain piercing through her stomach. Her vision slowly cleared and a thousand yellow lights came into focus, swaying above her.

She was lying on the floor somewhere, gazing at beautiful lights swirling above. It was peacefully quiet at first, but then faint sounds greeted her ears, growing gradually louder until they coalesced into a dissonance of high-pitched screams of terror mingled with low moans of pain. As if responding to the sound, her mind was reminded of the sensations slicing through her body. The slightest attempt to move—breathe even— magnified the excruciating pain.

Jiao turned her head slowly to the side. She was surrounded by a nightmarish collage of sight and smell. Bodies strewn across a red-streaked floor. Bloodied hands reaching toward heaven, splayed fingers clawing the air. Men and women wreathed in fire were dancing under the ballroom lights, collapsing onto the floor, their charred features shrouded in an orange flickering haze. The scent assailing her nostrils was foreign but unmistakable: the stench of burning flesh.

A few feet away, Jiao's father lay on his back, his neck at an awkward angle, his eyes frozen open. Just out of reach, Huang was facedown, a dark stain spreading out from under him across the white carpet. Jiao felt warmth ooze across her stomach, moving up her chest and down her legs as liquid saturated her wedding gown. She looked down at her tattered garment, and as her thoughts faded into darkness, Jiao wondered when she had changed into her red dress.

WASHINGTON, D.C.

A light rain was falling from a gray overcast sky as a black Lincoln Town Car merged onto the 14th Street Bridge, fighting its way north across three lanes of early morning traffic. In the back of the sedan, Christine O'Connor gazed through rain-streaked windows at the Potomac River, flowing lazily east toward the Chesapeake Bay. She ignored the rhythmic thump of the sedan's windshield wipers, focused instead on the radio, tuned to a local AM news station. As she listened to the morning's headlines, she wasn't surprised the most important news of the day was absent from the broadcast.

As the president's national security advisor, Christine was briefed daily on events occurring around the world with the potential to affect the safety of American citizens. This morning, she was returning from the Pentagon after her weekly intelligence brief with Secretary of Defense Nelson Jennings. Near the end of the meeting, the discussion had turned to yesterday's assassination of China's prime minister. There would be instability within China's Politburo Standing Committee as its eight remaining members determined the replacement for the second most powerful person in China. Concern was voiced about the loss of Bai Tao, a staunch opponent to using military force to resolve China's conflicts. Considering what the United States was contemplating signing, that was not an insignificant issue.

The MAER Accord—the Mutual Access to Environmental Resources Accord—was the exact opposite of what it purported to be.

Instead of ensuring every country would receive their fair share, the MAER Accord included complicated price calculations that favored the United States and its allies. Less fortunate countries, including China, would be forced to pay much higher prices. Additionally, it included a military defense assurance between the United States and the Pacific Rim nations, who were fearful of an aggressive China, which had been rattling its sword and staking claim to many of the region's natural resources. The future lay in vast Asian offshore oil fields, and the half-century-long MAER Accord assured America and its allies would have access to the natural resources their economies would require for the next fifty years. In return, America would respond to any attempt by another country to claim the natural resources of another.

Christine's Town Car turned right on West Executive Avenue, bringing her closer to the White House and her final meeting on the accord with the president and

Kevin Hardison. The mere thought of the president's chief of staff threatened to bring on a migraine.

The Lincoln Town Car pulled to a stop under the West Wing's north portico, next to two Marines in dress blues guarding the formal entrance to the West Wing. Standing between the two Marines—almost a head taller—was a Navy Captain, wearing the Navy's version of its dress blues, with four gold stripes on each sleeve. Steve Brackman was the president's senior military aide, with whom she had forged a close working relationship. Christine had called ahead and asked him to meet her when she returned to the White House. As she prepared for battle with the president's powerful chief of staff, she preferred to have the military on her side.

Brackman greeted her as she stepped from the sedan, polite as always. "Good morning, Miss O'Connor."

Christine returned the Captain's greeting, and Brackman followed her to her corner office. She entered and dropped off her leather briefcase, but Brackman stopped at the entrance to her office. Christine returned to the doorway.

"I'm sorry, Miss O'Connor. Mr. Hardison requested I meet with him in a few minutes. Is there something quick I can help you with?"

Christine frowned. Hardison apparently had the same battle plan she had. She answered, "The president is going to make his decision on the MAER Accord today. Hardison is pushing the president to sign it while I'm advising against it. I wanted to spend a few minutes with you, so you fully understood my concerns."

"I think I understand both sides of the argument," Brackman replied.

Christine pressed her lips together. As the president's senior military aide, Brackman could tip the scales. "And your recommendation will be . . . ?"

Brackman's eyes searched hers for a moment, and it seemed he was about to answer, but he checked his watch instead. "If you'll excuse me."

Christine watched him disappear down the hallway, then decided to wait where she could keep an eye on the Oval Office's doors. She headed down the seventy-foot-long hallway, turning left into the Roosevelt Room. While she waited, she took the opportunity to admire the two oil paintings hanging on opposing walls: Alfred Jonniaux's portrait of Franklin Delano Roosevelt seated behind his desk, and Tade Styka's equestrian portrait of Theodore Roosevelt titled *Rough Rider*. In accordance with tradition, the incoming administration had reversed the two portraits, placing the image of FDR over the fireplace and Theodore Roosevelt to Christine's right, on the south wall.

As Christine examined the portrait of Theodore Roosevelt, she reflected for a few minutes on his conservative policies, then on his famous slogan—*Speak softly and carry a big stick*. If the president signed the MAER Accord and China responded as she predicted, the United States was going to need a big stick indeed.

There was a knock on the Roosevelt Room's open door, and Christine turned to spot Chief of Staff Kevin Hardison, who tapped his watch. "The president's waiting."

* * *

Christine followed Hardison into the Oval Office. Captain Brackman also joined them, and Christine took her seat in the middle of three chairs opposite the president's desk, with Hardison and Brackman flanking her.

The president addressed Christine. "Any details on the assassination of China's prime minister?"

Christine answered, "Our Intel agencies have narrowed the potential motives down to the two most probable. The first is a terrorist attack by one of the separatist organizations from the Xinjiang region in northwest China. The second is internal strife within the Politburo, with one of the junior members taking matters into his own hands. In that case, Shen Yi is the leading suspect. He's the longest-serving Politburo member, yet sits third in the power structure behind Xiang Chenglei—the general secretary of the Party and president of China, and Xiang's protégé, Bai Tao—prime minister. Shen is getting up in years, and the death of Bai Tao is fortunate from his perspective, making him the leading candidate to replace Xiang when he steps down." Christine paused for a moment. "Or if something happens to Xiang."

The specter of Politburo strife plunging China's leadership into chaos couldn't have come at a worse time. The instability would make an accurate prediction of China's response to the MAER Accord impossible. In concert with Christine's thoughts, Hardison changed the subject.

"We need to discuss the accord, sir. The terms expire at the end of this week, so you need to sign it before you leave this afternoon for Camp David."

"What are the current projections?" the president asked.

Hardison replied. "Without price constraints, world demand for oil will increase by eight percent per year, with oil production increasing by only one percent. To reduce oil consumption to within production capacity, the price of oil will double over the next three years. We crafted the accord to prevent skyrocketing prices, and the terms we negotiated are more than fair, restricting each country to an appropriate percentage of the world's oil supply."

"The terms are *not* fair," Christine replied. "The method used to calculate each country's fair share is flawed, and you know it. The accord will strangle China's economy."

Hardison shrugged as he turned toward Christine. "And that's a bad thing? They had their chance to negotiate a better deal, and failed."

"They failed because we bribed our way to favorable terms, offering over a hundred billion dollars in military grants."

"We negotiated," Hardison jabbed. "*Negotiated.*"

Christine folded her arms across her chest. "Bribed."

Hardison leveled a malevolent gaze at Christine before turning back to the president. "Gasoline prices have doubled since you took office and will double again before the reelection if you don't sign the accord. If you want another term in office, you don't have a choice."

"I don't recommend it," Christine interjected. "The main question is whether China will use its military to obtain the resources it needs. They won't be able to buy the oil and natural gas they require, and they might use their military to obtain it by force. It'll be Japan and Pearl Harbor all over again. In 1941, the United States placed an embargo on oil and gasoline exports to Japan, cutting off eighty percent of their oil supply. Japan did in 1941 what China will likely do today—they moved south to secure the natural resources they required."

"China wouldn't dare start a war," Hardison replied. "They know we'd come to the aid of anyone they attacked. And another thing to consider, Mr. President," he cast a derisive glance in Christine's direction, "is that Christine has a track record of being wrong, so I recommend you factor that into your decision."

Christine leveled an icy stare at the chief of staff. She hadn't kept tally, but was pretty sure it was Hardison who was wrong most of the time. His long list of flaws apparently included a short memory.

The president clearing his throat brought Christine's attention back to the commander-in-chief. He looked toward Brackman. "What's your assessment? If China uses its military, can we defeat them?"

Brackman didn't immediately respond, and the president's question hung in the air as Brackman cast a sideways glance at Christine before focusing on the president.

"If China starts a war over oil," Brackman answered, "we can defend any country they attack. Although they've significantly modernized their military over the last decade, they're still no match for our Pacific Fleet. With five carrier strike groups off China's shore along with our Marine Expeditionary Forces—two Marine divisions and their air wings—any attempt to seize oil reserves in the region will be defeated."

Christine gave Brackman a frosty glare as the president absorbed the Captain's words, his eyes canvassing each of the individuals seated in front of him. Christine felt a deepening uneasiness as the president moved toward his decision.

Finally, he spoke. "I'll sign the accord."

FUJIAN PROVINCE, CHINA

As the sun slipped behind the Wuyi Mountains, shadows crept east from the red sandstone slopes, sinking into the lush green gorges of the Jiuqu Xi River before encroaching on the Pacific Ocean. Not far from the coast, a lone figure ascended a narrow trail toward a grassy plateau overlooking the East China Sea, its frothy-white waves crashing into the rocky shore six hundred feet below. With a steady gait, the elderly man moved toward a smooth outcropping of rock. Upon close examination, he spotted a rectangular seam in the side of the protrusion and knocked firmly on the heavy metal door. A few seconds later, a cover over a small window in the door slid away, revealing the face of a Shang Deng Bing, the green epaulettes on the young man's shoulders proclaiming him a Private First Class in the People's Liberation Army.

Even in the dim light of dusk, Xiang could see the blood drain from the young man's face when he recognized the man standing outside. Xiang waited patiently as the lock mechanisms rotated, and the door swung inward. Standing next to the Private was a Captain who saluted crisply, as did the Private a split second later.

"Greetings, comrades."

"Greetings, leader!" both men replied in unison.

The two men stood rigidly at attention, awaiting Xiang's next words. He offered a warm smile instead, and the Captain and Private dropped their salutes.

"There has been much progress since your last review," the Captain said, accurately assessing the purpose of Xiang's visit. "We are now fully operational, and have many new men who will be proud you have visited us."

Leaving the Private behind, the Captain turned and headed down an eighty-foot-long hallway. Xiang and Captain Zhou reached the end of the long corridor and turned left, delving deeper into the mountainside. The opening led to a twenty-by-twenty-foot room crammed with electronic consoles, the blue glow from the displays illuminating the faces of the soldiers seated behind them. The Captain called out as Xiang entered and the eight men snapped to attention, awe evident in their expressions as they stood in the presence of China's supreme leader. After Zhou ordered them To Rest, the men settled uneasily into their chairs, exchanging glances as Xiang and the Captain stopped behind one of the consoles.

"I believe it is dark enough to bring the battery online," Zhou said. It was more a question than a statement, and Xiang answered with a nod of his head.

Zhou turned and issued orders to the enlisted man seated at the console. The Shang Shi acknowledged, and as his fingers flicked across the glass surface of the touch-screen display, Xiang knew that above them, radars were being raised from recesses in the mountain's surface, beginning their rhythmic back and forth sweeps. A three-dimensional image of an island appeared in the center of the display, separated from the mainland by a two-hundred-mile-wide swath of the Pacific Ocean.

"With our new *Hong Niao* missiles," Zhou proudly announced, "we have complete coverage of the Strait. Nothing can enter without our permission."

Xiang nodded again. China had spent the last decade developing advanced anti-ship cruise missiles, deploying them along the coast in forty concealed bunkers like this one. The People's Liberation Army had done their task well, camouflaging their construction from American satellites in orbit. The United States had no idea what awaited them.

The Captain added, "Each man controls one of the eight launchers, selecting the desired target. Come, the launchers have been installed since your last visit."

Zhou led Xiang out of the control room, crossing the hallway. They entered a second room containing eight quad-missile launchers, the fifteen-foot-long missiles pointing toward a closed portal measuring four feet high by sixty feet wide. The Captain tapped a control near the room's entrance, and a twelve-inch-thick section retracted slowly upward, revealing the Pacific Ocean, providing a flight path for the thirty-two missiles.

As Xiang stared through the portal of the casemated bunker, the horizon melting into the darkness, he recalled the times he stood on the plateau above them in his youth, straining to see the distant shore of

Taipei, the island referred to by the West as Taiwan. It was to Taiwan that Chiang Kai-shek's forces, defeated in China's civil war, retreated in 1949. If the Politburo Standing Committee approved the People's Liberation Army plan tomorrow, there would be many benefits; one of them being the long overdue unification of the two Chinas.

Zhou interrupted Xiang's rumination. "It is an honor you have visited us again."

"The honor is mine, Captain. It is the dedication of men like you, who serve the people, that keeps our country safe and prosperous."

Upon uttering those words, Xiang's thoughts returned to the MAER Accord. The United States had restricted China's access to vital oil supplies, strangling its economy. Although America's aggression hadn't been formally approved by Congress, its proclamation was just as clear.

America had declared war.